I0784339

JOAN T. WARREN

The Bent Tree Path, Book One

A Secret Trail of Tears

First published by A Book to Grow On, LLC 2024

Copyright © 2024 by Joan T. Warren

All rights reserved. No part of this publication may be reproduced, stored or transmitted in any form or by any means, electronic, mechanical, photocopying, recording, scanning, or otherwise without written permission from the publisher. It is illegal to copy this book, post it to a website, or distribute it by any other means without permission.

Joan T. Warren asserts the moral right to be identified as the author of this work.

Joan T. Warren has no responsibility for the persistence or accuracy of URLs for external or third-party Internet Websites referred to in this publication and does not guarantee that any content on such Websites is, or will remain, accurate or appropriate.

Designations used by companies to distinguish their products are often claimed as trademarks. All brand names and product names used in this book and on its cover are trade names, service marks, trademarks and registered trademarks of their respective owners. The publishers and the book are not associated with any product or vendor mentioned in this book. None of the companies referenced within the book have endorsed the book.

This novel is a work of fiction. As most historical fiction is rooted and based upon true characters who are no longer alive. Any known public figures represented herein are now deceased and their portions of the story are fictionalized, with every effort given to respect their reported ethics, manner and positions as found in current research.

All other characters are fictional, and any actions or deeds, though some may be based on real occurrences, are modified and fictionalized to protect privacy and innocence. This book is not intended to hurt or malign any person's reputation.

CAUTIONARY STATEMENT:

This book is for mature audiences only. Readers be advised that the content, though not explicit and written with sensitivity, necessarily covers topics which may be triggering for some. Please see the back of the book for a complete list of areas of sensitivity that may be of concern in the text of this novel.

If, at any point in the reader's experience, he or she finds difficulty with the material, such as troublesome memories of a painful past, the author asks that the reader seek help from a qualified professional. This book is not intended, nor can be expected, to be responsible for one's personal mental, physical or emotional health. We encourage personal responsibility and initiative for one's own health and recovery as a healthy way of life.

Short quotations, lyrics and title references are used with permission from their copyright holders and are not to be reproduced without express permission from copyright holders. Fair use laws apply where the work's copyright holders were unreachable (as commentary). Some quotations are public domain (for works over 95 years old without a renewed copyright on original material).

First edition

ISBN: 979-8-9877746-2-5

This book was professionally typeset on Reedsy.
Find out more at reedsy.com

This first book in the series
The Bent Tree Path
is dedicated to the downtrodden.
May your journey be easier for having read it.

Prologue

In the lone woods stood a stalwart
Driven and bent by the wind
Bidding astute to press onward
Regardless of how men had sinned.

My Dear Ones,

I was a sapling, bent to the ground, pierced, wounded, held in the dark. Light reached me there, in the shadow of secrecy's shield, in furtive ground for shame. I grew toward Light, and now, I stand, a trail marker. I lead the way to nourishment, connection and the deep waters of Love. Read my story of secrets, a trail of tears untold. We hold seven generations, before and after. Our choices clear the path for future generations.

✳ ✳ ✳

In the lone woods stood a stalwart
Driven and bent by the wind
Bidding astute to press onward
Regardless of how men had sinned.

My Dear Ones,

I was a sapling, bent to the ground, pierced, wounded, held in the dark. Light reached me there, in the shadow of secrecy's shield, in furtive ground for shame. I grew toward Light, and now, I stand, a trail marker. I lead the way to nourishment, connection and the deep waters of Love. Read my story of secrets, a trail of tears untold. We hold seven generations, before and after. Our choices clear the path for future generations.

With Love,
Orb

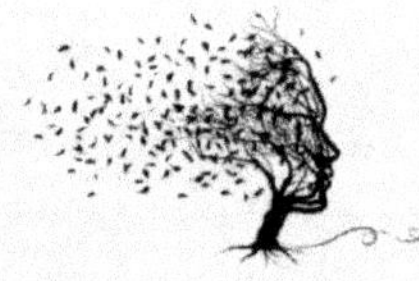

1

Becca

"War is not healthy for children or other living things."
-Lorraine Schneider, Another Mother for Peace

Kensington, Maryland. 1971

On any given night, on any given street in Becca's middle-class neighborhood, everyone chose to stare at a box that spewed violence and hatred and war onto their otherwise clean carpets.

Becca screamed so they could hear her from the kitchen. "Turn it off!"

Steadfast in their nightly ritual, lined up on the furniture like sardines in a can, their gray-cast eyes adhered to the box, absorbing its blast of destruction. Their souls numbed, no one noticed. No one cared.

Molotov cocktails shattering storefront windows crashed into Becca's home, through that horrid box. Angry mobs rocked and up-ended cars, families coiling within—Becca, too. Police maced the crowds. Becca's eyes burned. Her throat seized. She resisted the impulse to flinch—to raise her arms as police wielded their long black sticks upon the crowd.

She slammed the dish towel on the counter like a gavel in court. "Enough!"

Storming toward the living room, Becca cringed as orange smoke billowed across the rainforest, leaving nothing but stumps, withered fronds, and death. Vietnam. A mesmerizing *whump, whump, whump* sent her cowering, as if the helicopter was just above her head, hovering to rescue soldiers. Then the daily death counts.

She launched her complaint at the box. "They're just boys—forced to fight. Why?"

Of the eight people in the room, only Dad stirred. The furrow in his brow deepened, his eyes flared red, and his lips turned down.

Here it comes.

As he opened his mouth, his finger jammed the air in her direction. "Don't you start. I've had enough of you kids disrespecting our country—"

"Ugh! Never mind." Bursting through the broken screen door, her hand stinging with waves of repercussion from striking against the wood trim, Becca plunked herself onto the front step. She covered her ears to mask the gut-wrenching clamor and squeezed harder, as if, by counterpressure, she could prevent an explosion.

A tangle of thorns tumbled in her gut like a bramblebush, catching and tearing at will. Her body tightened against the points of rough concrete that poked their chilling spurs through her low-cut jeans. A cold shiver jerked her spine, lifting her head.

The maelstrom blared through open windows all up and down her otherwise quiet suburban street. She rubbed the shudder from her arms and stomped to the back yard.

Spring's new leaves on her tree flickered in specks of moonlight. They beckoned, offering solace. Becca hoisted herself up the tree and nestled into a crook. The branches squeezed her hips like a vice—comforting, compared to the pressure of living with her family in a hate-torn world.

The scent of freshly cut grass coalesced with the redolence of maple bark. She breathed in its soothing magic. How many times had she taken refuge in this crook while her family puttered below, not realizing she was above them?

The nightly battle would soon begin. Her parents' daily arguments, embedded splinters in Becca's mind, vexed and vied against calloused skin to press their way out. She fixed her mind to pluck them, sort them, discard them.

Mom aggravates Dad. He threatens her. She keeps nagging, bringing up the past. Rehashing. Re-thrashing. Until he sprays us all, insults thundering out of his vein-popped red face, like machine gun fire splaying from his B-17. Becca shifted her position off a small branch that poked her from behind. *It's not World War Two anymore, Dad.*

Her stomach growled. She'd stormed out before dinner. Not that they had an official meal time. *He storms out the door to get drunk. Mom locks herself in her bedroom. And us kids—* The kids often scraped dinner together from cereal or peanut butter and jelly.

I'll eat when I go back in. She shuddered—not from cold, but at the thought of going in. *If I go back in.* The loss of either parent's temper was reason enough for the kids to seek shelter. Who could predict if they'd be ignored or punished? Old scores could be called to settle more than once—and hard. When the brash air of punishment loomed, blame could land anywhere.

A high-pitched squeak caught Becca's attention. Her eyes shot to the source—a bedroom window cranking open. Cigarette smoke wafted out, along with songs of love and peace blaring from the radio. *Just Emily.* Becca crossed her arms and blew out a sigh. In the chasm between hate news and love radio, hippies, like Becca's older sister Emily, waved signs on the street corner on Saturdays, entreating the world to make love, not war. Tonight, their melodies *drip, drip, dripped* with love Becca did not have.

She shimmied down the tree, stretched one leg to the top of the rusting swing set, and swooped down into the yard. The family collies, King and Queenie, bounded from the doghouse and leaned against the fence, whining with excitement, tails wagging and tongues hanging out the sides of their mottled mouths.

"Aw, you're happy to see me. Didn't you hear me when I climbed the tree? Were you sleeping?" As she spoke, she unwrapped the coiled metal wire to crack the pen's gate open. She squeezed through the gap so they couldn't escape. Closing the gate, she knelt and hugged them. Their matted manes tickled her face and neck and their tails wagged their entire bodies side to side, knocking Becca onto her bottom in the dirt. She held on tighter and laughed. "You're such good doggies."

Fetid fumes met Becca's nose as King licked her face. She scrunched her nose and turned her face away. "Pee-yew!" Hugging King tighter and rubbing his ears, she kept his breath at bay. "Tomorrow, a bath and teeth-brushing for you, buddy."

King and Queenie had been Becca's best friends and confidants since early childhood. She could spend hours with them. Brushing mats from their fur with tender care, their soft manes soothed her in return. She would sit in the pen with them, relaying her innermost secrets to their empathetic brown eyes. And why not? They were loyal friends, greeting her with gusto whenever she came. Snuggling against her, pushing their noses under her hand, pawing her to say, "Don't stop petting me." They were the ones who cared.

Yet, they were the ones called animals. Sequestered to a portion of the back yard, they lived as prisoners, jailed from the amazing scents and greetings they longed for when someone in the family bothered to leash them and take them for a walk. Or be taken for a walk, rather. "It isn't right, doggies." Becca smoothed the fur over their heads and down their backs as she whispered to them. "You deserve the house more than we do. Yes, you do." She stood up, brushing the fur from her jeans. "I tell you what—I'll take you for a walk tomorrow, too."

It was quiet when she slipped back inside, the TV volume low. The black and white show *Combat!* had not been enough to keep her father awake. His snoring head dropped onto the top of the boxy vinyl couch, the reason for the sticky stains in the center of each cushion. Brylcreem. Erect in his hand stood his quart bottle, on duty to awaken him when he fell into a deep sleep.

She shook her head, amused by the sight. How many times she'd seen his bottle start to spill as he drifted off, followed by his jerk awake, fumbling to set the brown glass aright, beer spattering about. He'd hold the bottle straight again and fall right back to sleep. *He never thinks to put the darn thing on the table.* Deciding not to risk waking him by going to the kitchen, she doffed her shoes and tiptoed past him toward her bedroom.

No strip of light from under Mom's closed door in the hallway meant she was asleep. Becca's brothers had likely settled into their rooms in the basement, and her sisters in their rooms across from Mom's. Becca slipped into the double bed she shared with her younger sister, Missy, who whined and turned over at the disturbance. Becca snuggled the blanket close under her chin. A deep breath and then a sigh released more tension. She had successfully avoided the night's furies. Her right foot, in customary style, stuck out from the blanket and jiggled side to side, keeping time, like a mama rocks a baby until she sleeps.

* * *

In the morning, Becca trudged the two miles toward school. Friction from every step frayed the edges of her soul as it did the hem of her bell-bottom jeans. She mentally projected the upcoming week's obligations.

Tests in four subjects this week. I'll have no time for anything else. King and Queenie's doting eyes flashed through her mind, along with her pledge to give her furry friends their much-needed bath and well-deserved walk. She chided herself for getting their hopes up. *It's better not to promise. Maybe at least I'll walk them.* Becca turned her mind to the day's schedule. *English, history, algebra, lunch, PE, art and science. I can skip out at lunch and not come back until art.*

When the lunch bell rang, Becca slipped out the back door and scurried across the field to The Hill. Nearby, Washingtonians called Capitol Hill 'The Hill,' but wayward students from Newport and Einstein ruled the world, in their own way, from this Hill. A neglected playground behind a small knoll in front of the high school and downhill from the junior high hockey field, The Hill was secluded from the road by trees and bushes—the perfect get-away for class ditchers.

Becca approached her brood of class-cutting peers sitting in a circle in the grass. Off to the side, a couple lay under the trees, wrapped in each other's bodies, making out. She glanced away, eyes twinkling, head shaking. *Those two. Always at it.*

Her foot nearly kicked a folded paper on the ground. Drawn to the cover image, she picked up the flyer. The woven design in the Indian's headband matched hers, as did his long straight hair. His headband sported an upright feather. Her feather hung, an earring. She read the brochure's front caption aloud to her friends.

> *"If our people fight one tribe at a time, all will be killed. They can cut off our fingers one by one, but if we join together, we will make a powerful fist. Come to Washington, DC, May 1-7."*

Glancing at one of her friends, her brows squeezed against her eyelids as she cast a questioning eye. "A fist? What's this about?"

Frannie looked up. "Protesting the war. Peaceful, blocking roads and such, but the government will have to shut down." She toked a joint and, holding the smoke in her lungs, offered the smoldering bit to Becca.

Becca handed Frannie the flyer. "But. . . Kent State." The news images of Kent State demonstrations gone awry had become a permanent fixture in her mind—National Guard firing upon demonstrating college students, a student prone in the street, bloodied. . . dead. . . a female on her knees, wailing over him.

Becca's stomach twisted as she imagined what he must have felt—and what his friends and family must still be feeling. She raised her hand against the flyer. "That's not for me. But this?" Motioning to Frannie's burnt offering, the musky fumes promising a mellow state, she received the joint between her thumb and forefinger. "Sure, thanks."

"Well, I'm going." Frannie's over-sized, bleached-blonde afro swayed, suspended mid-air, as she waved her hands around, emphasizing her speech. "We can't just sit around and take it. We gotta stand up against those fascist pigs."

Becca headed toward the swingset and fit her slight frame into the rubber sling seat. She propelled herself slowly to and fro in the gentle breeze. The swing worked magically, even in this tiny hollow surrounded by schools and parking lots and two-way street traffic—the same magic as her foot-wag in bed, the crook of her backyard tree, or the warmth of her collies' manes.

This wayward teen didn't skip school to get high. All Becca really wanted was to be away from the clanging metal chairs, harsh fluorescent lights, haughty voices of authority, and hard-angled brick buildings of school. . . to nestle into the green of nature.

"But it's cool." Frannie's lanky arms stopped flailing. One hand slipped in her pocket, and she followed Becca toward the swing. "There's a free concert this weekend. Demonstrations don't kick off 'til Monday. Come for the weekend, for fun. You need some fun, chick."

"A free concert?" Becca reached for the flyer and confirmed it. "Cool. Maybe. For the music."

2

Lena

"A smile is something sacred, to be shared."
-Cherokee proverb

Sandy Spring, Maryland. 1917

Lena shrieked, waved her arms and tore at the murder of crows. "Shoo—you leave those babies alone."

Their cacophony faded. The black wings receded into the distant morning sky.

The young woman stooped beneath the nest, examining the pink fledglings that wriggled in the grass—their mouths gaping with inaudible cries for help.

"Hang on, little ones. You can't smell like a human." She picked up a leaf and used it as a barrier between her hands and the baby birds to re-nest them. "There you go. Shush now, your mama will be back soon."

Lena backed away and stood watch from her bench near

the dogwood, brushing the dust from her pinafore. *Those old crows—why don't they pick on someone their own size?*

The cardinal swooped in from a nearby tree, bringing food to her babies. The brightest of the two red birds flew close to Lena and chirped, flitting side to side and eyeing her.

"You're welcome. Now keep an eye on them, will you?" Lena winked, and with an exhalation of relief, she picked up her belted stack of books and strode toward the driveway.

Henry Burriss brushed mud clumps from the horses' hooves. "Be sure to watch out for holes in the road after all this rain. And tie the horses up good once you get there. Be sure they have water and hay."

"I will, Daddy." Lena lifted the hem of her skirt, and, seeing mud on her neatly laced boots, stomped on the pebbled driveway to clean them.

Mama carried the lunch basket toward the wagon. "She'll do fine, Henry." Leaning her head close to Lena's, she whispered. "Sometimes it's just hard for him to think you're not a little girl anymore." She snugged the basket under the seat.

"I heard that." Daddy's gentle manner turned his chiding into play.

Mama called toward the house. "Come on, kids, load up."

The little ones came running.

"Let's go," Lena's brother shouted. "We're gonna be late."

A bit late, yes, since Lena had stolen some extra time in the garden reading a chapter for English class. She'd usually read on the way, but today was her first day as the official driver for her younger siblings. The ninth child of fifteen, the honor finally came to her as, one by one, her older siblings married and moved away.

"Daddy." Lena placed her hand on his shoulder. "You taught me well, so there's no need to worry. I'm not gonna do anything stupid that might mess up my big plans."

"Just be careful—"

"I got all my stuff." Sister checked her lunch bucket. "I didn't forget nothing. Got my pencil and an apple for later." She hugged Mama goodbye, chatting all the time. "Hey, look—a rainbow!"

Lena followed her sister's pointing finger, over their farmland, to the sky. Golden beams splayed across the blue, their source hidden behind lavender clouds. A wispy, full-spectrum pastel archway framed the rows of corn along the way to the road. A quick breath preceded her whisper. "It's beautiful." A frown turned her side-glance at Sissy and sharpened her tone. "But it's anything."

"Huh?" Sissy tilted her head at Lena.

"I didn't forget *anything*, not nothing."

"You didn't forget nothing, either?"

"Never mind. Climb in." Her cheeks rounded, crinkling her eyes at the edges as she waved her arm to direct her passengers into the wagon. She climbed into the front seat and took the reins. "Okay, we're off."

With a flick of the reins, they clip-clopped off the farm, waving goodbye and turning south on the turnpike for the five-mile journey to school.

A new layer of stones on the century-old dirt road failed the test of the weekend's deluge. Deep ruts and puddles slowed the bumpy course. Lena commanded the reins as she'd been taught, speeding up over the shallow puddles but avoiding, or slowly navigating through, the deeper ones.

Her siblings enjoyed bouncing up and down, watching the mud splash from the buggy on every side. They pretended they were in an old stagecoach traveling across the west, watching out for 'Injuns,' as they called them, hiding in the trees.

"Get down." The older boy crouched low. "Watch out for them arrows."

The youngest pushed up to her knees in the seat and raised a defiant fist toward the empty forest. "You ole Injuns won't git us today."

Reading Wild West stories to her siblings the night before must have inadvertently fueled their imaginations. Now their game scraped like iron on the rough edges of Lena's contemplation. She hushed them. "Remember, Grannie said the story books mixed up the truth. The Indians were the ones afraid—afraid of us white folk."

Not long ago, Lena had lived to play. The desire had lessened these days. As her formal education churned alongside Grannie's tales, her longing for the truth of the matter grew. But the Indian Wars had long faded—and jaded—into glorified tales of how the West was won. Her school lessons had moved on.

She reviewed her memorization work—each American state and capital, from the Atlantic to the Pacific. Her mind skidded to a recent radio broadcast, President Wilson calling for a million men to join the war in Europe. *A million men? There's barely a handful of age around here.* Her eyebrows furrowed and her eyes narrowed.

She slowed the horses as they approached Crow-Town, as folks called it—the spot along the turnpike where the Smith kids sat on the split rail fence, cawing at passersby.

We oughtn't call them crows. They're not after anything but a good laugh. And that older one is so. . . Shifting the reins to one hand, she twirled a tuft of hair around her finger. Her eyes drifted off the gravel, into the distance.

As they rounded the bend, a loud thump jostled them in their seats. The horses whinnied, drew back, and halted. Her siblings yelped.

Lena hooted a burst of laughter. She hadn't planned on the buggy's wheel lodging in a rut, but the happenstance proved quite convenient. As if on cue, she waved to the 'crows' on the split-rail. "Excuse me, but could you help us, please? We need to get to school." She stepped from the buggy, carefully holding her skirts off the messy road.

"What're you goin' to school fer?" The older boy smirked and didn't budge. "You already look pretty smart."

"To learn, of course." Lena felt her nose tip toward the sky. *Maybe I don't like him at all.* "And why are *you* not in school?" She raised an eyebrow.

The tallest fence-percher flicked specks of hay off his overalls. "The farm don't run itself."

Lena surveyed the group. The girl, about ten, the boys about twelve and five, all sported haircuts that looked as if their mother put a bowl over their heads and chopped away. They wore baggy farm clothes and no shoes. She *tsk*'d and addressed the eldest. "Well, you may need to farm, but why are the children not in school?" Her shoulders drew back. "I have a year of school left. I'll drive them." Gathering the hem of her skirts, Lena lifted one foot onto the buggy's step, as if to climb in.

The oldest Smith snickered, jumped down from the fence and headed toward the buggy. "You won't be driving nothin' if we don't free this wheel from the mud." He gathered some hay and sticks from the side of the road and forced them under the wheel, just in front of it. He called his siblings to join him behind the buggy to push. "Okay, now give the horse a holler and snap the reins. On three, ready?"

Lena jumped into place, grasped the reins, and followed his count.

The group grunted and pushed, their feet slipping behind them in the muddy road. The buggy lunged forward.

Lena retracted the reins. "Whoa." She turned to the mud-splattered squad and addressed them collectively. "I owe you thanks." Stepping down from the buggy again and extending her hand to the eldest, she formally introduced herself. "Lena Burriss." A curtsy, holding her skirt from the mud with the other hand, accompanied her proper act of gratitude.

The young man smiled with confidence, as if he'd forgotten the mud on his face. He removed his thread-worn flannel cap, reached for her hand, bowed, and graced the dorsum of her hand with a light press of his lips. "Clinton Smith, at your service, ma'am."

Taken aback by beams of light shimmering from the golden-brown rings in his eyes, Lena caught her breath. Goosebumps tickled their way up her arm and flushed her body, subsiding at her insistence. "Nice to meet you." She withdrew her hand and tucked a curl behind her ear.

The sun peeked through the clouds again in the east, drawing her attention. "Well, I'd best be going—almost time for the bell. But I meant what I said about giving the little ones a ride. They'd love the new schoolhouse. It's huge and built with brick—big enough for all the grades.

They have baseball and soccer for the boys, tennis for the girls, and even stables for the horses." She patted one of the horses and checked the reins. "Besides, it'd be practical. They're likely just underfoot around the farm."

"I'll speak to my folks about it. We've been busy since Gramps took ill. Much to do. This farm's been in our family for hundreds of years and we won't be the ones to lose it."

Her feet lodged deeper in the mud from standing too long in the road as she looked beyond the split-rail fence to survey the vast property. Cattle and horses grazed upon rolling green hills, framed by verdant woods at the horizon. Closer in, a donkey nudged its nose through litter and rusty machine parts by the barn. *Hundreds of years?*

Local history came to mind. Most of the land in and around the Patuxent had been granted to British colonists in the 1600s—the largest portion to a ranger who served the Crown. Families later divided inheritances and sold off portions to make ends meet. *Is this what's left of their original land grant?*

Thinking chronologically, as Lena preferred, her mind skimmed across lessons conveyed from the 1700s, when Quakers moved to the area. Decades before the Civil War, they had freed slaves and set them up with farms, businesses and schools. They'd become part of the Underground Railroad in the 1800s, not far from the famed Uncle Tom's Cabin.

I'm proud of my little town for that. But which history goes with this farm? She studied Clinton's face and clothing. *Probably not Quaker.*

Sissy piped up, her squeaky voice jarring Lena back to the task. "Come on, let's get to school."

"Oh, I, uh, okay." She curtsied again. "Well, wave me

down if you want me to pick them up tomorrow."

Clinton kicked a stone. He donned his hat and adjusted it. Turning away, he paused midpoint and looked back at her. A savvy smile lit his face. "What if I just wave you down so's I can see you again?"

Climbing back into the buggy, Lena's hands quivered. She shushed her snickering siblings, cleared her throat and summoned her dignity. Giving the reins a snap, she nodded her reply. "That'd be all right, too."

* * *

The next morning, the family gathered around the table and held hands to pray.

"I wanna say it," the little one squealed, to which Mama smiled and nodded. "Dear God, thank you for this food. And may the little crows come to school with us today. Amen."

"The little crows?" Mama raised her eyebrows as she scooped fresh scrambled eggs onto each plate.

Lena patted her sister's arm. "Let me tell it."

As the family ate, she relayed the story of what had happened as they'd passed the Smiths' property, and how they'd hoped that at least the little ones could go to school again.

Daddy raised an eyebrow, peeking up from his Farmer's Almanac.

Mama paused, looking first at Daddy, then Grannie, who tightened her lips together. Mama smoothed her apron in her lap and cleared her throat. "Do you know why they quit school?"

"To lend a hand when his grandparents got sick."

"Oh. . . but that was years ago." Her eyes darted toward Grannie's, then back to Lena. "They need schooling. Be careful, though. If they say no, don't insist."

"Yes, ma'am. But wh—"

"Ew, what is this?" Her brother squawked, pulling something out of his mouth. He held the thing for all to see, which, though covered in mushed egg pieces, looked like a bug. "A chunk of wood whittled to look like a bug." He turned a stern eye toward the younger boy. "Another of your pranks?"

The lad giggled. "Wasn't me."

"Sure was. Who else would'a done it?" He eyed everyone around the table.

Lena placed her napkin over her mouth, but laughter burst out the edges. Her azure eyes sparkled with childlike teasing.

"Lena!" He stood and went for her.

She raised her arm to defend herself, then grabbed him into a hug. "Gotcha back, that's all." Tickling his side as he pulled away, she added, "Come on now, you know you deserved it."

"Yeah, you did," giggled Sissy.

The twelve-year old puffed out his chest and sat back down. "Okay, okay. Now it's my turn again." Through a sideways glance and a pointing finger, he uttered a playful, "Beware!"

"All right, kids, that's enough." Daddy's brief chuckle at the morning prank ended as he set the booklet beside his plate and rose from the table. "Come on, boys, we've a few things to do before school."

"Yes, and girls, let's get these dishes washed up. And don't forget to brush your teeth this morning." Lena threw a telling glance at the usual guilty party. They finished the dishes and Lena ducked out the back door to enjoy her few free minutes reading by the cardinals' nest.

* * *

Again, Lena slowed the horses as they approached Crow-Town. She transferred the reins to one hand and slipped the other hand up to gently pinch her cheeks rosy. This time she would steer clear of the mudhole, now dry, but deep, nonetheless. She crossed fingers on both hands, then crossed her feet for extra good luck. *Please let him be there.* She counted the heads of silky black hair glistening like iridescent crows' feathers in the morning sun. *One, two, three. . . four!*

Clinton jumped down, followed by his brothers and sister. They were dressed properly, including shoes. They ran to the edge of the turnpike, waving.

"Whoa." Lena pulled back on the reins and the buggy came to a gentle stop. She waved back, grinning. "Good morning. So, your folks agreed?"

Clinton lifted the smallest one into the back of the wagon. "They did indeed. Said it was very neighborly of you to offer. Maybe we can get more done with the little ones out from underfoot."

"So, you're not going? Wouldn't you like to see the new school?"

"Nah. I have a lot to do. I'll meet you back here after school. Fair enough?"

"Fair enough. . . but you're dressed like you're going with us."

Clinton shuffled and looked back toward his farm as he

donned his cap. "I'm on my way to the corner store. We have a bike shop there. On Tuesdays I check to see if there are any bikes for us to fix. We repair them and return them each Friday."

Lena remembered seeing the new sign—half as big as the store's front porch. "Oh, that's your shop?"

"Well, my father's, but he's been learnin' me the trade. Says if we do well with this, we just might learn to fix motor cars next."

Her eyebrows arched. "How exciting!"

"Yeah. He says, what with the war comin' and all, folks are gonna need things fixed instead of buying new stuff. Could even help us save the farm, like I said."

"Oh, good idea. At least you're putting your mind to use. Are you keeping up your reading and arithmetic? You used to be pretty good at school."

Clinton took his turn raising eyebrows. He pushed the brim of his hat back to get a better look at Lena. Through squinted eyes and cocked head, pleasure hid at the edges of his mouth. "So, you remember me from school?"

Her face warmed. "Well, yes. You were in eighth grade when I was in sixth."

Clinton grinned full-out and stood taller. "Well, I'll be." Stubby fingers clutched his hat, sliding it from his head. He held the cap to his chest. "Would you like to meet me, say, at the library. . ." His other hand smoothed his hat hair. "Saturday?" We could read together. You can tell me if I'm up to par." One eye twitched as a sunbeam caught it. "We could grab a soda pop at the store." His eyes held her gaze.

Lena's pulse quickened. Her first invitation to what may be a date—and from the boy she'd been dreaming of, wishing for. . . the boy every girl in school would envy her for capturing, if ever they saw him. She leveled her response, not too excited nor overly aloof. Casting a sugary smile, she launched a coy twinkle from her eye to his. "Well, thank you. That'd be nice." Her parents'—and Grannie's—faces inserted themselves into her mind's eye. At the breakfast table. . . they looked at each other as if. . . *Wait. Were they suspicious of him—his family?* Snapping the reins, she faced the road ahead. "But I'll have to check with my folks, of course."

3

Becca

Saturday morning, Becca joined her friends near Wheaton Plaza and hitched a ride downtown to Sylvan Theater. Hitching saved the fifty-cent bus fare, money that may be needed for phone calls or cigarettes.

Once there, they ambled among the grassy spaces surrounding the National Mall, the White House, the Capitol, the Washington National Monument, and the long Reflecting Pool. Throngs of like kind—young people with long hair, dressed in fringes, flowery prints, and bell-bottoms or flowy skirts—filled the streets and parks. Some older hippies had already abandoned their clothes and waded through the pool as though no one else existed. Wisps of smoke suspended a musky, sweet-sour diffusion of patchouli oil, pot, hashish, and tobacco in the air. Music pounded through stacked loudspeakers affixed to scaffolding, where a few people climbed to improve their view of the stage.

As Becca neared them, the pulsing music forced her heart to keep time. She claimed a spot with her group, where she spread her blanket on the ground. Their backpacks propped together in the center created backrests.

The sun well above them, Becca shed her second-hand Army jacket. Laying her head on the jacket-turned-pillow, she closed her eyes, glad for the warmth on her face.

The crowd filled in, casting shade. Her sense of being surrounded forced her eyes open. She joined them to stand.

Frannie leaned in and yelled over the music into Becca's ear. "Hey, I just thought of something."

"What's that?" Becca shouted back.

"What's the difference between a rock and a hard place?" Frannie's chin jutted forward and back to the beat of the music.

Becca didn't bother trying to think of an answer. Frannie was known for her stoner jokes. "I dunno. What?"

"You can dance to rock." Frannie elbowed Becca. "Come on, time to get down."

"That's awful." Becca grinned and rolled her eyes, but took Frannie up on her offer to let her body move to the music.

The crowd jumped and swayed to the music, raising their arms, and chanting lyrics to both live bands and piped in music. As afternoon brought greater heat, Becca stripped to her tank top and jeans and kicked off her shoes. She swayed to the music but held herself back from dancing in abandon amid the crowd.

In between live bands, a popular recorded song blared. The singer asked what war is good for, and, in response, the crowd shouted in unison, raising their fists to the drumbeat. "Absolutely nothing." Becca joined the chant.

The crowd circulated apple and strawberry wine, pipes and joints and pills of unknown variety. Becca took a swig of Boone's Farm and passed the bottle along. Wiping her mouth, she waved off a joint.

Chester. Her friend Chester had died just a few weeks prior. He smoked killer weed and got so out of his mind that he ate his parakeet. At least that's what her friends said happened. She doubted the story, but nonetheless, Chester was gone.

And Liam. He passed out, drunk, in the middle of the road—and got hit by a car. He died too. And Melinda. She fell from the side of a truck as she and her friends took a "sky-high" joy ride through back-country roads. Dead. And the famous ones—Janis Joplin, Jimi Hendrix, Alan Wilson.

Country Joe and the Fish lyrics floated through the smoky air and met her conscious thought. ". . . and it's five, six, seven, open up the pearly gates—well ain't no time to wonder why, whoopee! we're all gonna die. . ."

Too many had been lost to drugs and alcohol, and Becca had no desire to annihilate herself. The thrill of breaking free from adult approval and acting out against all she deemed wrong with the world exhilarated her, but moreover, she wanted to survive her teens. She would get a little high, no more.

"I've gotta whiz," Becca shouted as she jumped, pointing over the heads of the crowd to the line of port-a-potties. The crowd did not yield. A tall stranger with a kind face offered to help. She agreed, and before she knew it, he hoisted her to his shoulders. Becca placed one hand on her hip and with the other, pointed the way. "To the John!" They forged through the crowd like a fine steed and his maiden, laughing all the way.

From the stage, a women's libber took the microphone and shouted something about freedom and shrugging off the restraints of the system. She tossed her bra into the crowd, who cheered and responded in kind.

Time slowed from this higher vantage point upon her steed's shoulders. The warm sun glistened, spreading fairy dust to glide along the uplifted hands, and washing Becca's heart in lovely release. Her arms unexpectedly wiggled out of her bra straps and she produced the under garment from under her shirt. She flung the symbol of restraint to fly among the people.

"Let freedom reign!" Becca laughed at herself as she paused to survey this momentous occasion. Not like her at all, to act so wild and crazy, but fine by her—today.

Arriving at their destination, she bid her steed to permit her dismount. "Thank you, kind sir." She curtsied with awkward giddiness and joined the line of bladder-full, joyous rebels to the wrong.

As she waited, the music transitioned into a 60s protest song. The guys began to chant and shake their fists in the air. "Hell, no, we won't go. Hell, no, we won't go."

Becca saw them, those scrawny, young, bearded, long-hairs, facing the draft. Maybe they had received their letters already and were waiting for their number to be called. *They shouldn't have to fight a war they don't believe in.* She wanted to hug them all.

The buzz in the air loomed heavy after that, laden with pending doom.

Late at night, music still blaring, most everyone had

settled onto the lawn of the Sylvan Theater and the surrounding greens. Some lit campfires to keep warm, burning anything nearby to stoke the fire. Her group, without a fire, huddled together in the center of their circle. Hungry and uncomfortable, but surprisingly safe, Becca turned to her side, curled into a ball, and drifted in and out of sleep.

At 6 a.m., the police moved in. The megaphones' static noise woke her. Becca forced her head up. Peering through strands of her tussled brown hair, she saw half-drunk and drowsy campers busily engaged, collecting their belongings. Some were leaving. "What's going on?" She pushed herself to a sit.

"They're kicking us out." Frannie shoved her blanket into her pack.

"I thought we had a permit for the weekend." Becca stood and began searching for her shoes.

An announcement over the loudspeaker clarified the orders. "Man, I know this doesn't seem cool, but the police are saying our permit expired at 6 a.m. Military police are all around, so be cool, everyone. Do what they say, and we'll figure this out. If you don't leave, they'll arrest you. Peace, everyone." He held up two fingers in a peace sign.

"Come on, let's split." Frannie tugged at Becca's sleeve. "There's no time to find your shoes."

"But I just bought them. My parents won't give me money for another pair this year." The putrid smell of burning rubber assaulted Becca's nostrils. She followed the scent. In a smoldering pile of ash, the charred remains of her missing shoe hissed and curled, consumed.

Hobbling across the manicured lawn toward Fourteenth

Street to catch up with her group, the sight of her one-shoe-off-one-shoe-on state caught Becca's eye. Dr. Seuss children's story lilted through her head, contrasting against lines of armed guards, appearing almost cartoon-like as they manned the streets of a nation built on freedom. She shook her head and laughed. "My foot is. . ."

Frannie ignored her friend's amusement. "Come on, keep truckin'." She directed Becca's attention ahead. "Don't mess with them. They'll shoot."

Frannie was right. They were not cartoons and this was no laughing matter. Militia—Marines, National Guard, and DC cops—hemmed the streets, delineating government property from public, clarifying the designated route out of town. Becca's chest tightened. Her eyebrows furrowed. Incredulous, she marveled at the show of force. Her thoughts spilled aloud. "Gas masks and shields? Don't they know we stand for peace?"

A horse-mounted patrolman circled in front of them, blowing his whistle, signaling Becca's group to abandon their shortcut across the grounds of the National Monument. Her group complied and joined the masses evacuating the city, walking between the solid lines of arm-linked, shielded officials who enforced the way. A shiver raced through her. *George Orwell saw this coming.* Having recently discussed his book, *1984*, with Frannie, Becca tipped her head closer and, under her breath, quipped, "Are they Thought Police, too?"

Frannie cast Becca a sideways glare, huffed a half-laugh, and whispered back. "Pigs. Oinkers."

Becca's jaw clamped as she checked Frannie's face and body language—her eyes fixed and lips pressed tightly together and her movements were stiff and forceful. Protesting the war was one thing, but Becca didn't want to clash with the law. Or be thrown into jail. Or be hit with a club. She loved the rebel yell, and the music, but especially the freedom this weekend promised. *This, though?* She tucked her head and walked in line. *This is not freedom.* "I was just kidding," she whispered to Frannie. "Be cool."

4

Lena

Sandy Spring, Maryland. 1917

When Lena announced her desire to visit the library on Saturday morning, her family decided to come along.

"You look mighty nice for a trip to the library, young lady," her mother whispered as they climbed from the buggy. "Your Sunday dress, ribbons in your hair." She leaned in and winked at her daughter. "Are you sure you're just looking for books?"

"Mama." Lena giggled. She meant to check with her folks about Clinton meeting her here, but one after another cat had taken ahold of her tongue.

The library, housed in a small building across the street from the Sandy Spring Store, paled in comparison to the newer brick buildings—the bank, the insurance company, and the meeting house. Comfy chairs welcomed visitors to settle in and read while deciding which books to take home.

Her father and brothers crossed the street, heading toward the store, while Lena, her sister and mother approached the library.

Once inside, Lena perusing poetry and classics, while Mama and sister found a seat among the children's stories. Lena ran her fingers over the lovely, embossed flowers on the cover of *Poems* by Emily Dickinson. *Are these flowers supposed to appear as though they're wilting?* Her hand stopped on a well-read version of Jane Austen's *Sense and Sensibility.* The cover's ruddy color reminded her of the clay soil by the creek on her family's farm. *Sounds like a good one—I wonder why she contrasted the two words. They seem to mean the same thing.*

"Hmm, looks like a sensible book to me." A familiar voice hummed from behind her shoulder.

Lena's shoulders tensed, then relaxed. Turning toward him, she took a half step away. "Mr. Smith. I wasn't aware of your interest in fine literature." She smiled to show her intent to tease with such formal language.

"Oh, quite so," Clinton played along, assuming a British accent. "Why, if you would be so kind as to accompany me to the porch, I would be delighted to recite from memory." He stepped aside and waved one arm toward the front door.

Lena stole a quick glance at the children's section, and seeing her mother engaged in reading a book to the little ones, she garnered her courage. Still playing the fancy game, she raised a delicate right hand toward his. "With pleasure, kind sir."

Lena strolled with him, glad to be wearing her Sunday finest, a faded white dress with tiny pink flowers. The dress boasted a full blouse with embroidered collar and long sleeves. A ruffled hem at the bottom of the A-line skirt ended an exact inch from the floor. A wide sky-blue ribbon cinched the waist, tied in a crisp bow in the back. In this dress, Lena became a lady.

When she sat, she made certain to tap her knees and ankles together, tucking her feet slightly to one side beneath her knees. She rested the two chosen books on her lap.

It seemed to her that Clinton had dressed especially nice for the day, wearing a slightly mismatched suit and vest over a nearly white shirt with a straight collar. His shoes seemed a size too small, his toes pressing protuberances in the leather tips. He sat on the bench with his legs apart, leaning his elbows onto his knees, his chin resting on one fist.

He stood, pointing into the morning sky, his other hand against his hip. Clearing his throat, he quoted Dickinson, in grand recital.

> "Read, sweet, how others strove, Till we are stouter;
> What they renounced, Till we are less afraid;
> How many times they bore the faithful witness,
> Till we are helped,
> As if a kingdom cared!"

He let his hand fall. A faint smile quivered his lips.

Lena clapped in girlish delight. "I do believe you've read this one." She lifted Dickinson's book. "And not only read, but committed to memory? I owe you an apology, Clinton Smith. Honestly, I thought you were kidding."

Clinton sat next to her. His chin seemed to rest a bit higher.

"See now? There's more to the world than just school. Lena, there's so much in these books. . . so much of the world. There are books about war heroes, battles, and quests. Why, if you ever want to travel, you just check out a book. If you want to learn a trade, there's a book that will help, like this one." He held up his selection, "It tells me how to construct things, from a bobsled to a moving camera. I'll be building engines in no time."

Lena relaxed. She'd been afraid that, as cute as he was, he might be intellectually inferior after dropping out of school so young. Instead, his initiative and tenacity impressed her. Her face grew serious. She let her eyes meet his. "That's so true. But the piece you recited. It's about war heroes, no?" She swallowed hard and pushed out the next question. "You're not old enough for the. . . war, are you?"

Clinton met her change in tone. "Oh, no, you needn't worry about that. My father might have to register, but I don't think they'll call him at his age." He sat back, straightening his arms and pressing his fists against his thighs, then drew a deep breath, his chest puffing out. "Although I would, if I were old enough. I can do a man's work. Don't know why they won't let me fight for freedom. Because I would, Lena."

Lena imagined the worst. Bloody tales of the Civil War and Spanish-American War still circulated when the older men gathered. Grannie's loss etched deep lines in the old woman's face and rounded her shoulders into her sunken chest. *Grannie must have been sad a long time. Maybe still.* Opposing sides battled within Lena—one ready to rise to protect those she loved, the other hesitant. *Clinton seems valiant. Admirable. But heroes die young. Should I let myself feel what I'm starting to feel? Stop, girl. He's looking at you, waiting for an answer.*

She formed one, a surprisingly decent one considering where her mind had gone. "Well yes, I guess that's where you related to the poem: 'Til we are stouter.' But you wouldn't have to do such a thing to prove yourself." She checked herself, attempting to bring her words under closer scrutiny. "I mean, after all, I just met you. I wouldn't want to see you running off to war." A slight gasp closed her mouth. *I said too much.*

"Nor would I." Clinton smiled again and reached for her hand. "We're a good family, Lena, I assure you. Even though I left school, I want you to know I'm a worthy suitor."

Lena blushed. The hand he held started to sweat. Would he feel the moisture through her white glove?

Clinton didn't seem to notice. He went on, his voice gaining excitement. "There's a dance next weekend at the Lyceum. May I take you? I'll ask your father, of course, but if he agrees?"

Before she could gather her thoughts, filter them, and choose sensibly, Lena's answer spewed out. "I'd be happy to." Her hand slid out of his as she suddenly stood. "Here comes Daddy now."

Across the pebbled street came her father, a tall thin man with a mustache too large for his face. He wore an old farmer's shirt, with suspenders holding his baggy pants in place. At his side strode two of her older brothers. The three of them, on a mission, headed straight for Lena and her newfound friend.

Lena moved toward them, Clinton behind her. They stopped mid-street.

"Daddy, I'd like you to meet Clinton Smith."

They exchanged introductions, Clinton showing proper respect. "Sir," Clinton started, "I've found your Lena to be most interesting, intelligent, and delightful." He straightened his back and cleared his throat. "I wonder, would you grant your permission for her to accompany me to the dance next weekend? I will treat her with the utmost respect and have her home before ten."

Mr. Burriss glanced at Lena as if in so doing he might determine her wishes on the matter before deciding. He sucked his cheeks in, his mouth tucking nearly into a circle as he considered the matter. Then he squared up to Clinton, lifted one eyebrow, and spoke. "Son of Thomas?"

"Yes sir."

"On the Patuxent?"

"That's our farm."

He nodded. "How is your family, these days?"

Clinton shuffled and looked at his feet. "Very well, sir. Except for my grandparents. They're getting on, in years, you know."

"Yes, I suppose they are. And you, what are your plans?"

"I work the farm and the repair shop. My father says I'll be taking over the repair shop soon, and, someday the farm, sir."

Henry nodded. "Come and have supper with us first, tonight. If all goes well, then you may take her to the dance—chaperoned, of course, and home before nine."

"Yes, sir, thank you, sir." He reached to shake Mr. Burriss's hand.

An unusually loud noise from behind the store interrupted the group, which still stood in the middle of the road. *Ah-*

roo-gah, the horn blared again, louder this time, its source emerging into view.

Lena's lower jaw dropped as she propped her hands on her hips. "A Ford Model-T, here in Sandy Spring?"

Clinton took her arm to escort her to the side of the road. He looked at the vehicle, then at Lena's reaction. "I'll have one of those soon. You watch."

Though thrilled to see one cruise through town, the thought of riding in a motorized vehicle unnerved her. "Ooh," Lena said, her chin sliding toward her neck. "No hurry on my account."

Lena's father and brothers, after completing the shaking of hands, left the young couple on the porch and disappeared into the library.

"Oh, I almost forgot." Lena led Clinton to the family buggy. "Here, I made this for you." Reaching under a blanket on the buggy floor, she produced a boxed pie from the morning's baking.

Clinton sniffed the enticing aroma. "You made this?" His lips spread across his face and his eyes glazed over.

"Indeed." She curtsied and assumed the drawl of a Southern Belle. "Why, so much is changing—and so quickly. As for me, sir, I will greet the mechanical age head-on, with lace, ribbons and home-made pie."

* * *

He brought flowers. "Good evening, Ma'am." Clinton offered the gay bouquet of Queen Anne's Lace, bluebells and daisies. "These are from my mother's cutting garden, with her greetings."

"Why, thank you, young man." Mrs. Burriss bid him to come in. "Mr. Burriss told me you'd be joining us for dinner tonight. Let me take your hat."

Lena approached them, coming from the kitchen. "Here, I'll get it, Mama." She placed his hat on the hook and walked with Clinton to the dining room, where she introduced him to everyone.

On his manners and polite conversation, Clinton endeared himself to Lena, her parents, her siblings and their spouses as they chatted through dinner and retired to their singing circle in the parlor.

"Go on, pull it." Clinton said to Lena's little brother.

"Why, what's gonna happen?"

"Pull it and see." He grinned, his eyes shining with impish glee.

The boy tugged Clinton's finger.

Out from Clinton's feet burst a giddy, double-paced bit of the Turkey Trot.

Everyone laughed and clapped.

"Do it again," the little ones begged.

By the end of the evening, several of the family learned the dance steps and Clinton was a hit.

After bidding him goodnight at the door, Lena slipped into the chair next to Grannie.

"Grannie, everyone seems to like Clinton, but you've been extra quiet. Is something wrong?"

Grannie reached over and patted Lena's forearm. Her eyes, deep between the leathery folds that time pressed upon her face, reached for Lena's. "They call the Smith family crows for a reason. Tricksters, they are. Watch. Choose well."

Lena tipped her head to the side. "You? I wouldn't have thought you would be one to judge him by the thoughtless things people say."

"Not judge, Starlight. See."

Choosing one of the bluebells from Mama's arrangement on the table, she fastened the flower in Grannie's hair. "You are wise, but sometimes I think you worry too much." She smiled, kissed her grandmother on the cheek, and, with a gentle but dismissive tone, concluded the matter. "Enough said. I've chores to do before bed."

* * *

The dance went well. He was quite the gentleman. Their relationship ensued, with Lena occasionally remembering Grannie's warning.

Clinton greeted her with a fistful of flowers every morning when she stopped to pick up his siblings on the way to school. Every Sunday after church, he held her hand and walked her home. As she sat poised in her Sunday finest under the dogwood tree, he read poetry aloud—in grand fashion. Around the table, he told funny stories, animated and imaginative, delighting her younger siblings and impressing her mother. He worked on the family's buggy and fixed broken things with her father. Tipping his hat into hand, he danced the soft shoe outside Lena's window, crooning delightfully silly and well-smitten love songs in the moonlight.

Lena watched. He was no crow at all, no trickster. *What was Grannie thinking?* He was a charming lad with bursting dreams and confidence enough for them both. He was smart

39

and thoughtful and kind and funny. He was resourceful and lively and dedicated and true. He, he, he. . . he was all she'd dreamed of, and more.

5

Becca

Washington, D.C. 1971

They plodded along the armed streets for twenty blocks until the blockade thinned to an occasional cop on a corner. Public transportation being suspended, the group stuck out their thumbs. Immediately, a motorcycle unit pulled up to them and redirected them.

Becca pointed "Look, there's a line of phone booths." The scruffy, tired, hungry, and broke group of teen-aged wayfarers stood in line to make collect calls home for a ride. Becca's father was the first parent to answer. She described their location, and he told them where to wait.

They tossed their backpacks in the rear window and squeezed into the station wagon for the door-to-door service Dad provided. The vehicle was quiet at first, and then casual talk and laughter replaced the silence. Becca's

Dad was warm and friendly, accepting of their situation. He told a few stupid jokes that embarrassed Becca but made her friends laugh.

Frannie was the last one to be dropped off. The car stopped in front of her house, a mid-century modern with a tall, wispy cedar tree hanging over an array of front windows that formed a two-story right triangle. She reached for her bag, opened the car door, leaned in toward Becca's ear and whispered. "He's cool."

Becca shrugged. "If you say so."

As Frannie waved from her doorway, the two of them drove away. The emptiness of the station wagon emphasized the space between the two remaining occupants. Being alone with him had never been easy. Her abs tightened, preparing for impact from the impending lecture. *If I keep quiet, he won't yell. Or maybe if I thank him for giving everyone a ride? Will that be enough to throw him off?* She fixed her eyes out the window as she weighed her options.

He didn't wait a minute to begin. His eyes squinched the way they did when he meant business, and pierced her through the rear-view mirror. "You were lucky." His tone reflected the look. A harsh breath forced out from his nostrils and his head shook side to side. "Things could have turned for the worst." His lips tightened as he turned a corner, and his eyes flitted back onto Becca through the mirror. "Your mother worries about you. You didn't tell her you were planning to stay all night. She's going to have a mouthful to say."

His pause met silence.

"You don't have to talk to me, young lady, but I want to know one thing. Why? Why would you do such a stupid thing as staying downtown all night?"

Becca seized the opportunity to use offense as defense. She raised her voice and ranted. "To protest this stupid war. I can't stand it. Boys being forced to fight a war they don't believe in, only to come home in a box. Your sons could be next, Dad. Or my friends. For what? Is Vietnam any of our business? And the politicians—sending young men off to die—why don't they just talk out differences, like adults? Or line themselves up to fight instead of sending kids to do it for them? I can't sit by and take it."

Her quickened breaths and pounding circulation came as a surprise. She had thought she only cared about the music, but now every word gushed from her heart.

Her father's deep breath and sigh lingered, creating several long seconds of respite. His voice deepened. "It feels wrong to me too, and I've fought for this country." His eyes caught hers again through the mirror. This time they softened. "I admire your passion, but I have one thing to tell you—something I learned after many years." He paused again, as if gathering the most concise version of an important lesson.

Becca folded her arms, crossed her legs, and bounced her cold foot with nervous fury. His words sparked curiosity, temporarily overruling her mistrust of anyone over thirty. She drew in a breath and forced it out. *Fine. I'll ask him.* Her voice snapped, snarkier than intended, but in sync with her body posture—"What?"

His eyes smiled at her through the rear view mirror. He had chosen to overlook her impudence. This time.

"You're never going to stop war. . . because war. . . comes from people. If you want to stop war, you'll need peace in every person. . . in every family."

Her errant foot bounced with renewed intensity. *Peace in this family?* She stared out the car window. *So much for ending war.* Trying to focus on each store, house, and person they sped by, the images blurred. She rubbed her eyes. Her hand smelled like pot, opening a portal to the past.

Becca had come inside from playing with her friends to get a drink. Passing, Emily and Carlton in the dining room, she looked to see what they were so engaged in doing together.

They were rolling a joint on the plastic tablecloth.

Shaking her finger at her older siblings, she threatened them with her best twelve-year-old, whiny voice. "I'm telling."

Emily laughed her off. "Try it," she said. "It's blueberry."

"You're just trying to keep me from telling. I'm not falling for it."

Carlton slid the joint under Becca's nose. "Really, smell it. Blueberry paper!" His face read genuine, like he'd found a pearl of great worth he wanted to share.

But this family didn't share.

Something about the fruity paper and the offer to share weakened her childish defenses. She sniffed the joint.

Telling had never made a difference. What was the point?

Carlton lit the joint and toked it long and hard. He handed it to Becca.

Emily provided the verbal instruction, as if Carlton's demonstration hadn't been enough. "Draw it deep into your lungs, and hold it as long as you can."

They're being nice to me. She followed Emily's instructions.

The car stopped at a red light. Becca glanced at her father again. He wasn't paying attention to her anymore. Looking down, she noticed her foot had stopped shaking. Her arms had relaxed onto her lap. *Everything changed that day.*

The light turned green, and with it, the blurred houses resumed their entrancing magic. Becca slipped back through the portal, searching for where she'd left off.

After a few tokes, she had wandered outside. Her friends played hopscotch on the sidewalk, two houses up, but she didn't join them. *A person who smokes weed doesn't play hopscotch.* Her head hung low as she turned and went back inside.

Emily and Carlton, giggling together, rolled another J.

"Em, can I borrow your fringed belt and embroidered top?" Becca's face felt funny, like a cartoon almost, but she was pretty sure her eyebrows were appropriately positioned to plead.

To Becca's surprise, Emily scurried to her room. Producing her hippie clothes and Carlton's elephant-bell jeans, she smiled. "Here you go. Until you get your own."

Why is she being so nice? Becca shrugged, grunted a thanks and changed her clothes. Wrapping a beaded string around her head, she stared at her new persona in the bathroom mirror. *Either be a goody-goody or this, but not both.* She cast herself to the hippie role.

Dad's cigarette smoke wafted through the car, drawing Becca out of her trance. She wanted a cigarette but dared not ask him. She clicked her thumbnails together, noticing her need for a good nail scrub.

She had been a good girl. Honor roll. Now here she was, dirty fingernails, coming home after a wild foray into the world of free concerts with freak flags flying and pot smoke for air and chants against war and government and pigs. Everything had changed that day—the day of the blueberry joint. It hadn't been because she got high—she didn't. She had entered a world beyond childhood. A world beyond her age or comprehension. A world in which she and guilt cohabited.

She'd rejected her parents' control over her, disregarding rules at home and school. No longer fitting in with her age-peers, she'd tagged along with her older siblings, hanging out at The Hill. Her grades had taken a nose-dive. Yet, Becca hadn't cared. Newfound apathy and guilt cohabited in Becca's muddled mind.

A grasshopper landed on the car window as they waited at the next red light. Becca ran her finger along its bottom side, the glass barrier between the bug and her flesh allowed the green insect to disregard her touch. She pondered its powerful rear legs, its sticky feet and huge eyes.

When trying to rescue a praying mantis from her older brothers' torture, Becca learned that caring came with a cost. The frightened insect, tender and pale and apparently defenseless, had rewarded her four-year-old innocent intervention with a sharp, stinging bite.

The car sped up, and the grasshopper's sticky feet released their hold on the glass, sending it careening toward some unknown landing. *Hopefully on soft grass,* Becca wished.

At the next red light, a church on the corner caught Becca's eye. Tall gothic doors swung open and well-dressed people filed out—the men wearing suits, and the women, spring-colored dresses and white gloves. Some wore dainty hats.

Becca scrunched her nose. *Man, do they live in a different world.* She determined to look away, but a small girl walking alongside her family held Becca's attention. The child stumbled, not watching her step, her nose tucked in a book. Becca's eyebrows tipped up. *I used to love to read, and visit church with Uncle.*

Seven again, the young Becca responded to an altar call, confessing the only sin she could think of—that of sneaking a flashlight to read under the covers after bedtime.

How silly of me. Her eyebrows squeezed together, and a bothersome tear wet the edge of her lashes. She blinked and rubbed the annoying droplet across her temple. *God. Hmph. Why believe in someone who never cared to answer my prayers?*

She had prayed for Terry to like her. And Jimmy. And Bill. And Tom. And Steve—pouring out her adolescent soul in prayer each night for years, asking for someone she liked to like her. Her child's prayers for Mom, for Dad, for sisters, and brothers, all unanswered. Not knowing if life could be better, she'd longed for it, to God.

But that was long ago.

They passed the car wash, about half-way home. The roar of vacuums sent her into another memory. She and her sisters, sequestered to clean their room—her sisters happily playing with dolls or reading comic books. They would have stayed there forever. Becca had cleaned meticulously, even all their messes, to regain the privilege to play outside. . . to climb her tree.

An ambulance screamed by, jolting Becca's mind back to the car again, and her father, driving. Becca let her gaze pause on her father from behind the front passenger seat, her favorite spot to claim when the whole family piled into the car, all the kids screaming, "I call window." His image, from this three-quarter rear angle, his high cheekbones, black-rimmed glasses, ruddy, leathery skin and peppered hair, etched a place in her mind alongside his words about war and peace.

Peace, within?

Through a tiny spot in his glasses, she could see a portion of the road ahead. The visage warped, as through a prism, into a blurry, disfigured mass. Again, she flashed back. As a small child, she'd mussed his hair and pulled the plastic-framed glasses off his nose. *He used to let me put them on. Everything looked so blurry.* The little girl had asked her Daddy, "Is that how you see?" His answer, she recalled in his gentlest tone, "No, they help me see the way you do."

Becca refocused her gaze to her nails, this time sliding one nail under the other, pushing the dirt out and flicking it onto the floorboard. *I wish those glasses really helped you see things like I do. If ending war means bringing peace to every family, then. . . have you given up, Dad? Is that what you want me to do?*

They rode through a nice neighborhood with two-story homes and manicured lawns. A small family played together in a front yard—parents and kids, together. *They look so peaceful. Not like my crazy family.*

For a fleeting moment, riding home from May Day in the back seat of their 1960 Country Squire station wagon, Becca connected with her heart. *I won't give up on peace—or love.*

The car turned a corner, then another, and onto her street. Lined by single-story ramblers with run-down yards, her street hosted an occasional long-haired teen, blaring music and working on old, rusty cars. She looked down at her foot with the missing shoe. Pushing off the other shoe and tucking both feet up on the seat, she wrapped her arms around her legs and rested her head against her knees. From the safe spot she created within her folded body, she quieted her turmoil with resolve. *I'll make my family better.*

6

Becca

Kensington, Maryland. 1972

Becca laid her pen down on the notebook and rolled to her back in the soft grass. Looking up at the sky, she wiped a tear from her face. *I feel so alone. Does anyone notice me? Does anyone care?*

A gentle wind teased Becca's eyelids closed. For a moment, she was twelve again, dancing with her friends at the sixth-grade, end-of-year party. She recalled her excitement to be going to junior high and her certainty that soon her life would include regular school dances and meeting new people, including her first love.

Becca had been proud of herself for making straight A's that year. She was the first in her family to do so, and her teacher sent home the most encouraging comments in her report card. *Great potential.* A flutter of joy brought lightness to her face—almost a smile. Her biggest worry that year was what to wear, and if she danced as well as Dawn. *All the boys liked Dawn.* The memory faded, as did her peaceful expression. *Boys. Now they're guys, not boys. And boy, did I get myself into trouble.*

Seventh grade had not lived up to its promise. Neither had eighth. Things had spun so out of control. She opened her eyes and watched a car go by—*That day in the car, driving home from May Day, when Dad said peace had to begin in each person, in each family.*

Becca had tried making peace at home. Instead of fleeing from arguments, she had spoken up, tried to reason with them, to mediate. She had taken on housecleaning, laundry, grocery shopping, cooking, and budgeting, since age ten, and Dad's words that day had churned within her, chal- lenging her to take on conflict mediation. But her parents wouldn't listen.

"Stay out of it," they'd shout.

Becca had turned to the school guidance counselor for help, who'd, as a result, sent a social worker to the house to interview the family and discuss the problems. That choice bit Becca back—even worse than the praying mantis she'd tried to save when she was but a child. Her father's face, red with anger and his voice, booming, replayed in her mind.

"How dare you tell someone else about our problems? It's none of their business. Don't you ever. As long as you live under my roof, you abide by my rules. We'll solve our own problems."

"But you never do! You just keep going over the same things, dredging up old mistakes and throwing them at each other. We need help here. It's horrible living here. Mom, Dad, come on, let's do this counseling she's suggesting."

"I work hard, long hours, to put a roof over our heads and food on the table. You will show respect, young lady, or you'll be out on your ass. Do you hear me?"

"There's no point," her mother had chimed in, fuming and throwing her hands up in disgust. "No counseling is ever going to change him. He's a hard-headed monster, that's all. Don't you go blaming me for this mess. I didn't ask to be stuck here all these years having baby after baby. You think I want counseling to make things better with him? You've got another thing coming. All I want is out, but I don't have a way out."

That entire exchange, in front of the visiting social worker, who had tried in vain to intervene while Becca and her siblings all threw their frustrations and gripes into the mix. Becca remembered sitting there, going quiet in the midst of the frenzy, realizing there was no use. She remembered wishing she could find love soon, marry early and start a new life. A better one.

Mom's words, the ones she'd hurled at Becca after the

counselor had left, vied for attention. She couldn't really understand what Mom had meant, entirely, but the words still bounced against each other like Newton's Pendulum in her brain.

> "Do you want them to throw your father in jail? Then we'd all be in the poor house. We'd end up getting separated, and you kids in foster homes. No. Just keep what's in the family in the family."

Having done all she could to make home better, she had given up—abandoning herself to wistful dreaming, willing herself older so she could leave. Like her grandmother once said, *'What can't be cured must be endured.'* She'd given in to her various boyfriends, enduring what they'd wanted, but hadn't thought it could happen to her. Not really. She'd dreamt of love and of creating a better family, but she hadn't planned on it.

Usually insistent on using at least contraceptive foam, just in case, Becca had figured she was too far along in her cycle to worry. In that moment, so in love, longing to marry him—she'd thrown caution to the wind.

Luis.

Becca's body tensed. Her lips tightened. She rolled back over to her stomach and sat up. Pulling her legs into crisscross position, she adjusted her t-shirt over the slight bulge below her waist. *I can't believe I actually wanted to marry him and have his baby.* She held her head in her hands, letting her hair cascade to her knees, creating a tent around her. *And now he's gone.* Her nose tingled. *No. No crying.*

She thought of the teasing rhyme she sang many times—

whenever she found herself on the pity pot. The song always helped her make fun of herself for how pitiful she felt. *Nobody loves me, everybody hates me, Guess I'll go eat worms.* The silly song did not work this time. *Stop, Becca. Just stop. There's no use feeling sorry for yourself. Go tell your mother. Ask for her help. There's no other choice.*

Becca pushed her hair out of the way and stared at the neighbor's brick house. The long wall had been covered by dark green ivy for years, giving Becca's eyes rest. The ivy's lush charm had been beautiful. Until the invasive roots, affixed in the mortar, put the structural integrity of the house at risk. *'We need a strong house, not a pretty one,'* her neighbors said when they pulled the ivy out, leaving the bare brick pocked with tiny holes and dead pieces of root.

But Dad. He's gonna kill me.

And he might have. He had beaten her before, lost control and reason, punching her in the stomach repeatedly just because she abandoned her chores in favor of seeing a boyfriend the last day before he moved. She evicted the vision of that memory, shaking her head and shoulders, her spine shuddering like a dog trying to free itself from the discomfort of being soaking wet.

Becca laced her fingers into the curtain of hair around her. She pulled the captive strands just enough to hurt but not enough to tear them out.

My friends say abort. But I still don't have the money, even after saving all summer. I lost my job because I refused to wear a phony wedding ring. The manager—he could see the bulge my parents haven't noticed. And the fake ID fell through. I need Mom's consent to—

She stood and took the familiar journey from front yard to back, where she slipped in the dog pen and snuggled with King and Queenie.

Gina.

Gina worked at Hot Shoppes with Becca that summer. She had seen Becca crying one day in the break room. When Becca had admitted what was wrong, Gina's empathetic manner had turned to tender excitement. "Keep her," she'd said. "She'll be beautiful. She'll have your eyes, and your love of life. I can just see it."

Becca's hand cradled her lower belly. *It's not fair that this baby doesn't have a say. But can I give this child life? A better one?* She slumped toward her mother's room.

* * *

"You can't." Becca's mother spoke emphatically. "At five months, abortion is not legal, not even with my permission." Cecelia's hazel eyes pierced Becca's.

"I heard they'll do it this far along in New York. I just need your permission."

"No, it's too dangerous that late. You could die." She picked up the phone. "I'm calling my doctor, he'll know."

Becca sat on her mother's bed, fidgeting with the edges of the pillow she cradled in her lap. Realizing she'd bit her lip, she reached up and touched the sore spot, pressing into her teeth. *I don't see another way.*

Cecelia finished speaking to her doctor and hung up the phone. She fixed a strand of hair back into place in her salt-

and-pepper French twist. "He said an abortion this late is too risky. But there's a place you can go until you have the baby. They'll help arrange an adoption. No one needs to know."

Somewhere in the back of Becca's mind, a tangle released. *I didn't want an abortion. Not really. This person inside me. I can feel it.* She resisted the urge to place her hand on her belly, which bulged only slightly even at five months. She knew the answer to her mother's proposal. "No. I don't want that. I wouldn't know who. . . or where. . . Even bad families adopt babies, you know. If I carry the baby, I'll keep it."

Cecelia turned, her body almost facing Becca, one knee on the bed and the other on the floor. "Do you know who the father is?"

The blood left Becca's head. *What does Mom think of me?* She wanted to mount a defensive flurry. Instead, she held her tone in check. "Mom, of course—there's only been Luis. But he went back to Columbia with his family."

"Do they know about this? They have some responsibility, you know."

Becca cringed. Above all, she hated conflict. "He knows. He said he would help me with money for an abortion. Then he left without even saying goodbye. I've been saving, working on the weekends. I have enough to buy a crib and some baby things."

Well, if you're thinking about keeping the baby, we'll have to tell your father. He's the one that will have another mouth to feed."

It's come to this. He will know. Spiders crawled beneath her skin, everywhere at once. She rubbed her arms and legs, pulling her knees toward her chest. "He'll kill me."

Cecelia exhaled with force and uncrossed her arms. "I'll tell him. Here." She reached into her wallet and pulled out a bill. "Take this. Go to a movie with a friend tonight. Call me before you come back. I'll let you know if it's safe to come home."

"Mom. . ." Becca sighed, her eyebrows tilting up in the center. *She's actually being cool about this?* "You'll do that?"

"We can't have him losing his temper, not with you pregnant. One blow and you could lose the baby."

Becca took a short breath in as her hand reflexively shot to her belly. Abortion was one thing, but to lose a baby at your father's hand? "Thanks, Mom."

Becca slunk out of her mother's room to prepare for a movie with Carol. Relief washed over her.

The baby kicked.

You get to live, baby. You get to live!

7

Lena

Sandy Spring, Maryland. 1918

Lena steadied herself against her front porch balustrade, gazing down at Clinton as he, on one knee, moonlight glistening on his face, waited for her answer with the anticipation of a child ready to unwrap a chocolate bar.

Is this sense or sensibility? She had always planned on higher education, not considering the cost or feasibility of such a lofty goal for a poor farmer's daughter. She had planned on becoming a teacher, perhaps a writer, but most certainly on inventing mechanical things that would help around the farm—with lace, ribbons and home-made pies. Yet, in the moment, her former aspirations seemed the insensible ones.

At once, she abandoned herself. Willingly forsaking her plans, she embraced the most sensible thing—the thing that filled up her senses. A giggle and two words spilled from her lips. "I will."

Clinton stood, pulled her into his arms, and kissed her. "I know I can't afford much. Not yet. But I promise you happiness. We can live at my parents' house while I fix up the little house on the edge of the property."

"But. . ."

"No buts, baby. Come on, I can't live without you near me." He flashed his brown eyes and pressed his nose against hers.

Eye to eye, face to face, body to body, Lena found no strength to resist his charm. "You!" She grinned. "Are you sure they're all right with it?"

"Sure, I'm sure. It'll just be a couple of months. It's a big house, so you'll barely even see them. I promise."

"Well, I guess Daddy can show my brother how to drive the buggy to school. He's been driving the plow since he was eleven."

"Then why wait? Let's get married this weekend! I've already talked to Pastor. He said he can do it."

Eyebrows raised in disbelief, she drew back. "This weekend? There's no way, Clinton. There's so much to do."

"What's there to do, really? Just you and me, promising to love and to cherish each other forever." He crinkled his eyebrows. A forlorn look filled his eyes. His lips pouted ever so slightly.

Lena rolled her eyes and gave him a playful shove.

He drew her back into his arms.

She wanted to please him, and his offer was mostly practical, considering her burgeoning desire for him. She wanted to be with him every day, all day, and never say good bye. Using her confident and sweet voice, she relented.

"Well, let me check with Mama first, at least. But the wedding must be at my house. Outside, on the hill. We'll pull the table and chairs next to Mama's flower garden."

"Now you're talking."

* * *

"No, Lena."

"But you like him, and so does Daddy. Why must we wait any longer?"

Mama pulled the needle and thread, stretching her arm above her head, then turned the needle and lowered her arm to start the next stitch. "If marriage is worth anything, it's worth waiting for. A commitment like that is the rest of your life, child, so much longer than you've even lived yet." She looked over the top edge of her glasses, which perched half-way down her nose.

"But I'm as sure as can be." Lena's eyes searched the room as her mind searched for points to sway Mama's thinking. A painting of Grannie's lost soldier cued her. "What if he's called up for war? Since they lowered the draft age, he could be gone—just like that. I might never have the chance to be in the arms of the man I love." She twisted the hankee in her lap. "There might not be any men left after that, Mama." Lena paired her plea with a pitiful look—the sort a toddler sports when trying to persuade a parent into an extra piece of candy. Her face morphed into the look of a puppy dog chided for tearing up furniture.

"Honestly, girl. You think I'll fall for that look after all the children I've had?" Aggie laughed and waved her child off. "We'll host no wedding before due time."

"You're impossible!" Lena stood and, in a fit of feminine fury, turned to her father. "Daddy, talk sense to her. You know a few more months isn't going to make a difference in how much Clinton and I love each other. You and Mama got married in just six months and look how happy the two of you have been all these years."

Henry looked up from his manual. He laid the booklet on the table and stroked his mustache and the edges of his mouth. "Settle down, Starlight. Your mother and I will talk about this and let you know our decision later. It's not the sort of thing we take lightly, you know."

"But all my older sisters and brothers, they all married the same, or not much older than I am."

He put his hand up. "That's enough, now. I told you, your mother and I will talk. Now go on, get yourself ready for bed."

"Yes, sir. I'm sorry, Mama." Lena followed Daddy's orders, slumping away. But her insides were storming off, huffing and puffing. *This house. These chores. Always someone, more than one someone, in every room, every space. More chores.*

Dressed in her nightgown, she propped her elbow on the windowsill and looked out at the family farm. She'd always loved home, but now? Flat squares. Scruffy old livestock meandering around piles of dung. Noisy hens and goats and donkeys. Paths worn thin where the dogs ran along the fence, laying bare the rust-colored dirt. Fenced in, the whole lot. Doubly—boxed in by trees on every side.

Her eyes traced above the trees, toward the moon, following her heart's beckoning. Beyond the farm, in the direction of the Smith property on the Patuxent, rich soil and verdant rolling hills, flowing with life. She could not see them from here, but she knew. *Clinton.*

A deep and heavy sigh darkened her view. She walked to her bed, lifted the covers and slid between them.

I bet Grannie told Mama and Daddy what she thought about Clinton. Now they're all against me.

* * *

After three more months of persuasive arguments, Daddy and Mama relented.

Clinton and Lena wed.

She wore the pretty white and pink-flowered dress she'd worn on their first unofficial date at the library. Her older brothers and sisters came home that weekend, and the Smiths made a special trip to witness the family event.

After the brief ceremony, the Burrisses arranged chairs in a large circle and brought out their instruments. As was their custom on Saturday nights, but this time outside, by the flower garden. The sound of this happy night filled the air for at least a country mile, and Lena and Clinton danced with nearly every family member.

Lena snuck into the house to freshen up before leaving for their honeymoon, a night in a Baltimore hotel and a day in the city. She paused to look around her room, running her fingers along the bed and the washstand. *I'm going to miss you, old room.*

Thoughts of Clinton swelled within her. This would be the beginning of their beautiful life together, and she didn't want to wait another moment. Heading out the front door, she paused only at hearing her parents.

They stood on the porch watching the festivities and hadn't heard her come near.

She didn't resist the temptation to listen in on their private thoughts.

"Well, you know, we weren't much older when we married." Aggie leaned into Henry. "They grow up so fast."

Henry put his arm around Aggie's shoulder and gave a light squeeze. "He'd better be good to her. You know there's something about him that worries me. Impulsiveness, maybe."

"Aw, now," Aggie put a finger into Henry's side. "Just youth. I remember you like that, too. And there wasn't any stopping us. Time will tell. We decided, and we'll stick to our decision. We'll stand by them, like we do all the others. They'll work things out."

Lena backed up and intentionally bumped into the doorway, alerting them to her presence. "I'm off." She hugged their necks and bounced out to join her groom.

Clinton took his bride's hand and led her toward the buggy.

* * *

The young Smith couple spent the first few months of their marriage living in Clinton's parents' house while he worked on their future home. He tried keeping her out of the old clapboard house at the edge of the property to surprise her, but she peeked a time or two.

"Come on, please, show me." She tugged on his shirt buttons, casting him the puppy-dog eyes she'd used on her parents. She was anxious to move out from under his parents' roof. They hadn't been as kind as Lena's parents, complicating her adjustment to a new family. Lena longed to move into this place. Even if the furnishings were bare, they could have a proper start to their lives together here. "I promise I'll love it—almost as much as I love you."

"Oh, all right. It's almost ready, anyway. Let's go have a look, together."

They walked hand in hand from his parents' house to theirs, carrying the picnic basket Lena had prepared for their dinner under the stars.

Clinton opened the front door and carried her over the threshold. Once inside, he lifted Lena by her waist, spun her around the parlor and back into his arms. "It's ours. I promise we'll be happy here." He squeezed her tightly, pulled back, took her hand, and led her into the room down the hall. "Look, I put a bed here for us, and over here, a wash basin." Leading her toward the kitchen, stumbling and laughing as they went, he opened the cupboard door, which nearly fell off its hinge. "Oops, I'll fix this, I promise." He laughed and kissed her again, took her hand and opened the back door. "From here, it's a short walk across the field. I can still work the family farm, fix bicycles, and whatever, no problem."

"I love it, just like I thought I would. You've done a great job." Lena stepped out onto the back porch and caught her breath. The pastoral scene, right out of a classic storybook, inspired dreams of their idyllic life to come—rolling green hills of Smith property as far as they could see, dotted with cattle and horses. "Is that the Patuxent I hear from here?"

"It is. Rich farm land, and the river's just beyond that

treeline."

Slipping her arm around his waist, she leaned her head onto his shoulder. "It's perfect."

"We'll be happy here. I will always take care of you, and that little one in the oven." He placed his hand on her belly, which was starting to protrude, ever so slightly.

Lena laughed. "One son, coming up, just as the doctor ordered." She squeezed his waist against hers. *At least I hope—a boy would make him so happy.*

The two stood on the back porch for a moment, taking in the dreamy start to their lives together. Lena broke the silence. "Let's start moving in."

"Whoa, now, you'll not be lifting anything heavy. Let me do most of the work."

"Understood. My brothers will help. Mama said anytime— just let her know and she'll send them over."

Clinton shook his head. "No need for that. I've got things well in hand."

Shrugging, Lena smiled. "If you say so, but you needn't do everything by yourself. No need to prove your manhood to me." She winked and patted her tummy. "I got that."

He squeezed her to his chest and lifted her chin, bringing their lips together. "Yes, you got that, and more where that came from."

The two christened the new bed and then, after snuggling for a few minutes, settled onto the back porch for their picnic dinner.

8

Becca

Bethesda, Maryland. 1973

Becca struggled for release, her eyes squeezed tight against the harsh fluorescent light. Her spine retracted from the cold metal gurney. Sweat rolled down her face, dripping into her ears. Her pursed lips blew out shallow puffs of air. The arches of her bare feet pressed against frigid strips of steel, curling her toes. She fought to squeeze her splayed legs together to stop the pain, but something prevented her. She opened her eyes, hoping for something, anything, to hold on to, to press against, to escape. Her arms strapped to the rails of the gurney, and her legs to metal stirrups, she writhed, pushed against the restraints, squeezed her eyes tight again, and let a blood-curdling scream wail from deep within.

A strong, commanding voice overrode her cry. "Bear

down, bear down!"

Becca could only resist, and that with every muscle in her body. *What is happening? Is this a nightmare?* She struggled to ferret out reality. The last she remembered, she'd been in a comfortable bed, where she'd drifted off after the injection.

The harsh command reiterated. "Bear down like you're having a bowel movement!"

The voice seemed to come from above her. Something pressed on her stomach. Her eyes opened to a nurse above her, leaning over and pushing her contracting belly toward the doctor at the end of the gurney, between Becca's widespread legs.

She tried to comply with the nurse's commands to push. Her muscles defied her will, tightening to resist the pain. Pushing would explode her into a million pieces. She was alone, no one to hold her hand, coach her, or tell her how to breathe. She was a captured alien on a cold metal table with strangers restraining and probing and hurting her. "I can't."

Someone from behind her placed a clear plastic mask over her nose and mouth.

Becca squirmed and wriggled as much as she could, trying to plead through the plastic mask to the unseen figure behind her. "No! I want to be awake!"

"You're not pushing."

Gasping for air, blackness edged in from the periphery and took over.

A pitiful, gurgling cry brought her back.

"My baby?" Opening her eyes, lifting her head, she saw dark hair—and blood. She saw the doctor and nurses busily engaged in pulling the baby from her body. Becca's head spun. She wanted to stay awake to receive her baby, but blackness took over. She was out again.

Ow! What is that? Sharp needles pierced her in rapid succession, drawing her out of her drugged state. "Ouch! Stop!" She tried to reach, to fight off the incursion, but her arms, strapped to the sides of the gurney, proved useless. "What are you doing?"

"We made a clean incision so you would not rip," said a voice. "It's called an episiotomy. The doctor is stitching you up. Hold still."

She blacked out again.

Her body lifted into the air, awakening her. She opened her eyes to the team transferring her to another gurney, this one with a mattress and clean sheets. They covered her with thin white blankets and began wheeling her out of the delivery room. Becca looked down at herself. Her legs were flat and straight against the mattress. Her huge mound of belly was gone, but her stomach wasn't flat, either. At least she could see the outline of her toes in the blanket—the first time in months.

"Where is my baby? Is my baby okay? I want my baby!"

"Are you keeping her?" The nurse redirected the question to someone else. "Is she keeping her?"

Her? It's a girl! "Yes, I'm keeping her! Why wouldn't I? I want to see my baby! Is she okay?" Panic welled in her voice.

"Are you sure you want to keep her? Giving her up for adoption is easier if you never see her."

"What are you talking about? Yes, I'm going to keep her. Is she alright? I want to hold her."

"Okay," the nurse relented. "We'll bring her to you in a minute. We need to get her cleaned up and monitor her stats for a few minutes. She's fine."

They continued wheeling Becca down the hall.

"No! I want to see my baby!" Becca tried to get up. The blankets, cocoon-like, trapped her. Her pulse raced. *Something is wrong. They're not telling me.*

The transfer team stopped. A nurse patted Becca's arm. "Hold on."

"Here, here she is." Another nurse carried the swaddled baby girl over and held her for Becca to see.

Becca's world stopped. The pain, the sounds, the bustle of the busy delivery ward all ended abruptly. She gasped. *There she is! Aw, baby girl, smushed little nose and creased lips, so adorable. And a head full of dark hair, like mine. An angel, so peaceful after all that.* Becca fell deeply in love in an instant. *This is my baby.*

"I want to hold her." She reached her arms toward the swaddled miracle of life.

"No, we need to finish up with her, and get you settled into your room. Then we'll bring her to you for her first feeding. You rest now."

Becca didn't understand. She just wanted to hold her baby. "Is she okay?" Becca asked again. She noticed her baby's head wasn't perfectly round. Her face had small bumps all over it. *Poor thing—she has my pimples.* Becca simultaneously pouted and smiled. She stroked her hair and ran a gentle finger across her face. As she reached out to hold her again, the nurse pulled her back.

"She's fine, we just need to check a couple more things. You rest. Don't worry."

They wheeled Becca away.

With no energy to fight the returning darkness, she fell back to sleep before reaching her room. When she awoke, groggily, as if from a long sleep, she looked down at her body and placed her hand on her stomach. *It really happened. My baby!*

She surveyed the dimly lit room. Curtain dividers hung from the ceiling, gathered at the wall, exposing the entire room's dingy blue-gray walls, and checkered linoleum tiles. Four beds aligned, two on each wall, with windows on her left and another bed, then the door, on her right. The two beds across from hers were empty, with light spilling over their pillows from the boxed valances on the wall above. Red switches, oxygen tubes and pull chains dotted the walls, giving the place an impersonal, cold feeling. On her right, a woman lay sleeping. Light from the hallway streamed through the door. The beeps and buzzes, steps and chattering voices came from down the hall somewhere to the left of the door.

How long was I out? She ran her hand alongside the bed. Finding the nurse call button, she pushed it.

After a few moments, a nurse came in. "Yes?"

"Can I see my baby now? They said I could feed her in a minute."

"Oh, you slept through her first feeding."

Becca wanted to cry. Or scream. Or get up and go find her baby. *Why didn't they wake me?* "I want to hold her. I only got to see her for a second."

"Okay, I'll bring her in a few minutes. The nurses are all busy right now."

The few minutes seemed an eternity. Becca chewed her

nails, hoping her baby was okay. She wanted her here, in the room, not down the hall in the nursery. At last, a figure appeared in the back-lit doorway. She held a bundle. Becca's face lit up. Then her heart sank as the nurse carried this bundle to the woman in the next bed.

The woman sat up and gushed with excitement. She spoke loudly, as if her baby were a toddler, not a newborn. "Let me see you, little guy!" She unwrapped him and inspected him head to toe, welcoming and praising him, and then scooping him into her arms to feed him. Looking over at Becca, the experienced mother let her eyes rest upon the young girl in the next bed.

Becca shifted her gaze, as if she hadn't been gawking. *I wish I had her confidence.*

"Babies are such an amazing gift. This is my fifth! I can't wait to get him home to meet his brothers and sisters.

And she's so positive about the whole thing.

"My God, girl, how old are you? You look like a baby yourself."

Becca felt her cheeks flush. She looked down and smoothed her gown over her swollen belly. This was not the first time someone stated the obvious about her being too young to be pregnant. Avoiding eye contact, she quietly told her truth. "Fifteen."

"Oh, my goodness, you're so young. Well, no matter. People have been having babies too young since the beginning of time. You'll do fine if you set your mind to it. I was seventeen when I started."

Finally, an adult who doesn't judge me for this. Becca settled a bit and watched her feed her baby. *My baby. Where is my baby?*

The nurse came in with another bundle, heading straight toward her.

With a shortened breath, her arms reached out for this precious, tiny human being, hidden in the swaddling of a soft receiving blanket.

The nurse instructed as she presented the infant to Becca's outstretched arms. "Be sure to hold her head. Her neck isn't strong enough yet."

I know. Having helped raise her younger brother since she was ten, she was prepared for this. She received her baby with one hand under her head, the other under her torso and bottom. Becca cradled her baby in her arms, a perfect fit, and held her to her chest.

She's beautiful. She's alive. And pink. And beautiful. Becca stroked the baby girl's head, smoothing her dark hair. *Hmm, her head isn't quite round, but I remember Mom telling me not many are, at first.* With a very light touch, she stroked the bridge of her nose and forehead. *Why are veins showing through her eyelids and across the bridge of her nose? No matter, she is beautiful. I can't wait until she opens her eyes.*

"I'll be back in fifteen minutes to get her." Nurse pulled the curtain closed between the two beds.

"Fifteen minutes? But I want her here with me. Can't you bring her bed here next to mine? I want to take care of her."

"No, you need your rest. You'll be home soon enough with her. Believe me, you might as well enjoy your rest while you can." The nurse laughed and waved a knowing hand.

"No, I want her here with me," Becca protested. The joy of meeting and holding her baby conceded to the flash of anger that rushed through her body—a reaction to the way she'd been treated since entering this place the night before.

"I'll see what I can do, but it's not our policy," the nurse shook her head as she backed out of the room.

Alone now with her baby—well, relatively alone, as the curtain blocked her from anyone's view, Becca's heart settled back into place. She gazed at the wonder before her and gently stroked her baby's face and hair. *I guess I should check her over like the lady next to me did.* Gently laying her down between her legs, she unfolded the blankets slowly. She didn't want her baby to be cold, so she checked her over quickly. Astounded by her perfect little body, Becca noticed her own skin was pale compared to the baby's. *Her father's skin tone. . .*

They'd met when he visited his cousin at Becca's school. Gorgeous and olive tan-skinned, with wavy brown hair, Becca's eyes locked on him at once. She still remembered what he wore that day. A Western-style green shirt with piped yoke and snapping pockets, faded blue jeans, and Frye boots. His hazel eyes smiled with obvious pleasure when their eyes met. His teeth were perfect, his smile confident and engaging. He spoke English with a dreamy Latin accent.

His gas-hog of a fancy car didn't impress her, but at least he drove, while Becca still walked everywhere. She soon learned it was his father's car, and his family would be in the United States temporarily, on Columbian business. The family lived in a lavish home in the best part of town, but Luis, in contrast to his family, seemed casual and at ease with Becca's crowd.

Becca waited for him while he chose to date her best friend first. With that fling over, and with her friend's consent (*You can have him*, she'd said), Becca soon fell completely for Luis, dreaming of marrying him and having his baby.

Only fourteen, she chided herself for thinking that way. But if they married, he could stay in the states when his family's appointment ended. In a few months, her whimsy turned reality. Part of it, anyway.

The baby part. But pregnancy changed everything. Hormonal changes made everything smell horrible, even Mr. Perfect. Her pregnant mood swings pushed him away.

How could we have made it, anyway? If we'd married, the stress would've driven us to divorce. I didn't want her to go through the pain of losing her father. It's better to never have known him.

There had been no need for such angst. The family returned to Columbia. Luis left with them, without so much as a goodbye.

Becca and her mother had finally tracked down their number and called to let them know her condition.

"Diplomatic immunity," Luis's father had said. "We have diplomatic immunity."

Back to reality, Becca gazed at her little beauty. *Ten fingers. Tiny, slender, perfect little fingers and fingernails.* Placing a finger in baby's palm, Becca giggled as those tiny fingers grasped her own. *Ten toes. Cute little piggies to count and tickle—soon enough.* Touching just under her toes, they curled around her finger too. *Sweet.* A bandaged umbilical cord covered her future belly button. *I hope you get an innie.* Becca swaddled her baby in the blanket to keep her arms and legs from dangling.

The nurse came in with a bottle. "Do you want to feed her now?"

"Yes, of course." Becca's heart ached now, at the thought

of not breastfeeding, but she had already decided, with her mother's insistence, that since she'd be going back to school in six weeks, bottle-feeding would be the best choice. In the flush of bonding with her baby, her mind changed. "But can't I breast-feed her for a few days?"

"No, you said you would bottle-feed, so we've already given you the pills that dry up your milk. You shouldn't try now." She placed the bottle on the bedside table and wrote in Becca's chart.

Becca sighed. *I have no idea how to breast-feed anyway. But in this moment, I want to. Now I can't.* Her brows furled over the bridge of her nose. *I'm not good enough for this baby. She deserves a parent like the one in the next bed—one who's confident, who can welcome her with ease and know just what to do.*

She picked up the bottle and tested the milk's temperature by shaking some onto the underside of her wrist. Snuggling her baby close again, she stroked baby's cheek and offered the nipple to her lower lip. Love washed over her again.

Baby woke enough to peer through squinting eyes.

"Hi!" Becca whispered. *Those eyes. Beautiful dark eyes. Oh, you're melting my heart.* "Hi, honey, I'm your mama. Happy birthday, little one." Becca smiled as she said more in her head. *Welcome to the world. I'm so glad you're here. I promise I'll keep you safe.* She was too shy to say all she thought all aloud, and besides, positive words seemed a foreign language.

Baby squinted in the light, peeking at her mother, then turned toward the nipple and began sucking.

The nurse stayed a few moments, giving Becca instructions about how many ounces, about pausing to burp her, then feeding her more.

The words faded into the background as Becca gazed at her beautiful little girl. *A perfect little human being from inside of me. Unbelievable.* "Okay, I got it." Becca forced a smile at the nurse.

The nurse left, wagging her head on the way out the door.

Becca's confidence swelled. *Why do they all act like I'm too young for this?*

They didn't know she'd been an adult since age ten. They didn't know she had been trying to teach her parents to get along. They didn't know she'd been cleaning, shopping, and cooking for her parents, brothers and sisters—for years. They didn't know she'd been reading all the baby books she could find at the library, or that she'd been painting, crocheting and sewing for the nursery, and making A's in school—all so she could be a good mother to her baby.

She stroked the baby's silky hair, bumpy forehead, tiny nose and pink-clothed shoulder. *I'm going to do everything I can to be the best parent I can be for you, little Christine. Yes, that's your name! Christine. You're going to know you're loved. I'll protect you with my life. Everything will be okay.*

Finally, seeing the baby's alertness, she whispered another welcome to the little one. "Hi, Christine, I'm your mama. I love you so much." Becca gazed at her precious girl. She lightly stroked the edges of her cheek with her forefinger while presenting the bottle. A song played in her mind. She hummed the tune, rocking her babe, lyrics cycling in her head—*"hmm, hm, hmm, thinking 'bout my baby, ain't got time for nothin' else."*

9

Lena

Sandy Spring, Maryland. 1918

Clinton lowered his voice and revealed the edge of a brown paper bag hidden beneath the front seat. "I have a little surprise for the first night in our own place."

Uneasiness pulled at her stomach, but she played along. "What is it. . . a bottle?"

"We'll cook up a couple of nice steaks and enjoy a glass of wine as we watch the sun set."

Lena put her hand on his arm. "I don't know. I never tasted any alcohol before, but a romantic dinner with only you sounds good." She looked around, as if anyone might see them in the middle of rural farmland. "But what'll your parents say if they see it?"

He laughed and jumped out of the car. Tucking the bagged bottle under his arm, he presented Lena with his other hand to help her out of the buggy. "Don't you worry your pretty little head, my darling. It's fine."

The steak, cooked to perfection, never tasted so good.

"Oh, that was absolutely delicious." Lena sat back in her chair and placed her hand on her belly. "But I couldn't have another bite."

Clinton poured himself a third glass. "If you're not going to have another, I will. No sense wasting the bottle."

"One was enough for me." Yawning, Lena stretched. "I feel so relaxed I could sleep now." She took up the empty plates and carried them to the kitchen.

"Aw, come on, sweetheart, the night is young. Let's put some ragtime on the phonograph and do some foxtrot. We can try the new one, the bunny hug." He gulped his drink and headed for the phonograph, dancing without any music.

"Maybe just a dance or two, but honestly, I don't feel so good." She sat on the sofa while he cranked the Victrola.

Half-way through the song, Lena begged off and started toward the bedroom. "Ooh, I need to lie down. My head is spinning."

Clinton pouted. "All right, sweetheart. I'll be there in a minute." He poured the rest of the bottle into his glass.

How can he stand the stuff? Lena held her head with one hand and traced the wall with the other. She sat while changing into her night clothes before slipping under the covers. As she drifted off, Clinton opened the door. The music blared, making her ears hurt.

"Sweetheart, this is our first night here. We at least need to christen the bed again." He kicked off his shoes and pulled his trousers down, letting them pool on the floor. Jumping into the bed next to her, he lay on his side and propped his head on his hand. "Prince Charming is here."

She opened her eyes from her wonderful, cozy place and squinted at him, lying there, inviting her to enjoy his offer. But his words slurred, and his face looked goofy. He leaned in to kiss her. "Oh, your breath!" Acting on reflex, she pushed him back. *Rotten fruit and garlic.* Lena spilled out of bed, ran to the wash basin, and retched.

Clinton stomped out of the room, knocking his shoulder into the doorpost on the way. "Is this how it's gonna be? A man's first night in his own house with his wife, and this?" He stormed toward the front door.

Lena followed, grabbing a towel to wipe her mouth. "Baby, I'm sorry. I wanted to celebrate, too. But I guess being with child doesn't go too well with that drink. Come on, come back to bed."

He stopped, fixed between the front door and his wife. "All right, then. But come on, I want you to give me some lovin'."

Lena, too tired to argue, waved him into the room.

Clinton had his way with her and promptly fell asleep, his hand lying across her neck.

Lena lay staring at the dark. She worried he'd be called to war before seeing his baby. Maybe he was too stressed from his work on the farm and in the shop, plus his pending status as a father, so soon after marriage. Maybe she hadn't pleased him enough. He'd pushed himself into her even when she'd shown no interest. *Must have been that drink. That's all.*

* * *

He came in the door and slumped into the sofa. "Called for duty," he said.

She sat next to him and placed her arms around him.

Everything happened so fast. He was gone. They sorted the men, suited them up, sent them out.

Lena's prayers took on new depth and desperation.

Over a million Americans joined the Meuse-Argonne offensive. In just forty-seven days, forty-seven days of no news is good news, forty-seven days of wondering, waiting, hoping, fidgeting, praying, and all the other things families do when their soldier is gone. . . forty-seven days, and the war was won.

Clinton came home.

He came back! But he came back different. Lena placed her hands across the table and spread them out for him to hold. "Talk to me, sweetheart."

Clinton, stone-faced and dulled eyes, just stared at her hands.

"We're all so proud of you."

The grandfather clock chimed.

She stood, placed a hand on his shoulder and squeezed it. "I'll make supper." As she chopped, kneaded, baked and boiled, Clinton sat and stared. *Whatever did he see?* Her lower back reverberated with a dull ache. A few minutes later, another, stronger. Another, just three minutes later. She turned the stove off and sat back down in the chair opposite her husband. "Clinton, please go get Mama. The baby's coming early."

His eyes slowly moved to focus on her.

"Clinton!"

"What? It's time?" He ran to do as she said.

In the weeks to follow, Lena had a tiny preemie to tend to. Less than five pounds, he was, little Shaw. Red and scrawny but alive and beautiful, Lena did everything Mama said to keep him alive.

They moved the bed near the fireplace and made an incubator, of sorts, by propping up the mattress and placing blankets all around him. This blocked the cold breezes that inevitably snuck through cracks around the windows, doors and eaves. They wrapped him tightly, swaddling to help him be calm and grow stronger.

"He'll have to push against the swaddling to start moving." Mama tucked him in and handed little Shaw to Lena.

Lena looked puzzled. "Won't that be too hard for him? He won't like it."

"Yes, he will. If he'd stayed inside your belly the full term, he would've been more squished in there. The pressure on a baby is good for them—makes them stronger."

She watched his face. "He does seem to like it. Puts him right to sleep."

"Yes, love." Aggie touched his cheek with her finger. "You might have to rub his cheek here a little. Tap it, even, to get him to eat."

Sure as Mama said, he turned his head, as if on cue, and his mouth made a sucking movement.

In the round-the-clock vigil of keeping Shaw alive, fed,

nurtured, comfy and cozy, giving Clinton his time in silence was easy. She was too exhausted to coax him into talking. Besides, she didn't mind that he left her to herself for a while. *At least he's alive, and home.*

10

Becca

Bethesda, Maryland. 1973

"You're going home," Becca whispered to Christine. "There's a cute little crib I painted for you. And I sewed a fuzzy yellow kitty for you. It's a crazy house for a little baby, but I'll make things as nice as I can for you."

Becca's mother entered the room, followed by an aide with a wheelchair.

"I have to ride in that?" Becca squirmed in her bedside chair, frowning at the wheelchair.

"It's a long way down there. You'll be glad for it." The aide locked the chair's wheels and swung back the footrests. "Come on, climb in, I'll give you a fun little ride."

Becca's mother held Christine while Becca sat in the wheelchair. She handed Christine to Becca, picked up the overnight bag, and surveyed the room. "Is this everything?"

"Yes, except those flowers. Can you empty the water from

the vase and put them here next to me?"

"It was so nice of your uncle to send flowers." Cecelia walked to the sink and let some of the water pour out. "It seems I only get flowers when I have another baby."

Becca watched Christine sleep. *No one's ever sent me flowers before.*

Cecelia tucked the vase of flowers between the arm of the wheelchair and Becca's thigh. "I think we're ready."

As they reached the end of the hall, the aide turned the wheelchair in the opposite direction from the main elevator.

Cecelia piped up. "Where are you going?"

The aide continued pushing the wheelchair. "We'll take the service elevator. The main one is down for repair."

They rode the service elevator down in silence. As they approached the main lobby, the aide turned toward a smaller exit. She suggested Becca's mother bring the car to the door, and she would wait with Becca and the baby.

Once in the car and underway, Cecelia spoke first. "I don't like that they took you down the service elevator and out the side door. It's like they were trying to hide you, like they were embarrassed to have a teen mother in their hospital."

"Why would you think that?"

"Because the main elevator was working fine. I had just taken it, and I saw people there when I passed by the lobby to get the car."

Becca's heart sank. She stared out the side window, the sunlight flickering through the trees as they sped by.

"Well, you might not care, but I certainly do. I'll call the head of the hospital and complain as soon as we're home."

Becca sighed. "Mom, please. Let's just enjoy this special time. We don't ever need to go back there."

They pulled up to the house.

"Wait here, I'll come around and open the door." Cecelia parked and walked around to Becca and Christine's side. "Do you want me to carry her?"

"I can manage, but can you grab my bag?" Becca winced as she rose to stand up with Christine. The pain of her episiotomy stitches forced her back into her seat. *Ow, this pressure.* A burning sensation signaled an urgent need for the bathroom. "Well, okay, maybe you can carry her in."

Her mother reached for Christine. "Come here, little one. Oh, you must be cold." She pulled the blanket over Christine's face in the freezing January air. They hobbled up the frozen sidewalk between piles of snow.

"The keys are in the front pocket of my purse. Everyone's at school or work, so it's just us three for now."

Becca fumbled for the keys successfully and opened the door for her mother and Christine. "Let's show Christine her room, then I need to lie down for a while."

Cecelia carried Christine into Becca's room and gently laid the sleeping baby in her crib. She turned to check on Becca. "Are you okay?"

Becca laid her bag on the floor and slid into her bed next to the crib. "Yeah, I guess so. I just ache, and it burns to pee."

Cecelia's brow furrowed. Her lips pursed. "They let you go from the hospital like this?" She shook her head. "That is the worst hospital I've ever known. All my babies were born either at Women's Hospital downtown or at St. Catherine's. I was treated like royalty. Well, I'll call the doctor and see how soon they can see you." Starting out of the room, she turned. "Didn't they tell you to use the special soap after every time you went to the bathroom?"

Becca glanced down. "Well, they showed me a bottle of dark red stuff to wipe with, but I didn't want to get myself all stained. I didn't know—"

Mom approached Becca and placed her hand on Becca's forehead. "You're burning up. You rest. I'll bring you some water and call the doctor."

Once her mother left the room, Becca let the quiet soothe her soul. She turned to her side and pulled her knees toward her chest as she hugged a pillow snugly pressed into her belly. From this position, she could watch Christine's breath make her little tummy rise and fall. The sight washed Becca in comfort. *She's okay. We're home, Christine. Well, until I can find us a better one.*

* * *

Becca settled into the routines of motherhood. Focusing on Christine helped ease discomfort while healing from the urinary tract infection and episiotomy.

She timed and measured Christine's feedings, every four hours, being careful to burp her after every two ounces to minimize gassy discomfort. When Christine napped, Becca sterilized bottles, boiling them fifteen minutes. Using tongs to scoop the bottles out to air dry, she'd boil another pot of water to become formula. Blending in correct measures of evaporated milk and corn syrup, she poured the formula into eight sterilized bottles and sealed them to store in the refrigerator.

Washing a load of diapers and, on alternate days, baby clothes and bibs, consumed what might otherwise be free time each day. These new chores, on top of her school work and general chores, left no time to nap. Catching up on the broken nights of sleep when Christine needed feeding, changing and rocking became impossible.

Some days, Becca didn't even take the time to dress herself. She didn't see the importance of dressing when she wasn't going anywhere, and she didn't want to fuss over herself when a little person needed her attention.

When Christine awoke, Becca's heart lightened. She held her and stroked her little hands and soft hair. Becca carried her around the house, showing her everything for the first time. Christine's every movement, glance and sound brought waves of delight through Becca. She had never known such love.

Sometimes, even though beyond tired, she would just hold Christine and gaze at her angelic face, whispering to her sleeping baby. "You are so beautiful." She'd run her finger over Christine's forehead. "The little white pimples are gone and your skin glows. You're perfect—your eyes, your nose, your lips, your ears. Your little fingers and toes send giggles through my heart." The foreign language became more natural when speaking to Christine.

When Christine's gaze focused on Becca, their eyes latched onto each other in blissful dreams of mutual adoration. Her eyes were deep, dark blue, which Cecelia said meant they would turn brown. Her wispy brown hair stood straight up, a comical sight. Becca applied baby oil to help the wild hairs lie down and to ease her cradle cap. "You have worse dandruff than me, little girl," Becca teased, stroking her daughter's head. "No worries, though. Grandma says that will go away soon."

Christine yawned, her mouth opening so big.

"Why look, even your gums are straight." Becca smiled. "I'm sure that means you'll have straight teeth."

Cecelia flipped on the evening news.

"No, Mom, please. You know I hate the news."

Becca's mother ignored her request. "Your father will be home soon."

Becca gathered Christine's things to head to their room, when President Nixon's voice gave her pause. She sat back down and looked at the box.

"We today," he said with gravity, "have concluded an agreement. . . to end the war and bring peace with honor in Vietnam. . ."

Tears flooded Becca's eyes. "The war is. . . over?" She pulled Christine into her chest. "Baby girl, I thought you might be an angel. And look now, just two weeks into the world, and you've brought peace. You're such a good girl."

* * *

Six weeks flew by in a sleep-deprived, blissful blur.

"I have to go back to school next week." Becca plunked on the couch near her mother after getting Christine off to sleep. She spoke her worries aloud. "How are we going to do this? I mean, I love taking care of Christine, but how can I manage going to school and homework plus all of this? The two a.m. feedings keep me exhausted."

Quitting school was permissible at sixteen, but Becca, still fifteen, had kept up with schoolwork with the help of a home tutor the county provided. Becca's tutor was great. She helped her adjust to pregnancy and the emotions that some-times overwhelmed her. Her kind support restored Becca's commitment to education. At six weeks after delivery that assistance would end.

"I want to finish high school, for Christine. A degree will help me be a better provider in the long run."

"You know I agreed to babysit during school hours, as long as you keep your grades and good behavior up." Cecelia looked away from her sitcom to face Becca. "She's six weeks old this weekend, so you can start adding some baby rice cereal to her night feeding. That will help her sleep through the night."

"I can? Oh, good! Will you show me how to do that tomorrow?"

Her mother was right—over the next two nights, after many trials of scooping baby cereal that Christine's tongue reflexively spit out at first, Christine slept nearly seven hours straight.

Becca awoke at five to feed and dress Christine, then showered and dressed herself, leaving for school by seven. Becca missed Christine each step of thirty-minute walk in the cold. She slipped into the back doors of school, hoping not to be noticed.

The last time she walked these halls, at five months pregnant, her nipples leaked through her bra and shirt. Becca had covered her chest by holding her notebooks in front of her and rounding her back and shoulders. The effort was to no avail, for gossip had spread its greedy, finger-pointing whispers quicker than a summer hail storm ruins a brand new car. Kids who'd never spoken to Becca pointed at her, their lagging tongues concealed behind cupped hands as they spoke. Their whispers caused the listeners' mouths to gape. She knew they whispered about her—about Becca being pregnant.

It had been a great relief to have the tutor, removing her from daily embarrassment and fear of cruel judgment. But now, buoyed by her intense love for Christine, she would be stronger. Still, she preferred to remain in the background, if possible. That hope dashed upon her first foray in the hall.

A classmate's eyes lit up. "Becca, you're back."

"Yep." She closed the locker and glanced up. *What's her name, again?*

"Wow, so, did you have the baby? Did you keep it? What is it?"

The tone of excitement caught Becca off guard and begged doubt of sincerity. Nonetheless, Becca couldn't keep her enthusiasm at bay. "It's a girl! She's healthy and beautiful. Here's her picture."

The baby in the photo could only have been beautiful to Becca—newborn Christine, squinting in the bright lights of the hospital, her skin still red and flaky and pimply, her oiled hair mashed against her misshapen head and her nose still smushed and bruised from birth. The student cleared her throat and handed the picture back to Becca.

"Wow, congratulations. That's so amazing. You should bring her in sometime."

"Thanks. She really is amazing. I don't know how the school would feel about show and tell at our age, though." Becca laughed at herself, clicked her lock closed, and twisted the dial. Shifting her books to her left arm, she turned. "Well, gotta go. See ya later."

As she headed to class, her steps held a little more pep. *She didn't seem to look down on me. That's a switch.* She felt her shoulders draw back and she held her head higher.

By the end of the day, Becca had shown Christine's picture and told so many about her baby that the telling came easily. No longer did she feel too uncomfortable being so different than the others. Not for this.

I can pull this off—school and mothering. I don't have to be ashamed. I got pregnant. Most of the girls in high school aren't virgins anyway. I'm just one of the few who got pregnant. I'm so glad I kept my baby. I can't imagine life without her.

* * *

By the end of spring break, Becca was feeling better about her body, too. She'd been doing her crunches, leg lifts and side bends daily since the doctor cleared her for exercise. She begged her father for a few dollars and sewed some new clothes in an updated style. Although her stomach still sagged a bit, she mostly returned to her pre-baby figure.

Becca looked in the mirror as she prepared for school. *Only a few stretch marks here and there, not too bad. Maybe a guy will still like me.* She took a moment to apply eyeliner and mascara, brush her hair, and don her favorite earrings. Placing Christine in the infant seat, she fed her a half-jar of pureed peaches and cereal for breakfast, while making faces with her for fun.

"Good girl, sweetheart. Now let's get you cleaned up and into the playpen. Mama's gotta go to school today."

Christine cooed.

Becca placed the infant seat inside the playpen, where

Christine would be safe from Becca's little brother who played with his trucks on the floor nearby. "I'm going now, Mom." She listened for her mother's acknowledgment from her room.

"Okay, I'll be right out."

She walked to school alone. The long walk each day provided time to think, to review, to plan, and sometimes, to dream. This morning, the cherry and apple blossoms blew in the breeze and gathered into small heaps along sections of the sidewalk like soft blankets for her toes. Becca stopped at a low stone wall along the way, removed her shoes and let her toes run through the blossoms.

This is where Carol used to meet me. She pushed a stray hair behind her ear and let her eyes fix upon other kids walking to school, first up, then down, the road, looking for Carol. *I miss her.* Carol and Becca did nearly everything together since Becca had joined the gang at The Hill. Just one year ahead of Becca, Carol was smart, pretty and confident—even confident enough that she planned to become a doctor. Why she had joined the weed-smoking group of misfits was a mystery. *We were so close. Her family was my second family. . . and my favorite of the two. Why did she give up on me so soon?*

Becca and Carol had dreamed of being roommates some-day. They had planned to break stereotypes and conventions for fun, to work at conventional jobs but host parties every weekend and own their own motorcycles to ride through the country. They had laughed about planning a double wedding and then having their kids at the same ages. *We were gonna be friends forever.*

Carol had replaced Becca with another best friend. Becca

had tried staying as part of the threesome, at first. The three of them had laughed about someday opening a doctor's office together. Carol would be the doctor, her new friend the front desk clerk. Becca had said she wanted to be the psychologist. The other two had laughed hysterically. *"No, Becca will be the streetwalker infecting the men in town with VD and keeping us in business."* Becca had laughed with them, but the joke cut deep. She remembered asking them, in serious tone, *'Don't you think I could be a psychologist?' Because I'm seriously interested in why people do what they do.'* They'd still laughed—to the point Becca doubted, and had since abandoned, her career dream.

She remembered asking Carol why she didn't call her back anymore. Carol had said something about the baby destroying their plans for the future together.

Becca shrugged. She pushed her feet back into her shoes and continued the long trek alone. *I guess I can understand. But I miss her. Our plans had to change, yeah, but that shouldn't have mattered. Not if she really cared.*

As Becca plodded through the hall toward her locker, a boy approached from the other end of the hallway. His wavy hair hung loose below his ears, just above his shoulders. *Hmm. He's kinda cute.*

He smiled at her.

Becca stifled her gasp. *He's looking at me.*

"Hi." He extended his hand to shake.

That's odd, a handshake? Becca waved a quick hand up instead. A slight smirk lifted her left cheek and squinted the eye, letting him know a handshake was corny. "Hi."

"My name's Noel. I've seen you around and wonder if

you'd like to go out sometime."

"Um, go out?" Becca shifted in her stance. "Do you know about me?"

Noel pushed a hand in his pocket. "Well, yeah. I mean, people talk, right? I know your name is Becca, and they say you have a baby."

"Yes, I do." She tucked her hair behind one ear. "That doesn't bother you?"

"No. I think it's cool you kept your baby."

Becca turned toward her locker. She fidgeted to open it, trying to think of something to say.

Noel leaned on the locker next to hers. He gave her a pouty look, widening his eyes and protruding his lower lip. "So, will you?"

Becca hesitated. "Well, I don't know. But we can hang out, get to know each other."

"Cool. I'll find you at lunch. Can I carry your books?"

Is this guy for real? No one's ever offered to carry my books. I don't know how to react to this. "Um, okay, Wally Cleaver." The playful jab about the old television sitcom fell out of her lips to the floor, awkward, but not to be retrieved. *I'm such a dork, making fun of him for being like the good kid from Leave It to Beaver. Nothing wrong with a Wally, but why would a Wally want a girl like me?* Becca cast a speculative eye at him, took a deep breath, and handed him her books. *Maybe he's more of a Eddie Haskell.* "I have English, over here." She pointed to the right.

They walked together to her classroom door. Handing her books to her, he leaned in toward her ear. "You're really cute." Not waiting for her response, he hurried down the hall, waving as he went. "Don't be late to class."

As they got to know one another, Noel and Becca challenged one another to a new vocabulary word a day. Noel, who was college-bound, said this would help him study for the SAT's. They tried to stump one another by finding a word the other didn't know.

No one in Becca's family had ever gone to college. Her older siblings had dropped out and Becca was determined to be the first to graduate high school. *Maybe the future can be good. But college? I doubt that's possible for me. But to have a real date sure would be nice—to go to a movie or take a walk and hold hands.*

Even though Noel was not Becca's usual 'type,' she started to like him—a lot. She found herself primping more often, especially before English, when he made his daily stroll toward her in the hall. Closing the compact after checking her makeup, she closed the locker.

"Your antipathy toward me is dissipating." Noel smiled and leaned one shoulder against the lockers.

Becca's eyebrows scrunched as her eyes rolled, scanning her memory for the meaning of the word. Recalling it, she smiled. "Antipathy, huh?" With a lift of her brows, she formed her response. "Perhaps you mistook my acrimony for animosity, while in truth it may be affectation."

"Well, we seem to have the A words down."

When Noel's eyes beamed at hers this way, Becca felt smart, admirable and. . . a little shy. The feeling put her off balance. She liked and eschewed these feelings at the same time—almost like being in seventh grade again, but smarter, and with higher stakes. She ducked away. "Gotta go, late to class."

* * *

When cards arrived in the mail, everyone in the house paid attention.

"Becca, a card for you, in the mail." Cecelia waved the letter for all to see.

"From who?" Becca's younger sister, Missy, pushed in to see.

Emily, the oldest sister, and thereby, always privileged, grabbed the envelope. "It's from someone named Noel. Who's Noel?"

Becca's jaw dropped. "Really?" She snatched the coveted item away, rushed to her room, slammed the door, and tore open the envelope.

She slid out a beautiful card, handmade, with a water-color painting of a garden and a gated wall. Recognizing Noel's handwriting from shared notes at school, her cheeks warmed and rounded as the edges of her lips pushed them up. *A poem? He really is like Wally Cleaver!* He'd scripted the letters of her name vertically on the page, then filled each in with a word to describe her.

Beautiful

Exquisite

Coruscating

Charitable

Amatory

Dang it, he got me! Two I don't know. Becca pulled out the dictionary. *Coruscating—emitting vivid flashes of light.* She took a deep breath and flipped the pages. *Amatory—of and relating to lovers, making love, expressing love.* Closing the dictionary, her face radiated heat. As tough as she'd been, as hard a facade as she'd tried to erect, his flirtatious ways cut through. He was cute and confident. He was awkward and dorky—but also cool and smart. Now she must add to his list of charming traits. Romantic.

Showing the card to her mother, Becca braved a query. "Mom, can you babysit Christine, so I can go out with this guy?" She grinned through her embarrassment.

Cecelia held the card and read it. "Becca, what does this mean?" She pointed at several words.

Becca provided the needed definitions.

"You oughta keep this one." Cecelia handed the card back to Becca. "But I don't know about babysitting for a date yet. It's only been a few months since—"

"But how am I gonna keep this guy, like you said, if I can't even go out with him?"

"I don't know, but you can't risk pregnancy again. And I already babysit all day, I need a break. I was almost finished babysitting when Jake turned five. I thought I'd have some free time again—maybe get a job, get a life. I've been raising kids for twenty years, and now I'm stuck at home, babysitting—again. I'm not doing this with another baby."

Stuck? You feel 'stuck' with your beautiful grandchild? The blood rushed to Becca's heart, which beat faster and harder. "Forget it, then. Just forget it!" Becca stormed off, slamming her bedroom door behind her, which woke up Christine. She picked up her crying baby and rocked her. "I'm sorry, baby." *I'm sorry you had to come into a world where your mama wasn't ready, your father skipped out, and even your grandma doesn't really want to take care of you. But you are wanted, baby girl. I want to be with you. I wish I could just stay home with you all the time.* Becca's thoughts settled as she rocked her baby. Her baby settled, too. Once calm, a plan came to her. *I'll convince Emily to watch Christine.*

"I promise I'll have her all ready and asleep before I go. I'll be back in time for her ten o'clock feeding."

Emily agreed, with conditions. "Okay, fine, but you clean my room for a month. No touching my makeup or borrowing my clothes. And be home on time. If Mom finds out, she'll be mad at me, and then—"

"I know, I know. I promise."

Date night came. When Christine fell asleep after her dinner, Becca quickly got ready and snuck out the back door. Noel waited on the corner, as they planned. She jumped into his sedan and slid next to him on the bench seat. Noel slipped his arm around her shoulder.

"Let's get some ice cream and play putt-putt."

Surprised at Noel's suggestion, Becca laughed. Going for ice cream and putt-putt seemed like something only the straight, rich kids did—the ones who didn't have any challenges in life. "Sure. That sounds good."

On the way to the ice cream shop, Noel parked the car by his house. "I need to run in. I forgot my wallet. Looks like my parents aren't home, so come on in for a minute."

"I. . . I don't know. I'll just wait out here." Her eyes scanned the dark windows of the two-story home.

Noel offered her a warm smile. "What, are you scared of a dark house?" He took her hand. "Remember how I told you I played t-ball when I was little? I have a picture I want to show you. Come on in."

He seems so innocent. You shouldn't be so suspicious. "Okay, just for a minute."

Once inside, he flipped on a soft light in the main rec room downstairs and pointed to his room. "My room's in here. I share it with my little brother. Come on, I'll get the photo album out." He put a record on and headed for the other side of the room.

Becca followed him into his room and observed the boyish decor. Sports memorabilia and toys lined the bookshelves, posters of famous players adorned the walls, and a set of bunk beds with baseball-printed coverlets all anchored by a large rug in a baseball design. "Wow, are you sure you're in high school?" She cast a teasing eye at him and picked up a framed picture from the dresser. "Is this you?"

Noel moved closer to see. He slipped his one arm around her waist and peered over her shoulder. "Yep. That's me and my brother at baseball camp a few years ago."

She turned slightly toward him, holding the picture next to his face. "You haven't changed a bit," she teased.

"Haven't I?" He pulled Becca in for a kiss.

"Oh! Well," she cleared her throat and smiled again. "Maybe a little."

He kissed her again, this time more passionately.

Becca drew back at first, ever so slightly, but the kiss felt so good, and his manner had been so kind and romantic that she let herself return his kiss. One kiss turned into another, and before long Noel tugged Becca into the bottom bed of the bunk.

Make-out sessions being common in high school, Becca told herself this was nothing to worry about. As she let herself enjoy the moment, her inward struggle amplified. *I don't really want to do this. Is he just using me? Did he plan to come here all along, never to go play putt-putt? But I haven't been touched or held for so long.*

Noel proceeded with rapid urgency to second base and wasted no time approaching third.

"No." She moved his hand away. "I have to get home before Christine wakes up."

A clamor at the door, followed by bright fluorescent lights in the family room, signaled the family's return.

"My parents." Noel sat up and handed a spare quilt from the end of the bed to Becca. "Hide!"

A firm female voice approached his room, snapping, "What's going on in here?"

Becca hid beneath the quilt.

His mother stopped at the frame of the doorway. "Noel. Who do you have in here?"

He bounced from the bed and led his mother out of the room.

"Is this the girl I told you to stay away from? The one with the baby? Get her out of here right now."

Becca heard him apologize. She heard him promise he would take her home and come right back. He promised never to bring her in the house again.

Everything inside her dropped. She was a spent cigarette butt flicked to the ground and trodden upon. Filthy pollution. Dung. She adjusted her loosened clothing, shook her hair over her face and slunk behind Noel to his car.

Noel spoke almost incessantly the whole ride home. "I'm so sorry for my mother. She doesn't understand. She's trying to protect me, but she thinks I'm still a baby. I can't wait until I'm out of there, in college. I'll have anyone I want there, anytime. . ."

Becca's outer shell held silent vigil, eluding his attempts to draw her out. When they arrived at her house, she forced a half smile, practically fell out of the car, and snuck inside through the back door.

The next day at school, he didn't seem cute anymore. *He's not really my type. I don't know what I was thinking. I'll never be the girl to take home to mother. He should go have a good, normal life.* She slipped him a note. "I'm sorry, but we're over."

11

Lena

Sandy Spring, Maryland. 1922

A clever yet fickle lover, early spring in the rural Maryland countryside woos winter's frozen heart to bask in the splendor of bright new beginnings. Promising warmth, life, and love, the season's first crocus blooms beckoned Lena, rendering her helpless in their teasing pursuit of her slowly hardening soul.

She loved spring, as she'd loved her handsome young man and the two brown-eyed boys they'd created together. Clinton had come home from the war different, but she was glad he was home. He worked both farms and the shop, and still found the energy to play with his boys at night. Shaw, now three and big brother to the toddling Elliot, had conquered his challenges from premature birth. Elliot was learning to talk and loved trying to keep up with Shaw in all they did. A third child grew within, joining spring's declaration of the proceeding nature of life.

"I'm off." He kissed her cheek, grabbed the bucket she'd prepared for his lunch, and shot out the front door.

"See you tonight." She watched him ride off at the front window, her neck muscles relaxing like butter as he rode out of sight. The buttery balm spread to her shoulders, settling them down where they belonged. The ball in her stomach let loose. Her foggy worries cleared.

Things will get better. He's just having a hard time of it, getting over the war, adjusting to parenthood, working so much. I need to make things easier for him here.

As she headed to the back door, Lena concentrated her focus on her blessings—her boys, the little one growing inside her, and the good land. The boys grew healthy and active. Elliot followed Shaw's every step. Together, always into something messy—they dug in the dirt, made mud pies, or chased the dogs around the farm. The one growing inside her thrived, Lena was sure. And the farm, as well. A small portion of what had been in the Smith family since the seventeenth century, the rich farming land stood ready. For all these things, she gave thanks.

Lena fastened her planting apron around her, the straps barely reaching to tie in the back. The tomato seedlings started in her kitchen window just a few weeks before the last frost were ready now, after being hardened off for two weeks under the glass-topped box near the back door. Seeds for spinach, peas, carrots and radishes would follow. She slipped little bags of seeds into her apron's generous pockets. Pulling her floppy hat over her tousled short curls and slipping on her worn garden gloves, Lena set out to the garden.

Balancing the tray of seedlings against her waist, she headed to the first row. The theme of Pastor's sermon from last week replayed in her mind. 'This, too, shall pass.' He'd repeated the line again and again, as he usually did with his three points and a prayer. This time, his message hit home. *This too, shall pass*, she repeated to herself. *Lord, help me press on.*

She started to sing. Lena liked to sing while she worked. She danced a bit too, though her movements proved less than graceful in the early bloom of this pregnancy. Her once lean and petite body had grown rounder and squishier everywhere, matching her plump rosy cheeks. Her new form pleased the boys, who loved to snuggle against her and nuzzle into her "pillows," as Shaw called them. Not so much, Clinton. But no matter—the distance Clinton typically displayed when Lena grew great with child provided a welcome break from his daily requirements.

She sang an old favorite love song, but the words rang shallow. Recalling how she'd loved him—in the beginning— now seemed a distant dream. They were just kids themselves when they started this family, bent on being together. Thoughts of their original excitement tugged at her through- out the days, a longing, but cloudy, lacking depth.

His bouts of drinking—and the meanness that followed— left her thinking she would never let him get close to her again. She had hoped that prohibition would change things, but Clinton set up his own still. She knew the illegal little shack was there, hidden in the woods. The home-made brew made things worse. She hoped it wouldn't make a criminal of him.

But he was so good at coaxing her to soften, at making her laugh again, at rekindling her affections. He'd shave his face smooth and put on his Sunday best and bring her breakfast in bed, a wildflower slipped into a tiny vase on the tray. He'd plead for her forgiveness and promise, 'Never again.' He'd shower her with praises and read poetry aloud to her over the bustle of little boys around the dinner table. He'd take her hand, spin her around the parlor floor, dancing without music, and sing her their song, 'A Little Love, a Little Kiss.'

Lena sighed as she reached for the next tray of seedlings. She sat back on her heels and wiped a single bead of sweat from her brow. The sun fully above the trees now, the place sparkled with promise of the coming season. The trees sported their new clothes, speckled with chartreuse buds—some of which had sprouted and rapidly become half the size they would be in a week or two. Spider webs, still damp from the morning dew, gleamed, showing off their maker's work with pride. Two squirrels played a game of chase by the property edge, running up and down the trees and abandoning themselves in impossible leaps from one branch to another, fearless in flight.

The boys played in the picketed area close to the house. Hearing their laughter and noises—for they seemed to make noise just for the sake of it—gave her the information her keen senses stood alert for—that they were safe and sound.

"Ten more to go," she said aloud, as if someone were listening. Sliding the tray closer as she scooted on her knees to the next plowed row, she remembered the first year she'd planted here. Lena had been anxious, so excited to start her life with Clinton—that she had planted her seedlings too early. The frost had beheaded her little treasures, as in Emily Dickinson's poem, "Apparently with no surprise." Lena considered those lines. She must learn to respect nature's 'accidental power.'

That's how life is. We sow, we plant, and tend the garden. We reap what we sow, except sometimes. Sometimes, things happen.

Lena learned from that year, after the hard work replanting everything and then reaping a less-than optimal crop. *I made so many mistakes that year. Could have been disastrous. I've got the timing now, though.*

A ladybug lit on her hand and tickled a trail up her arm. Lena pushed herself up from the ground. Placing one hand on her lower back, and stretching to relieve the pressure, she lifted the arm where the ladybug crawled. Peering at the little red and black beauty, she spoke aloud to her little friend.

"Oh, you are a pretty one. The fairies painted you just right." The ladybug tale—how they got their spots—had passed from generation to generation through her mother's side of the family. Her heart lightened. *I must tell the boys that story tonight.* "Thank you for coming to visit me. Stick around, because we're going to have plenty of good crops for you to protect this year." She knelt back to the ground and transferred the ladybug onto the plant. Slipping her glove back on, she reached for another seedling.

"I see you have things quite in hand." A voice approached

from the front yard. "Here I thought you'd need some help, but look at you. You're almost finished and the sun's not even half-way up the sky."

The startle raced to light up Lena's brain. *Mama.* Her eyes turned to see. The sight of her mother turned up the edges of her lips. She pushed herself up from the ground. Slipping off the soiled gloves and wiping her hands on her apron, she turned to greet her mother. "I'm so glad you could come. I didn't think you'd be able to steal away."

"Well," Aggie replied with a grin, holding out a basket, "I couldn't let these fresh pies go to waste, could I?" She set the basket on the back porch and exchanged a shoulder-to-shoulder hug with her daughter.

Lena's olfactory glands went right to work, detecting sugar and. . . "Ooh, Mama, what kind is it? You know I need some pie." Her mother would appreciate her lack of restraint.

Aggie let out a slight laugh, as Lena expected. "Your favorite, of course. We're finishing up the peaches from last summer."

"You angel, you. I'll fetch us some plates and forks and make some more tea."

"And I'll go visit these—what are they—boys or mud-pies?"

As Aggie hugged her muddy grandsons and listened to their renditions of the morning's building and road construction, Lena brought what was needed for brunch to the porch. "A bit dusty, but come on, we can eat here."

"Pie!" the boys shouted, one after another, and headed for the porch.

"Wash yer hands first," their grandmother insisted, directing them to the water pump.

The boys obeyed their grandmother, gobbled up their snack and ran back to the play yard.

"Mama, thank you so much. I felt the need to see you today."

"Oh? Is something wrong?"

"No, not really." Her throat tightened and the hair on the back of her neck betrayed her determination to keep things in hand. *No, don't say it.* Lena folded her napkin and laid the tidy rectangle on the table. "I guess I'm just a little lonely sometimes. Clinton's been off working a lot lately, and there's nobody around for miles. Well, except for the Smith's." She stared off toward the next farm.

Aggie stacked the dishes, scraping the crumbs onto the top dish. "I don't expect anything else, really. A young woman does get lonely, surrounded only by children." She paused, laying her hands on the table. "I remember, dear, even though it's just been a few years since you moved out. And now, the younger ones are in school or working the farm all day, so usually just me and Grannie are home. At least I have her, but I miss you. I wish you and Clinton had a place closer to us."

"Me too, but being closer to his folks saves time. They need lots of help on the farm. His father's back is so sore now, and his mother's legs and feet have been swelling up— of what, they don't know. Always scowling over something, anyway. I tell myself she must not feel good."

"And how are you feeling?" Aggie reached her hand over to the crest of Lena's belly. "Is there still plenty of kickin' goin' on in there?"

Right on cue, a little kick pressed against Lena's belly.

Lena smiled and took her mother's hand to the spot. "There. Oh, and there. Yes, plenty of showin' off for you."

"There you are—keep up that action, little one." She sat back in the slatted wood chair and looked across Lena's field. "That's some beautiful soil. I'll stay for the afternoon and help you plant."

Lena showed her approval with a glint in her blue-green eyes. "Here, I just happen to have an extra pair of gloves and an apron." Lena handed the items to Aggie. They walked the furrowed rows to where she'd left off less than an hour before. "We may be able to finish before nap time, with two of us working."

Aggie knelt and began to place tomato plants in the ground. She spread a little bone meal, pinched off the lower branches, laid the seedling deep into the furrow, and covered the stem to just below the first set of leaves. She pressed in a stake to support the tender shoot when the rains came. "Grannie tells me she has a gift for you."

"For me?" Lena turned to her. "Whatever for?"

"I'm not exactly sure. She wouldn't say. Said she thinks you're going to need it more than she, but not quite yet."

"Sounds like Grannie, so mysterious. I wonder what I'll be needing?" Lena sprinkled spinach seeds in a row and spread a thin layer of soil above each line. *The only thing I really want is for my little ones to be safe and happy.* As her work continued, Lena mulled over the idea that she might need something more. She'd assumed her future would be secure, but something began to stir in her gut.

Emily Dickinson's 'blonde assassin' passed through Lena's mind. *Please God, don't be approving anything like that.*

"Mysterious." Aggie started again after several minutes of silence. "I suppose that's a good word for her. But you know, her quiet ways are not really mysterious as much as— unassuming, I'd say. She likes to give each person space and time, to be who they are, rather than pressuring them into paying her mind or trying to please her in any way. Grannie is quite astute."

Lena shrugged. "I guess." Grannie, Eliza, seemed to live in another world. She was sweet, kind, and loving, but, most of the time, quiet. *So quiet—like she's dreaming of some other life she wishes she had.*

"Truly, Starlight." Aggie's tone said she meant what she'd said. "I wish you could spend more time with her. We never know how long we'll have with our elders. Or with anyone for that matter. But Grannie, she carries a mountain of wisdom inside that lil' body of hers. Now that you're here on your own farm, spending most of your time raising your children, you'd probably love her company."

"Mama, are you trying to pawn Grannie off on me? Don't tell me you and Daddy want some time alone, at your age." Lena laughed and poked Mama in the side with a tickle.

Aggie laughed in return, catching herself from nearly falling over from the unexpected tickle. "No, chile, no— " She gave Lena a playful push, not enough to make her lose her balance. "Although now that you mention it. . .we'll have her here by noon Saturday."

"Oh, Mama, you are a card." Lena lowered herself to sit in the dirt. Switching her legs so that they both bent off to the side, she leaned on her left arm. "But if you were even slightly serious about that, I'd love to have her. Except on the weekends. Clinton might not like me having to tend to anyone else when he's home. He's so tired after working hard all week. He just wants to relax."

Aggie's lower lip turned out. Her eyes tilted up and to the left, squinting. She drew a deep breath and squared her eyes with Lena's. "Yes, I do understand. I'll let you in on a little secret, my darling."

Lena's eyebrows perked. "You know I love secrets."

"Husbands are a lot like children. In the first few years, you either spoil 'em rotten, or you raise 'em to be the men their future wives will need."

Lena dropped her jaw, taken aback by this unusual scheming from her otherwise pure-as-the-driven-snow mother. A burst of laughter followed. "Why, Mama, I do believe you've got more surprises in you than I ever imagined."

12

Becca

Becca fastened Christine into the stroller and stuffed her overnight bag in the basket beneath it. Their evening stroll, which she and Christine both enjoyed, took a different turn about a mile down the road. Becca stood at the bottom of two flights of concrete steps.

"Well, honey, I hope I don't wake you as we bump up these steps." She turned the stroller around to approach the steps backwards and bumped the stroller up one step at a time—gently so as not to jar Christine awake. *Step, step, pull, step, step, pull.* "You must be really tired tonight," Becca whispered toward her sleeping toddler.

They reached the top landing. Becca felt her deep breath expand her chest and relax her from within. She opened the screen door and knocked.

Her brother answered the knock. Music, talk, and smoke

wafted out of the noisy house. "Becca? What are you doin' here with the baby?" Doug pulled the door closed behind him and stepped outside onto the expansive front porch.

"I need some freedom. Can Christine sleep in her stroller in one of the bedrooms while I hang out here? I'm so tired of always doing everything Mom should be doing—shopping, cooking, cleaning—and also working so hard in school and trying to be mother and father to Christine. Please, I need this. We won't be any trouble."

Doug's blue eyes rounded and his brows tipped upward as he gazed first at Becca, then at the sleeping baby in the stroller. He shrugged his shoulders. "Yeah, I guess. I don't know how these guys feel about it, but come on in. She can sleep in my room for a couple of hours. But then you've gotta go home." He held the screen door open. "No way they'll let you stay here for good, though. This house is full of party animals."

"Oh, I've never seen a party animal. Unless you mean like Eeyore and Winnie at Piglet's birthday?" She forced her eyes wide with innocence while she awaited his response.

He rolled his eyes. "Very funny. Get in here, you silly."

Becca giggled with pride for her stab at humor. It didn't come easily to her, especially at times like this, but she and Doug had enjoyed silly banter together during many hot and boring days of summer before he moved out. "Thanks, Doug. Don't worry, it's just a little break. You know how things are at home."

He shrugged and rolled his eyes again. "That I do."

One of the roommates looked up from under his mat of stringy orange hair as Becca and Christine entered.

"Guys, you remember my little sister, Becca. She wants

to hang out for a while if that's okay with you. The baby's asleep, we'll put the stroller in my room."

"We ain't babysitting, and it's loud in here." He pushed his hair out of his eyes. "But yeah, go ahead." Turning back to check his fingering on the guitar, he continued to play.

Becca parked Christine's stroller in Doug's room and quietly closed the door behind her. Joining the guys in the living room, she slunk into a comfy chair and pulled her feet up beneath her.

Doug snuggled with his girlfriend on the couch, their lanky legs and arms intertwined. His roommates played music, and the evening proceeded in relaxed manner.

This feels like another world. Becca sipped her beer. *A better one. I can't wait until I can move out and have a place like this.*

More people streamed in throughout the evening, all casual and fun-loving. Some danced in the living room, some played cards at the kitchen table, and some coupled up and headed down the hall for privacy.

Becca danced and talked with those she knew. She checked on Christine often. By two in the morning, she threw some pillows on the floor next to the stroller and slept.

As she strolled Christine home the next morning, her feelings battled, bouncing like a ping pong ball between two sides of her brain. One side enjoyed the freedom of hanging out with friends—no rules, arguments or other breeches of privacy—and the other delivered chiding pangs of guilt for taking Christine to a party house. Once home, she chose the peaceful, easy feeling over the guilt.

"You didn't come home all night?" Her mother's verbal assault began as soon as she entered the house. "You kept that baby out all night?"

"I told you we were going to Doug's."

"But I expected you home. When I woke up this morning, I was worried sick that something had happened to you or Christine."

Becca rolled her eyes. "Mom."

"Don't you Mom me. It's not right for her to sleep all night in a stroller. And you should have called."

"I didn't decide to stay until after eleven. I figured you were asleep by then."

Cecelia's eyes narrowed. "Your child deserves to sleep in her own crib." A blast from her flared nostrils accentuated her reddened neck and face. "You can't borrow my stroller anymore."

"Mom? How could you?" Becca's jaw stiffened. She paced the floor. "How am I going to take her for her evening walks?"

"You're lucky I didn't call the authorities on you. They'll take this baby away from you, and you'll never see her again." Cecelia picked up Christine and put her in the high chair. "I bet she hasn't even been fed yet, and here it is, nearly eleven." She went to the refrigerator and retrieved a jar of baby cereal with fruit.

Becca moved quickly, inserting herself between Christine and her mother. "I fed her breakfast already." She picked Christine up and headed toward her room. "She needs a dry diaper, and then we're going to the park, even if I have to carry her the whole way."

We've just got to find another home, baby. Call the authorities on me? For what? Would they. . . take you away from me?

"Hold still!" Becca held both of Christine's ankles in one

hand and slipped out the wet, and on the dry, diaper. She fastened the safety pins and pulled rubber pants up over Christine's diaper, all no small feat when a toddler twists and turns, insisting on anything but lying still. "There. All clean. Wanna go play at the park?" Becca, in high-tone, sing-song baby voice, and blowing blubbers into Christine's neck. "You deserve to be out of this crazy house. Let's go."

But how?

Christine held Becca's finger and toddled along, stopping at every flower, bug and rock to inspect it. They walked toward the park at the end of the block.

I've got no money, no way to earn more than minimum wage without a degree—and no one else to watch Christine. What's the use?

They arrived at the park. Becca pushed Christine to and fro in the swing, alternating between laughing with her daughter and plotting their escape from what was supposed to be home.

Just lay low until you get your degree. Then you can find a decent job—one that pays enough to rent a room. Maybe you can find some friends to share rent on a house—like Douglas does.

For a season, Becca spent as much time as possible away from her parents' house, staying with friends for the week-end, here and there, Christine in tow. Buying a used stroller, she stuffed Christine's blankee and favorite stuffed animal into her backpack and made a bed for her wherever they ended up for the night.

Landing in party houses meant rocking Christine to sleep while gently humming or whispering bedtime stories behind a closed door. Music, laughing and loud talking carried on outside the door. Not the best place for a toddler, but better than insults and arguments outside the door.

Christine didn't always seem to agree. Sometimes she sobbed into Becca's shoulder. "Uhngo home."

"I know you miss your bed, honey. But home is with me, wherever we are." *This is the best I can do, until we can make one of our own.*

* * *

While her classmates read *Wuthering Heights* and *Stranger in a Strange Land*, Becca read books on parenting, books that confirmed her parents didn't know everything.

She looked up from her book and stared out the window into the school courtyard. Her mother's interference and threats to call authorities rang in her ears. *How dare she try to tell me how to raise Christine, when she messed up so bad herself?*

Becca turned her eyes back to the book, where the author proposed the idea of setting limits, even for a baby, to show good care. *Limits? Maybe if Mom had supervised me in the first place, I wouldn't be in this mess. But no, she gave up on me. There I was, thirteen, out doing whatever I wanted. Mom doesn't care about me. She doesn't care about any of us. She even told me she only wanted three kids. And me? Number four of six. Doesn't she think I can do the math?*

The minute hand on the clock dropped to six. Two-thirty—the bell would soon ring for the end of the school day. She pushed her hair out of the way and returned to her reading. The next section focused upon the importance a father plays in a child's healthy development.

Christine needs a father. But I can't just go get that for her. I won't marry someone for that. I won't use a good man that way. She squirmed in her seat. *I would feel like a prostitute if I married for anything other than love.*

The words on the page blurred as her thoughts wandered. *Is there really such thing as a good man? Dad puts food on the table, but that's about all he does.*

A memory of Luis replaced these thoughts. They sat on the rocks watching the roaring waters of the Great Falls course by. Luis pulled her close to his side and she leaned her head against his shoulder. *Christine has a father. I'll reach out to him.*

The bell rang. She closed the book and strode to her locker. Gathering all she needed for the weekend, she decided to mail Luis a package with pictures of Christine. The two had shared occasional letters. She'd begun dreaming of reuniting with him. *Maybe we can make a real family after all.*

She tucked a present for his birthday into the package and topped it with pictures of Christine. After dropping it off at the post office, Becca checked her mailbox daily for weeks. Over a month. . .

Finally, a letter came, one with wispy blue paper lined in red diagonal stripes. *Air mail! From him!* Becca opened the overseas letter with extra care. Her heart warmed at his beautiful handwriting filling the page.

Dear Becca,
I received your letter and gift. Thank you so much.

You didn't have to do that. I wish I could send something for Christine, but when you convert what money I have here into U.S. dollars, it doesn't amount to much. I spoke with my parents, and they said that if you want to, you can bring Christine to stay here with us. I'm afraid I cannot provide much for you. I am studying engineering. I should have a good income by Columbian currency, but not by U.S. standards. Inflation is killing us. I hope you are well.

    Sincerely,

    Luis

Becca held the letter to her heart. Tears welled up and began to run from the corners of her eyes. *He wants us there.*

She read the letter again. *We'd have to stay in his parents' apartment. Just a year ago, his parents swore off responsibility. Would they be kind?*

Taking the letter to her mother, she presented it. "Mom, Luis wants us to come to Columbia."

Her mother read the letter, stone-faced. Setting the blue paper down, she picked up Christine, and stroked the baby-fine curls that swirled at her neckline. After a moment's pause, she shook her head. "No. You can't take Christine there. You have no idea what those people are like. For all you know, they could take Christine and not let her come back. The letter. . . doesn't say *you* can stay there. It says Christine can stay there with them. They might turn you out on the street, then what would you have? You'd have no rights there. Don't do it. Tell him that if he wants you, he has to come back here."

Becca read the letter again, her mind a swirling tempest.

Confusion collided with unbelief, despair with desperation. She let the letter fall, its tissue-thin paper wafting in the air. "Maybe you're right."

"Of course, I'm right. Don't you remember that episode on *60 Minutes* the other night? That sort of thing really happens. Americans don't have rights in other countries. You absolutely should not take this baby there. We might never see you again."

I do remember that show—grown women held captive in other countries because the father of the child had primary rights and the women didn't want to leave their children. Wow. I hate to say it, but Mom's right this time. Going to Columbia is too risky.

Becca wrote Luis and asked him to come back to Maryland.

13

Lena

Sandy Spring, Maryland. 1922

Lena stood on the back porch by the table with her hands on what used to be her waist and her legs spread wide, observing the fruit of her hard work. The luscious red tomatoes sagged from their staked branches in plentiful clumps. Lena would gather them now for canning. She smiled, shaking her head in amazement. "All this, in only two months."

Well before her due date, Lena's girth reached ungainly proportions, as if competing with the tomatoes. She spoke aloud to her belly, laughing. "Child, you must be stretching your legs straight out." Laying her garden gloves atop her table-shaped belly, she reached for her glass of tea before heading out into the morning sun. Using the condensation on the glass to cool her forehead, followed by a wipe with her hand-embroidered linen towel, she picked up a nest of baskets and set out to gather tomatoes.

"Boys, come and help your mama," she called. "Shaw, you take Elliot by the hand and head on over to the tomatoes. Here's a basket."

"Yes, ma'am," Shaw responded, reaching out for Elliot's hand as they descended the two steps into the back yard. "This way, El. Help Mama get some 'maters."

When they reached the garden, now overflowing in greens, reds and purples, Lena pulled the stool she kept outside to sit next to the vines. She sat, placed her basket on the ground and reached her arms open to the boys. "Come here, big guys." Hugging them both together, she spoke to them with wonderment in her tone. "Mama loves you so much. Thank you for being good helpers. Now, listen close."

She leaned back, keeping her hands on their shoulders. "Here's what I want you to do. Take a nice red tomato and cradle your hand around it. Gentle, no squeezing." Letting go of Shaw to demonstrate, she continued. "Now, twist, like this, and you've got yourself a tomato." Showing them the sample, she bit in like an apple. "Here, have a bite, but just this one. We'll save the others for later."

Shaw took a bite first.

Elliot imitated his big brother. "Mmm, yummy," he blurted through a full mouth dripping with fresh tomato juice.

"I need salt." Shaw wiped his mouth on his arm.

"Fair enough. But now, go slow, and only pick the ones that are all red. Then put them in the basket. Be as gentle as if they were lil' babies. They'll smush if you toss them around. They're not balls."

"Ball?" Elliot reiterated, moving his arm as though he

would throw the tomato he held.

Lena reached to stop him from throwing it. "No, not a ball." She accommodated her instructions into fewer words and guided his hand toward the basket. "Gentle. Tomatoes here."

The three of them worked in sync, Shaw helping his mother and his little brother, and Lena helping them both while doing most of her work seated on the stool. Three baskets filled up with tomatoes in very little time.

"Oh, my goodness, just look at these beauties. We'd better carry them up to the house before those dark clouds over there start to spill a bunch of rain on us. Now, Shaw, you carry this basket, and Elliot, you carry this one." She placed a large basket in Shaw's hands and a small one in Elliot's. With a squeeze of her legs to help herself stand from the stool, she picked up the largest basket. "Okay, let's go."

She waddled back to the house, the boys following in imitation. Lena turned and caught a glimpse of her little ones behind her and giggled. "We look like a mother goose with babies waddling along in a row. Come along, little goslings."

As they reached the first stoop, Lena dropped her basket, one hand grabbing her belly as the other hand caught the step. She grimaced, her eyes, nose and mouth tightening as though squeezing into a smaller space.

"Oh, ooh, Shaw," she grunted.

Shaw put his basket on the ground and ran to his mother's side. "What's wrong, Mommy?"

Liquid ran down her legs and spilled out beneath her. Her uterus contracted. "The baby's coming. Now listen. Run as fast as you can across that field and get Daddy, or Grandmom or Granddad Smith. Bring anybody who can come and hurry back. Tell them your mama's having the baby. This one's coming fast."

Shaw obeyed. Lena called Elliot to her side.

Elliot, eyes wide with wonder, sat next to her. He patted her on the leg. "Booboo, Mama?"

"I'm okay, baby. Just stay right here with me, you hear? Sit here with Mommy." She controlled the flow of air in through her nose and out through her pursed lips. *Ooh, this one's coming fast.*

It was on this stoop Lena realized, perhaps too foolishly and too late, that something terrible could happen. Amid acres upon acres of rolling hills with only a few farmers scattered here and there, anything could happen—and so far from anyone's help. Her job to protect her children could be lost with her consciousness, lost with the breaking of her water, lost in excruciating pain. She lay there on the splintered wood planks of her own back porch, with pursed breath, and a two-year old relying on her.

And Mama was gonna be here tomorrow.

14

Becca

Wheaton, Maryland. 1974

Months passed. She didn't hear from Luis. Becca slipped out one night to join her friends. They hung out in a parking lot by the corner convenience store, where some of them worked—including Craig.

Her instant attraction to Craig drew her to the hang-out several nights a week. His silky black hair, gleaming blue eyes and sexy half-smile left her breathless. Even in his goofy-looking red and white work shirt, he carried himself with surety. She could just sit and watch him work. It would be enough.

But it didn't have to be enough. The two of them clicked— hit it off—and within weeks, became a solid couple. Inter-twined, touching, laughing. Hanging. Where Becca was timid, Craig was certain. When Craig saw things simplisti-cally, Becca saw their complexity. For Craig's stupid jokes,

Becca returned a phony laugh and a roll of the eyes.

"What's the capital of Maryland?" Craig asked.

"Annapol—"

"No, stupid. The letter M."

"Ha." Becca rolled her eyes. "So funny."

Hanging out with friends, laughing, listening to music and enjoying their mutual admiration, Craig and Becca's togetherness enlivened her otherwise miserable summer nights. Becca would find and embrace life in the sweltering heat of black asphalt, under the buzz of harsh florescent lights that zapped moth and mosquito alike if it flew too close, like Icarus to the sun. What else was there to do before returning to the pressures of the upcoming school year? All too soon, the fall semester's prerequisite class of suffering— necessary to carry her to adult independence and success— would arrive.

"I've been saving up to go to California to visit my cousin," Craig said. He pulled her by the waist into his lap and nuzzled his face into her cheek. "Wanna come?"

"California?" She drew back in bewilderment. "Wow. For how long?" Becca had never dreamed of taking that long of a trip. She'd never been further than a few hours' drive from home.

"Just for a couple of weeks. If you can come up with three hundred dollars, you can join us. We need another rider to pay for gas. Frannie and Karen are headed to Arizona, so I figure we can ride there together and then catch a bus the rest of the way to L.A."

Frannie and Karen were fun-loving, no-worries people, which Becca emulated. "California or bust, then!" Becca threw her arms around Craig. "This'll be so much fun!"

She argued with her parents about the trip. Disregarding their worries—or perhaps fueled by their disapproval—she withdrew her savings from the bank. When Frannie arrived in her small station wagon, Becca squished their bags, Christine's car seat, Christine, and herself, all in.

"Off on our grand adventure!"

City traffic and highways disappeared behind them as they took to curvy roads over the Appalachian mountains. Even with the constant need for chewing gum to keep her ears from popping, and the scary turns around deep drop-offs, Becca fell in love with the views. "I want to live here someday," she said.

Then the plains, long and boring, stretched out before them. . . and into the dessert. The hot, crowded—and hot, and crowded—vehicle closed in around them. Driving through the desert with no air conditioning became more like hell than adventure.

After five days crammed into a small car with four full-sized people and one screaming toddler in a very large car seat, Becca wasn't sure they were friends anymore. Christine cried anytime she couldn't be right next to, even touching, Becca. Frannie, Karen, and Craig each had turns fussing at Becca to make Christine stop crying.

Becca did everything she could think of to appease her fussy daughter, from reading stories to playing with toys, mostly to no avail. As a last resort, she surrendered her shyness and sang, as animated and as silly as could be, along with the radio, changing the words to America's *A Horse with No Name*.

"You see I been through the desert in a car with no name,

it felt hard to be stuck and in pain." Becca scrunched up her nose as she put her finger on Christine's nose. "In the desert, you can't go out to play 'cuz it's way too hot for your body to stay."

Her friends chimed in for the long la-la-la part of the song. Christine stopped crying to watched everyone, her face awash with great interest and delight.

"You know your mama, well, she wasn't too bright when she thought that a trip would be all fun and right. 'Cause the truth is that you're way too young and ya just can't see why there's naught to be done."

The group joined her song again, and Christine joined in with her best baby-talk singing voice. This turning point hastened their arrival in Flagstaff, Frannie and Karen's destination.

Once Craig and Becca said their goodbyes to Karen and Frannie, they spent their first night of the week's drive with just the three of them. As they settled into the room for the night, Christine in the hotel port-a-crib and down for the night, Craig turned to Becca and smiled.

"I'm glad that's over. What a trip."

"Yeah, so much harder for Christine than I imagined. And for all of us!" Becca pulled back the covers and slid into the clean sheets.

"You were great, though, turning the mood around the way you did with that song."

"Christine's always loved music. I guess I just needed a few days to get over being too shy to sing in front of everyone." Becca laughed at herself. "And desperation."

Craig climbed into bed and wrapped his arms around her.

"I think I'll get you singing again." He slipped his hand over Becca. He caressed her with gentle strokes, his hand pausing below her belly to apply a swirling massage.

Becca's body rose and tightened at his touch. She placed her hand over Craig's to keep it there. Waves of tingling sensation built one upon another. Her muscles clenched as a wave of intense flush spread through her veins, leaving her awash in pleasure. Trembling, she let go of his hand and looked up at him.

He smiled back, an impish grin. His eyes offered pools of pleasure and satisfaction she could wade into and stay, forever.

At sixteen, three years after first giving in to sex with a boyfriend, and eighteen months after having her first child, Becca had her first experience with what everyone had been talking about. . . with what everyone must like. . . about sex. And Craig rose to a new level in Becca's heart and mind. *This must be love.*

The bus pulled into Los Angeles after a long ride from Flagstaff.

Craig's cousin met them at the station. Vicki, thirty-something, staunch of jaw and sparse of words, barely said hello

They pulled into the parking lot of a tiny Hollywood apartment—a boxy brick building with a pool and common grill outside, and no grass. They walked the narrow path by the pool to the back entry, climbed two flights and entered. Inside, a simple living room with a black and gray plaid sofa, chrome and glass tables, and an eat-in kitchen with counter seating stood empty.

Bertie and Vicki's kids joined them from their bedrooms. Bertie's manner, short hair and masculine clothing distinguished her as the man of the family. She shook hands and sat in a side chair, reading. Craig's niece, a lovely young teen, seemed innocent for her age compared to Becca when she was fourteen. His nephew, a lanky ten-year-old, showed himself both funny and smart.

They chatted past midnight, until Vicki insisted everyone must get some sleep.

"You didn't tell me," Becca whispered to Craig once they settled into their assigned room.

"What, that they're gay? I didn't think it mattered." He held her gaze with his.

Becca spread the blanket over the bed.

"Does it?" Craig put his face closer to hers, begging an answer.

"No, of course not. It's cool. I just thought you'd tell me something like that."

The next night, Becca overheard Vicki complain to Craig about having a baby in the house. She gave Becca a cold shoulder and soon complained about everything, like she was mad at the world.

Puzzled by Vicki's coldness and complaints, Becca grew uncomfortable with their plan to stay in her house for the next two weeks. *I'll just try to keep things pleasant, keep Christine from getting upset. Maybe it'll be okay. But I wonder why she doesn't like us.*

On the third night, Vicki yelled at Becca for leaving a soda in the living room. Her rant continued, and she revealed that she was mad that her kids had been displaced, one sleeping on the couch and the other sharing her room, to make room for the extra visitors that Craig hadn't told her he was bringing.

Becca glared at Craig. "You didn't tell her we were coming with you?"

He smirked, a smug air emanating from his nostrils. His drawn back shoulders and lifted chin completed the message.

Becca sped into the kids' room, where she, Craig and Christine slept, and shut the door. *No wonder she's been giving us the cold shoulder. I could just die of embarrassment! Here we are, on the other side of the country, unwanted, and no money left to get a hotel. Now what?* She folded her arms and paced the room until deciding her best choice was to climb into bed and pull the covers up to her neck. *I sure won't leave any messes around to get her mad again.*

Craig entered an hour later and shut the door behind him. He slid into bed next to her.

Becca rolled to face the wall, away from him. After what seemed hours laying awake, she rolled onto her back and whispered to Craig. "You awake?"

He mumbled. "Sorta."

"I want to go home. Vicki's mad that we're here. You should have told her."

"It'll be fine, don't worry." Craig stroked Becca's hair "Hey. Why do you never get mad?"

"I don't know." *I didn't even realize I never got mad. Is that true?* Her next words seemed to pop out before the next thought formed. "Guess I'm afraid."

"Afraid? Of what?"

"I don't know. Maybe that you'll blow up, or that I'll drive you away."

"Well, that's no way to live. You have feelings and you should get mad if you're mad."

"Hmm." *Maybe so.* "But you changed the subject. I'm tired. I don't want to stay here."

"I'll get some money soon. Vicki said she'll drive us to San Diego to see my mom. I'll ask Mom for a loan."

Becca couldn't tolerate staying mad, but Vicki didn't seem to mind being, or staying mad. She insisted they vacate the apartment until at least noon every day so she could sleep. Craig decided he wanted to stay in California. Since his mother denied his loan request, he left to job hunt every morning.

Becca, with no funds, friends, or family, took Christine outside from when Christine awoke until afternoon. Walking through Griffith Park or sitting outside the grocery store with nothing to eat or drink, Becca saw a different side of Hollywood than she'd imagined. Regular sights on her morning walks with Christine included hookers walking their beats in their 7-inch heels and short-shorts, a man dressed like Superman making his rounds along Hollywood and Vine, looking for unsuspecting tourists to flash, and male couples sunning together in the tiniest Speedos she'd ever seen, rubbing lotion on each other's backs. Bars showcasing drag queen acts lined every street. The streets were dirty, busy, and noisy. Even Mann's Chinese Theater was grungy and underwhelming in the heat of the day. Hollywood wasn't at all like it seemed on TV. And not at all like Maryland.

Becca forced herself to complain to Craig, a painful task for the peacemaker in her. "It isn't right that we're left to fend for ourselves here. I'd rather go home than have to walk Christine all around town every morning. This is no way for me to raise a child."

"I want to stay," he insisted. "Once I get that bank job downtown, we can rent a nice place. It's great here, really. You can go to the beach and the mountains all in one day."

"I've seen neither beach nor mountain. We have no transportation. The only places I've seen in weeks are within the six square blocks I walk with Christine every day."

Craig rolled his eyes. "You're making a big deal out of nothing."

"Nothing?" Becca waved her arms emphatically and her voice grew louder and more desperate. "Today I got scared to death. I had to grab Christine and run down an alley to get away from the Superman flasher. Then a cab driver followed me, stopped and told me—and I mean *told me*—to get in. Even after I told him I didn't have money, he insisted." Becca's heart raced. She looked away from Craig, off into the distance. "His face. He was up to no good. I ran off with Christine to hide. As I turned the corner, I tucked into a small courtyard surrounded by tiny cottages."

Craig laughed and moved to put his arm around Becca. "He probably just wanted to give you a ride."

"No, he was no good." She swallowed her frustration at not being taken seriously. Calming herself with a few deep breaths, she crossed her arms and turned back toward Craig. "Anyway, after he drove off, I looked around, and the courtyard wasn't bad. It had a lush lawn, a picnic table and some shade. One of the cottages was for rent. If we're gonna stay in California, we should look. A tiny place like that can't be too expensive."

After a few exchanges back and forth, Becca holding her ground about needing another place to live, Craig conceded.

The tiny cottage needed a lot of work, which Craig said wouldn't be a problem. "We'll refinish these counters, bomb out the bugs, get some furniture, it'll be fine." He agreed to borrow money from his brother to pay the security deposit and first month's rent.

Impressed that she'd made ground by asserting herself, Becca let herself adjust to the idea of staying in California. *Maybe we can build a future here, together.*

While Craig went job-hunting, Becca set out bug bombs and, once the fumes were bearable, placed covers on the floor as beds. She sanded the gunky wood kitchen counter. Crafting tables and chairs out of boxes for the living room, she played with Christine. They colored with crayons and made imaginary toys from rocks and twigs.

Craig didn't come home until after dark. He said he was job hunting and got stuck in traffic. This happened three days in a row, with a different excuse each time.

On the fourth night, Becca met him as he snuck into the dark house after midnight. The stench of stale beer wafted about his wavering stance as he looked at her, dumbfounded. Hands on her hips in a wide stance, she dared let her pounding heart pound away and her mouth speak her mind. "You told me to tell you when I'm mad, right? Well, I'm there. You expect me to believe you've been job-hunting for over twelve hours a day? Where have you been, really?"

Pressing him, she exposed his lie. He had been watching TV at his cousin's house.

"We're here with no television, no air conditioning, no furniture, and barely anything to eat, while you're over there with your feet on the coffee table, watching TV in the air conditioning, drinking beer? How dare you?"

At the confrontation, he blew up, ranting and calling her names, accusing her of taking advantage of him. "You need to bring some money in, Becca. What you brought is gone. And control that kid of yours. Everyone's tired of hearing her cry. You give in to her all the time. If she doesn't want to eat, you make her something else. If she cries, you baby her and hold her. She's spoiled rotten."

"She's not even two, Craig. What do you expect? I've been trying to appease her so she wont' bother you all with her crying."

Their loud voices woke Christine. Her crying added to the sounds of fury.

Craig turned on Christine, yelling at her to shut up, to stop crying. When this made her cry more, he spanked Christine—hard.

Becca snatched Christine from Craig, held her tight and yelled at him. "Keep your hands off of her. Get out of here!"

"Gladly!" Craig left, slamming the door and leaving a trail of expletives down the sidewalk.

Becca held and rocked Christine, stroking her head and patting her back. Through welled eyes, once Christine calmed, she examined her little bottom. Bruises in the shape of Craig's hand had already appeared, the reddened areas dotted with purple vein lines. Becca's tears stopped.

15

Lena

Sandy Spring, Maryland. 1922

Shaw came running around to the back yard. "She's back here, Daddy."

Clinton and his father hurried on Shaw's heels, overtaking him.

"Lena?" Clinton called. "What's wrong?"

Lena tried to sit up, but another strong contraction drew her back to her curled state. "The baby's coming—hard and strong." She grimaced and squeezed herself tight. "It's too soon. Something's not right."

"Dad, we'll take her to the hospital. I'll get her up while you bring the car around." Clinton sprinted to Lena's side and knelt beside her. He reached to place one arm beneath her as he guided her one step at a time. "Put your arm around my shoulder." Helping her sit up on the steps, he used his calm voice. "Can you stand?"

"I can try." She forced air through her clenched teeth.

He supported her as she rose to her feet, then he took most of her weight by putting his shoulder under her arm. They inched toward the waiting car. "Try and stay up if you can."

"The car." Lena managed to speak as she hobbled toward the metal monster, leaning on Clinton. "I'm glad for a car now. A godsend."

"At least my father had the good sense to buy one."

They sped six miles to the new hospital, past the town, over bumpy dirt and gravel roads. Lena lay in the back seat, her children nestled beneath her on the floorboards. The model T reached the hospital in less than twenty minutes. The trip would have taken well over an hour in the buggy.

That precious time bought Ruth's life.

But there were two. One was lost to where there is no time. And Lena almost followed.

* * *

"She's wrought with fever and pain, and very weak after losing so much blood."

Too groggy to open her eyes or speak, Lena listened to the conversation just outside her door. She heard a man's voice.

"She should stay here for now. The nurse will go over the details with you, but you'll need to arrange things for the children for the next week or two, at least."

Lena fought to open her eyes. Her eyelids were heavy, as if something was sticking them together, weighing them down. She tried again. This time she managed to pull her eyelids apart just enough to make out who stood in the doorway. Clinton. He looked stiff, worried, his hat pressed to his chest, his legs spread wide to keep himself steady.

"Sir, that can't be."

"She needs to rest."

Clinton and the doctor, Lena confirmed to herself, seeing his long white jacket. The doctor shifted his feet like a jack rabbit ready to scurry off.

"We're lucky she survived. Here, let the nurse show you how to care for the baby, and leave Mrs. Smith to us." The doctor hurried off, waving Clinton toward the nurse, who stood ready in her long white dress, round veiled hat, white stockings and shoes. The nurse held a baby.

My baby's alive. Her eyes closed, against her will.

The nurse waited for no introductions. "Sir, have you any experience feeding a newborn? This one is very small, but she can take the bottle like this. . ."

Lena drifted in and out of consciousness as she strained to listen. *Why do I feel so tired? I hope everything is okay.* Clinton seemed to be staying for instructions, though he didn't say anything. She felt him kiss her on the cheek as he left.

A week later, he brought the baby back. He stopped outside Lena's door when the nurse approached him. "She won't eat. Here, you all keep her until Lena comes home." He held the baby out toward the nurse.

Lena opened her eyes and saw the nurse reach out to receive the child from Clinton's outstretched arms.

"Oh, dear. Haven't you anyone in the family who can help?"

As though timed from above, footsteps sounded on the hall floor and Cordelia joined the nurse at the door of Lena's room. Her sister removed her jacket and folded it over her arm. "Clinton," she nodded. Her focus turned to the bundle in the nurse's arms.

"Cordelia," Clinton said, his voice rising with excitement. "Am I glad to see you."

"I've come to visit Lena. How is she?" Cordelia continued her attention to the tiny bundle the nurse held. "Is something wrong with the baby?"

Clinton cleared his throat. "She refuses to eat."

The nurse addressed Cordelia. "She's terribly small. Are you relation, ma'am?"

"I am Lena's sister. I'm nursing my five-month-old. Maybe I can help this little one along. Here, let me take her. I'll do my best."

"I'd be much obliged," Clinton offered.

The nurse tendered the tiny newborn to Cordelia at Clinton's cue.

Cordelia pulled the baby close. Her face would typically light up upon meeting a new family member. This time, though, a contracted brow and gnawed lip accompanied her glance into Lena's hospital room. Cordelia addressed the nurse. "She will recover soon, won't she?"

"I've seen many a mother bounce back. She just needs more time to rest. And, like I said earlier, it's best not to tell her yet. Let her use all her strength to recuperate first."

Cordelia nodded. She pulled the swaddling blanket tighter around the baby and turned her gaze toward Clinton. "And the boys? Where are they?"

"They're with my parents. Quite a handful, and there's much to do in the fields."

"Bring them on by, too, then. The more the merrier, we always say." Her countenance lightened.

"That'll be fine. You live closer to town than I do, and you two have a telephone in your house, right? If you need me, call the little store at Smith's Corner. They'll send someone out to the farm for me, right quick."

* * *

By mid-July, under the heavy heat of day and the over-powering crescendo of cicadas in unison, Lena came home. Cordelia's husband, John, drove their car down the dirt road and into the front drive, which was overgrown now from the wispy sprouts of weeds and grass gone to seed. He and Aggie helped Lena transfer inside the weathered, wood-slatted home, where Lena dropped to the couch with a sigh.

"It's good to be home, I bet," her sister said. Cordelia had been there with Ruth since John and Aggie left that morning to pick up Lena. "I came over earlier to tidy up the house. Since Clinton was living here alone all these weeks, I figured he just might have left the place a bit on the unlivable side of clean." She waited for a response.

Lena stared straight ahead, looking at nothing.

"Do you want to hold Ruth?" Cordelia moved toward the cradle near the rocking chair. "She's doing well now. I ended up having to put drops of cocoa water on my finger until she finally started to eat." Cordelia lifted Ruth and held her up for Lena to see. "But she's taking a bottle now."

Lena received her. She held her to her heart and rocked her, but her expression remained flat and her eyes as dim as the sky on an overcast day.

* * *

Lena forced her lips to curve up as she perused her little girl. "They just told me yesterday," she spoke softly to the little one. "I'm so sorry about your brother. And I'm sorry I haven't been here for you." She brought the sweet angel to her cheek. "But I'm here now."

Aggie sat next to Lena. "We'll be taking turns staying with you until you're strong enough to manage. No worries, now, we've already cleared the matter with Clinton. Your sisters are banding together to take turns." She patted Lena's knee.

Those words and the gentle touch merged, wafting slowly through her body and into her mind as though they were written in a letter from some faraway land. The meaning settled in, creating a tiny nest there in her mind, where she could curl her knees up, wrap her arms around her baby, and lay her head onto Ruth's—both together as if in a womb.

A ray of sunlight crept toward her face, warming her eyelids. *The sun proceeds unmoved. . . to measure off another day. . . for an approving God.* The great poet's words had new meaning, yet their value escaped her. *Approving?* A shadow cast over her like a hawk flying over the safety of her nest. The chill of that sudden darkness alerted her to the parlor. Realizing she had not yet responded to her mother's comforting words and touch, Lena pulled herself out from this inner world and nodded.

* * *

That night, her husband climbed into bed next to Lena. Clinton snuggled in close and wrapped his arms around her. He nuzzled her neck and breathed her in. "So good to have you home again."

Lena lay on her side, facing away from his side of the bed. She had slipped on her oldest, raggediest nightgown, hoping to avoid any sense of appeal to her husband. *I'm not ready, that's all.* As he offered his body to hers, snuggling against her backside with his warmth, his tender touch, and his heavy breath, Lena's insides rent in two. One side of Lena—desperate for his comfort—longed for his words to soothe her waning heart. This side of her wanted to turn toward him and let her head rest on his chest to release a torrent of tears. The other side of Lena could not face comfort nor the risk of discovering that all he wanted was a physical release of his pent-up manly craving. The second side prevailed.

"Clinton, Mama's right outside the door. I just. . . can't."

"I'll be quiet."

"No."

He pressed on.

He's been without this all that time, some distant part of her mind reasoned. A voice in her head spoke, with authority, like an expert, maybe a voice on the radio, or something in a book. *A wife needs to keep her husband satisfied or he might look elsewhere.*

Where had she heard it? A book? The radio? Some distant relative? No matter the source, that fearful reasoning overrode the more needy part of her, the part she couldn't connect with. . . the part of her that longed for a place to rest. A place to feel safe. A place to feel loved, not just needed.

The warring parts of Lena were distant from her mind, as though she were not there at all, as he got what he wanted, while Lena was off somewhere in a dream, in a beautiful wildflower garden, rocking the baby boy that had passed to where there is no time. Did anything else really matter?

* * *

The muggy days of July melted into the sweltering heat of August. Thankful for quieter days since the cicadas finished their mating calls, Lena brought a pitcher of freshly-made sun tea to her mother on the back porch. She reached for the fly swatter hanging from a rusty nail on the post, ready to swat any intruders who would dare land on the table while they had their brunch.

Just as Aggie promised, the women of the family had been taking turns staying with Lena until she was strong enough to manage. Grateful as Lena was, the constant company had become all too much. She took a seat and poured her mother's glass to the brim. "I'm alright now," Lena said to her mother, as she set the pitcher down. "I can't keep you all away from your families forever. I appreciate all you've done here, but weeks have gone by. You must need your time at home."

"Are you sure, Starlight? I'm hoping to see that light in your eyes again soon." Aggie picked up her glass. A twinkle leapt from her eye to Lena's as she sipped.

Lena couldn't send one back. Instead, she looked across the property and watched wisps of clouds disappear behind the tree line. Her stomach, like a pit of quicksand, sucked her heart into an abyss. *What is this weight inside?* It reminded her of how she'd felt when she'd sneak a cookie out of Mama's jar, only a hundred times worse. *Guilty.* Climbing from beneath it, she defied the heavy weight and spoke.

"Mama, how long did you. . . when you lost—?" She couldn't bring herself to say her siblings' names—the ones they'd buried in the back of Mama and Daddy's property.

Some were lost at birth, some in their first two years. They were each so precious, despite the ample size of the family. Twelve of the fifteen Burriss children survived.

Aggie looked down at the diaper she folded in her lap. She smoothed it, then looked back at her daughter. "Some say you never get over it. I'm not sure I ever did. But you go on, for you have others. And they need you. You will find your spark again."

The sad idea lit a candle in a dark corner of Lena's mind. In the willowy grey shadows that flickered nearby, she gathered her wits like a hen her chicks. *Mama still hasn't gotten over it, so I shouldn't be too hard on myself about how hard this is.* A breath shuddered into her lungs. "I am glad there's Ruthie." Lena forced a half-smile.

"That baby is a delight," Aggie affirmed. "And the boys have been extraordinarily good—like they know you need them to behave." She sat her glass on the checkered tablecloth and glanced at her grandsons.

Lena cast her fixed half-smile at her boys. Today they played in the yard with their older cousins. "I'll be whatever the kids need, Mama. You needn't worry."

Aggie squeezed Lena's hand across the table, then stood and reached to hug her. "Alright. I'll go. Check back on you tomorrow."

Lena watched her mother hug Shaw and Elliot goodbye and climb into her carriage with two of her other grandchildren. Listening to the horses clop off down the road, her heart sank even further. Their company had helped, but she must resume living. She hadn't had a chance to really talk with Clinton since all this happened. He had seemed sullen, as she was, and distant.

Clinton's daily routine all this time was to go to work, come home late, and dismiss himself to bed early, while the women sat folding clothes, mending, and talking in the parlor. Now she would face him completely alone. Her mind spun ideas for the discussion all afternoon and evening. *We've both been struggling so, since the baby. I haven't been myself. But if we talk, we can find ways to help each other. Let's try, Clinton. Please, I don't want to go on feeling this way forever. Besides, our kids need us to be strong. . .*

But that night, it wasn't Clinton who went to bed early. Lena read Shaw and Elliot a story and sang them a song. They wanted the one about the hole in the bottom of the sea, but she begged off, being such a long song, and her heart felt too much like that hole in the bottom of the sea, with the log, and the knot, and the frog, and so on, atop it. Instead, she sang "Jesus Loves the Little Children." Then she fed and rocked baby Ruth to sleep.

After sitting at the kitchen table for over an hour, wondering when he would be home, Lena left his plate on the table and cleaned up for bed. Her head on the pillow, she dropped her weary arm to his side of the bed. *Still no Clinton.*

The clock had struck eleven a while back when he stumbled up the steps and let the screen door slam behind him. The sound of grumbling and drawers slamming in the kitchen drew Lena out of restless sleep. Groggy, she pushed one arm, then the other, through the sleeves of her summer night robe, and gathered the belt into a knot as she went to see what was wrong.

"Well," he slurred, "at least no one's here but us, for a change. But, my Lord, couldn't you keep the food warm for me?" He held his fork full of cold pole beans toward his wife, then stuffed them into his mouth. He rested his head on one hand while he chewed.

"You're drunk!" Lena's arms crossed her chest. The skin between her eyes tightened. "Clinton, you promised." *Have I neglected him too much? Is that the problem?*

"I just had a little of that cider in the barn. A man's gotta do something, working all day and comin' home to a bunch o' hens on his nest."

Hens? Insecurity gave way to pride and possessiveness. Lena bit her tongue. Talking was never a good idea when he was in this condition. But to hear him insult her mother and sister that way—when they'd been her life's blood the last two months—was more than she could take. Her teeth released their hold on her tongue. "Hens? I'll not have you calling them hens, for Pete's sake. They are my family, and they've been a huge help. I couldn't have survived without them." She turned her back on him and stomped toward the sink for a drink of water. "Nor Ruthie."

Clinton stumbled toward her and slid his arms around her waist. "This rooster's gotta crow!" He leaned into her and laid his sloppy wet lips on her neck.

She retracted from his hold and stepped to the side. Turning to face him, her hand shot up between them. "No. Not like this, you don't." She mustered all she had to cut him off.

His face turned sullen, then pouty. His eyebrows tipped in a sorrowful plea as he put his hands out for her. "But it's been so long, baby. I thought I'd lost you."

"I said, not when you're drunk." She moved to pass him by, meaning to leave him in the kitchen and head back to bed before she caved to his wishes.

"Don't you do that to me!" He reached for her, grabbed her by the arm, squeezed and pulled her back into his arms, barraging her with violent kisses.

His forceful manner sickened her, making her stomach threaten to heave through her chest and land on the floor. Her skin crawled at his touch. Lena struggled to free herself from his grasp. "Stop it. No." She wanted to shout but feared waking the children.

"Don't you love me anymore, darling?" He kept kissing her face, her neck, and holding her tightly.

"Don't you love *me*?" She pushed back hard on his chest, freeing herself. "Because this ain't love to me." *There. I said it.*

Clinton opened his belt and began slipping the long leather strap out of the belt loops. "You're mine, you understand? Mine. If I want you, I'll take you." He staggered as he lurched toward her.

Energy poured into Lena's feet. Afraid to run into the bedroom where Ruth slept, she sprinted to the parlor and out the front door. The screen door slammed behind her. She ran toward the buggy.

The screen door slammed a second time. Clinton followed, picking up his pace with the wind that preceded a summer night's storm. Even drunk he was faster than Lena. He overtook her by the buggy. Picking her up, he tossed her into the back seat and pressed himself against her, pushing one hand around her neck.

Lena fought to free herself, twisting and kicking the air, and trying to pry his fingers off her neck. Then his body went limp. She heaved the weight of his stone-cold drunk body off hers. He rolled onto the floorboard and lay there, snoring.

Lena noticed her body, which had been tense, began to relax. Climbing down from the carriage, she straightened her nightclothes and went inside, leaving him to sleep off his drunken stupor.

As she neared the house, she noticed lightning and thunder and a mass of dark clouds above. She raised her fist at the sky. "That's right—pour what you've got out on him."

At breakfast, she looked out the window and saw him still sleeping in the carriage. Following her usual routine, she spooned his eggs onto his plate and turned to finish her work in the kitchen. *Maybe he doesn't even remember.* Warming a bottle for Ruth, Lena kissed the boys and praised them for eating so well, then shooed them out the back door to play. They knew now to go right into the fenced play yard and shut the gate behind them.

The baby cried. Carrying the bottle, Lena retrieved Ruth from the bedroom and took her to the parlor. She snuggled onto the couch, pulling a pillow under her elbow. Ruth accepted the bottle happily. Half expecting Clinton to be kind again, to beg her forgiveness again, Lena determined to remain silent. Waiting.

Clinton came inside and went right to the table. He showed no regard for Lena or his wet clothes. He finished his eggs, sucked down his coffee, wiped his mouth, took a deep breath and pushed back his chair. Without a sound, he stood, puffed out his chest and straightened his spine, then strode toward his wife and daughter on the couch. Stopping in front of them, he loomed over them, breathing hard.

Lena's stomach churned, as if caught in a meat grinder. A frantic heartbeat sent electricity to quicken every muscle. Her eyes scanned the room for an escape route. *He's doing this sober.*

Raising his right arm across his body, the back of his hand facing Lena, he paused, threatening to strike. His eyes narrowed like arrowslits in a castle, turned on their side, and his voice rumbled, gruff and low, delivering his threat. "I'll take you both down, I swear."

She had seen this side of him before, but only when he drank. Lena drew her baby closer to her chest. Her eyes welled with tears. Refusing to let them spill, she let anger take their place. *No, you will not.* Seeing no way to protect Ruth, she froze.

He slowly lowered his arm to his side but retained his powerful stance over them. His breathing grew harder, faster, flaring his nostrils. The arrowslits sent a message so intense he didn't need to say it, but he did. "You brought me a girl, but you let the boy die." He pointed at Ruth, poking his finger toward her with each word. "That girl killed my boy."

Her hand instinctively covered Ruth's head. "Simmer down," she said, using her tone to lasso the pain that had driven him mad.

He turned and paced the floor. "What am I gonna do with a girl, anyway? Boys work the farm. We've got no money to pay workers since the war. We're short on everything. I'm doing all the work—or trying to, anyway. My family needs boys to save the property. Hundreds of years, Lena. I won't be the one who loses it." His pacing seemed to provide momentum, fueling his outburst.

He stopped at the door, turned back toward Lena and jabbed his pointing finger in her direction. "I give you my seed, you make me boys." Like cannons in the distance,

Clinton's voice boomed from the porch as he stormed off. "And I won't tolerate no more of you standin' up to me, either. You got that?"

Lena pushed up from her spot on the sofa and looked out the window to watch him leave. She saw Shaw and Elliot at the edge of the front yard, both standing with stunned faces. A short breath caught half-way into Lena's chest. *They heard it. They saw.*

16

Becca

Hollywood, California. 1974

Morning relieved the sleepless night. Becca carried Christine a few blocks to the payphone, where she'd seen the Yellow Pages hanging from a hook. The office location confirmed by a call, she set out. Walking miles of cracked, steamy sidewalks, Becca alternated between carrying Christine and holding her hand to plod along at toddler's pace.

By afternoon, she transferred her Aid to Families with Dependent Children payments from Maryland to California.

"The check should be in the mail within a week," the social worker said. "They come the first of each month. Be sure to let us know if anything changes."

"Thank you, I will."

When she reached the sidewalk again, Becca held Christine and wept for her lie. She would not be transferring permanently to California, and she knew it. It was the quickest way she knew to get the money to leave.

For the next week, Becca kept things on the low with Craig, biding her time. He stayed away most of the time, which helped. When the check arrived, she cashed it, took a cab to the airport, bought a ticket and flew home.

* * *

Wheaton, Maryland.

The five-hour flight was bumpy enough to spill Becca's drink as it approached Washington National Airport. The pilot's voice followed a crackle in the speaker above her head.

"Not to worry folks, just a little turbulence as we descend through that thunderstorm. All should be clear now, and as we approach passengers on the left should be able to see the now famous Watergate Hotel."

Becca kept watch, but with a distant, sarcastic eye. *Politics. Burglars. Reporters. Cover ups. Accidentally erasing eighteen and a half minutes of a tape recording.* She'd heard enough about Deep Throat—or rather, the associated sexual innuendo satirized on Hollywood Boulevard, where hookers and triple-X rated films strutted like proud peacocks with shredded feathers. Licentiousness on the west coast and pretentiousness on the east—none of it impressive.

Her parents met the two waifs at the airport. On the otherwise silent drive to the house—the one that wasn't a home—the radio filled the void. Nixon had resigned. His men took the fall for the Watergate scandal.

Every man's a liar. She stared out the window, the neon lights of the city blurring into wavy lines as they sped along Capital Beltway.

Becca returned to her parents' house and convinced her mom to babysit again. After consulting with the school guidance counselor, she started her senior semester in the half-day work/half-day school program designed for apprentice work. Without a trade to apprentice in, the counselor made an exception for Becca so she could work half-days to support herself and Christine.

She banished her dreams of marrying Craig, like bits of discarded love poems, purposefully torn and scattered in the wind. Becca left school at noon and headed to work, head down, and brow cinched with plans for the evening—making dinner, doing homework, reading to Christine.

Her steps across The Hill provided a quick respite on the way. Just a short cut now—no stops to hang out or get high—the shade trees offered gentle rest from the sweltering September sun. Her eyes embraced the play of shadow and light as she traipsed across the empty playground. The wind lapped at her hair, bringing slight relief from the heat—and the absence of Craig's touch on her face.

Ahead, toward the road, a figure stepped out from behind a tree. Becca gasped and squinted.

It was Craig. He leaned against the old oak, folded his arms, and beamed at her. "Hi."

Her heart quickened as her feet slowed. "What are you doing here?"

He pushed himself off the tree and headed toward her, hands out and palms facing up. "I realized what an ass I was." He shook his head, smiling. "I miss you. So, I'm back."

"Yeah, and Nixon's not a crook." Becca put a hand up against him as she snapped away from his path. A warm flush filled her face. Her feet prepared to run. Her hands waxed sweaty—the way they did when peering over the edge of a high cliff.

Craig reached for her. "Come here. Becca, I love you."

Frozen in the icy chasm between repulsion at what he had done and elation to hear those words, Becca retained a response.

He begged forgiveness and for another chance. His eyes fixed on her, pleading with the intensity of sincere sorrow, his eyebrows tipped up, one higher than the other, and his lips slightly puffed like a child begging for a lollipop. Watching her face, he moved to sit on a swing and motioned for her to sit next to him.

Her feet slowed. *He does look sorry.* Her heartbeat calmed toward normal. *Hear him out.* Curiosity triumphed over anger, pushing her toward the hope of love. She sat on the next swing.

They talked for a while. Before long, Becca believed he was truly sorry for how he'd behaved. After all, she reasoned to herself, he wasn't even Christine's father, and he was young. Craig made a mistake. *I've made mistakes. Shouldn't he have another chance?* He seemed willing to try to do better. *He even promised to let me do all the discipline going forward.*

Becca's whimsical belief in a fairy-tale kind of love—the sort that overcomes all obstacles, the sort that learns and grows through mistakes, the sort she'd never known—might just be happening, now. *He flew across the country for me. He's literally begging me. No one has ever pursued me this way.* Her grip on the swing's chains loosened and a smile crept onto her face.

* * *

"He's a freeloader. You can't go back to him." Becca's father slammed his fist on the table. "What kind of a man would let his girlfriend pay for the food—and with food stamps, nonetheless? Those food stamps are for you and your child, not for a grown man. He's no good, I tell you."

"He's not freeloading, Dad. He has a job. He's saving all his money so we can get an apartment. I share my food stamps for groceries since I'm not working."

"As long as you live under my roof, you'll do as I say. He'd better not set foot in this house again."

Becca's fuming, defensive anger got the best of her. "Then I won't either!" She packed their few things and headed to Craig's place, a basement room in his brother's house.

A government program helped pay for a local home-based sitter, which Becca arranged in less than a week. Becca and Christine walked to the sitter's each morning, then Becca walked on to school, then work. They walked back to the basement apartment together each afternoon.

Becca played with Christine, made dinner, and studied. Craig's brother's yard was perfect for playing ball or swinging. A niche under the basement stairs, filled with pillows and a clip-on light, became a perfect spot to snuggle up to read stories together. She'd peruse magazines to find new recipes and cook a thrifty dinner, all before Craig came home from work.

He came home with a kiss and a gift—a flower from the yard for Becca, a balloon or a piece of candy for Christine. "For Beauty, from your beast." He bowed and kissed her hand as he presented the rose.

"You're so goofy." Becca accepted the supple offering with a curtsy. She stroked the velvety petals. "But don't stop." She backed away, a come-on look in her eye.

He pursued her, meeting her invitation with an equally cunning gaze.

"Christine's watching a movie." Becca ran into the bedroom, giggling, and shut the door behind her.

He followed, shutting and locking it behind them.

After dinner, Craig watched television or read. Some evenings he went upstairs to visit his brother.

Becca spent the evenings with Christine, getting her bathed, combing her hair, reading bedtime stories. Once Christine went to sleep, she had a few minutes to do homework and prepare for bed herself.

Craig didn't share Becca's bedtime routine. He could stay up after midnight and still have no problem waking up for work in the morning. Before a month of the new family living situation, he slipped out after dinner more than he stayed in.

"Come with me." He combed his black hair, which immediately fell back into his eyes.

"That doesn't work for me." Becca pouted. "I can't leave Christine here. We go early every day. We need our sleep. Stay with us."

He picked up his keys and jammed them into his pocket.

Becca stood in the doorway. "You told me to let you know when I feel angry. Remember? I'm starting to get mad about this. I don't want to be here alone while you're out. You came all the way back from California for me. You said how much you loved me."

"I know, and I do." Craig squeezed her body into his and kissed her. "You're the only one for me. You're beautiful, and sweet, and I love you so much. I just need to go out for a little while. I go crazy sitting at home. When I get home, we'll make love. I'll take you soaring. You'll feel so good you won't want to let go." He slipped his hands down her back and held her by the bottom, grinding closer.

His sweet talk—and hands—could melt an iceberg. "Okay." She sighed and slapped his bottom. "Go on. But hurry home."

Complaints soon followed. Craig didn't like when Christine left toys around. He didn't like that Becca didn't want to party anymore, or if the dishes were still dirty when he got home.

Arguments grew commonplace, leaving Becca crying and Craig storming out.

"It otay, Mommy," Christine said. She patted her mother on the shoulder.

"Mama's okay." Her baby wasn't even two yet, and already she'd taken to playing the Mommy role. Becca's stomach twisted. She sucked in her tears and hugged Christine. "Thank you, Sweetie. You're such a good girl. Don't you worry. When I finish school, we'll find a better place to live. You'll have your own bedroom, a really pretty one, just for you. Come on, let's play."

* * *

1975

Becca walked across the stage to receive her diploma, the first in her family to do so. Inside she glided, her feet not touching the ground.

But a high school diploma did not ensure a great job. Neither did her prior experience as a car wash attendant, a fitting room clerk, or cafeteria line worker. After a month of job hunting, Becca faced reality —without a college degree, she still would make no more than minimum wage. Not enough to cover a sitter, medical bills, rent, and food.

Staying on public assistance would be more to her financial advantage than a menial job, since the government provided food stamps and free medical care. But this was no way forward, so Becca took a job as a cashier.

When she and Craig finally found an apartment complex that would rent to first-timers, it was an hour's drive from their town, in Frederick. Becca purchased an old clunker from a friend for six hundred dollars so she could keep her job.

"I should take the car to work. You can go back on public assistance and stay home with Christine." Craig cast her his best "I'm-more-sensible-than-you" look. "You'd like that, wouldn't you? Just until I find a job closer to home, or we can get another car."

Becca sighed. They'd already moved. He hadn't found a job nearby yet and neither had she. His job in Kensington paid more than hers. "Okay. It would be nice to have a chance to stay home with Christine for a while."

Craig continued staying out late again, but now he didn't come home for dinner first.

"What?" Craig reasoned over the phone. "It doesn't make sense to drive all the way home and then back to Kensington to see my brother. The car is old, and gas is too much."

She and Christine were almost always alone without transportation and an hour from friends and family. After a few arguments over the subject, Becca chose silence over the issue. *He needs to feel welcome when he comes home, not attacked. I'm just going to be happy when he's here.*

Until Sheri, one of Becca's friends, called her, in tears and a slurring voice. "I'm so sorry, Becca," she cried.

"What?" Becca asked. "What's the matter?"

"I'm sorry about Craig. I didn't mean to do it."

"Do what? Is he okay?" Becca grew concerned. Sheri sounded drunk.

"We were just hanging out, drinking, and I swear, I'm not like this. I really am your friend, but—" She sobbed and slurred, "before I knew what was happening, we started doing it."

The room grew blurry from the outer edges, in. Sounds took on a surreal, slow pace. Becca's mind raced. She bit her lip.

"Then again. Three times now. I feel so guilty. Betraying you was wrong. I couldn't hide the truth from you any longer."

Becca heard music in the background coming through the line. *Craig said he was working late.* She gathered her wits and her voice. "You guys have been partying together?"

Sheri sniffed. "Yeah, he's been down at the Hole almost every night."

"Oh." Becca envisioned him at the Hole, where she and Missy and their friends hung out to party. *All of them. They all saw Craig with Sheri, knowing I was home with Christine. No one told me.* She mustered a response, ready to hang up the phone. "Well, I'm glad you told me."

"Can you ever forgive me?" Sheri pleaded, her sobs growing more uncontrollable. "I'm so sorry. I never should have done it. I'm so weak."

Forgive you? Forgive you for sleeping with my boyfriend not just once, but three times? Forgive you for breaking my heart while I sat here at home not even suspecting Craig was with anyone else? Forgive you? What does that even mean? Am I supposed to act like it didn't happen? She blew the toxic air from her lungs as if her anguish would ride along the wind. *Neither one of them is worth fighting over.* She forced a response. "He is very persuasive. I tell you what—you can have him." She hung up the phone.

17

Lena

Sandy Spring, Maryland. 1922

The familiar *clop clop clop* of the Burriss' horse hooves grew louder, paired with the distinct crunching of gravel as the wagon wheels curved onto the driveway. *Mama, checking on me, as promised.* Lena rushed to the washbasin and splashed water on her face. She looked in the mirror as she patted dry. *Red. Puffy. She'll know.*

Aggie stepped inside and called out.

Lena walked toward her in the parlor, pretending to be engaged in reading a magazine. "Hi, Mama."

Her mother took her by the shoulders and stood back, squaring eye to eye. Her lips tightened upon her teeth and an exhalation flared her nostrils. "Starlight." She pulled Lena in for a hug.

Lena's head filled with fluid that rushed to her eyes, her forehead, her nose. Forceful spasms nearly pushed her heart into her throat. She let go of what she could no longer contain and sobbed in her mother's arms.

Her mother stood, holding Lena and stroking her hair. When the upheaval of sobs started to wane, she squeezed her tighter, then led her to the sofa. "Sit with me."

Lena took a handkerchief from her apron pocket and blew her nose. She inverted and folded the cloth, then dabbed her eyes with the corners. "I'm sorry."

"Nothing to be sorry about."

"It's just. . ." She buried her face in her hands and sobbed again.

Aggie scooted closer and placed her hand on Lena's shoulder. "Sometimes there are no words."

Lena looked at her mother. "Loosing the baby is hard. But Clinton. He's so. . . angry."

Mama's look grew more concerned. "What do you mean?"

Lena held herself. *Will telling help or worsen the situation?* She bit her lip.

After giving Lena time to answer, Aggie regrouped. "If there's reason for me to know, please tell me. But I will say that many people feel angry when they lose someone. This passes, after a while."

Lena seized this as an opportunity to lessen the impact of Clinton's words. She sat up, wiped her face again, and pulled her emotions in. "Yes, that's probably all it is. I'll try to be more understanding. I've only been thinking about how much I need him. He needs me too."

"Helping each other will ease the pain. Talk with him. Think about what you both can do to say goodbye to the twin who was called home. Maybe give the boy a name and have a little ceremony. We didn't do that, since you were in the hospital, and then, since you've been home, we never felt the time was right."

"You're right, Mama. This has all just been too much."

* * *

Lena lugged baskets of the last vegetables into the kitchen. She peered out the window at the fields she tended. The boys, after helping carry in the harvest, had run back outside to play. Lena turned to Ruth, who had become her tiny confidant and constant companion. "There. That should be enough for a while. Now's the time we all go for a ride."

Ruth cooed, flailing her little arms from the basket near Lena's feet. She was growing now, but at four months old she seemed only two.

Lena pushed open the screen door to the back porch. "Boys, come on, we've got the buggy today, we're going to Grandpa and Grandma Burriss' for a visit."

"Yay!" Shaw's face lit up, followed by Elliot's. The boys ran around to the front yard, where they met up with Lena and the baby.

As they pulled into the Burriss farm, Lena felt her body relax. *Still feels like home.* She saw her mother hanging linens on the line. Grannie lay nearby in the grass with her youngest granddaughter, pointing at shapes in the clouds, as she had done with Lena and her siblings when they were young. *Dear Grannie. Will she ever declare she's too old to be laying in the grass?* Lena grinned at the sight. *When I'm a grandmother, I want to stoop for my grandkids like that.*

Aggie saw them approaching, stopped her work and waved. She helped Grannie to her feet, and they met by the front porch.

Grannie extended her worn and bumpy hands. "Now give me that precious bundle."

"Sit here in the rocker, Grannie, I'll hand her to you."

Receiving the swaddled infant worked like an elixir, bringing joy and youth to Grannie's face. Her brown eyes, cast grey from age, shone through as she gazed at the little miracle.

"Oh, little Ruth, you are a going to light up this world." She quieted for a moment as she rocked her great-granddaughter. "And dance. This one will dance." Grannie grinned, her old, wrinkly, half-toothed grin, and peered at Lena. "Starlight, this one is meant to be here. She's a fighter."

"Yes, I believe you, Grannie." Lena bent down to take Ruth from Grannie's arms. "Let's all get inside. The boys will be screaming for lunch soon, so we'd best be ready."

* * *

Once the boys were fed, Lena's younger sister took them out to play in the fields behind the house. She was good with them, a little mother, and held their rapt attention with her verbose ramblings about every detail they came across while exploring the fields or skipping stones across the pond.

"How are things, now, Lena?" Aggie's eyebrows raised as she placed her elbows on the small round table on the back porch.

Lena's eyes flitted. *What do I say? How do I say it?* She stared off into the fields, avoiding eye contact with both of her elders.

Grannie sat quietly by, sipping warm tea on this brisk October afternoon. Her long dark dress and white crocheted collar, worn dutifully, like a uniform, for as long as Lena knew, frayed at the cuffs.

Grannie fussed with the edges of her cuffs, tucking the frays underneath. "Lena." Her deep voice vibrated, emphasizing the 'nah' part of her name. She cleared her throat and pushed a stray hair into the tight bun on top of her head. "Some things are hard to tell." Her head bobbed slightly, up and down. "Mm hmm." She fixed her gaze on her granddaughter.

With that, Lena's eyes and nose tingled. Her brain was a hot cauldron with weeks of dirty laundry churning in murky water, and her tightly closed lips, the wringer. *What do I let out? Dare I?*

Placing her hand on Lena's forearm, Aggie gave her daughter a comforting squeeze. "What have you tried?"

"Everything." The word slipped out. Her chest heaved. She reached for her hanky, squeezing it, hands in her lap. The wringer opened, letting too much out. "Talking. Pleading. Ignoring. Giving him whatever he wants, whenever he wants—even before he asks, sometimes. But what he used to do only when he was drunk, now he does all the time." Lena forced herself to stop speaking, for the onslaught of murky liquids from her eyes, nose, and mouth made breathing a nearly impossible task.

Mama rubbed Lena's shoulder, waiting for her to get everything out.

Grannie spoke, her grave voice cracking a little. "Is he hurting you?"

"In every way." Lena clutched her handkerchief tighter.

"But worst of all, I'm scared he'll hurt Ruthie."

Grannie drew a deep breath and sat back in her chair. Her hands folded in her lap. "Chile. I have something for you." She reached into her apron's large pocket, pulled out an envelope, laid the mysterious packet on the table and pushed it toward Lena's plate.

Surprise and curiosity led to Lena's composure. "Grannie?"

"I've been holding this for you for quite some time. Open it."

Inside was cash and a ticket. "What. . . why?"

Aggie answered. "Grannie saved a long time for a trip to see her sister. But when you and Clinton wed, she told me this was for you, not her. I don't know how she knew."

Lena's head shook side to side and her eyebrows pressed downward. "Grannie." She looked into Grannie's eyes. "How did you know?"

"I just knew. I think this will be enough for you all, for a while. So, go. Stay with my sister. Caroline will be good to you."

Lena sat back in her chair. *Could I?* A flash, Clinton harassing her parents, angry and drunk, stopped her. *No. I just can't.* Returning her lips to their tight stance, she pushed the envelope back across the table. "I couldn't possibly. You haven't seen your sister since you were a girl. You should go."

18

Becca

Kensington, Maryland. 1975

When Craig returned, Becca waited until he fell asleep. She took the car keys, carried Christine and a bag, and left.

Driving through her tears late at night, unsure where to go, she drove toward the streets she knew. An occasional raindrop splashed on the windshield. Then another. She turned on the wipers, but they didn't make wipers for her eyes.

She turned on the radio to take her mind off things. As she was about to switch from news toward music, the reporter's emotion gave her pause.

"A handshake in space. The two spacecraft—one from the Soviet Union, one from America, united. Amazing, folks. Just amazing."

She turned onto a side street and shifted the gear into park. Flipping from station to station, the news reports confirmed what had happened earlier that day. The space program, of all things, ushered in peace and brotherhood between the U.S. and Soviet Union. Becca's face fell into her hands and she sobbed.

All of her life, she'd wanted peace. She'd given up hope for peace on earth and taken up the hope of making peace in her family. In herself. But she'd left her family. She'd left Craig. She wouldn't leave herself. . . or Christine.

Becca reached, twisting nearly out of her seat to put her hand over the back of the carseat and rest it on Christine. She looked around, wondering which way to go from here. The rain had stopped and her eyes were clear. Though driving aimlessly, she'd parked just a few houses up the road from Trista's.

Trista was also a single mom. Her house had been a place where friends sometimes crashed for the night. She carried Christine and knocked on her door in the middle of the night.

Trista answered, her hair in a wild tussle, her green eyes squinting. "Come in, honey, what's wrong?"

Becca entered, carrying Christine, and followed Trista's lead to sit on the couch. "Can we stay for the night? We won't be a bother."

"Yes, of course. Here, I'll get some sheets, and a quilt, and we'll make up the couch."

They settled Christine comfortably, placing pillows around her on the floor in case she rolled off the couch.

Trista prepared them both a mug of decaf. She sat in the dining room chair, tucking one leg under her, and lit a cigarette. Blowing smoke off to the side, she pushed her hair out of her face. "Now tell me. What happened?"

Becca spilled the whole story to Trista, through her tears.

"Oh, honey." Trista's eyes emitted compassion as she shook her head. "Men can be such jerks." She pulled a pillow onto her lap and squeezed it. "Here's how I see it. My parents helped me get this house, and I want to help others. You stay here as long as you need to. I mean, as long as you do what you can to pitch in."

"Really? You must be an angel or something."

Trista laughed. "No, not that." She raised an eyebrow and lit another cigarette. "Want one?"

Becca accepted and lit up. She had no money for cigarettes but craved one bad enough to start again.

"You should know this." Trista's voice grew lower and more serious. "Just six months ago, I was in the hospital." She held out her arm and pointed to the scar. "I let myself get so messed up over my boys' father and his cheating that I sliced my wrist."

"Oh my gosh."

"Yeah. I'm okay, though. I had counseling for a while. I think I just did it as a cry for help. If I'd really wanted to kill myself, I'd have cut the other direction." She used her finger to draw a line up her forearm. "Never again, though. I'm over him, and I need to be here for my boys. They mean everything to me."

"Wow, Trista. I had no idea. I always thought you had it all together."

Trista blew smoke off to the side through pursed lips and smushed the tip of her cigarette into the ashtray. "Nice acting job, huh?"

"I almost walked Christine and I into traffic one day, on purpose. I was so upset over a guy and my parents and my situation. I was heading up the street toward the main road, crying my eyes out, thinking I should just put us both out of misery."

"Oh my God, Becca."

"Yeah. But then something made me stop. I imagined the person who would hit us. How would they feel? Or, what if only me died? What would happen to Christine? What if I didn't die, but was paralyzed and couldn't care for Christine? What if only Christine died? The possibilities swirled through my mind. I turned the stroller down a side street and walked away from the main road. I just kept walking—for miles, down side streets, until I finally went home. Ever since, I walk off my frustration whenever I can. I take Christine and we just go. I live for Christine just like you live for your boys."

"Well, you know what?" Trista's tone perked up. "I had a job offer today, but I didn't have a sitter. If you'll watch my boys, I'll try out the job and you can stay—rent free. I won't make much money, but I think we can make ends meet."

"I'll drink to that." Becca raised her mug. "Oh, and did you hear? We shook hands with Soviets today!"

Trista clinked her mug against Becca's. "Yes, I saw. As the cosmonaut said, 'Very happy, my friend.'"

Trista and Becca became fast friends, as did their kids. They understood each other and enjoyed many of the same things, not the least of which being their mutual dedication to make life better for their kids.

Their coffee talks became a daily routine, growing deeper with time.

"I used to think, if there is a God, He certainly hasn't done me any favors." Trista poured them each a fresh cup of coffee. She pulled her feet up under her in the chair and blew on her coffee as she took the first sip, her wild curly black hair spilling over her face. She straightened her head and pushed aside the curls. "But then I started to realize, He really did. Okay, so I messed around and got pregnant in high school, and my husband cheated on me on our secret wedding night—the first of many times—but then again, both my boys are healthy. We have a roof over our heads, food to eat. We're doing okay."

"On your wedding night? Wow, that must have torn you up." Becca sipped her coffee. She raised her cup to Trista. "How could anyone cheat on a girl who makes such good coffee, anyway?"

They laughed.

Becca grew pensive. "When I was little, I begged God to make this boy or that boy like me. He never answered my prayers, so I decided He wasn't real. But then, when some of our friends at The Hole became Jesus Freaks, I reconsidered. They said since I'd accepted Jesus as a child, I was still saved—whether I wanted to be or not."

Silence danced in their midst for a few seconds, carrying the coffee's aroma in swirls that tickled Becca's nose.

"I was touched by the idea that maybe there really is a God. What if He really does love me, even though I'd given up on Him?"

"I know." Trista fixed her eyes on the bird feeder hanging from the tree out front. "I'm not crazy about church, but Jesus touches my heart." She turned her eyes to Becca. "I was thinking, what if we both read a little bit of the Bible every day, just to start learning about it?"

"I don't know about that. I've never been able to get

through all the who-begat-who parts."

"Well, you can pick up anywhere you want. Maybe in the New Testament, or in Psalms."

"You can read the Bible that way? I always thought you were supposed to start at the beginning—like a regular book."

"No, I think you can. I mean, I often turn to the back of a book to see the end before I read it."

Becca raised her eyebrows at Trista. "You do?"

Trista put her feet on the floor and leaned forward, placing her hands on the arms of the chair. Her porcelain-doll face morphed into an impish grin. She stared Becca straight in the eyes. "I know. I'm sooo bad like that."

Becca laughed. "You daredevil!" Used to taking herself—everything—all too seriously, sarcastic humor helped her lighten up.

"Let's do it." Trista picked up her mug and headed back to the kitchen. "I mean, if we are starting to have a relationship with God by praying, we ought to know what His book says."

"Okay. But don't ask me to go to church. Church is for hypocrites and ladies in white gloves." Becca followed Trista into the kitchen and wiped counters while she washed dishes.

"Hey, This Catholic-raised girl is with you on that. I'm a bit wild to fit in there. I still love to party after the kids go to bed. I don't want to have to act all prim and proper or wait 'til marriage for sex. I like sex. How will I know if a guy is any good if we don't sleep together first?"

"The Bible says not to have sex until after marriage?" Becca's eyebrows raised in utter surprise. "I didn't know that. I always figured if God made us, including sex, then why would sex be wrong? I mean, for me, love makes the difference. If I love the person, and both of us want to, then I guess sex is okay. Well, as long as we use contraception, that is."

Trista snapped a dish towel at Becca's backside and laughed. "You're forgetting one thing. Drunk can feel a lot like love."

Becca raised her eyebrows again and laughed in wonderment. "Oh my gosh, you're right. I never thought of that."

* * *

Trista folded the bed linens to put them away for the day. "I've been thinking. You're great with the kids, and I'm doing well at work. This house is too small for the five of us. I think you deserve your own room instead of sleeping on the couch. Let's look into getting a bigger place."

"I'm used to it, though, don't worry about it. I've been sleeping on a couch on and off for years. Besides, how could we afford an apartment?"

"Well, maybe we both can work, and share a sitter for all three kids."

Before long, they secured a ground-floor, three bedroom apartment. Plain, but decent, the place suited them both. Sliding glass patio doors opened out onto a small, but fenced, neighborhood playground—perfect to watch the kids play. Becca found a job, and her sister Emily agreed to the job babysitting all three kids.

The two friends worked all day, then came home and made dinner, cleaned, and played with the kids before bedtime, when they'd trade turns reading a bedtime story to the three children. On weekends, they'd shop for inexpensive home decor and plants to fix the new place up. They created a gallery wall in the living room, arranging large, inexpensive nature photos in an aesthetically pleasing design. They hung a grow light over a table by the window with plants. The furniture, though old, was comfortable, and large floor pillows added extra seating.

With a tight budget, they were careful with grocery plans. Since the kids wanted bread at breakfast, lunch and dinner, they learned to bake homemade bread. Every Sunday, they'd mix a large batch of dough from scratch. They'd let the dough rise, punch it down, and let it rise again, then divide the dough into six loaves. The aroma of freshly baked bread from the oven inevitably drew the five of them to the kitchen table to devour one entire loaf, still hot from the oven, smothered with gobs of real butter.

One evening, after they'd put the kids to bed and washed the dishes, Becca turned on the television. "What are we gonna watch tonight?"

"Well, that's a silly question. This is Friday night, so *Rockford Files*, of course." Trista teased. "You know I think James Gardner is kinda cute."

"I guess, for an old guy." Becca switched channels to find the show. "It's not quite nine, so we've got *Chico and the Man* for a few more minutes.

Trista headed toward the kitchen. "That's good. I want to get a snack ready anyway."

"We're like an old married couple, staying in to watch TV on Friday nights."

The doorbell rang.

Becca opened the door, then stiffened in place. "Craig? What are you doing here?"

Craig looked shocked as well. "You live here? I met this guy at the store." He pointed to the stranger next to him. "And he invited me to come with him. He said his ex had a roommate."

The stranger stood there with a big grin, holding a case of sodas, a scrunched up brown bag laying atop it. He handed the case of sodas to Craig, tucked the bag under his arm, and extended his hand. "Hi. I'm Bob, Trista's ex."

She returned his shake, dumbfounded.

Bob breezed by Becca, entering the living room with a loud, "Kids, I'm here!"

"Well, come on in, I guess." Becca let her right arm open, a little late since he'd already passed her and entered her apartment.

Trista entered the living room from the kitchen, responding to Bob's loud entry.

"Shh. The kids are asleep. What're you doing here so late?"

Bob kissed her on the cheek, took the sodas from Craig, and headed into the kitchen. Trista followed him. Becca closed the door and motioned for Craig to sit.

He sat on the sofa, spreading his legs wide and clasping his hands behind his head.

"Wow," Becca sat diagonally from him in a single-seat chair. "What are the chances?"

"Yeah, weird, right?" Craig straightened, leaning forward. "So, how ya been?"

"Well, good, really. Trista and I are great roommates. We're both working and Emily babysits for us. What are you up to these days?"

"I'm back in Kensington, working at the station again. Broke the apartment lease and moved back into my brother's."

Bob and Trista returned from the kitchen.

"Hey, since the kids are in bed, let's party." Bob turned the music on, the lights down, and poured shots for all.

With a quick glance, Becca checked Trista.

"Well, just one." Trista reached for a shot.

Becca followed suit. "Here's to old flames."

Before long, the four of them were laughing and dancing together. Bob made moves on Becca, slipping his arm around her waist and pulling her hips toward his. Craig danced with Trista, running his hands along her torso while she swayed to the music, pulling her hair up in full-on seductive mode.

Trista nodded her approval to Becca.

Becca conceded, letting herself get into Bob, knowing full well he was a lady's man, not to be trusted.

The party lasted until everyone fell asleep sometime in the wee hours—Bob and Becca in Trista's room, and Trista and Craig in the living room.

Becca awoke alone. Bob was in the living room playing the Great Daddy role to his boys. His gregarious nature entreated everyone to love him, especially the kids. He treated Christine with similar excitement and attention as he did his boys.

Becca noticed Christine enjoying his attention as she shuffled into the kitchen to make coffee. Christine hadn't seemed to notice Craig sleeping on the floor, facing the wall.

Bob followed the kids into the playroom.

Craig stumbled into the kitchen. He picked up the coffee pot. "Did you sleep with him?" His gravelly voice lingered.

Trista looked up, pushing her tousled hair behind her ear. She moved from the dining room chair into the kitchen, closer to Becca.

Becca noted how Craig's left eyebrow rose, his nostrils flared, and his breathing increased in pace. *He's got no right.* "What? No. We fell asleep. And even if I did, what would that be to you? You were with Trista anyway. Did you sleep with *her*?" She moved past him and poured a cup of coffee.

"No. I cried to her about you."

She saw his body tense. The energy of his rising temper palpably filled the room. Becca stirred the cream and sugar into her mug as she shot Trista a questioning glance.

Trista's face was hard to read.

"Come outside." She motioned and headed toward the patio door. *I don't want him acting like this in front of the kids.*

Craig followed her out the sliding glass doors and onto bench in the playground.

He cried to Trista about me? Is he lying or does he actually still love me? I don't know what to say.

Craig solved her quandary with his next utterance. "You did sleep with him, didn't you? Of course, you did. You're just a tramp." His voice raised as he pointed his finger into her chest. "A self-righteous whore!"

"What? Oh my God, how can you say such a thing? I don't belong to you. And besides, you were the one cheating on me while I was home like an idiot, believing you were working your ass off."

"Oh, sure. I bet you were screwing all the neighbors when I wasn't home." Craig turned and stormed away. He shouted behind before turning the corner. "Good-bye, bitch. I hope you enjoy your holier-than-thou life."

Becca stood in the center of the playground watching until he disappeared around the side of the two-story building. *What the hell was that?* She rubbed her head and pressed her palm firmly against a point of pain on her forehead. Moving to sit on the swing for a while, Becca tried to process the events that unfolded since nine o'clock the night before.

She slipped back inside. Pouring a second cup of coffee, she curled up in a chair and drank in silence, while Trista and Bob and the kids went on with a seemingly happy Saturday morning. Bob play-wrestled with the boys and then lifted them into the air. Christine stood by excitedly, asking for her turn.

How can they act so normal after all this? Don't they have hangovers too? Becca tried to ignore them, tune them out. Her inner turmoil made enough noise without them adding to it. *This will be the last time I ever let him come around. Self-righteous? Holier-than-thou? What in the world is that? I feel bad lying about Bob. I feel even worse that I did sleep with Bob. Ugh! Why did I do that? I guess I wanted to make sure I didn't sleep with Craig. God, now what do I do? I screwed up. I don't feel righteous. I sure don't feel holy. Do I act that way, really? Or was he just trying to find something to throw at me, to guilt me into being the sorry one?*

Trista entered the kitchen to make breakfast. "You okay?"

Becca excused herself to take a shower. The water ran down her head, shoulders, body, and into the drain. *God, please forgive me. Please wash me clean.* She could barely manage to use soap. She propped her arms on the wall, leaning her weight onto them, and let the water run over her. *This hangover, and this dirty feeling. Ugh. Help me not drink anymore. Help me not sleep with anyone anymore. This feels awful, God. Help me remember how this feels, so I never do it again.*

She ruminated, not feeling like herself, all day.

Once Bob was gone and the kids were in bed, Trista brought Becca a soda and snuggled in next to her on the couch. "I couldn't believe he just showed up like that after all this time. I hadn't seen him in so long. But that's the way he is. He's off doing whatever the hell he feels like doing, and then, when he comes around, the kids love him anyway. He's like Santa Claus to them. One day a year and he's the hero." She leaned harder against Becca's arm. "Hey, you okay? I've been worried about you all day."

Becca's inner world spewed out, like a volcano erupting, but with tears instead of lava. She told Trista what Craig said and how horrible she felt about everything that happened.

"Oh, sweetheart, don't let him make you feel bad. He's an ass."

"But I thought you liked him. You two were hitting it off."

"Well, he did start crying to me about you, but not for long. As soon as he saw me care, he leaned in to kiss me. I just stayed with him so you wouldn't."

Becca wiped her face and blew her nose. "So, you didn't?"

"Listen. Let's just forget them. From now on, we'll date decent guys and help each other. You hear me? We don't have to be with anyone who tries to make us feel bad."

"I don't know if there are any out there like that. I feel like guys just want to use me, whether they're from good families or not. With Craig, I settled. I thought he was in my league, but he still just used me." Becca leaned her head on

Trista's shoulder. "I wish I could have a good relationship with a guy—as good as you and I are together."

19

Lena

Sandy Spring, Maryland. 1923

Autumn's golden, orange, and burgundy splashes across the landscape tried to warm Lena's soul. Soon they withered and fell, the frost taking not only the color from the trees but also the tender flowers in the garden. The bleak and frozen winter days forced everything inside, including Lena's heart.

Buried within the confines of her grief and fear, she performed daily chores and childcare, but devoid of joy and whimsy. She excused herself from family gatherings, church and socials. Having exhausted attempts to reconnect with Clinton, she feigned sickness to keep him away.

But he kept coming. He relied on her for meals, to lend an ear to his frustrations, to provide a receptacle to his pent up urges, and to sustain the household while he left to work on bicycles, motorbikes, and automobiles, and his parents' farm. Mostly, he came for his physical needs.

When she didn't meet his needs, she was sure he looked elsewhere. Arriving home late many nights, smelling of alcohol and perfume, and marked with lipstick smudges on his neck, he didn't try to hide his waywardness. He was trying to show her, to provoke her to jealousy, to coerce her into doing the things she didn't want to do anymore.

Lena turned a blind eye to his effort. She tucked her heart behind her logic. *I prefer him to look elsewhere. I can't get pregnant again.*

Love was a memory, a dream skirting the edges of her mind. If only he were the Clinton she had known when they first met. *Where did he go?*

The door closed.

Lena turned away from the doorway, and pulling the covers around her, she forced her muscles to relax and slowed her breathing. *Asleep. I am asleep.*

"I've had enough of this," he said, his gruff voice looming above her.

A sharp breath caught in her lungs, as quiet as a caged bird under night's cover.

His voice boomed. "You're my wife. There's no reason why I should come home and find you already sleeping in the bed. I've been working hard all day—what have you been doing? If not your stomach ache, you're coughing, or you're weak, or sore, or tired. What's wrong with you? Are you going to act like a wife, or are you just trying to make me mad?" He slammed his hand against the bed post.

She held her breath and anchored her position.

His weight, his breath, his hands, all rushed upon her.

She tried to push him away, to scream, to get words out

of her mouth. Her efforts met with his brawny, thick hands around her neck and his barrel chest atop hers. Nothing to say, nothing to do, no way of escape.

His tirade faded into a distant, faint sound, as though she were standing outside the window, from afar, looking on. From that place, she saw him take her. Ruth cried out. She saw him go after the baby. He shook her. . . almost threw her against the wall. Lena saw herself step in his way. . . begging him to give her the baby. She saw him drop Ruth, like a sack of potatoes, on the bed, before he stormed out the door.

Hope's wispy threads are the tattered flag after a bloody battle. Lena recalled Grannie's poetic words, written after she lost her husband in the Civil War.

From the unknown outskirts of her defeated soul, as she rocked her crying baby in the darkened room, she found courage to grasp a tiny thread of hope that floated across her mind. A thread of hope—not for Clinton's redemption, no—not anymore. The hope of freedom. Freedom from this good dream gone bad.

Lena reached for hope, catching the silky threads in her fingers, and drew the promise of freedom to her heart, embracing power. She would take Grannie's offer.

* * *

Lena tucked her carefully worded letter under Clinton's cup on the table, then paused to look around. Simple and small, but home, this was where she'd first begun marriage with the love of her life. *He was gentle then.* Taking a deep breath and swallowing hard, she pursed her lips. Her eyes skimmed over the crocheted doilies on the arms and backs of the hand-me-down sofa and chairs. *I put so much of my heart, and hands, into this place.*

She scanned past the parlor, over the old floorboards in the hall, and into the small bedroom at the back of the house, where she and Clinton spent their wedding night. *I didn't even know about intercourse until it happened.* She shook her head, partly at herself—for her former naivety—and partly at Clinton, for his bullheadedness. She had other memories of the bedroom. Shaw and Elliot were born there—both prematurely.

The pain of losing Ruth's twin stung Lena's heart. That pain had become unbearable when Clinton took his anger out on Lena, blamed her for it. But now he took his wrath out on little Ruth, too.

Lena clung to the wispy threads of hope in her heart as she sat on the borrowed suitcase, bounced until it closed, and pushed the brass clasp locked. Standing to smooth her dress, she noticed her hands trembling and scolded them for betraying her resolve. She hoisted the large suitcase upright on the floor and pushed her worldly belongings to the door.

"Goodbye, house," Lena sighed. She wrapped up her baby and went through the door. The freezing cold air sent shivers down her spine. Lena told her spine to relax. All the locals learned this trick as youngsters to make the shivers stop. She closed the front door with resolution.

Brushing the frost off the baby carriage stored on the porch, she tucked Ruth in with extra blankets and baby items. She slid her suitcase onto the buggy's lower shelf. Backing the carriage down the front step, she turned to face the path that led to town.

She called the boys to her side. *They never seem to mind the cold.*

They came running, leaving off their snowballs for another day, and climbed to hold on to the rails of the carriage. Elliot squeezed himself onto the lower shelf with the luggage.

"We goin' on a big 'venture?" Shaw bounced up and down, holding onto the push bar with Lena.

"Yes, baby. A big adventure."

She pushed and they headed toward the road. A thin layer of pure, white snow blanketed everything—the grass, the mess of broken yellow-brown straw that had been her flower garden a few months prior, the top edges of the wood fencing, and the bare tree limbs that lined the path toward town. This was usually a peaceful scene, but not today. Lena clenched her fists around the carriage handle and pressed forward. *Hard as ice. Don't look back.* She turned the carriage out onto the path and set on her way.

Under the trees on the path, frost clung to buds on some of the trees. *Will this late snow damage the buds?* Like spring's first chartreuse buds rapidly burst into full foliage, fear of frost behind them for the summer, Lena's sons had grown into lads so quickly. Shaw was nearly five now, the man of the house. Elliot almost four.

They will miss him. How excited they grew when their father came home. *"Where's Daddy?"* They would whine each evening, peering through the window, watching and waiting to see him strolling down the path toward home. *"Daddy, Daddy, swing me, Daddy!" "Daddy, fix my toy,"*

"Daddy, can I have a horsey ride?"

Clinton had taken their buggy and hadn't come home for two days, a relief. She didn't want to have to face him again after that night. She had gone to her parents' house, accepted Grannie's gift, and come back home to prepare their things.

I don't know how to tell them this.

Tears streamed down her face, trickled onto her neck and landed in her scarf, defying her determination to harden. She wiped them and pulled her scarf closer around her neck. The tightened scarf elicited soreness. *These bruises. His hands tight around my neck, holding me down. One quick move and I'd be dead now. Where would my babies be then?*

In town, three miles down the road, she'd board the carriage that would carry her to Takoma Park. From there, she would take a train south, to her great aunt's home in North Carolina, where at least they would be safe. She didn't know what she would do after that—not yet.

Sunbeams penetrated the wooded path, highlighting delicate ferns as they unfurled in morning's early light. The frost melted, allowing patches of moss to sparkle in the sun. She slowed the carriage to make eye contact with a frightened doe, grazing by the way. Betraying her aching heart, the edges of her lips turned slightly up. She loved woods, gardens, wildlife, and little things—perhaps for the unexpected joy they brought. Lena was a child again, just for a moment, playing at the edge of the wood as her mother tended the garden nearby.

Her childhood memories were sweet. Images of those times rolled through her mind—seemingly endless days playing in the grass with her siblings, exploring the woods, helping with baking, singing, and making music with family in the parlor of their tiny farmhouse. The Burriss family created a loving home, full of kindness, respect, and affection. How could she have known of the life she'd have with Clinton?

Clinton. What is wrong with him? She had wondered this so many times. She spent years trying to understand him, help him, nurture him, hoping he would find a happy life. Her efforts had fallen like sand through her fingers—falling, falling, never turning, or leading anywhere—but down. Then she herself had begun to fall like sand, falling into an abyss of immovable, oppressive weight. Her once loving, faithful heart now churned resentment for the man she had loved. *Resentment.* Lena didn't believe in living a resentful life. She couldn't bear the thought of becoming this. Nor could she bear the thought of her children living this life. More tears, wiped away, she pressed on.

"We're almost there, kiddos." She consoled Ruth, propping a bottle into the crying baby's mouth. "Almost there."

Arriving in the center of Sandy Spring, which was more a crossroad than a town, Lena pulled the baby carriage into the market. The market housed not only groceries but also the town clerk and police station. Delivery trucks and wagons stopped here every few hours. A carriage taking passengers to larger towns came each morning at ten. They arrived just in time.

It would have been a fun experience, if not for the circumstances. Lena had never been into the city. Within a couple of hours, they'd passed several towns and arrived in Takoma Park, a bustling city just outside of Washington. There were people everywhere—more than she'd seen in one place at one time. Trucks, cars, carriages, and horses competed for a spot on the road. Ladies in pretty dresses walked along near the shops.

She made her way into the station, where the faint smell of wood and dust combined with the perfumes of several ladies. A few people sat on benches. They kept to themselves, most of them reading. Posters with maps of the railway system and advertisements for local shops lined the walls.

Shaw and Elliot found a new store of energy and climbed up on the bench to see the posters.

Seeing the ticket booth at the far end of the corridor, Lena picked up her crying baby and used one hand to push the buggy to the window. "Good morning, sir. I have a ticket to Charlotte, North Carolina." She presented it.

"Yes, ma'am. Train should be here in less than an hour."

Ruth settled into play, sitting up in the carriage, and Lena read to the boys. A thousand thoughts vied for her attention as she did her best to concentrate. Reading the same paragraph four times over, she asked Shaw to "read" the book to Elliot. She leaned onto the side of the carriage, shaking a rattle for Ruth.

The train whistle blew the myriad of thoughts away. The mighty engine roared into the station, brakes screeching loudly. Ruth cried at the sound. Shaw and Elliot's faces lit up.

"The train!"

Lena, nearly dumbfounded, gaped at this monstrous machine. Reading about trains in school had not prepared her to hear and see the real thing. "Jeepers!"

The screeching brakes quieted, and a loud puff of steam

signaled the end of the train's forward movement. Lena progressed to the train, pushing the carriage and holding the boys' hands the best she could all at once. "Shaw, hold Elliot. Hold him tight. Elliot, hold Shaw's hand. Don't let go."

It heaved and hissed, like a living thing—a monster from a storybook.

"All aboard!" The call came.

A man helped load her baggage and the pram. He helped the boys up and gave Lena a hand to climb the steps, Ruth in arms. She found her way to a row of seats with room for them all, enough to fix blankets as a bed for Ruth.

Clang, screech, swoosh, then the gradual roll forward, with a gentle sway—all new sensations. The boys held onto the windowsill, their faces pressed on the glass.

"Here we go," she whispered to her little troupe.

The steady *clack, clack, clack* of the rails and the flicker of light as they sped past trees in the evening sun became a lullaby for them all. She read first to the boys, and once they nodded off, she tried to read the novel she'd brought. Cather's words in *One of Ours* blurred in and out as Lena's head dropped to one side, and she drifted into sleep.

20

Becca

Aspen Hill, Maryland. 1975

Trista and Becca did just as they had resolved. Months passed, enjoying being roomies, dating different guys, hosting parties for their friends, and quietly slipping in a little Bible reading at least once a day. Their kids were close, like siblings, and stayed busy playing together most of the time.

Becca still hadn't found anyone to date regularly. If a guy thought a lot of her, she found something wrong with him. If she started having feelings for a guy, he didn't feel the same about her. Frustrated with the boyfriend situation, Becca sat on the swing outside their apartment watching the children play and letting her thoughts be prayers. *Lord, why is finding a good guy so hard? Will there ever be someone who feels about me the way I feel about him? Someone who will be good to Christine? Will you please help, God?*

Something caught her eye from off to the right, just out of

view. A person, a man, approached. As he came closer, she recognized him.

Craig walked back around that corner, the same place he'd left almost a year prior. He held something behind his back.

Becca froze. *Oh my God. What's he going to do?* "Kids, go inside, quick." She shooed them in.

He smiled and waved. He slowly offered what was behind his back. Flowers. "I moved to California, but I felt bad about the last time we saw each other, so while I'm here visiting my brother, I thought I should come back to see you."

"What? We've been down this road. Why keep trying? Is there no one else you can torture?" A coy blink of the eye told him she teased with the truthful cut.

"I've changed. I got that bank job in Los Angeles. I found God. Come on, let me just take you out to dinner and tell you about it."

Curiosity sparked Becca's interest. Hope, like an aggravating ray of sun after a late night drinking, prodded her heart. *Found God?* She agreed to dinner. "But nothing else."

"I don't think you should do this." Trista watched Becca put on her makeup for the evening.

"I promise, I'll be good. I'm never going to get in his trap again. I just want to see what he has to say about finding God. I just hope he's doing better now, not that we'll get back together."

"Still. I don't think so." Trista stood in the doorway blocking the way out. "Be careful, honey."

"I will," Becca pledged. She picked up her purse and scooted past Trista's blockade.

Craig arrived on time, picking Becca up at six. A rental

car, he said. He took her out to a nice dinner—a first—and caught her up on all that was new in life. He said he'd picked up a Bible and started reading. He'd decided to ask God to forgive him and help him start anew. Craig listened as Becca described the events of the last several months and her hopes for the future. She confessed her developing faith as well as some ongoing misgivings.

They talked like old friends, like old lovers, through steak and potatoes and the gooiest, most scrumptious, death-by-chocolate cake ever. They laughed as chocolate dripped down Craig's mustache, Becca instinctively reaching to wipe the spot away. Then they sat, napkins on their laps, and gazed into each other's eyes for a moment.

God, I haven't been able to get over him. Why do I love this guy so much? I can't, though. I just can't. He's no good for me, and he's certainly not good for Christine. She intercepted her thoughts, remembering her promise to Trista. "Well, I'd better get back. It's getting dark. Christine's not used to me not being home at bedtime."

Back at his car, Craig produced a bottle of wine. "Come on up to the room first. We'll have a glass, talk things out."

"You got a hotel room?" Impressed that he had enough money, and was trying so hard, she conceded. "Just one drink, then I really have to go."

A glass later, Craig laid the sweet-talk on heavy. He always had a way of making her feel like the one.

He usually follows his sweet talk with reassurance that no one will ever be able to make me feel the way he did. At this memory, more negative memories floated to the surface. Becca drew back. She headed to the door, picked up her coat and pushed one arm into the sleeve.

Craig took her by the hand and pulled her into his arms. He held her like he'd been craving her all this time. "Please, baby," he whispered, "there's no one like you." Pressing his lips lightly upon her shoulder, her neck, then her jawline, he implored her. "Just one kiss."

Her coat slipped to the floor as their lips met. Betraying herself, she melted into his arms, and returned his kiss.

Immediately his hands groped her body, her breasts and between her legs.

Her body on fire, Becca nearly caved, but memories resurfaced, practically screaming at her, *Stop!* She pictured him taking her food stamps and her car and leaving her, for Sheri's arms. His insults swirled atop the pictures in her mind. Becca pulled back and resisted, her hand up against him. "No," she said with blunt force. "No."

Craig's face distorted into a that of a pitiful puppy-dog. The worst kind—a puppy dog with blue eyes. "But what about God? What about forgiveness?"

Becca took his hands together in hers, her eyes piercing his. Surprising even herself, she responded with boldness. "You say you have God now. Let's pray." Not waiting for his answer, she prayed aloud. "God, I thank you for helping Craig. I thank you for helping me. I thank you for what we had together. Now I ask you, if we ever see each other again, help us remember what we had, and remember what you've taught us, and help us let that be that."

That *was* that. *Forgiven or not, he is not good for us.* Becca walked to the hotel desk and called for a ride. Two years of trying, and finally, the break was clean. Clear. Searing all the way through the young woman's heart.

Safely home with Trista again, she relayed the whole story.

At the end, she threw the pillow off her lap and stood up. Hands on her hips and a smile on her face, she quipped, "Turns out, absence makes the heart grow. . . harder."

Trista smiled. "That's good." She picked up the pillow Becca had cast aside, pulled her feet up into the chair and hugged it.

But Trista seemed too quiet. "What's wrong?" Becca sat back down, next to her.

"I struggle whether to tell you this. I have been afraid to tell you, because I didn't want to hurt our relationship." Trista squared her eyes on Becca's. "Our relationship is more important to me than anything. I want you to know that."

"What?" Becca put her hand on Trista's knee. "Tell me."

"I slept with him."

Becca sat straighter as air rushed into her lungs. "What, with Craig? When?"

"It was a long time ago. You remember that night when we all partied together?"

Becca remembered. They both had been vague about whether they'd gone all the way with each other's exes.

"It didn't stop there," Trista confessed. "He came back other times when you weren't home."

Tears welled up in Becca's eyes. She averted her eyes, not wanting to look at Trista as she told the story, but also not wanting her to stop telling the whole of it. "More times?"

"I felt terrible. I took a while figuring out how to stop. I knew you two had broken up, but you were still in love with him. I think maybe in some weird way, I hoped being with him would keep him away from you, because he's no good, Becca. He's just no good."

I slept with her ex, too. But I didn't keep doing it. Becca wanted to crawl under a bridge somewhere and hide forever—or scream at Trista for not telling her sooner. *My best friend. . . betrayed me. But not really. We weren't together anymore. But she didn't tell me. And he is hard to resist.* "I slept with Bob that night, too." Becca put her hand on Trista's shoulder. "Look. I don't know why you didn't tell me before, but you told me now. Honestly, I can't imagine losing our friendship over this. You're more important to me than he is."

Trista wiped the wet edges of her face and sat to the edge of the sofa. "Girl. You are too much. I thought you'd hate me forever."

"Let's just get away from here, somewhere we never have to see him again."

"Funny, you say that." Trista headed toward the kitchen. "Wanna a soda?"

"No, thanks. What's funny?"

Returning to the living room with a soda bottle, Trista took a long swig and set the bottle on the table. "My parents called today. They want us to move closer to them, at the beach. Dad even said he'd buy a place and I can pay him rent toward owning it."

"Seriously? Wow."

"So why don't we? We can get away from all this craziness. Who'd drive three hours on a whim to see us, anyway?"

"Let's go."

21

Becca

Berlin, Maryland. 1976

They chose an old farmhouse a few miles from the Ocean City, where Trista's parents had retired. While Trista's father complained the house lacked insulation and a decent heating and air system, the place met Trista and Becca's dreams of living a quaint country lifestyle.

On an acre lot, the clapboard house at the end of a quiet street welcomed them with a grand front porch in Victorian trim. The antique front door—a gorgeous mahogany with hand carvings and a cut-glass window—provided an inviting centerpiece. Inside, Becca and Trista were surprised by the odd mix of old and new. Velveteen wallpaper in gold brocade gave the home an overdone, creepy, funeral-home feel, and autumnal-colored shag carpeting brought a 60s vibe.

Trista laughed. "This place is us, for sure." She dropped

her purse and spun around in the middle of the empty living room. "We'll have so much fun decorating."

Becca, half stunned and half amused, with her mouth agape, took longer to warm up to the idea. "This?" She sat on the shag rug and ran her fingers through its orange and green fibers. "I suppose it is sort of cool. In a very tacky way." She sputtered a laugh and exaggerated a 60s-speak. "All right, then, groovy, baby."

Up the carpeted stairs were three bedrooms, perfect spaces complete with flowery wallpaper in one, striped in another and zoo animals in the kids' room. Back downstairs, a large oil heater jutted out into the middle of the dining room, the only heat source. The single bathroom, though resting upon a worrisome slanted floor, delivered instant charm via a footed bathtub and antique brass fittings.

"Let's see what's out back." Becca creaked the screen door open and stepped down the two concrete steps. "Wow, kids, a chicken coop!"

They followed the kids and peeked in the screen windows, inspecting the abandoned, rotten mess.

Trista turned up her nose. "I don't know about chickens." She pushed the half-broken door open. "Looks like they've used this more as a shed."

"And this huge tree—what kind is it?" Becca bent her head back and squinted at the leaves above. They were large, almost rubbery in texture, with brown on the bottom and green on top.

"Mahogany, or Magnolia? I don't know." Trista walked ahead, scoping out the far end of the yard. "This will be perfect for a vegetable garden, and the rusty old swing set seems sturdy enough. Just needs sanding and a coat of paint."

With the sale complete, Trista and Becca packed their things into a rented truck and moved three hours away, into the quaint, quirky home. Finding rustic antiques, like the folding wood chairs in the dining room and the wrought iron beds they refurbished for the kids, became their new hobby. They hung ruffled calico curtains in the play room and dining room, and accepted an awful lemon-yellow vinyl sofa a well-meaning family friend bought them at a yard sale.

They found jobs nearby, alternating their hours, and settled in for a picture-perfect new life in this small town on the Maryland's Eastern shore.

"Ah, this is home." Becca leaned back in the cushioned wicker sofa and propped her feet up on the old trunk serving as a coffee table. A warm summer breeze tickled hair into her face. She breathed in the peaceful feeling, savoring the treasure like a king does his gold. "I never want to leave."

Christine curled up next to her. "I love it, Mama. We stay?"

"Yes, sweetheart, we stay." Becca opened a book stored on the side table and began to read to Christine.

Blaine and Billy piled in around them, all of the children snuggling against Becca, all in their jammies, content to be waxing a little sleepy from the cozy lull of Becca's reading voice.

The next year went down as idyllic in Becca's book of life. Satisfied with the present, while still hoping to have the same peaceful family experience in marriage some day, she kept her dating struggles mostly to herself. And Trista, of course. As she wrote to her parents, she reflected on the year in ways she hoped would bring them to believe life could be better.

Dear Mom and Dad,

Sorry I haven't written in a while. Christine is blossoming here. Trista is like a second mother to her, and Billy and Blaine like brothers. Billy leads the pack in their fun adventures, from which Christine, as the youngest, suffers the brunt.

Once, she got stuck in a tree that Billy challenged her to climb. Blaine came rushing inside, yelling for help to get her down. She was only a few feet up, so it tickled me more than scared me. Another time, Billy persuaded Christine to ride down the carpeted stairs in a box, not thinking of the fact that the stairway turned at the bottom and her box had no steering mechanism! Poor Christine learned the hard way. (Don't worry, Mom, she's fine).

We made sweet summer memories with bedtime stories in jammies on the front porch, all nestled around either Trista or me, whichever of us had the evening off work. Now that the days are cooler, the kids help us bake bread together. We love devouring the first warm, delicious loaf from the oven. They make faces together over the yucky soups they have to eat when the budget doesn't stretch far enough for us to make a full meal every night. The soups are good the first night, but after three days of the same thing, the kids act as if we're torturing them. We grew our own veggies in the garden. Christine even tasted sautéed radishes. She's a brave little buckaroo.

On really cold nights, the five of us huddle together under blankets to sleep near the oil heater in the dining room. Old houses aren't known for good insulation. A neighbor said the plaster walls in this house only have horse hair for insulation. Imagine that. We cover the curtains with extra blankets, as well as the doorways, to trap the heat in the center room.

All is well here. How are you all doing?

Love, Becca

* * *

Then Trista fell in love. He was a friend of a friend, and they connected instantly. He was great with the kids, easy to get along with, and perfect for Trista in every way. In what seemed like no time at all, the two lovebirds wed.

Becca cried her way through the reception. Trying to hide it, she ducked out of sight as much as possible. When she snuck into the dining room to fix a small plate of food, one of their friends noticed Becca's puffy eyes and pulled her aside.

"What's wrong, Becca?" She held her by the elbow and patted her forearm.

Becca took her hand and led her upstairs, away from the party. "I don't know. I don't understand why I'm crying like this. I'm happy for Trista. Really happy." Even these words came at the cost of more tears. "But I can't stop crying."

The friend held Becca's hands in her lap. They sat together, in silence at first. "Did you and Trista have, um, you know, *that* kind of relationship?"

The emphasis on the word, *that*, clued Becca to what she meant. "Oh, no. I mean, I guess we looked like *that*, and, to be honest, we thought about *that*, but no, we aren't gay. But I do love her. I'm happy for her, but now that she's married, things will never be the same."

"Oh, I see. Did they say you have to move out?"

"No, but—" Becca pushed the wadded tissue onto her lower lip to suppress the trembling. "I've been so happy living here with Trista. Christine has been happy here, too. I'm sure they'll want me to go so they can establish themselves as a family. I dread the thought of being on my own again, of having to take Christine away from what has become her home and her family. I feel so. . . lost. . . and alone."

Becca's friend tried to comfort her, assure her, assuage her fears, but truly, there was nothing she could say. They both knew the truth—life would be hard again. There were no easy answers.

Becca's heart-knowledge proved right. Everything did change. Trista clammed up. She wouldn't talk to Becca. Not to say what was wrong. Not to say what was right. Becca tried getting Trista to talk, to work out their problems, but met a silent protest. After two weeks of living this way, Becca answered her own question. *She just can't bring herself to tell me to go.*

Trista and her new husband took the boys and went away

for the weekend. "We just need some time to ourselves," he explained, shrugging his shoulders and tilting his eyebrows as if physically sending an apology for his wife's behavior.

"But Christine's fourth birthday is tomorrow—"

Waking early the next morning to an empty house, Becca kissed her sleeping birthday girl on the forehead, and tiptoed up the stairs to her prayer spot in the attic. *Jesus, I don't know what to do. We don't belong here anymore but I don't know where. . . Is there a place for us? For Christine and me?*

She folded herself forward onto the rug, holding the empty ache in her belly and closing her eyes. The smell of her grandmother's perfume, like a wisp of ambrosia, lifted her spirits. Warmth embraced and rocked her.

The sound of Christine's feet squeaking the old wooden rungs of the attic ladder drew Becca's attention. Her timid voice followed. "Mama, you okay?"

With a quick wipe of her tears, Becca sat up. "Yes, honey, Mama's just having some prayer time. Happy Birthday!" She stretched her arms open to Christine as she headed toward her. "Are you hungry for breakfast?"

"Where's Blaine and Billy?"

"Oh, they went on a trip with Trista and their new daddy for the weekend."

Christine tucked her chin. Her eyes cast downward.

"But we'll make your birthday special, just you and me. You want your favorite pancakes?" Becca hoped to distract her from sadness over the others being away on this special day. "How about a pancake with bunny ears?"

Christine started to cry. "I want to see my grandma."

Becca's heart melted for her little girl. Poor Christine

wouldn't have anyone with her on her special day except her mother. How special would that be? She wanted to create a happy memory for her daughter's birthday, not a sad one. *Maybe this is the answer to the question I prayed.*

"Okay, then, you will." Becca purposefully forced a bright face and cheery attitude. "After breakfast, we'll pack our things and go to Grandma's! How about that?"

"Really, Mama? Really? Yes, yes! And yes, bunny pancakes!"

As light returned to Christine's countenance, Becca turned to how she would keep her impetuous promise with no trans-portation and very little money, and on Saturday—when the bank was closed. She packed some things, suppressing her tears at leaving, knowing this would be the end of her roommate era with Trista.

Becca scribbled a note of explanation and an I.O.U. She tucked the note in the soup tureen, swapping with the shared funds hidden there.

As they started out the door, Becca turned to look one last time at the home she'd loved so dearly. *It's the people, not the house. Without them, this is just a quirky, cold house with mismatched furnishings.* Christine's new toy ironing board leaned on the wall by the playroom. *She just got that for Christmas, I hate to leave it. But there's no way I can carry all her toys. Maybe we can get someone to drive us back to pick them up.*

"Let's go, Mama, let's go!" Christine, on the front porch step, jumped up and down in excitement.

Becca sighed and closed the door. She slung a bag over one shoulder, took Christine's hand and picked up their suitcase with the other hand. They trod through the slush toward the main road. Two feet of snow lined the yards and covered many of the cars on their street, but the sun was out, and the wind wasn't too hard on that cold January day in 1977.

People hitch-hike everywhere. We'll be okay. She tried not to notice the sound of her heart beating fast and hard in her chest. *God, please protect us.*

Their first ride was from a sweet old lady. "Where are you going, dears? Hitchhiking isn't safe, you mustn't."

"My little girl—all she wants for her birthday is to see her grandma."

She drove them to a bus station and insisted on buying them tickets to D. C. "Just sit here and wait," the kind woman insisted. "Promise me you won't get back out on the road hitchhiking again. Why, anything could happen to you two."

"Yes, ma'am." Becca nodded and smiled. "Thank you so much." She sat with Christine on the bench in silence, watching the woman drive off. *What am I supposed to do, make Christine sit here all day, on her birthday? The bus doesn't leave until so late that she won't see Mom until tomorrow. I can't face going back home. Leaving was too hard. The old lady was sweet, but I've hitched rides before. Most people are kind. There aren't mass murderers everywhere. People exaggerate with fear. Besides, I need the money from that ticket.* Feeling as if she were in someone else's body, Becca walked to the counter and traded her ticket for cash. She picked up her bag, took Christine's hand, and headed out to the highway.

It was cold, freezing cold, and much windier on the highway. Becca kicked the stiff bank of dirty snow to create a small nook. She placed Christine sitting on the suitcase and stuck out her thumb.

Christine imitated her mom, laughing at the idea of putting out her thumb to get a ride.

"No, no, sweetheart, that's Mama's job. You just sit."

Protruding her lower lip, Christine conceded, but made up for the concession by complaining. First the cold. Then the suitcase handle was uncomfortable to sit on. Then she was hungry.

Finally, an old pick-up truck pulled over, the color of robin's eggs, with a rounded cabin and a little rust around the edges. A man jumped out and moved swiftly around the back. A big man with extremely dark skin and yellowed eyes, he wore shabby work clothes and muddy work boots. A little stick lodged between his teeth on the left side, protruding an inch out of his mouth. Without eye contact, he heaved the suitcase into the truck bed and scooted past them to open the passenger door. "Hop in."

He's probably okay. I did pray about this. Becca paused to reconsider her plan.

Her hesitation must have spoken loudly, because he spoke again before she could respond to his offer. "What's the matter, scared of a Black man?"

Afraid to admit her fear, she reacted without thinking, asserting herself as neither prejudiced nor fearful. "No, of course not," she laughed. They climbed in. Becca held Christine on her lap as the bench seat had stacks of assorted wrappers and boxes in the center. *I'd rather hold her, anyway.* She snugged her arms around Christine's middle.

Christine rested her head onto her mother's upper chest, her shivers relaxing as the heat of the vehicle warmed her muscles.

"Where ya off to?" He ground the truck into first gear and

pressed on the gas pedal. Casting a sideways glare at her, he popped the truck into second gear. "Runnin' away from yer ole man?"

"Oh, no, nothing like that." *Why would he pose such a question? Is he a man who's been left?* Breakfast stirred in her gut. Or perhaps something else churned there. She delivered her well-considered words in a light, airy tone. "No, there is no man—he left us long ago." She glanced at him, watching for signs of emotional reaction.

He nodded.

"My girlfriend, roommate, got married, so we're heading to my parents' house, near Silver Spring. Plus, today is my little girl's birthday." Becca called upon her most confident and excited voice, holding Christine close. "She wants to see her grandma for her birthday. I didn't know what else to do but hitchhike because the bus doesn't leave til late."

The man grunted, more of a consensual growl under his breath, but he seemed to relax. "I'm goin' as far as Easton."

They drove without conversation for about twenty minutes.

Well before Easton, flipped his turn signal on and put his foot on the brake. "I can take ya further, another hour, to Easton, but I gotta stop in here first to get something."

Becca stiffened as the truck headed down a rural road through vacant farmland, pine trees and snow. Nothing ahead—no stop signs, no houses—nothing. The truck clipped along at about 45 or 50 miles an hour. Becca's mind raced. *Should I jump out with Christine? Even if we landed in that hill of snow, we'd be defenseless. And he'd be mad. He could just stop the truck and come after us.* Her heart pounded harder and faster. *Are we going to die today? Please, God, not on Christine's birthday!*

He turned the truck into a long dirt driveway to a house where several other men stood around a barrel of fire. The lone house amid fields bore signs of serious neglect. Ripped screens hung loose from their windows. Clapboards hungered and thirsted for a good sanding and painting. A patchwork of varied colors and textured objects stood in for a roof. Rusty old vehicles gave way to the vines and weeds in their final resting place around the property.

The driver killed the engine, took the keys and got out. "Wait here. Don't get out." He went inside the house.

The men around the barrel stared at Becca and Christine as if they were a meal, and they—hungry wolves. Starving, even. One of the ragged men left his place at the barrel, shoved his hands in his pockets and approached the truck window on Becca's side.

If they don't smell fear. . . Becca cranked the window halfway down and tried to act nonchalant. "Got a cigarette?"

"Yeah, sure." The man lit a smoke and handed it to her. He paused there, his hand on the edge of the window, and leaned in. His squinted eyes weighed them, up and down, as if they were goods to be purchased. . . and consumed.

Becca took a drag and blew the smoke toward the driver's side of the truck. "Thanks." *We're about to be raped. Maybe killed.* She felt her foot shaking and pressed her toes into the floorboard. The energy provided a gentle bounce of her knee to calm her innocent child. *Christine, my baby. I'm so sorry.* Becca's heart pounded harder. *Why did I do this? I'm so stupid, trusting everyone. God, please, please, help us. Please forgive me, and save us, God, I'll do anything. I'll serve you forever. Anything. Just please get us out of here.*

22

Lena

Lena disembarked the train in a new, yet ancient land. A balmy breeze caressed her face. *Hmm. Warmer here than at home.* She closed her eyes and raised her face toward the sun, absorbing warmth and light. Shaw and Elliot stayed close to her legs, holding on to her skirting. Settling Ruth in the baby carriage, she pushed forward, looking for someone who might be her grandmother's sister.

Surely that's her—tan skin, shining eyes, crowning brows, round cheeks—the same as hers, her mother's, and her grandmother's. "Aunt Caroline?"

"Lena! Come here, darlin' chile, lemme see yah." Caroline held Lena by the shoulders, at arm's length, and beamed as if Lena was a fine piece of sculpture. Pulling Lena into her embrace, she cried, "Eh, Law, chile. I'm so glad you're here."

Caroline's lips tucked inside her mouth and her eyes lit up with mischief. "And who might you rascals be?" She pointed a long, weathered finger to tickle each of the boys in their bellies, sending them further behind Lena's skirts. "They's cuter than speckled puppies."

She turned to Ruth, who squawked from the carriage. "And this, your usdi. A gem from the river. May I hold her?" She extended her arms toward Ruth.

Lena lifted Ruth and handed her to Aunt Caroline. "Usdi?"

"Baby."

Ruth calmed at Caroline's touch.

Their brown eyes met, gleaming one to another, as Caroline began a sweet melody, singing ever so gently—straight into Ruth's eyes.

> *"You bright mornin' star,*
> *Oh, how you shine!*
> *I see you dancin' in the rain*
> *and singin' with your might*
> *soarin' 'bove the pain*
> *like an eagle in flight."*

A moment suspended time as the prophetic word settled upon them. Aunt Caroline had improvised a new song, as Lena often did when she sang to her babies, as her mother had done, and her grandmother.

"Thank you, Aunt Caroline. That was precious."

"Yes, Lena, yah know my heart rejoices to see you both. Now," she said, turning Ruth back over to Lena, "let's getcha on down the road where suppa's cookin'."

Lena nestled Ruth back into her spot and pushed the

carriage alongside Caroline.

The boys kept a tight hold of their mother's long skirts, practically running to keep up as they absorbed the new sights and sounds around them.

"I'd been wondering what nickname to give Ruth. Grannie and my folks call me Starlight. Now I have it, thanks to you. Ruth will be Bright Morning Star."

"A bright morning star, that one."

"Maybe just Morning Star for short."

Lena followed Caroline to a horse-drawn wagon, where they loaded their things and climbed up. They made their way northwest of town, Caroline chatting away with the boys, who started coming out of their shell.

Lena took in every sight ahead while often checking over her shoulder. Confirming that no one followed them, she settled herself, still fidgeting with the edges of her lap blanket.

Caroline told stories about herself and her sister. They called themselves "Aniyunwiya," she said, "the real people. We spent much of our early lives traveling through mountain trails, never staying in one place long. Uncle said if we were captured, the soldiers would take us far away. We learned to be quiet." Caroline stopped the horses at a curve in the road. "Look here, ya'll." She pointed.

An old tree stood at the juncture in the road. The tree seemed to have run into some trouble in earlier years.

"What happened to that poor tree?"

"Taint poor, darling.' Tis showin' the way." Caroline shook the reins and the horses started off, following the bend of the tree.

Lena wondered how long the tree had been there, and

what forces could have shaped it so. She didn't ask because Caroline went right on with her stories.

The monotonous *clop, clop, clop* and gentle jostling of the long wagon ride put Shaw, Elliot and Ruth to sleep. They curled up together just behind Lena and Caroline.

Though Caroline's stories were rich, Lena could not stay with them. Her mind cycled around the past—the day she decided to leave home.

"I had to go," Lena blurted, no sooner realizing she'd spoken right over Aunt Caroline.

Caroline pulled the reins. "You had to go? Well, now, tell me. There ain't no reason not to, not here."

Ruth awoke and wailed a hungry cry.

"Go on, ain't nobody for miles. You can feed that youngin' and talk at the same time. The horses need to rest a spell, anyways."

Lena gathered Ruth into her arms and snuggled her onto her breast. "Oh, she's hungry, alright," Lena smiled. "All right, I'll try to tell you, Aunt Caroline. This may take a while, though."

"There's time enough."

"I don't know where to start."

Caroline pulled out a snack and offered some to Lena. "With the first thing that comes to your mind, gal. The rest'll come."

"Yes," Lena acknowledged. She looked down at Ruth's peaceful face and glanced back to ensure the boys were sleeping. "He. . . was at work, I guess, when I left. I couldn't even tell him to his face. I left him a note." Tears welled, threatening to spill. "I don't know if I can tell it, just yet." She bit her lip and glanced behind them again. "But I can talk more about the trip."

"You'll get no conniption from me. Good company makes the road shorter."

Lena told the story, checking the road behind them as she spoke.

"Is there something back there, darlin'?"

"No." Lena's face warmed. "But I keep feeling there is." *I said too much. Time to change course.* "Aunt Caroline, I'm very tired. Do you mind if we just think for a while?"

"Thinkin's good." The wagon team pressed on, advancing out of a wooded strip of road into a broad expanse of rolling hills—as far as the eye could see. "And now there's a bonny eyeful to go with it," chuckled the old woman.

Lena's eyes wandered across the hills, landing here and there on a distant cow, a fence, some sheep. The peaceful view provided comfort for her troubled mind. She drifted back again, to the day prior, replaying the stream of thoughts that vied for her attention.

I need my children with me, safe and away from Clinton. Maybe he'll finally change when he sees I'm really gone. Maybe he'll quit drinking.

The wagon bumped over a large rock on the trail, jolting Lena to her surroundings. As the sun dipped behind the vast mountain range ahead, splaying pink, lavender, and golden light across a rich and vibrant blue, the mountains glowed. Golden threads edged the clouds, bursting into rays so bright and magnificent one might think heaven's gates had opened to let the glory stream out. Lena caught her breath.

Caroline, noticing Lena's awestruck state, smiled and patted her work-worn, aged hand upon Lena's light and tender cheek. "This place is good medicine, Lena."

Lena acknowledged, "Yes. Better than any man's invented."

"These hills, they're rolling in blues and purples tonight. That's a good sign—the Little People donned their finest royal colors to welcome you."

Lena recalled her grandmother's mention of the Little People. Legend said they lived in the rocks and caves. Most believed them to be good spirits, teaching people to care for the land. Some said they were mischievous or even outright evil. *Apparently, Aunt Caroline believes the best.* "I've never seen any Little People, but this is the finest sight I've ever laid my eyes upon." Her soul resonated with connection to this land.

"We're almost there," Caroline said. "Around the next bend."

The wagon turned and drew close to a small wooden shack amid meadows. A loose web of split-rail fencing delineated the yard. Two boys, about 8 and 10 years old, played ball with sticks. Smoke billowed from the chimney and carried the essence of wood-smoked roast with garlic, onions, and vegetables.

With the fervor of a hungry teenager, Caroline announced, "We're here. . . and I smell suppa."

The family approached them. First, the two they'd interrupted from a lively game of what Lena learned was stickball, named Adohi and Enna. Then came their parents, Bette and Tom, and Gatlin, Caroline's son. Warm greetings, introductions and gushings over baby Ruth ensued, while Shaw and Elliot ran after the ball with the older boys.

Caroline called out to her great-grandsons. "Boys, take the reins up. Give the horses some water and a rub-down. They worked hard today." She handed them the reins. "Let's the rest of us clean up." She worked the stiffness out of her joints as she hobbled across the yard and climbed the stoop.

The place was homey—a simple, rustic, cozy log cabin.

"Come on, grab and growl. I lit a fire to this stew before settin' off for you." Caroline routed Lena to the front of the line, shewing back the others who clamored to fill their bowls with the steaming, aromatic lamb stew. "Let Lena go first."

Amazed by her aunt's stamina and fortitude, Lena beamed in awe at the preserved beauty before her—brown, weathered skin, ruddy cheeks, and ashen hair pulled into a knot atop her head. *She must be 80 or 90, but she acts more like 30.* Lena had imagined Aunt Caroline would be sitting in a rocker on the front porch, quilting and watching children play—not making supper before driving horses across bumpy terrain for ten hours in a single day. *I wonder why Gatlin didn't come to meet them in Charlotte, or at least come along to protect his mama.*

Her unspoken question was soon answered at the supper table.

"I sure wish you would'a let me fetch Lena today, Mama," Gatlin said. "It ain't as safe as you like to think."

"Now, now, son, don't go frettin' like that. You know I'm as spry as ten men!"

Everyone laughed, clear who was in charge here.

Lena learned much about this hearty family. Caroline's husband, when his first wife died, needed someone to care for his children. He sent for Caroline, knowing only that she was a strong and quiet woman. She grew to love him and his children as they raised their family and farmed the land. When he died, her stepchildren moved to the city to raise their families, while their son, Gatlin, stayed on to help.

Gatlin was a grandfather himself now, but Caroline wouldn't think of having him do for her. A woman had her role, and a man, his, no matter the age.

Aunt Caroline tended farm chores and fended off predators, animal or human, with tenacity—and taught children the old ways.

"In the old days, females were the strength and center of the Cherokee home," Caroline said. "Men trained to hunt and do battle. Women managed the farm and home. Woman carried the blood line, too. So, Eliza's children, like mine, are *Aniyunwiya*, even if their fathers were white. Aggie was Eliza's only young'un, but Aggie had so many that we call Eliza 'Unilisi.' Means 'grandmother of many.'" She laughed at herself and shared the reason for her chuckle. "We say she started her own tribe in Maryland."

They laughed at the thought—a Sandy Spring, Maryland, Cherokee clan.

"I know almost nothing about the Cherokee, even though you say I am one." Lena leaned in. "But I want to know more. My heritage is a part of my family. Why all the secrecy? Grannie won't talk much about it, but we could lose our heritage if we don't."

Her words silenced the table. Gatlin stopped mid-chew and sat his fork down.

Was I rude? Did I overstep my bounds as a newcomer? She looked at each member around the table, down to her hands. She crunched the napkin on her lap. Her face must have turned red, for she felt aflame. A lifetime passed in a breath or two.

Caroline broke the silence. Setting her tea-stained, linen napkin on her plate, and pushing the plate a few inches away from her, she leaned onto her forearms on the table. "Look up, chile."

Lena let her eyes rise to meet Aunt Caroline's. Tears now spilling from the edges, her eyes begged forgiveness.

"Yes, Lena, our ways are at risk. A weight to carry, but we are strong. We carry seven generations behind and ahead."

23

Lena

Southern Appalachians. 1923

While the children slept in the loft, Lena gathered up the mending and joined Aunt Caroline in the main room. Sitting in one of the two upholstered armchairs beside a round table, she set her hands to sewing.

Putting her hands to work eased some of the awkwardness of mustering courage to share her story—as did the ambiance in the main room. Cozily nestled inside foot-thick log walls, the room glowed in the golden light of well placed candles and a roaring fire in the hearth. The essence of pine, sassafras and sweetgrass—a vanilla-like sweetness—infused the room with calm. A colorful braided rug warmed the space and framed their gathering spot. Scattered without rhyme or reason along the walls, portraits of family members, mountain scenes, and botanical embroideries represented their collected history. Resting her feet on the footstool, her eyes met Aunt Caroline's.

Aunt Caroline, a skilled storyteller, turned chores into pleasure. Since Lena's arrival, she'd spun many a tale—how the world began, how a water spider brought us fire, how the animals sent diseases when they got fed up with humans killing them. Fortunately, she'd said, the plants had mercy and decided to provide a cure for every disease. Their evenings together came alive with Jack tales about animals in all sticky situations who maneuvered out of their troubles.

"Tonight is my turn." Lena kept her eyes on Aunt Caroline. "I'm ready to tell my story."

"Very well." Aunt Caroline nodded, looking over her glasses at Lena.

Snug in the blanket of time and distance, her story made its way into the warm light of this quiet setting. The telling took on form, nearly, swirling in the air, a smoky tempest, before settling into a slowly burning ember on the floor by the fireplace.

"The right choice, to leave," Caroline said. Her lower lip protruded before finishing her point, emphasizing her choice of words. "It is time for safety."

From the kitchen, where he sat reading the news, Gatlin spoke. "Any man who would take his hand to a woman is a coward." He leaned forward and looked at her over his glasses. "And nuttier than squirrel scat."

Lena, realizing he overheard her story, leaned forward to see him better. "Yes, Gatlin, you may be right. I'd been thinking of myself as the coward."

"That coward will back down from your father and brothers. Keep them with you when you return. If you return.

We've a saying here—never move so far away that you can't see the smoke from your parents' chimney."

"I'm not sure what to do." Lena placed the mending aside. "I'm afraid to go back, but I do miss my family. And the boys miss their father, though I can't say I'd want them with him ever again."

Gatlin turned the page of his paper, glancing toward Lena as he did. "In our culture, a woman's children are her children. They do not belong to the man. Is this not so with your family?"

"The women rally for their rights. Just got the right to vote three years ago. But you know that." She stood to freshen her cup of tea.

She returned to the main room and freshened her great-aunt's cup. "I think I missed some of your stories on the wagon ride here. My worries distracted me."

Aunt Caroline waved her hand. "Ah, don't you worry, gal. I know I can talk up a storm."

Lena laughed. "My little sister has that gift." She took her seat again and sipped her tea. "But I am curious about what led you here while Grannie went to Maryland. You said something about being afraid soldiers would take you away." She placed her teacup on the table and started on a new piece of mending from the basket. "I learned about the Indian Wars in school. Grannie doesn't say much, but she told us she saw things from another viewpoint."

"Be careful, Lena, you'll start me up and I won't stop." Caroline closed her eyes as she took a sip of blackberry tea. "Europeans fled to this land after being victims in their homeland, but here, they made victims of us. Many of them were nothin' but tricksters. All vine and no taters."

Lena's brows furrowed and her head tipped to one side. *Grannie used that word—tricksters.* "Where I'm from, most people seem kind. . . and helpful."

"Mm-hmm." Caroline nodded. "Your grandmother told me of the kindness she met in Sandy Spring. They were good to her, for the most part. Cherokee helped Europeans, too—taught them how to fight in this territory. Even fought for them in the Revolutionary War, and others. Many died, too. If not, this might could still be British territory." She readjusted her position in the chair, reached for a quilt and laid the soft, time-worn patchwork across her lap. "Our help was not returned in kind. They promised food, clothing, money, land, rights. . . many times, but that is not what our people received."

Lena set her darning down. "Aunt Caroline, I knew some Cherokee fought in the Civil War, but I didn't know about the Revolutionary War. Are you sure?"

"No doubt, chile, and before. Cherokees publish a newspaper—have, for a long time. This might not be in your schoolbooks, but all the records are here. Uncle Ezekiel taught me to read the newspapers he'd smuggle into our camp."

Caroline leaned back in her chair and, laying her sewing aside, took another sip of tea. "Before my time, Cherokee prospered here in business, building big, fancy homes in European style and sporting fancy clothes. The women traded food from farming, and the men traded their goods from hunting—all sorts of business. White folk saw the land had gold. They liked gold, so much so, a person might think of gold as good medicine." She chuckled and winked. "But they'd be wrong."

Lena twisted her gold wedding band. "I didn't know that."

"We're close to the part you asked about." Opening her eyes, she leaned forward. "I warned you about starting me up on this. See now, I can't stop." She chuckled. Her tone transitioned, growing resolute. "When Andrew Jackson found out about the gold, he set his mind to drive us all out of the homeland. Greed got the best of him, I reckon." Her manner grew more animated. "One of us, a warrior who had saved Jackson's life, tried to meet with him, to negotiate. He wouldn't even speak with him."

Lena spewed a drop of tea from her mouth. "What?" Her interest piqued, alerting her to the edge of her seat. "Why didn't I learn this?"

Aunt Caroline smiled at Lena. She looked down at the floor. Her voice became serious and low. "Our people divided over the matter. Some took to fighting. One group wanted to accept the government's land and money in the west. The other one warned of a trick, a lie, slippery as a hog on ice. They said we should stay and fight. A group snuck off to keep making treaties in Washington, without the approval of the clans—without the chief." She sat back in her chair, her lips pressing together.

"Is that when the Indian Removal started? Is that what separated you and Grannie?

Aunt Caroline's head nodded. "Mm-hm. But I think I'll stop for tonight—if you don't mind. My bones had the lick."

Lena wanted to beg Aunt Caroline to finish her story but chose to respect her wishes. "Yes, of course. You go ahead and rest. I want to know more, and I want to know why Grannie and Mama never told me these things. Tomorrow?"

"I'll say this 'afore I go. When you come from dark into

light, your eyes need time to adjust. Me, I've been living close to native land, while she's been up near Washington City. The light may be a whole lot different there."

This answer satisfied Lena's curiosity—for the night. Maybe Mama and Grannie had tried to tell the story before, and she didn't listen. When she'd lived at home and the elders started talking about the past, she'd often excused herself. She'd been more interested in new inventions—the automobile, the phonograph, the soda fountain. And books. . . with library books, Lena lost track of eons of time absorbed in the classics. *Sometimes I think I acted as if my family didn't know a thing.*

24

Becca

Somewhere near Easton, Maryland. 1977

The screen door slammed. Becca's driver reappeared from inside the dingy clapboard house. He shouted a slurred nickname toward the truck as he approached the men around the barrel, flames bursting above from their fresh stoking. The man at her window backed away from the truck and hustled over to the men at the fire.

They exchanged words, the driver pointing at Becca and Christine in his truck and waving his hand toward his companions.

A wintry wind swept across the field, picking up ashes from the fire. The miniature tempest swirled, freezing the ash into a snow-like mist in the icy air and landing on the windshield.

Becca's foreboding froze, suspended midair and drifting as she watched. Her eyes scanned between the men at the barrel, items in the truck and objects scattered in the yard, searching for something to aid their escape.

The driver approached and entered his side of the truck. Starting the engine and shifting the truck into drive, he made a three-point turn and headed out the way they'd come.

Becca could not completely hide her sigh of relief.

"What, did ya think I was gonna do something?" He chuckled. "Nah. Could'a, though." He shot a piercing glower. "Changed my mind. I'll take you to Easton so you can get your young'un back to see her grandma."

He drove them to Easton, about half-way toward their destination, Christine filling the awkward space with chatter about seeing Grandma and what she got for Christmas.

"Thank you so much." Becca forced herself to say as he pulled her suitcase from the bed of the truck and placed it next to Becca.

"Yeah, be careful."

"I will." *Wow. That was so close. But thank you, God, for saving us. Please just help us get to my mom's and I promise I'll never hitchhike again. Never! I promise, and I really mean it.*

Their next ride was an older couple, on their way to Bethesda. When they heard Becca's story, they drove many miles out of their way to take them all the way to Becca's parents' house. Arriving by dark, Christine got to see her grandma for her very late birthday dinner.

* * *

Becca secured a job pumping gas at the corner station. Her mother agreed to babysit *"for a month, no more."* She began the search for a room to rent and a sitter for Christine.

Dialing phone numbers from newspaper ads and notices at the grocery store, she soon found that potential renters declined renting to a child. Only one invited her to come and see the room. She borrowed her mother's car to check the rental out. This time, it was Becca who declined.

"Mom, that place gave me the creeps. At first, the house seemed perfect. A huge place on a horse farm. The room was beautifully decorated in pink, with pictures of a little girl all around. And a woman and boy, too. But the man lives there alone. He said his wife and kids went to visit family in Holland and they'd be gone six months to a year. But he was evasive about it, on edge, and he seemed desperate to have us there, which was so weird. I got the creeps, like he was a murderer or something."

She sat at the table and rested her chin on her palm. "This is so frustrating. Life was so good with Trista. Now I feel like there's nowhere for us."

Becca's mother shook her head. "You should live with Emily. She has an open bedroom in her apartment and could babysit again. The extra rent money would help her."

"Emily?" Becca cast a a furrowed brow at her mom. "You know I can't stand how messy she is. And we don't get along—she's impossible." She reached for the paper and circled another ad to call.

Becca's father, whom she thought was asleep in his recliner, opened his eyes and threw his opinion in the mix. "Emily's your family. Family helps family. You should rent the room in her apartment. Two single mothers, helping each other, what more do you want?"

"Dad, you don't understand."

Becca awoke from her spot on the living room floor with the feeling that someone was watching her. She opened her eyes to find her suspicions verified.

Her father leered at her from a lofty position in his recliner.

"What are you looking at?" She knew her voice sounded snappy and disrespectful, but the way he looked at her made her skin crawl.

"I'm just admiring my daughter."

"Well, stop it."

"I can look at my daughter if I want to. There's nothing wrong with that." He held his position, eyes on her as she lay on the living room floor in her usual sleeping attire, a tee shirt and underwear.

Becca rolled, turning her back to him, and pulled the covers tightly around her. *God, please get us out of here soon.* She lay awake the rest of the night, on high guard. *Tomorrow I'll see if I can sleep on the floor in Mom's room, and I guess we'll have to move in with Emily. We can't stay here.*

Becca's mother tapped the spoon on the side of the pan. "We're waiting on your dad for the milk. I think he's home by now, but he hasn't come up yet." She fixed a plate for Christine, who sat at the table coloring. "He's just sitting out in his car. He does that all the time."

"I'll go down and tell him dinner's ready." Becca grabbed her coat and scooted down the stairs of the apartment her parents had moved to a year prior.

When she approached the car, he was sitting in the parked car, his head down. *What's he doing? Is he okay?* As she got closer, she realized her mistake.

He masturbated, a pornographic magazine on his lap.

Becca swallowed hard and moved along, as if she hadn't seen it. *What a sick bastard.* Disgusted, she picked up the pace away from his car. The horror and disgust unlocked a memory she'd stuffed away since the age of thirteen. *Mom was away, visiting her parents. He left that book in the bathroom, spread open on the side of the tub. . . the book with incest and bestiality.* She stopped near the picnic table and leaned against it, fighting the urge to retch. Her hands shook. She recalled their conversation, when she held the book at him and raged at her father. *"Why would you read such crap? And why leave it out where we can see it? You never do that when Mom's home."*

His answer, so flippant, and with that demented smile, haunted her. *"It's just my choice of reading material. You can't slight a man for what he likes to read."*

She sat on the picnic table bench and held her head in her hands. Her body shivered uncontrollably, whether from the bone-chilling January air, or from the onslaught of awareness of her father's true icy nature, Becca could not tell, and didn't care. Helpless to stop the flow of the gut-churning truth, she let the vision run its course. *Later that night, he jumped on top of me, said he wanted to make love to me—more than any other woman in the world. I pushed him off. I curled up on a chair in the living room and chain-smoked, trying to figure out who I could tell, where I could go, waiting for him to fall asleep. I was frozen in the middle of the summer.*

Becca stood and pulled her coat tighter around her waist. *This is what I have for a father.*

An icy wind drove her back inside. *We've got to get out of here, but how can I take Christine out in the cold again? Where would we even go? Miles from everyone I know. I won't hitchhike. No more of that.* Entering the apartment, she removed her scarf and coat, and plunked herself on the couch.

"Becca, you look like you've seen a ghost."

"I just saw Dad. . . in his car." Seeing no one in earshot but her mother, Becca locked eyes with her and kept her voice down. "Masturbating."

Cecelia drew a deep breath and pursed her lips, then forced air through her nostrils—like a dragon, but lacking fire. "That disgusting monster." She crossed her arms. "Jake said he saw him doing that, too. He parks his car, and instead of coming in for dinner, he just sits out there and does that. Just stay away from him."

"Then why'd you let me go out there?" Becca's face grew hot. "You could have told me before I had to see that."

Cecelia's hazel eyes flared. "How dare you blame me for that? I've been stuck here for years with no way out. How do you think I feel?"

Oh my God! How many years Mom knew about him—and she stayed? How could she so easily berate—and then dismiss— Dad's behavior? Becca couldn't fathom it. *I have to get out of here. I have to get Christine out of here.* "I don't know," she retorted, "but if I were you, I'd get out. I'm going to."

"Ha, you have no idea." Cecelia shook her head and turned back toward the dining room. "Easier said than done."

The next day, Becca and Christine moved in with Emily.

As her mother drove away, Becca watched Christine play with her cousin, Molly. Christine readily shifted to being the 'big sister' to her two-year old cousin. She noticed how naturally kind and patient Christine behaved toward the little one. *She's such a good girl.*

Emily watched television.

Becca looked around the place, pinching her nose. *What is that stench?* Piles of clothes lined the furniture and sections of the floor. Stacks of plates with hardened food bits seemed to add new layers of mold before Becca's eyes. Under the dining table she spotted the kitty litter box, its contents overfull and spilling out onto the floor. *The culprit.*

"Emily, what is this, some kind of science experiment? This place is a mess. It's not safe for the kids."

Her sister looked away from the TV just long enough to acknowledge Becca's presence. "You're welcome to clean if you want to." She waved a nonchalant hand and turned her attention back to her show.

As spoiled as ever. Becca and Emily had never been close the way she and Missy were. When they were young, Emily always got out of chores. Her excuses worked on Mom and Dad. Becca couldn't stand sloppy. She gathered plates from the table and carried them into the kitchen, where she stopped mid-step.

Now I understand why they were still on the table. The kitchen counters, stove and sink—all cluttered with dirty dishes, open boxes, cans with food sticking to the inside, wrappers, and. . . "Ew! Roaches! They're everywhere, Emily. How can you live like this?"

No response forthcoming from the living room, Becca set the stack she carried atop another. She opened the windows, found a can of bug spray and commenced to exterminate the dreadful, patent-leather-backed foes. Next, she changed the cat litter, took the trash to the dumpster, washed the dishes, dried them and put them away. After a thorough spraying and scrubbing the stove, counters and sink, she reentered the living room.

"My rent should be lower if I'm going to be the house-keeper."

Emily stood from her chair, changed the TV channel, and sat back down. "Mom said you want me to babysit while you work. That's worth more."

"That's nowhere near an even deal. Look, Christine's been babysitting Molly this entire time."

They looked at their children. The angels had been playing well together the entire time Becca'd cleaned the dining room and kitchen. Molly's wet diaper swelled, drooping to her knees.

"Do you change diapers at least?" Becca bent to pick up laundry from the floor. "Where's the vacuum cleaner?"

"I don't have one. There's a broom in the hall closet."

Becca slumped toward the closet. *Life. Here? God, did you really mean to send me back here, or am I just a complete fool?* Visions of life with Trista—the flow of shared routines, organized living and peaceful interaction—wafted through her mind as she cleaned. *I miss her. So much.* The chasm in her heart squeezed in, craving to be filled.

Christine's growing up without a father. I want to love and be loved. God, please send us love.

When Becca had enough extra money to pay Emily to babysit, Becca met up with old friends. They streamed in and out of local parties, most looking for fun, but Becca also for love. Being physically wanted, caressed and held, even if but for a night here, and one there, eased her pangs. Yet none cared to be with Becca during the day.

Becca pushed aside the piles of dishes and opened mail to make room for her coffee mug on the table. She pushed her hair behind her ears and blew out a puff of smoke. "What man in his right mind wants a package deal, a ready-made family, anyway?"

"Date someone older," Emily said.

She had. One—fourteen years her senior—showed his maturity level with petty jealousy and physical rage. "Age is no guarantee of maturity," Becca said in return. "Take this, for example." She spread her hand across the messy visage. "You're older than me, but you still live as messy as you did when you were a kid."

"Hey. If you don't like it, leave it. This is my place." Emily folded her arms. "And remember, I don't have to babysit."

Home life with Emily was far from idyllic, but it was all she had. Becca pushed herself to swallow that one. "I'm headed to the library today. Wanna come?"

"What, for more parenting and psychology books? Or did you want to get me a book on how to clean house?"

Becca took Emily's snarky response as a no. "Suit yourself. I'm taking Christine to the playground later. I'll take Molly too, if you want."

"No. By the time you get back from the library, Molly will be napping."

"Come on, Christine, time to go inside." They'd been at the playground most of the morning. She'd been reading while Christine played with a little girl from the apartment complex.

"Aw, I wanna play. Pleeeeeease?"

Becca pressed her lips together. She looked around. Their apartment was across the parking lot, in view. Seeing no one else around, she relented. "Okay, you stay inside the fence and play with Jasmine. Don't talk to anyone. I'll go grab us some lunch for a picnic."

"Okay." Christine ran toward the sandbox.

"Promise?"

"I promise."

Becca never let Christine out of her sight when they were outside—not since the days she and Trista's boys played together in their yard. Hurrying back to the second floor apartment, she checked the playground through the living room window. The girls appeared safe and happy. She slapped together two peanut-butter and jelly sandwiches, tucked them into a brown bag, poured a thermos of lemonade, and headed back to the playground.

It was empty. Both girls, gone.

"Christine!" Becca cupped her hand around her mouth to shout in every direction. She searched behind every car. "No hiding, Christine, you're scaring Mommy. Come out!"

Nothing. Frantic, Becca ran back upstairs to get Emily to help her look. They started knocking on doors, up and down stairs, three floors in each building.

"Do you know which apartment is Jasmine's? I can't find my little girl. They were playing together."

Finally, one person pointed to the next door. Becca ran and pounded on the door. She heard noise inside and pounded again. "Jasmine? Christine? Is she in there?"

Jasmine opened.

"Where's Christine? Is she here with you?"

Jasmine opened the door further, and Christine stood

beside her. Her eyes cast down, a look of utter shame.

"Christine, come here." Becca stooped down and hugged her tightly. "I was so scared. I didn't know where you were." She drew back, holding Christine at arms length to scold her. "Don't you ever do that again. You never go away from where you're supposed to be. Always ask me first. Do you understand me?"

Christine nodded. A tear dripped from the outer corner of each eye and splashed on the concrete floor.

Becca hugged her again, took her hand and walked her back home. Christine remained quiet, even after their next meal together. She wouldn't play or watch TV or talk—she just sat and stared at the floor.

"Come on, honey, I'm sorry." Becca sat next to her and pulled her in to her side. "I was so scared, but I shouldn't have yelled at you. I love you, honey."

Christine stiffened.

It was not like her to be unresponsive to her mother's entreaties. "What's wrong, sweetie? Tell me."

Christine started to sob. "He hurt me."

"What? Who hurt you?"

"Jasmine's brother."

"What did he do?"

"He took off our panties and pushed on us with his thing. She said he does it to her all the time."

Becca froze. Every emotion clashed within. Outrage. Horror. Contempt for him, for herself, for the world. Sorrow. Empathy for Christine—and Jasmine. She quelled her anger. *Christine will be confused and hurt if I get mad.* She pulled Christine into her side, wrapping her arms around her. "Oh, honey. He shouldn't have done that. Where was Jasmine's mother?"

"He was watching Jasmine. She told me to just pee on him, he will stop. So, I did, and he stopped." Christine let out a cry of shame and confusion. "I'm sorry I didn't pee in the potty."

Becca swooped Christine onto her lap and rocked her. "It wasn't your fault, honey. You did good to try to stop him, even if you had to pee on him. I'm so sorry this happened to you. He was the bad one." She sat holding Christine, until Christine seemed ready to let go.

"Now, honey, you stay with Emily for a minute, I'm going to talk to Jasmine's mother. She needs to know. And Jasmine's brother needs to stop."

Becca knocked on the dark brown metal door. A petite Hispanic woman partially opened the door, letting only her head show.

Becca started to explain what happened, but the woman pleaded.

"No hablo Inglés, por favor, no hablo Inglés."

Becca struggled to remember her Spanish from high school. "¿Puedes Jasmine hablar para me?"

Jasmine's little head appeared from behind her mother's dress. In the heated moment, she saw no other choice than to let a four-year old translate such horrible subject matter. *But maybe Jasmine needs to learn the words to tell.* Becca tried to choose age-appropriate terminology to help Jasmine interpret what her brother had done, both to Christine and to Jasmine. *But will she even know the words in Spanish?*

It appeared she did. The child used hand motions to supplement her translation.

Jasmine's mother waved her hand and shook her head at

Becca. "No. No, no, no. Es. . . good boy. Por favor, no police. Te lo suplico."

Becca stood, torn between pity for them and anger at what was happening. *I don't know what to do. I don't know what to say. I have to say something.* She flashed back to her own brother. Eventually, he had stopped. . . when he had a girlfriend his age.

"Don't let him do that again. Jasmine, tell her I said don't leave him alone with you. You can tell me if it happens again."

Jasmine nodded and looked at her mother.

"Si, gracias." The woman quickly shut the door.

As Becca walked back to her own building, everything went numb. The parenting books had not prepared her for this. *Is sexual sickness like this everywhere? My baby. . . what do I do? Do I call the police?*

When Becca returned to their apartment, Christine's attention snapped to, her big, brown, doe-eyes begging for a sign of what happened.

"I talked to Jasmine's mommy. She'll make him stop." Becca sat with Christine. "But, honey, you can't go over there anymore, and I can't let you play outside without me or Aunt Emily with you, watching you. We have to keep you safe."

"Okay." Her innocent reply, followed by hugging Becca's neck, seemed to restore Christine's joy. She returned to play with her dolls, almost as if nothing happened.

But Becca couldn't forget. Laying in bed, she traced every swirl, nick and stain on the ceiling as her thoughts cycled with indecision. *Could she really be okay? Should I call the police? They would question her, maybe press her to testify.*

*She'd probably feel embarrassed, scared, and punished even—
when none of this was her fault.*

* * *

"Come to my baptism." Becca's younger sister Missy
beamed, leaning her head against her newfound love's
shoulder. They stood in the doorway to Becca's room. "Get
out of bed and come with us. A friend of Jimmy's leads a
gathering of Christians, all our age group. It's really cool,
Becca. I'm gonna be baptized in a lake, Jesus-style!"

Becca pulled her head off the pillow and sat to the edge
of the bed. *Missy. So happy. Not a care in the world.* "Okay,
sounds cool. Lemme get dressed."

"Can I pick out a dress for Christine? You know I love
dressing up little girls."

"Yeah, sure. They're hanging here, in the closet."

The gathering didn't seem like church. Outdoors, twenty
or more teens and young twenty-somethings, along with
a few older people, meandered through tall grass and met
together by the edge of a small lake. The leader played his
guitar, singing songs about Jesus and the disciples and love.

Missy, Jimmy, Becca and Christine joined the others,
sitting on the ground in a circle. Several people spoke up
about what the Lord had been showing them in the Bible.
One by one, several of the group waded into the water and
the leader baptized them, fully immersing them and lifting
them up.

Becca enjoyed watching this very different group. They made music on their instruments, sang, talked and, after the meeting, some played frisbee while others tossed a softball. Fun. Good, clean fun. *These people are different. The guys talk of love, and their eyes seem to shine pure—not full of lust. The chicks seem cool, too, though awfully innocent. Maybe there is such a thing as a church I could fit into. Maybe Missy's onto something here. This way of life looks a whole lot better than mine.*

As she watched, she reviewed her life, all the times she'd tried to make life better for Christine and for herself, but failed. Again—and again. Everywhere she went, everything she did, nothing worked. But these Christians, their lives seemed good. They had happiness and peace. They didn't seem ashamed to love Jesus and follow His ways.

Becca's heart cried out. *I've never known life this way. I didn't have the guts to follow you on my own. Instead, I made excuses, because I didn't want to be weak, to give up, or be ostracized for being a Jesus Freak. But my way isn't working. I've been looking for love, but I just keep getting hurt. I've been trying to protect Christine, but I've failed. Miserably.*

She brushed away the tears and drew in a breath. Christine romped in the field with two other children from the fellowship group, playing tag and laughing. Missy snuggled into Jimmy, who held a huge towel around her wet dress as he spoke with the group leader by the food table.

Becca closed her eyes. A sincere prayer sprang from her heart, like fresh water from a spring. *I feel like I just met you, Jesus, even though I've been talking to you for so long. You are good. You want goodness. There is goodness in this world. I give myself to you, if you'll have me. Cleanse me and make me* pure. Make me whole. Teach me your ways and I'll walk in them. Please help me to know you more. Open my eyes, open my heart. Give me a new heart and a new mind. A new life, for you.

25

Lena

Gatlin returned after riding into the nearest town to check the post office. He waved a letter above his head as he slowed his horse. "Letter for you, Lena."

Lena sprang from her seat on the front porch, where she had been laughing at the boys playing stick ball. "For me? Oh!" She ran to meet Gatlin, pulled open the letter, and devoured the contents.

Dearest Lena,

Your father and I are well, except for missing you and the children. Somehow, three weeks passed since your travel began.

Clinton approached the farm yesterday, inquiring for you and the children. We relayed to him how your great-aunt needed tending. He said that was no reason for your departure—especially without warning. I doubt he'll be back, since he knows you are not here.

Sadly, Grannie's health has taken a turn for the worse. We hope she will recover soon. Doc says she needs rest.

Please write and tell us all about Aunt Caroline and her family, yourself and the children.

With Warmest Regards,

Mama

Lena held the letter to her chest, her face like stone, her stance as well. *Grannie. I have to get there. But Clinton. The kids. What do I do?*

After supper, the family gathered again in the main room for songs and stories. Lena shared the letter and declared they would leave on the morrow.

"Are you sure?" Aunt Caroline's eyes narrowed.

"I am. Like Gatlin said, I'm not the coward. My father and brothers will help me stave off Clinton. I have to see Grannie again. I just have to."

"Hard to tell." Aunt Caroline nodded. "Might just fly over a clover field to land on a cow pile. Eh law, chile, go on, then."

The rest of the family clamored a while over the news, extending their sadness at Lena and her children leaving, and they reciprocated.

Lena turned to Aunt Caroline. "Before we go, please do finish your story about you and Grannie. Do you mind telling more? If not, I understand."

"I don't mind. Our story must be told, for generations—if we've any chance as a people." Moving the sheepskin drum from her lap, she placed the instrument on the table. "I don't feel like music tonight, anyway. We're going to miss you when you go."

Lena settled Ruth on her lap. "I hope Grannie will tell me her story when we get home, but just in case she doesn't, honestly, I *must* hear it. I feel like a part of me is suspended out there in the past with you, and I must know, or I'll just die!" Lena laughed, hand over her heart, knowing her exaggerated feelings entertained the group.

The family chuckled along with her.

"The boys and I have some chores in the barn. Can Shaw and Elliot tag along with us?" Gatlin picked up Elliot, who seemed excited at the idea.

"Horsey, horsey!" He reached for the top of Gatlin's head.

Gatline flipped Elliot up to ride on his shoulders.

"Yes, of course. Be good, boys." Lena kissed Shaw and mussed the top of his head.

"We will, Mama."

A sparkle danced from Aunt Caroline's eye. She cleared her throat as the boys left, then turned to Lena. "Well, your Grannie and I were born in those days, when Jackson aimed to remove the Cherokee. A dangerous time, especially for those with young'uns, so our folks hid away, so's nobody would know about us." She waved an arm in the direction of the mountain range. "We stayed in caves. Didn't come out in the day until after they scouted to be certain no one was about."

Lena's eyes perked open, wider. "You lived in caves?"

"Sure did. Our family taught us the Cherokee ways, to

247

keep, and pass on to future generations. *Edutsi*, uncle, was with us, too—Ezekiel by name. They took turns sneaking out of camp to gather, trade, and hunt."

Lena searched her memory for anything Grannie might have said about her parents or *Au-duh-chee*, as Caroline said it, Uncle Ezekiel. Her search returned empty.

"The soldiers surrounded every village. Rounded up thousands of people and penned 'em like hogs, but worse. They took over their lands, properties. . . rights."

Lena shifted in her seat. As a school child quells the urge to raise a hand for permission to speak, she slipped her free hand under her thigh. *But Aunt Caroline tells me to speak my mind.* She spoke, risking foolishness. "We learned a bit about that in school—The Trail of Tears."

"Mm-hmm." Aunt Caroline's eyes waxed distant. "The trail where they cried." Clearing her throat, she regained her composure. "Many died in those pens, from diseases. They couldn't go to the water each day for cleansing. Or to gather simples. The soldiers forced them away to the west, to the darkened land. By wagon and by foot, old and young alike, many walking the whole way—through the winter across the mountains." Aunt Caroline leaned forward in her chair. "Most of them didn't make it and got no proper burial. Soldiers forced survivors to keep going."

Her story paused again. Looking out the window, her breathing staccato for a moment, Aunt Caroline blew a deeper breath out slowly, then continued. "The few that survived found no freedom on that barren land. The whites took children from their parents, forcing them to learn their ways. And punishing Cherokee ways." Her face flared as her eyes narrowed. Squeezing the armrest, her tone deepened.

"I don't mind saying, learning what happened to them made me madder than a wet hen. A thorn lodged in my heart."

At last, she looked back at Lena. Her head nodded and her face paled. "But we two girls, we stayed hidden. They didn't find us. Wasn't til many years later we learned what happened to our people. . . to our parents."

Lena interrupted. "Your parents? I thought you said they hid with you and raised you in the mountains."

"For a while they did. Until one night, they didn't come back. Later, Uncle Ezekiel admitted he thought they were caught up by a posse and taken west, but we never knew for sure. We stayed hidden with him for years after that."

"Years? So, you grew up hiding in the mountains?"

She nodded. "Until we were old enough to marry instead of being taken in as slaves. Our tribe fought the old wars with some of the better whites. Ezekiel knew some of them, all up and down the mountains, from Georgia to Connecticut. He knew which folks to trust, and which not, after they enforced Blood Law. He arranged—"

"Blood Law?" Lena asked. "What's that?"

"Oh, mah deah." Caroline took a deep breath. "Cherokee Blood Law said if anyone traded away our land, they'd pay with their life. So, three of the leaders who signed the treaty that started the Trail of Tears were killed, all on the same day."

"Oh! I didn't know any of this. Were they our relatives? Is that why Grannie moved near Washington? Is that why she hides her Cherokee?"

"My mouth's drier than Gatlin's jokes." Aunt Caroline took another sip of tea. "That's a long story you're asking. For tonight, I'll say that Uncle arranged our marriages, but not together. My sister can tell you more once you are home."

The room grew quiet, amplifying natural background sounds. The family breathed. A lone cricket chirped from outside the window, the short bursts punctuated by the sound of rain droplets joining a puddle as they released their hold on the roof's edge.

"Do you think she hurts when she recalls it?"

"Who, Eliza? Could be. But she is strong. She can handle you asking." Caroline brushed a tear aside. "It does hurt to think about again, but where love is, one can bear it."

26

Becca

Rockville, Maryland. 1978

"Twenty-one! Here's to being a grown-up." Becca clanged her lemonade glass with Christine's. She lit the candles on her cake, sang the chorus, and blew out the candles.

"Happy birthday, Mommy. Time for cake?" Christine set her cup down and held up her plate.

"Which piece do you want?" Becca cut the corner piece, the one with three sides of icing and big, sugary flower.

Christine's eyes opened like saucers. "That one."

"Here you go." Becca placed the slice with an icing flower on Christine's plate, added a scoop of ice cream, and handed her a spoon. "Now for mine." She snagged the other corner piece and sat down to enjoy this precious moment with her favorite person in the world.

"Mmm, so yummy."

Christine's smile, accented by pink and green icing at the

edges, must have held magic, for in seeing it, Becca's entire world lit up. "Honey, you make everything yummy to me. I love you so much." She touched the tip of Christine's nose.

They two laughed and giggled together as they devoured their cake and ice cream. Christine produced a homemade card with the perfect sentiment, obviously aided by some other adult's help spelling suggestions.

> *Happy Birthday Mama.*
> *You are my sunshine.*
> *I love you forever.*
> *Love, Christine*

"Oh, babe, this is the very best birthday card I've ever had—in my whole life!" Becca swooped Christine into her arms and kissed her with wild, tickling pecks around the cheeks and neck, causing Christine to writhe in giggles. "Thank you, thank you, thank you."

"You're happy, Mama?"

Becca smiled and leaned her head against Christine's. "Yes, I'm happy. Are you happy?"

"Yes, I'm happy."

"Good. Then let's take the bus and go to the zoo today."

"The zoo?" Christine bounced up and down. "Hooray!"

Life was indeed happier since deciding to give her whole self to Jesus. Devoting herself to prayer, Bible study, and fellowship, she saw the world through fresh eyes. New friendships in the fellowship group replaced old ones, which had proven themselves empty after all. Old parties, drinking and such behind her, she chose inspirational music, movies and reading material—desiring to renew her mind and live according to God's instruction manual.

Growing in the sense of being loved by God didn't replace Becca's desire for a healthy relationship with a man—a life partner—but her choices narrowed to find one with shared faith and values. One of the group leaders seemed a good choice. He was kind, talented, handsome, a strong leader, and personable. He was the type she'd been dreaming of all these years. *But would a man like that ever love me?*

Missy and Jimmy wed. Any self-respecting hippie or Renaissance gent would have loved the bride—flowers woven into her long blonde tresses, which loosely trailed over her lacy Gunne Sax dress, past her trim waistline. They were married in a field, surrounded by a chosen few, and danced long into the night, Missy showing no signs of caring that the hem of her dress became permanently soiled from spinning through the long grasses and muddy dance floor.

A month later, Becca folded laundry with Missy at the newlyweds' place.

"I'm so happy for you two." Becca sighed—a heavy sigh that gave away her mixed emotions. "But I wonder. . ."

Missy gave Becca's shoulder a slight shove. "Stop, now, you'll meet somebody." She shook out Jimmy's jeans and pushed the wrinkles flat.

"There is someone I think about. All the time." Becca raised an eyebrow, waiting for Missy's inquisitive nature to take over.

"Hmm." Missy walked toward the kitchen, a corner of the garage apartment, with a small refrigerator, a cooktop, a table and chairs.

"Aren't ya gonna ask who?" Becca threw a towel at her.

Missy caught the towel midair. "Well, you don't have to start throwing things." She hurried to sit next to Becca, her brown eyes full of anticipation. "Who then?"

"If you insist, I'll tell you." Her face flushed and her eyes beamed with excitement. "Luke. He's so amazing. He's everything I've dreamed of—and more." Becca waited for Missy's response with bated breath.

Missy's facial expression dropped. Her voice deepened. "Becca, we are not his kind of people."

"Huh?"

"Just look at him—his family has money, they all love each other, they even sing songs together like they're in a Broadway musical. Then look at us. Our parents fought all the time. We wore hand-me-downs, no sheets on the bed." Handing Becca a soda, she sat next to the laundry basket. "Face it, Becca. We live in a different class than they do. Luke would only marry a virgin, anyway."

Missy's words spun in the room and slammed Becca's heart. As she tried to recover from the blow, she glanced around at all that Missy had now. She and her new husband rented a garage apartment on his sister's property. They had furniture, a truck, a little garden outside—even a puppy and a kitten. All Becca dreamed of, they had. . . and so easily. Marriage and independent living had not come easily—at all—to Becca.

"But. . . I want to be. . . his kind of people." Becca placed the folded tee shirt in the basket, sat in the chair and sipped her soda. "And we can be. We don't have to live like Mom and Dad did."

"You read too many fairy tales. That life is a fantasy, Becca."

"No." Becca sat her drink on the coffee table. "I refuse to accept that. We can do better. This is twentieth century America, not a caste society."

Becca staved off Missy's crushing blow with greater determination to succeed. She would become a stellar Christian. Someone worthwhile would see her value. The rest of her life would not be lived as lower middle class, feeling less than others, always struggling to make ends meet. Christine would not be raised as less-than anyone. Missy might be prettier. And more loved—married, even. But Becca would prove Missy wrong.

And while she was at it, she would save her entire family. She would defy her shyness and get down to the business of spreading her message of love and peace, of cleaning up this messed-up family.

She told everyone about salvation through Christ. . . Emily, Douglas and his wife, Carlton and Jake. She witnessed to her parents, her aunts and uncles, and cousins. Becca seemed to be the only one impressed with Jesus. Her talk with her father went exceptionally bad.

"So, you're getting all holy on us now?" A swig of beer, followed by a knowing grin, ensued. "We'll see how long that lasts. How many men will be after you if you're not interested in sex?"

Becca swallowed hard. "Well, if by holy, you mean pure, then yes. God designed sex to be special, in committed marriage. I'm going to wait until marriage before sleeping with anyone again. He forgave me and justified me, which means just-as-if-I'd never sinned." Becca smiled at herself for making good use of the terminology she'd read in one of her Christian primers.

"Why would you want to do that? Human beings are no different than animals. They get a feeling and act on it. It's nothing to be ashamed of. You should be free to have sex with whoever you want."

"Wow." Becca sat back, stunned. "Dad, you don't understand." Uncomfortable with overstepping the bounds of propriety for a father and daughter talk, Becca ended the conversation. "I don't know where you learned to think that way, but that life won't satisfy you. God loves you and wants better for you."

She left the room.

But she struggled to leave the argument in her head.

I never sought out sex. I was looking for love and approval. I wanted to be wanted but had no idea about enjoying sex. I gave myself up for what they wanted. Only occasionally did I ever have an orgasm—for which Craig made me pay. No one else ever made me feel—

She shook the thought away. *I will have a good sex life someday, with a good man, who treats me right.*

At fellowship group that night, the leader asked if anyone had a prayer request. The group would agree in prayer, asking God for help with any concern.

Becca wanted to talk about what was going on in her parents' home, what her father said. She wanted to tell how horrible living with Emily had been, what the neighbor boy had done to Christine, how she had to get out of there, but now was stuck at her parents' place again. Which was in many ways worse. Having someone's help would be nice.

But I can't say those things, not here. They'd think I'm a low-life, more messed up than anyone here. But I want better. How do I get there?

She heard herself speak. "Um, I do." Her feet shuffled, calling her to look at them. "I need to find another place to live. Will you pray for us?"

After prayer time, one of the older men in group motioned for Becca to meet him off to the side.

He smiled politely. "We believe a single woman should be sheltered by her parents. She should stay with them until marriage and honor them. God will bless you if you do." He nodded, a smug air of confidence delivering his advice.

Becca's heart sank. *If only he knew. But how could I tell him? None of these people would understand.* Forcing her eyes to meet the elder's, she nodded. "There isn't room for us. They have a two-bedroom apartment and my little brother lives with them." This part of the truth was easy enough to share.

"Well, in that case, I'm sorry. Then find a room in the home of a good Christian family, who can give you an umbrella of safety until you marry."

"I'd like that." Becca shifted her stance and perked up. "Do you know anyone who would take us in? I keep things clean, and Christine is a good girl. We wouldn't be any trouble."

"Well, no, but we'll keep praying for you." He turned his body toward the door and touched Becca's upper arm to lead her out. "Please let us know how God answers our prayer. Thank you for sharing."

Becca shuddered as she left, an odd feeling she hadn't

experienced here before.

Her search continued. She posted notes on church bulletin boards and answered newspaper ads for rooms to rent. Longing for a Christian family to take them in, or to be roommates with some of the young women in the fellowship, Becca prayed and searched and asked around daily. To no avail. Taking a child into one's house seemed to be beyond the average sacrifice, like asking for a room in a crowded hotel in Bethlehem.

"I'd be happy to just have a barn we could legally sleep in. I'd turn a little shack into a haven for you, my girl." Becca snapped Christine's picture as they walked through the woods. They walked in the woods every chance they found these days, to get away from the crowded apartment with her arguing parents.

"Lemme take your picture," Christine said.

"Okay." Becca showed her how to work the camera, then stepped back and smiled.

"Hold my bear." Christine handed her mother her stuffed bear. "Okay, say cheese."

"Cheese!" Becca squeezed the bear and smiled for the camera. They walked on.

"What's a haven, Mama? Is it like heaven?"

"Good question, my dear. And I'd say, yes, sort of like heaven, but on earth. A haven is a place where you feel safe, loved, and happy."

"Oh." Christine poked her walking stick onto a large rock and stepped up, her face even with her mother's. "Then this is our haven. We love the woods."

Becca laughed. "Yes, we do. You're so right."

A week later, Becca landed a decent job as a grocery store clerk, earning well above minimum wage. Knowing she had to do something to make a better place for Christine to live, she convinced Missy, her husband and a cousin to lease a four-bedroom townhouse together. They pooled their resources, creating a better lifestyle in a nicer neighborhood. Though not the haven she dreamt of for Christine, it was closer.

Christine was growing up without a father. Luke was engaged, so Becca let that idea go. Any little spark for other guys in the fellowship soon fizzled out. She wouldn't accept a date for the wrong reason. Becca would wait. God would come first. He would provide.

27

Lena

Southern Appalachians. 1923

After breakfast, Lena and the boys gathered their belongings and placed them near the door. Lena picked up Ruth and opened the door. She saw most of her Appalachian family gathered by the wagon—all but Gatline. Shaw and Elliot ran ahead.

From behind, Gatlin swooped up her bags and followed her out. Helping them all into the wagon, he kissed Lena's cheek. "Write us, cousin. Stay in touch."

Adohi and Enna hung on the side of the wagon, as if to climb in. "Can we come with you?"

"Not this time, young men, but come see us in Maryland someday."

Tom and Una exchanged glances and nodded.

"Someday," Una laughed.

"Yay!" They shouted, jumping about, their arms in the air. "We'll go to Maryland some day!" They all waved as Caroline led the team away. The older boys ran alongside as if they could outrun horses.

"See you later." Lena called to them as the wagon pulled ahead of the panting boys.

"*Stiyu*, never good-bye." Aunt Caroline winked.

On the way, talk came in waves. They reviewed their visit, going over good medicine and herbal remedies Caroline had taught her. They engaged in lighter talk of weather, of the times, and fabrics for dresses Caroline wanted to purchase when they reached town, to make pretty dresses for Ruth.

"I'll send them by post."

Lena turned around, her head resting on her arms on the back of the seat. Watching the mountains grow smaller behind her, sadness and longing merged with the joyous splendor they forged in her soul. Rich blue greens became a haze of purple in the horizon. Her deep sigh must have reached Aunt Caroline's ears.

"The mountains will miss you too, darlin'," her great aunt whispered. She tapped Lena's knee and squeezed it. "Come back to us when you can—by travel or by dream—we'll give ya a good squeezin' either way." They pulled into town, stocked up on necessaries and made their way to the station, with little time to spare. "We said more in a couple of weeks than most folks do in a lifetime." Caroline laughed.

Lena's body felt lighter. *True.* "I feel rich now," Lena smiled.

"Good—you are. Rich in spirit. Stiyu."

"Give my love—and good medicine—to my Eliza. And all of her clan."

On the train, once the boys settled into the ride, Lena snuggled Ruth close to her heart. She sang what she remembered from Aunt Caroline's song.

> *"You bright mornin' star. . .*
>   *I see you dancin' in the rain. . .*
>   *. . . soar above the pain*
>   *like an eagle in flight."*

* * *

Sandy Spring, Maryland.

"Home again." Lena let go of Shaw's hand and lifted Elliot out of his perch next to Ruth in the pram as they approached her parents' farm.

Mama saw them coming and called out. Family ran to greet them from all about. They smothered Ruth and Shaw and Elliot with kisses as they led them into the house.

"Where's Grannie?" Lena doffed her jacket and hung it on the hook near the door.

"She's in bed. Had an awful spell. But you can go in, she's been waiting for you, calling you."

Lena sprinted up the stairs and peeked into Grannie's room. She lay sleeping, her long grey hair splayed out like a crown around her head. How much she looked like her sister, her nephew. She crept in and sat beside her.

Grannie stirred and opened her eyes. "Starlight?"

"I'm here. Aunt Caroline and all the family send their love."

Grannie cleared her throat and moved one shoulder. "Love received. You must write them for me, soon."

"How are you? Mama said you had quite a spell, but are you better?"

"Getting stronger."

"Caroline sent some medicine for you. I have it, here. She taught me so much—"

Eliza reached for and grasped what Lena held, then brought the paper bag to her nose. "Ah, yes. Make the tea for me."

"I will."

"I'll just rest a few minutes."

Lena tiptoed out, leaving the door open an inch. In the kitchen, she put a kettle on to boil and began to hear the family news since her departure. Tea steeped and ready, Lena begged her leave. "Mama, do you mind, if once I take the tea to Grannie, I lay down a moment? I'm exhausted."

"Of course not, go on, get some rest. We'll tend to the little ones. We've missed you all, so." Mama squeezed Ruth, whom she held on one hip, planting a kiss on her cheek.

Lena placed the tea cup at Grannie's bedside. She didn't stir, so she crept to her old room down the hall. She landed in her childhood bed, splayed out like a teen. Overwhelm supplanted the relief of being home. *Home.* It struck her, full force—Clinton's downfall robbed her of home—her home, her children's home. *I can't go home again.* Tears flowed. Unable to suppress them, she turned into her pillow and wept.

Her mother entered the room. She leaned over, wrapping her arms and laying her head over Lena's back. She held Lena through every shudder of sorrow, every stilted breath, up and down. "Let it out, my girl. It'll all be okay."

A safer place in the world could not be found than her own bed, the one she'd known all her life—with Mama holding her. She cried until her tears emptied, until the light of her mother's assurance shone in her darkness, until trust in her mother's love cast out her pain. Her touch soothed deeper than words could reach. At last, Lena waded in calm. She sat up and wiped her tears. "Thank you for sharing my heartache, Mama."

"A shared heartache is a soothed one." Aggie took Lena's hands in hers and looked straight into her eyes. "The trip did you good. I see light in your eyes, even through the tears."

"Yes, Mama."

Aggie let go of Lena's hands and spread the wrinkles out of her apron. "Good. How about we head down to the kitchen. You can tell Grannie and me all about it."

"Grannie's up?" Lena's face lit up.

"She is! Come see."

Lena stood, walked to the wash basin on the bedside mirror, dipped a washcloth in the water and squeezed it. She held the cool wetness over her eyes, wiped them, and looked in the mirror. "I can't do anything about these red eyes. They'll just have to do."

As they entered the kitchen, Lena took an apron off the hook and tied it around her waist.

Grannie stirred the pot on the stove. "Starlight." She sent Lena an eye-to-eye twinkle, the edges of her eyes wrinkling up in glorious delight.

Lena returned the twinkle. Grannie had always called her Starlight. Lena had imagined the nickname came from the blue in her eyes. Her siblings had green or brown. Now she knew better. Grannie sent powerful light from her brown eyes, too. The twinkle of joy they brought to one another could light the sky on a moonless night. Throwing her arms around her grandmother, Lena squeezed her. "Musta been some good tea."

"Indeed. Now, grab a knife and chop those carrots, gal." Grannie poked Lena in her upper arm with her elbow, pointing toward the carrots with her eyes.

Carrots, potatoes, onions, and green beans, staples in this kitchen, always needed chopping, peeling or snapping. Lena grabbed a knife and some carrots and obeyed. "Where's Daddy?"

"He was fishing." Aggie picked up Ruth. "You might not want to hug him when he returns."

"Thanks for the warning."

They peeled, chopped, stirred, and chatted in easy manner. Lena relayed news on Aunt Caroline and her family. "Grannie," Lena turned to face her grandmother, "I never knew."

Grannie, who had since taken a seat at the table to sip more of her tea, looked up. "Never knew what, darling?"

Starlight's look spoke for her.

Grannie grew somber. "Oh."

"I want to hear your story, please. I've been with you all my life, yet I never knew the life you led before you came here. Please tell me. Tell me all you can stand."

Grannie patted Ruth in the cradle next to her. She showed no sense of urgency to respond. Turning, she picked up some green beans and commenced snapping.

Silence—for too long—caused Lena to worry she'd asked too much, too soon.

At last, Grannie spoke. "I will, Starlight. I will. I thank you for asking."

Quiet, again. *Snap. Snap. Chop. Chop.*

Aggie looked at Lena and back at Eliza. The three generations looked down at their work, engrossed in thought, waiting.

Grannie broke the silence again. "In droplets, though, not a torrent. Send torrential rain on a tender shoot and you'll uproot it. The rain will carry that shoot way down the river, where no roots can take hold."

Snap. Snap. Chop. Chop.

"I understand."

"I thought you would."

"Anything you can."

Grannie chuckled. "I was a girl in the mountains a long time ago. But it was. . . yesterday. Before too long, I'll be back again, to rest."

A chill went through Lena's spine. "You're okay, aren't you, Grannie?"

Grannie looked up, startled. "Oh, I'm fine." She waved her hand off to the side. "But when you reach my age, you never know."

How old is Grannie? To Lena, she had always been the same age. Working in the kitchen, in the garden, telling stories, singing, she always did the same. She always wore her long house dress, still from last century's style, under her big-pocketed apron, and spun her soft hair into in a loose bun atop her head. Grannie had rocked Lena as a babe the same as Ruth, today.

"What do you remember about home, Grannie?"

Grannie's eyes wandered, looking off center of the beans she snapped. Her nimble fingers stopped for a moment as she closed her eyes. "Purple." Her face lightened and glowed. "Blue and purple mountains with golden skies. A misty haze in the morning, giving way to shades of green. Ferns and laurel, growing wild—everywhere. The sun streaming through the leaves, tiny beams directing one's focus to a leaf unfurling by the creek. The sound of water flowing over rocks. Quail taking flight. Squirrels chasing one another across the trees."

Lena knew the scenes Grannie drew upon, first-hand. She treasured these precious mountain memories along with her.

"Caroline and I," Grannie continued, "stringing necklaces of clover gathered from the meadows before we hid away at nightfall. 'My sister forever,' she said, as she donned me with a clover crown. 'We'll be here forever, won't we 'Liza?' Ah, and I thought we would." Eliza opened her eyes. *Snap. Snap.* She cleared a catch in her throat. "It won't be easy telling."

"As you can, Grannie."

She straightened her back and held her chin higher. "One thing I will say is this: We are Cherokee. You come from generations of strong women, and you will carry on this family. We are not easily extinguished. The fire is in your eyes." *Snap. Snap.* "Here. Carry this pot of beans to the stove, please."

Lena smiled, put down her knife, hugged Grannie's neck, pecked her cheek and carried the pot of beans to the stove.

Daddy came in the back door, carrying—and stinking of—fresh fish. "Well, lookee what the cat dragged in," he announced, his eyes on his catch of the day. Turning to see the ladies' response, he saw Lena. "Leenie!" He charged her, his arms open for a bear hug.

"Ew, Daddy, not the fish!" Lena squealed laughter and took off running.

Henry lit after her, fish flapping around in hand.

He caught her and they all enjoyed a good laugh as Lena suffered an odoriferous hug from her dear Daddy.

"Girl, you stink! You better go clean up for dinner," he teased, beaming with pride for sharing his stench. He placed the day's catch by the sink.

"After you, Daddy." She guided him to the stairs. "It is good to be home again." She held Daddy by her side as they climbed the steps to clean up for supper.

At her door, Daddy's tone waxed gentle and serious. "Leenie, I have a sense about what happened. You birthed a family young, which happens. Why in the world God made kids able to feel the drive to loving before they've the sense to handle what comes of it, I don't understand. But we're here for you, and it'll work out."

"I was foolish, dreaming of Prince Charming."

"Okay, no more, young'un. Go freshen up. Glad you're home."

Lena closed the door, undressed, and washed up with the fresh bowl of water Mama had placed in her room. The scent of their family's soap, once so familiar she barely noticed, now elicited olfactory bliss intense enough to be a fragrant offering for ancient Greek gods. Mint and rosemary to freshen and liven the soul, and lavender to calm the day's nerves, blended in a happy, foaming lather. Her eyes paused upon herself in the mirror, where she saw Daddy and Mama and Grannie in her face. They pulsed in her being. She breathed a prayer of thanksgiving. Donning a clean dress, she headed down to the table. *It's so good to be home.*

* * *

No one ever expected dinner to be a quiet event in the Burriss home. Brothers, sisters, nieces, and nephews streamed into the farmhouse, hugging necks, shaking hands, all begging to hear of Lena's trip.

Lena began her story several times, but each time another family member would enter, grab a plate, and ask her to start again. Their questions would interrupt her story and send her down various streams of thought.

Mama put an end to the barrage of questions. "Settle down, y'all, give her a chance to eat her dinner, poor soul. Lena's been through a hard time, and she's made a trip most of us will never make in our lifetime. She's met family we've never met. Does she have a lot to tell? Yes, indeed, she does. But in due time. So, hush up and eat. Let Lena say what she can when she can."

Everyone in this house respected what Mama said. The table fell silent, save for the clinking of forks, the gulping of water and the occasional, "Pass the salt, please."

The little ones finished quickly, as little ones do when they want to run outside to play.

"Can we be excused?" One asked.

Daddy delivered his edict with kindness. "Yes, you all can, but don't go far."

Once the room belonged to adults, Lena volunteered. "All right, you all, all right. Now that everyone's here. . . I'm going to be completely open with you , but I only want to tell you my personal story once."

All eyes fixed on Lena.

"I left Clinton. I was afraid for my life, and for Ruth's." She paused to take a breath, and to read the room. Finding all still, and listening, she continued. "Ever since the war, especially, he's been drunk much of the time. When he's drunk, he gets crazy. Mad. Violent. We went to Aunt Caroline's to be safe, to figure out what to do."

Their mouths hung open.

"But as for Grannie's family there, we met with a wonderful welcome. They're a good family. I wish you all could have come. I wish you all could know them. We have plenty to be grateful for, especially considering what our elders have been through."

Another sip, a bite of fish, and Lena looked about the table. All eyes still on her, all forks down, all mouths hanging open—the sight of which made Lena laugh. "What? You all are looking at me like you've seen a ghost or something."

Her eldest brother, George, composed a response first. "We've never heard you talk that way."

Everyone nodded in agreement.

"Clinton, though." George sat forward in his seat and banged his fork upright on the table. "I'm ready to take him out."

28

Becca

Rockville, Maryland. 1979

Becca chose a red bandanna to complement her blouse's embroidered neckline. She placed the triangle over her hair and tied the bandanna at her nape.

"Almost time to go, honey. What do you want to wear today?"

"My favorite." Christine swiped her hand across the billowy skirt of her corduroy dress as it hung in the closet.

One eyebrow lifted in playful questioning. "Again?" Becca slipped the plaid dress from the hanger. "You sure do love this dress."

Christine had worn her find almost daily since trying it on in the thrift shop. She wriggled her arms and head through their respective openings. "Zip?"

Becca pulled the zipper up the back.

Christine twirled around the room. "My dancing dress."

Her eyes lit with delight as the skirt rose into a full circle from her waistline. She spun until falling from dizziness. "The room's spinning," she said, her finger in the air, imitating the motion.

Becca seized the opportunity to help Christine with her socks and shoes, then pulled her up to stand. She wrapped her little girl in her arms. "All better?"

Christine nodded and smiled. "Again!" She began a twirl.

Becca caught her hand. "Time to go, sweetie. We volunteered to set up for church today."

Becca and Christine arrived early, along with two other volunteers. One person started the large coffee pot brewing while the others carried folding chairs to the center of the room, arranging them in a large circle.

Christine giggled as she wrestled with the taller-than-her chairs. She would be their master, Becca figured, and so insisted on carrying and unfolding each one she claimed— all by herself.

Others arrived, hugging their greetings and chatting in small groups. As the clock above the cafeteria service windows approached ten, they filled in the seats. An opening prayer and quiet guitar music set the mood for reflection.

The dust glistened and danced in the air, lit in magical wonder by dappled light streaming through spotty windows. Like miniature fairies at play, they rode the sunbeam to the cup of wine and loaf of bread in the room's center.

Becca's heart settled as she considered these symbols. The fruit of the vine and the sustenance of life represented Jesus giving his all to prove God's love. She considered those around her. Most were her age, or thereabouts, except for three older couples. This ragtag group—akin to Jesus's first disciples—presented no pious trappings or religious airs. They didn't seem to judge by what a person wore, or how a person had lived before meeting Jesus. Becca embraced this simple, come-as-you-are style of church.

The double-door creaked open, drawing every eye. A sunbeam flashed across the room. A few dried leaves rode in on the wind, tumbling along the linoleum floor and settling near the corner of the cinder block walls.

In the doorway stood a newcomer—a slight young man with black hair lapping in waves around his neck and ears. Backlit in the morning light's aura, he could have been Jesus—except for the casual jeans and striped polo.

Becca's interest piqued.

He hunched his shoulders forward, his expression begging pardon for his late arrival.

The leader, Luke, stopped playing guitar and greeted him. "Great to see you, Mike. Grab a chair."

Several in the group scooted their chairs to make room, and Mike pulled a chair into the circle.

Luke's eyes crinkled at the edges as he introduced the newcomer. "Everyone, I met Mike on campus. We had some interesting discussions, so I invited him to come check us out."

Mike nodded, his hand waved a quick hello. In a soft voice and sincere brown eyes, he entreated their pardon. "Sorry for being late. I had a little trouble finding the place." His glance around the circle returned to, and paused on, Becca.

Becca nodded, then averted her smiling eyes to hide her instant attraction.

Luke resumed playing his acoustic rendition of "Sometimes Alleluia," by Chuck Girard. Voices joined. Laura, a new friend of Becca's, created her own harmony in high soprano.

Becca tried to focus on the Lord by closing her eyes and turning her palms upward. Her heart fluttered like a schoolgirl's. Having had a few crushes on guys in the fellowship, but nary a date in the year since joining, she downplayed her attraction to the newcomer. *I don't even know him. I'm here for you, Lord, not for a guy.*

After scripture reading and communion, they broke into four smaller groups. The Sunday School teacher led Christine and three other children to another room. Mike pulled his chair into Becca's circle.

Jack, the small group facilitator, opened the discussion. "We'll dive into John, chapter sixteen."

All around, Bible pages fluttered to the passage.

Jack continued. "Jesus was preparing his disciples for the time he knew would soon come—when he'd leave them for the cross. In verses 23 and 24, he says—

"*In that day you will no longer ask me anything. Very truly I tell you, my Father will give you whatever you ask in my name. Until now you have not asked for anything in my name. Ask and you will receive, and your joy will be complete.*"

Jack made eye contact with Laura, then Becca. "When you pray, do you pray to Jesus, or do you pray to the Father in Jesus' name? What's the difference?"

Becca's chair creaked as she adjusted her position. She hoped someone else would answer.

Laura broke the awkward silence. "I'll share."

Everyone turned to Laura.

"I think Jesus wants us to relate to God as close and loving, like a father. In the Old Testament, only the high priest could enter the inner temple, after specific sacrifices." She smiled and leaned in. "But because of Jesus' sacrifice, we can be just as close."

Another said, "I was raised to pray to God as my heavenly Father."

A third person contributed. "My family taught me to fear God. We weren't supposed to bother him with our little stuff any more than we were supposed to bother Dad when he was working."

Becca compared their comments to her own perspective. *I prefer Creator, or Lord.* She didn't want to say why.

"I'm new at this," Mike said. "I just asked the Lord to set me free the other night."

Several people responded at once. "Congratulations."

"Thanks." Mike glanced down, then surveyed the group. "Luke told me to read the Gospel of John. Chapter eight says, 'Who the Son sets free is free indeed.' I want to be free. So, I asked Jesus into my life. I'm here to learn how to live in freedom, but I haven't thought much about the difference between praying to the Son versus the Father." He smiled and leaned back in his chair.

Becca regarded him as the conversation continued, endeared by his openness and his unassuming manner. She forced her visual attention to the next speaker, and then to her Bible, where she read, 'Ask and you will receive, and your joy will be complete.' *Could I ask the Lord for Mike? But what if someone else asked for Mike? Not so simple.*

Luke strummed a few quiet notes on his guitar, signaling time to wrap things up.

"There's no simple answer to the question. But, that's all the time we have today, so we'll talk more about this next week." Jack thanked everyone for sharing. As they folded their chairs and headed back to form one large circle, he addressed Becca. "I'm sorry we didn't get to you this morning. Maybe next time?"

"It's okay." With a sigh of relief, she smiled. "Really."

***

Six months passed. Becca's interest in Mike swelled as he continued to attend fellowship and grow in his relationship with God and others in the group.

After an evening out with friends from the fellowship, Becca carried her sleeping daughter into bed, pulled off her shoes and tucked the covers up to her neck. After kissing Christine's cheek, she returned to the living room and tossed her coat on the sofa. A yawn overtook her face, scrunching her eyes and drawing her hand to her mouth. *A drink of water and then bed.*

She flipped on the kitchen light. Something out of the ordinary drew her attention. By the sink, a paper plate faced her, propped upright by salt and pepper shakers. Moving toward the note, she recognized Missy's handwriting in blue crayon. "Mike called. He wants to take you to a concert Friday night." His phone number completed the message

As if touched by a fairy's wand, a spark flickered in Becca's heart, enlivened her limbs, and lit her face. She grabbed the note and read again. Almost skipping down the hall, holding the paper plate of dreams to her heart, she knocked on Missy's door.

No answer.

She nudged the door open, raising the paper plate note.

"Missy! Is this for real?"

"Huh?" Missy lifted her head, her face covered by blonde curls. She wiped aside a strand and squinted at Becca. "Oh, yeah. He called about 9:30. What time is it now?"

"10:30. Sorry I woke you, but—"

"Okay, great, now shut the door." Missy pulled the covers over her head and rolled toward Jimmy.

As Becca obeyed, she repeated her apology. "I'm just so excited. I've been hoping for this for six months. Eeee!"

* * *

Progressing from group dates to being a couple, they grew close. Their mutual admiration grew with each walk, talk, and prayer together. They enjoyed going out to eat and listening to music. They took Christine on short hikes along the Potomac River, the C & O Canal, and nearby Sugarloaf Mountain.

Becca and Christine packed a picnic lunch and met Mike for an afternoon at the park. Christine ran off to play with the kids on the playground while Mike and Becca sat to watch her and talk.

"What a great spot this is." Becca reached into the picnic basket and pulled out a soda.

He brushed away a bug that buzzed and landed on his face. "Yeah, perfect."

Becca drew a deep breath of the fresh air. "Mmm, I smell wild ginger! Where is it?" She turned, scanning the understory of nearby bushes.

"Seriously? You know the names of plants by their smell?" Mike popped the top of his soda.

"And a lot of their medicinal purposes." She picked a leaf and brought it close for Mike to smell. "I don't know where I first learned, though. My mom wasn't into flowers, except zinnias, roses and four o'clocks—and only those for how easily she could grow them."

"I guess in your case, the acorn didn't fall so close to the tree."

Becca laughed. "Thank God! Some squirrel must've picked that acorn up and carried it away."

"You don't talk much about your family."

"Well, you have met them." Becca rolled her eyes and poked his ribcage.

"My family was Catholic." Mike nodded toward the Catholic church building on the other side of the park.

"Oh? My mom was Catholic, Dad protestant." Becca checked for Mike's response. His eyes remained on the building.

"All was good, until I questioned the faith." He looked at his feet. "Which didn't go over too well."

"What do you mean?" Becca tucked a stray hair behind her ear.

"Having been on the debate team in high school, I knew how to argue points, but for the first time I stood up to my parents. They grew more upset with every counter point I made. " He shook his head. "I pulled away from them when I went to college, but my life spiraled downward from there."

Becca nodded. His description of family troubles seemed trivial. Her toe wiggled against a tiny pebble in her shoe.

She pulled off the shoe and shook the offending bit to the ground. "That must've been hard for you."

"It was."

"Have you all made up since?" She slipped her toes back into the shoe.

"Yea, pretty much. I've visited a couple of times. The first year we still argued. I questioned everything. You know, they say never discuss two things with those you love—religion and politics. I pushed them on both." He shook his head and stared into the woods. "Even got involved with an underground communist movement on campus."

Becca's eyebrows raised and her chin tucked. "What?"

Mike chuckled. "Yeah." His eyes returned to Becca's. "I left them when I joined the fellowship. I agreed with some of their ideas, but not enough to join them." A bug landed on his knee and met with a brush of his hand. "Just a rebellious stage."

Becca nodded and patted his forearm. "I understand. I rebelled earlier in life than you did. Did a lot of things just to defy the rules I didn't understand."

Becca watched Christine, who had wandered from the edge of the playground. She picked wildflowers and placed them in the middle of the merry-go-round. "Do your parents know you've joined our fellowship group?"

"Yeah. We talked about it on my last visit. They're worried I'm in a cult. I assured them that I haven't committed all my money or moved into a commune." He grinned.

"What money?" Becca laughed and elbowed Mike. "I'd be all in on a commune, though. I love the idea of everyone sharing what they have and contributing their abilities to build successful community. But truth be told, I can barely stand sharing an apartment with my sisters and brother-in-law."

Mike reached his arm around Becca and pulled her close. "I couldn't live with them, either." A wink tagged along with his teasing smirk.

Becca poked him with her finger. "Hey, hold on there. They're my sisters, only I get to knock them." She chewed her lip and watched the children.

Christine lay in the center of the merry-go-round, sprawled like da Vinci's *Vitruvian Man*. Each hand and foot anchored around a bar, she steadied herself. Her companions ran around the device, lending their force to spin the grand, metal circle of childhood fun. She screamed with glee. "Faster, faster."

"That's my girl." Becca pointed at Christine, smiled, and shook her head.

"Makes me miss being a kid." Mike sighed. He leaned back against the picnic table. "Everything was so easy then."

"Yeah?" Becca turned to study his expression. For a second, he appeared much younger. Dreamy. Then his brows furrowed, and his adult face returned.

"At sixteen, I volunteered to work the crisis hot line at church. I talked to a lot of pregnant teenage girls, and my heart always went out to them." He watched Christine as she moved to the swings.

Becca followed his line of sight. "Don't swing too high, honey."

"My experience there drew me to you."

One eyebrow raised, her head tilted toward him. "Huh?"

A hint of light sprang from his eyes to hers. "Being alone and pregnant at fifteen must've been so hard. Yet, you kept your baby. . . and you work hard to be a good mother. I respect that."

Her heart warmed. "Thank you." Her gaze averted, landing on Christine. "It was a tough decision. Not everyone respects me for it, I assure you. Truth is, I think Christine saved me, not the other way around."

They leaned against one another and watched the kids playing.

Christine's friend propelled the swing high enough to run beneath, with Christine calling out, "Higher."

"Careful, girls." Becca intertwined her fingers with Mike's and squeezed. Their hands fit together with ease. "I hope I made the right choice for her because she deserves a good life. You need to know I love her more than life. If you're interested in me, I come with her. A package deal."

"I know. And I know I'm young for this, so I'm not sure I'm ready. But I do like you—a lot." He drew their interlaced fingers to his face, kissed the dorsum of her hand and pressed it to his cheek. His doe eyes met hers.

She sighed. *He is sweet, kind, gentle. . . but. . . too young. I shouldn't let him get too attached to me.*

29

Lena

Sandy Spring, Maryland. 1923

"Son, settle down. No need for such. Any of you." Daddy looked around the table with a stern eye. "You'll throw your lives away, in jail." He drew a deep breath and redirected the family's energy. "Fighting, no. But we won't live in fear, either. That's even worse than fighting. When we go, it'll be civil. You understand me?"

"Yes, sir," several of the brothers resounded.

Picking at food resumed.

Lena cleared her throat. "We'll figure out what to do about Clinton. Remember, he is my children's father. One thing I've learned is that secrets can make things worse. Let's all be honest with each other. At least in this family, we're here for each other."

"Here, here," Daddy lifted his glass. "We'll cool down. We'll talk. We'll decide what to do. All in good time."

Lena nodded. "I don't mean to change the subject, but speaking of keeping secrets, I want to talk about our Cherokee history. After the long secrecy here, we missed learning what Grannie and Aunt Caroline went through to survive. We need to know how strong and clever and savvy they are."

"Clever and savvy is right. They are more than this Scotsman ever dreamed." Henry winked, reaching over to squeeze his mother-in-law's hand on the table.

Lena yanked off a bite-sized piece of bread. Adding a generous spread of butter, she popped the warm goodness into her mouth. Preferring to speak of her trip to Aunt Caroline's, she talked right over the bread as she rolled it side to side in her mouth, savoring the fresh, grainy flavor. "Aunt Caroline told me stories—some myths, but some true, from her memories." She turned, directing her speech to her grandmother.

"Grannie, I want to hear what you remember, too. I am sorry if I didn't listen before, but we all need to know your story." She looked around the table. "I'll never be the same, ya'll. I found new strength inside. I'll make it, and so will my kids. And I'm glad to God to have you all."

Grannie nodded in approval. "I'll oblige you that. Perhaps not tonight, though. I'm still quite tired. I tell you what. How about you all tell me what you remember that I've taught you thus far?"

The family clamored with chatter about the table, asking questions and relaying their personal recollections of Grannie's Cherokee ways as they gulped down the delicious meal. Lena sat in amazement that she'd missed as much as she did.

After dinner, the extended families heading off in their various directions, Lena laid Ruth down for the night and took Grannie by the arm as she headed to bed. "Can I ask you one more thing tonight?"

"Yes, of course. Come on into my room."

Lena admired the lace curtains over the window and the fresh lilacs brightening the windowsill in their pretty vase. She ran her fingers over the soft quilt at the end of her bed. She recalled Grannie sewing the quilt, incorporating salvaged scraps of the children's old clothes as they outgrew them. Grannie told her the quilt meant more to her than anything she could buy from a catalog.

"Sit down, Starlight." Grannie patted the spot beside her on the bed.

Lena snuggled in close. She hadn't been this close to Grannie in years—since she was ten or twelve years old— about the age when kids think they're too old for such affection. After all she'd been through, she treasured the opportunity. "Grannie, why did you not tell us straight on about your Cherokee history?"

Grannie's lips pursed and relaxed, in turn. She nodded in the way older people do when their thoughts take them far away—to the places they seldom consider after storing them away in the dusty shelves of the past. "It's hard to know what to do when you're in the thick of a matter. I chose to hold back once, which became the easier choice, then habit. Plenty of reasons. At first, fear—and with good reason, mind you."

"Fear? I get that. I wouldn't have thought you afraid, though."

Her eyes narrowed and linked with Lena's. "Most of my

kin were lost in the Great Removal." She glanced down and fidgeted with her quilt. "Hmph. Removal, yes. But great? No. Not in any way." She shook her head several times after she uttered the words. "After many broken promises, trust eludes a soul."

Lena nodded. "I understand losing trust, too."

Grannie patted Lena's hand. "When I arrived in Sandy Spring, I blended in without question. Folks were easy-going, due to the Quaker ways. They believed in hard work and letting God be the judge. When I became a mother, I let Aggie grow up with nary a word about it. If I told my young'un a secret, when young'uns blab without a care, that telling could'a put her life in danger. I worried some might call her a red girl, if she told them she was Cherokee. Kids can be mean like that, you know?"

"Yeah, I know."

"Also, I didn't want someone from outside of these parts learning about us being Cherokee. They could take us in the night, never to be seen again. Lots of Cherokee went missing that way, all up and down the trails. Happened again in Virginia, not long ago."

Lena shook her head. "I didn't know. Not at all. I always felt safe here."

Eliza closed her eyes. "I wanted you all to be safe, and to feel safe. I kept my past a secret to protect my loved ones. Many times, I wished I could tell you all. I want to keep the light of my people burning forever. I grieved that loss. But I am here. They are far away, spread everywhere. If we will be a nation again, I don't know." She shook her head. Looking at Lena, she exhaled. "I lost them, but I have you. To be good to my kin, here, I can do." She looked down at the wrinkled hands in her lap. A tear splashed on her weathered knuckles.

A tender hand, porcelain white, wiped the tear, took Eliza's chin and lifted her face. "My dear Grannie. How I admire you. You've been a solid rock in this family, and we all know it. You're the center of warmth and love. You've brought us all life. What you did, I'm glad of it. I'm proud to be your granddaughter, your Starlight, and I'm proud to be *Aniyunwiya*."

"*Aniyunwiya*." Light sparkled from Grannie's eyes. "Well said." She smiled. A few more tears spilled over her smiling eyes and trickled down her bumpy cheeks, onto the hand still cupping her face. A moment passed, twinkling eye to eye.

"Alright. You sleep," Lena mustered, kissing her cheek.

"And you too. Morning comes swiftly."

"Yes, indeed. Goodnight, Grannie."

Lena lay in bed, her eyes resting on a spot on the ceiling she'd known since childhood. Questions spinning in her mind dissipated, as fog in the light of day, no longer dominating her thoughts. The mountains of their ancestral heritage awakened a primal instinct. Her future would not be what she dreamt in her childish whimsy—dancing with her handsome young man in the moonlight, riding in automobiles with wind in her hair. Instead, she would ensure her children's survival. Making her way as a woman in a man's world, she would raise her children without their father. They would know the value of love, kindness, hard work, and goodness in family. *Great-Aunt Caroline did it. Grannie did it. I will do it.*

30

Becca

Rockville, Maryland. 1979

Becca left Christine in Emily's care so she could spend an evening with Mike, just the two of them.

All through dinner and their stroll through the snow, Becca planned her words. She'd find the right time—an opportunity to thank him for caring for her, but to break off their relationship. He was two years her junior, and she had no business letting him get so close.

A shiver sped up her spine. Was it the cold, or the thought of breaking up? She leaned in toward Mike's shoulder as he placed his arm around her, capturing warmth between them. They stopped beneath a street lamp and watched the snow, lilting, in weightless, effortless journey toward the earth. Light from the lofty orb glowed, enshrouded by misty rainbow hues.

They embraced, shivering in the cold yet basking in the

warmth between them. Pure as the fresh layer of snow that glistened on Mike's beard and kissed Becca's lashes, Becca's heart longed for him. She dared let her eyes leave the beauty around them and tarry on his.

He smiled, a warm smile that defied the frosty tips of his beard and mustache. He leaned into the moment—the opportunity.

Their lips met, tentative and tender, matching in desire and cautious restraint.

He pulled her into his chest and held her tight for a moment.

Becca held the moment as eternity.

Retreating slightly, he locked his eyes on hers again. He smiled, this time with an awkward blend of what seemed both pleasure and embarrassment. "Let's go inside and warm up. I'll make us some hot chocolate."

"Your roommate is home?"

"Yes. No worries."

The couple scurried into his apartment where Mike made good on his promise of two mugs of warm deliciousness. His roommate excused himself to his room.

Mike lit a candle and picked up his guitar. He played his guitar and sang several light-hearted popular songs.

Becca swooned in contentment to have met a man with such goodness, heart and talent. And to have such a delight-ful cup of hot chocolate warming her nearly numb fingers.

His guitar softened, and he sang in tender tone, looking straight into her eyes.

Becca watched and listened, rapt, yet guarding herself. She nearly forgot her intention for tonight. *You're supposed to be breaking up with him.*

He sang. "So, I guess I'll say, I love you, with this song." Mike finished the last note and held his hand on the strings, absorbing their vibration as if to catch himself from saying more. His face beamed.

Becca stuttered over her words. "Wait, are you trying to say. . ." Her heart fluttered, radiating to her neck, then pulsing in her ears. "That you love me?"

He stirred and shifted his position. His face pinked like a little boy caught being 'in like' with a girl. "What if I am?" His rounded eyes begged her to save him from utter embarrassment.

"Then. . . " Becca scrambled for a proper response—one that would save him from his risky position while also guarding herself. "the feelings might be. . . mutual." Warmth tingled her neck and face.

He leaned his guitar against the wall and moved to sit next to her. "I do think that what I'm feeling for you is love. It scares me, I admit, but yes, I think I love you."

Becca gathered herself. *He thinks he loves me. Thinks? I'm not sure how to take that.* "Well, then." She raised her eyebrows and decided to emit an air of aloofness. "I *think* I might love you, too."

* * *

The two grew almost inseparable. They talked on the phone when they couldn't be together. They planned their schedules around when they could next talk or be together. Whether watching a show or reading a book—they longed to be together.

Becca eyed Mike from across the room as she and Laura

chatted in their small group. She pushed away her tendency to push away her feelings, just as she'd been doing since the night he declared his love. "I think I'm in love." Becca crossed her legs and sipped her soda. She would test her friend's assessment of the age difference.

"I knew it," said Laura. "The way you always watch Mike during the games. The ball is in play on one side of the court, and your head is still turned to the other end of the court, where Mike is."

Becca laughed. "Oh, I didn't realize I was being so obvious."

"Yeah," said another. "He'd be watching you in left field when the softball was in right field."

"Ah, young love."

Mike approached them. "So, where are we going after church today?"

Becca stood and folded her chair. "How about the ball field? I need to practice."

"Could be dangerous, Becca." Laura chided, an elbow to her ribs. "You really think you can keep your eyes on the ball with him there?"

"Hmm. You have a point there." Becca chuckled. *Laura didn't judge me for it.*

As they headed to the door, one of the elders called Mike over to talk. The elders, so named not necessarily for their ages, were well-schooled in the fellowship's doctrines, and had been entrusted with guiding the group's younger Christians.

He went to them. They encircled him.

Becca took Christine's hand. "Let's wait outside, honey."

When he came outside from the cafeteria, a puzzled look stayed with him.

Becca motioned to Christine that she could join her friends, who were playing hopscotch while their parents stood around outside the school building to chat. She turned to Mike. "What was that about?"

Mike laughed and shook his head. "They wanted to know my intentions toward you."

"Oh my gosh." Becca's arms stiffened against her torso. *Are they trying to scare him off?*

"It made me think about my feelings and our future before I normally would have. We've only been dating three months, but I realized—"

"And two weeks." Becca smirked. "Three months and two weeks."

He paused, swallowed hard, and cleared his throat. "I realized that my intentions are to marry you. I mean, if everything keeps going well, then yes. I certainly don't intend to do you any harm. But do you know what they said next?" His brows furrowed.

Becca was stunned, unable to speak. *To marry me. . .* Her head spun. *Wait. What they said next?* She fixed her eyes ahead, steeling herself for a blow.

"They said, 'Are you sure? There are plenty of young women here who deserve your attention more. Women who saved themselves for a man of God.' I couldn't believe it. I mean, here you are, doing everything you can to make the best of what someone else did to you, and they go and disparage you for what happened years ago." Mike's face contorted with disbelief.

Becca looked away. *He wants to marry me?* Her heart

began to float like dandelion seeds in a gentle breeze. A swift, stormy wind cast the imaginary dandelion seeds tumbling. *The elders. They think I'm not worthy? And the—supposed—virgins?* A forceful exhalation blew any remaining dandelion seeds away. *One of them probably would be better for Mike than me.* She should do the right thing. Let him go.

Mike opened the car door. "Come on, let's go."

Becca called Christine. They climbed into Mike's car and buckled up.

But Mike's not all innocent. He told me many things he did wrong before he met the Lord. Becca's stomach soured recalling his tales. Her vision blurred at the edges. *I never did things as bad as he did.* She pushed away her thoughts and faced him. "What did you tell them?"

"I told them I would pray about it, but that I want to date you, not the others. They said if marrying you is God's will, then my parents will give their blessing. That's how we left it."

Becca stared out the car window. *His parents. I bet the elders doubt his parents will approve. And why would they? I mean, I'm already super young to be a mom, and he is younger than me, and still in college.* She cleared her throat. A timid question slid out. "Do you think they ever would?"

"Well, we'll see. We're not there yet." Mike reached across the stick shift for Becca's hand. "They would want me to finish college."

"And you should." Becca held his hand. "I'm glad we don't have to decide right now. It's just nice to be in a good relationship with someone who feels the same."

Mike turned the steering wheel, guiding the car to park along the side of the road. "Let's pray together, right now."

"Okay." She closed her eyes and bowed her head.

Sitting in the car on an unnamed residential street, Mike and Becca dedicated their relationship together in faith. They laid their love for one another in God's hands and received peace.

"You two are getting married." Christine giggled from the back seat.

"Christine!" Becca laughed and twisted her body to see her daughter clearly. "Don't scare him away, silly. We don't know yet."

***

Becca watched Mike with Christine. Over time, he showed himself consistently gentle, unassuming, and kind. She checked to see if they agreed on how Christine should be raised, including matters of discipline—just in case. His responses checked her boxes, and everything fit into place.

Everything.

Except his parents. Convinced their son was marrying too young and taking on too much responsibility for his age, Mike's parents insisted he should finish college first.

"I knew it." Becca bit her lip. "Of course they wouldn't want you to marry me."

"They haven't even met you. Once we visit, they'll change their minds. I'm sure of it." Mike rolled a small section of his shaggy beard between his index finger and thumb.

First the elders, now his parents. Her focus landed on a potted plant near the window and stayed there. The plant blurred, but no matter. Becca turned the situation over and over again in her mind, as if she could better swallow and digest by rumination.

* * *

The glow of a much-coveted shiny toy, longed for and beloved at Christmas, fades. By summer's lazy days, the prized possession lands in the bottom of the toy box. Becca's childlike excitement about Mike took a similar turn. The more they talked about their future as husband and wife, the more Becca harbored second thoughts. She'd struggled with misgivings for months when he noticed.

In his car outside Becca's place, they kissed another goodbye. Mike whispered, for the second time in as many seconds, "I love you."

A heavy sigh snuck out of Becca's chest.

"What?" Mike tipped his head to one side. "Don't you love me too?"

Becca stammered, clicking her nails together in her lap. "I just said it, like, one second ago." Her eyes averted his. *Don't rock this boat.* Searching for a reason to hurry out of the car, she forced a coy smile.

Mike's countenance dropped. He leaned toward her, placing his face squarely in her view. His forlorn eyes begged her. "I know, I just can't help it. I'm so crazy about you." He held his position as if demanding she look at him and return his phrase.

"I do love you, Mike." The reticence in her voice betrayed her.

"Then what's wrong?"

Becca looked down at her hands, which had become heavily invested in tying and untying knots in the fringes of her scarf. *This feeling isn't going away, so I'm just going to say it.*

"I—" Her voice caught in her throat. *No! Don't ruin everything for Christine. He's the one good thing that's come along. Get with it. He loves you.* "I. . . don't know. . . what's wrong with me." She stressed the *me* part of her sentence—shouldering the blame. "I'm not comfortable with all the 'I love you's.' You say it like, every other second."

"What's wrong with that? I mean. . . if we're in love."

"Nothing. There's nothing wrong with it. I don't know what's wrong with me."

Mike sat back into his seat and turned his gaze out the front window.

"It feels like, as much as you say it, that you're always needing to hear it, like you're lacking. . . confidence. . . or something. I'm just not sure about being with someone who's insecure, maybe because I'm insecure enough on my own."

He swallowed hard. "You think I'm insecure because I love you so much? Come on, Becca, that doesn't make any sense."

"Maybe we just need to take a break." Becca's hands stopped knotting the fringes. Her breath, her heart, her stomach, all settled. *I said it.*

He dropped his face into his hands and wept. Audibly.

Becca's eyes opened wide. Her head shook in disbelief. She placed a hand on his shoulder.

Gathering himself, he spoke through his stunted breath. "I don't understand. My last girlfriend broke up with me on prom night. That was heartbreaking—and humiliating. She didn't even have a reason. And now you're breaking up with me—for loving you too much?" He reached into the glovebox, pulled out a napkin, and wiped his face. "You say you love me. Maybe you just don't know how to be loved."

Tears pooled in Becca's eyes. Both sorry for Mike and angry at herself for causing him heartache, she focused on consoling him. "Mike, I don't know, maybe I'm just scared. Marriage is a big thing. I don't ever want to have to go through a divorce. Please, just give me some time."

"Alright. Alright. I'll try to back off. Let you think."

Becca breathed a sigh of relief. She opened the car door.

"So, how about dinner tonight, is that enough time?" One side of mouth curled up as Mike sent his doe-eyed plea.

Becca stiffened again. She wanted to roll her eyes and storm off. But he was joking. Sort of. Instead, she chided herself. *You waited so long for him.* Propping the car door halfway between opened and closed, she placed one foot on the road. *If I break up with him now, who knows when I'll find love again? Christine could grow up with no father or stepfather. All because I can't handle being loved. Shake off this funk, Becca.*

Shoving the car door all the way open, Becca sprang out, closed the door, and turned to lean in the window. She lightened her tone, conceding to his playful request. "How about tomorrow?" Knowing her eyes wouldn't lie for her, she spun quickly and headed inside.

Mike called out behind her. "I'll call you tonight."

31

Becca

Rockville, Maryland. 1979

Mike called that night. She didn't answer. Another call, and another, tossed Becca between numbness, devastation and determination as she avoided his calls for a week.

Then the phone stopped ringing. He was gone—*for good?*

Another week, and Becca missed him. She wiped away tears and turned her pillow over to the dry side. *I'm not good for him. Please, God, send him someone who will be good for him.*

No one ever came to the door of Becca's third floor apartment. When the sound of the knocker resounded through the sparsely furnished place, Becca's feet sent her sprinting. "I'll get it, Missy." The dish towel spilled to the floor.

The power of his grin could have lit half the country for a

week.

"God said yes." Mike reached for Becca and pulled her into his arms, laughing.

"Wha—"

"I surprised my parents, showing up on their doorstep. They were so impressed that I'd driven a thousand miles for their blessing that they gave it. Plus, a wedding gift."

Speechless, Becca pulled him into the apartment and led him to the sofa.

He reached into his pocket and produced a check. "This, and they're sending a hundred dollars a month for the the first year of our marriage!"

Becca held her cheeks, pressing against them to keep her eyes from popping. She swallowed hard.

Mike stooped to one knee, reaching into his pocket again, and produced a small black velvet box.

Becca's hand slid to cover her gaping mouth. A tear welled to the brink of her lashes and held on.

He opened the box, facing the contents toward her. "I love you, Becca. Will you be my wife?"

A spectrum of light danced from the diamond and teased the brimming tear, bidding it to jump into the abyss. Abandoning itself into the unknown, the tear raced down her cheek and landed on her left hand, just where the ring would be.

"Yes, Mike. I will!" She threw her arms around him and kissed him with grateful abandon.

* * *

In the surreal mist of a new day, one droplet released its

hold on the edge of a leaf and splashed into the dried basin of a bird bath. Then another. The droplets fell, creating a pool. A lone bird perched at its edge and drank, then sang its morning song.

Some choices are like that. One good movement spills onto the next. Enlivened by the unexpected turn of events leading to their engagement, Becca resumed her search for a real home.

She turned down a road not usually taken and saw an apartment complex under construction. After being on a waiting list for subsidized housing for over a year, she recalled reading about a new law committing ten percent of all new construction to subsidized housing. She took the initiative and knocked on the door of the site's mobile home.

Becca was the second person to inquire. As soon as construction was complete, she and Christine received a brand new two-bedroom apartment with income-based rent. After six years of trying—six years of unsuccessful endeavors with roommates, of moving back in with her parents, of looking for just a room to rent, of sharing a place with a houseful of sisters and cousins—six years of trying to make a normal home for Christine, and finally, her prayers were answered.

Becca looked around the apartment from her used dining room table. The living room furnishings were sparse. A neutral plaid sofa borrowed from Missy lined one wall. Two five-dollar square tables pushed together formed a coffee table. Brown and white lamps, also borrowed from Missy, completed the ensemble.

She'd had her eye on a pair of lamps she'd seen at the mall—modern tear-drop shaped ceramic lamps, with dark streaks of teal. *Maybe I'll be able to afford those someday.*

Above the couch, she'd hung her original artwork, a large pencil drawing with the focal point a gentle lion. A lamb curled up to its mane, and around these slept other animals, commonly known to be predators—a leopard, a wolf, and a cobra. She'd practiced calligraphy to copy prophetic verses from the book of Isaiah to the side of the drawing:

> The wolf will live with the lamb,
>   the leopard will lie down with the goat,
>   the calf and the lion and the yearling together;
>   and a little child will lead them. . .
>   They will neither harm nor destroy
>   on all my holy mountain,
>   for the earth will be filled with the
>   knowledge of the Lord
>   as the waters cover the sea.
>   -Isaiah 11: 6-9

She sipped her coffee while reading those lines. *That's how I want this home to be. Safe. Peaceful.*

Sunlight streamed through the sliding glass doors, drawing her attention to the balcony, where her house plants thrived. Becca loved nurturing plants. Buying tiny, affordable specimens, she tended them carefully and they flourished. Each had a name. Charlie. Edna. Violet. Ramone. *They're happy here. Like me.*

To the right of the balcony doors, the galley kitchen connected to a sunny breakfast nook. Decorated with thrifted items in blue and white, this area felt like quaint, like an old European kitchen. The well-worn character of her old table and mismatched chairs provided a welcome contrast to the charmless new cabinets and appliances. Items collected during the years completed the nook's homey feel—various patterns of blue porcelain dishes and service ware, a cow-shaped creamer, and embroidered linens repurposed as cafe curtains.

She rinsed her coffee mug and set it on the counter. *I'll take Christine to gather fresh wildflowers by the edge of the woods today.*

A distinctive sound resounded through the open balcony door. Footsteps, and then the mailbox cover opened and closed.

She grabbed her key and flew down the stairs. Excitement brimmed into her fumbling fingers as she opened the mail-box. *Yes.* She gently removed the package, skipped up the steps and went to the table. *The invitations.*

So many of her friends had married. While Becca thoroughly enjoyed a good wedding cry, touched by the sentiments of unfailing love, she had long wondered if the dream would ever come true for her. *It's my turn—finally.*

By evening, Becca finished addressing the envelopes in her neatest handwriting. When Mike stopped by, they folded and inserted the invitations into envelopes as they discussed wedding arrangements and colors.

Mike said he'd like to wear a white tuxedo, cummerbund, shirt, tie—everything white.

"White? How about ivory?" Becca shifted in her seat. "I have a child. Everyone knows I'm not a virgin. I was so lost all those years, equating love with sex."

Mike's brows came together. "Becca, you're as pure as the driven snow." He smiled. "We both are, in Christ. Let's not worry about what anyone thinks."

"You're right. And we have waited all this time."

The couple had often behaved like horses at the fence, reaching beyond, as if their allotted acres of beautiful pasture weren't enough. When they'd come too close to consummating their passion, heavy clouds of guilt weighed upon Becca for days. Her prayers, full of remorse, easily slipped into shaming self-talk. She'd told Mike she couldn't handle it, that she'd have to back off again.

They'd moved the fence further back from the edge of that cliff—a simple kiss, no making out. Their pre-marriage counselor suggested they limit dates to being in groups with others, and in daylight. Since the new apartment afforded too much privacy, they'd agreed Mike would leave before Christine's bedtime.

Becca brightened. "White, then. I'll sew the dresses to save money." She showed him the pattern she'd chosen for Christine's flower girl dress. "But you can't see mine yet."

They gazed into each other's eyes from across the table.

"I can't believe you're going to be my bride." His smile matched his eyes in intensity.

Becca's cheeks warmed. How she had changed. After hardening against crudities as a child, she'd rarely blushed as a teen. Nor had she dreamed someone would ever feel amazed to marry her. Jesus had renewed her innocence. They would have a marriage made in heaven, blessed, ensured by their love and dedication to Christ. She gushed her response. "No, Mike, I can't believe I get to marry you!"

Rockville, Maryland. 1980

Standing outside the sanctuary doors, Becca watched her bridesmaids, ring bearer and flower girl begin their slow procession toward the altar. She peeked at the guests from behind the door, all waiting for her entry.

Becca's father extended his elbow toward her. His white suit and tie complemented the white in his hair. His apricot shirt enhanced his skin's ruddy tone. He looked distinguished.

But his eyes. Nausea swept through Becca, nearly causing her to faint. She leaned against the wall, closed her eyes, and suppressed the gut reaction.

"Are you sure about this? You can still back out."

"I'm sure."

"Then let's go."

The ornately carved double doors opened. The song changed pace. The crowd stood, turning, all eyes on Becca.

Becca laid her hand on her father's arm and stepped in. Her eyes first landed on the cross at the top of the altar. The flowers, simple, not overdone, led her eye to the altar, and Mike. His smile. She returned his gleaming look, held her head high and proceeded toward him.

Beside Mike stood the pastor, bridesmaids and groomsmen. Coming onto the platform and turning around, her flower girl—her beautiful Christine—took her place. A vision of delightful simplicity in her apricot dress with white lace trim, holding a little flower basket tightly with both hands, she watched her mother approach. Her face spoke of innocence, shyness and uncertainty.

Becca smiled at Christine, trying to send her beams of light and joy. *I'm so proud of you, honey. You're such a good girl.* For a second or two, Becca wished she could jump right out of her body and hug Christine, comfort her, tell her how much she means to her, and how everything will be fine. *I've given her too little attention in the flurry. . .*

Becca and her father reached the end of the aisle.

Mike picked up his guitar and stepped toward his bride. He played a song that made Mike and Becca's hearts soar, a song by a musician whose concert they'd attended on their first date. The words expressed their feelings perfectly on this perfect day.

Becca's eyes locked on Mike's as he serenaded her. For a moment in time, all was beyond what she'd dare to dream.

The song ended and the pastor questioned, "Who gives this bride?"

Her father's voice quivered. "Her mother and I do." He held on a little too long and a little too tight, but placed her hand into Mike's, then took his seat next to Becca's mother.

Becca watched her father until he sat, stunned that he had such difficulty giving her away. *I wish Mom and Dad could be happy.* Becca turned back to Mike, and they ascended the altar steps. *Lord, let them see you in us.*

Readings from I Corinthians 13, and others, ensued, each groomsman and bridesmaid reading a passage. The pastor spoke of love, marriage, and community support for the couple—the family.

It was time for their vows. Mike and Becca had written their own vows but had not yet heard what the other had written.

Mike's vows were valiant and strong. "Becca, I promise to

love and cherish you forever. I will always love you, always defend you, always be there for you. Divorce is not an option for me."

An audible gasp from someone in the crowd created an uncomfortable pause.

Becca hoped that whoever had gasped would witness the agape love that is possible in Christ. She wished for the power of true love to prove to doubters that love until death is possible, in this day and age, no matter what.

Next, Mike turned to Christine and made a vow to her. He promised to love her as his own, to do his best to be the father she needed, and to always love her mother with all his heart.

Christine listened, looking up at him, expressionless.

He kissed Christine on the cheek and handed her a flower.

The congregation whispered an extended "Aw."

Becca took a deep breath. Having written her vows with much prayer and contemplation, nervousness now threatened to erase every word from her mind. *The beginning, start with the beginning.*

"Mike, I promise to love you, to serve you and honor you all the days of my life." She cleared her throat and continued, including portions she'd borrowed from the Bible's Book of Ruth. "Where you go, I will go. Your people shall be my people. . ." She paused, searching for a forgotten line.

In the seconds she paused to remember, the pastor must have thought she was finished, for he spoke again. "I now pronounce you husband and wife. You may kiss the bride!"

It was too late now to go back and say the last line of her vows. *May God deal with me, ever so severely, if anything but death, or the coming of the Lord Jesus Christ, separate you from me.*

The kiss, and everyone clapped. The newlyweds rushed out the door.

In the vestry, they embraced with tears of relief and happiness. With her arms still around Mike's neck, she slipped her rings off, turned them, and slipped them back on. The wedding band should be closer to her heart than the engagement ring. They kissed again.

The wedding party poured out around them, followed by family and guests. Swarmed with well wishes, Becca and Mike greeted and thanked guests until the best man pulled them toward the car to head to the reception.

32

Lena

Sandy Spring, Maryland. 1923

"He's coming, he's coming!" Lena's nephew yelled, running into the house from the front yard.

Grannie looked up from cooking. "Who's coming?"

"Clinton! He's coming up the road."

"Run out back and call some more grown-ups to come in. I'll go tell Lena and tend to Ruth."

Lena had settled Ruth in for a nap when Grannie tapped on her door. Flustered and nervous to hear of Clinton's approach, she bit her lip. Her eyes begged Grannie for advice.

Grannie settled her, taking her by the arm and patting her shoulder. Hearing some of the men in the family assembling downstairs, she sent Lena down to talk with Clinton. "It'll be alright, we're all here."

Lena opened the door to him. "Come in." *Hold strong, Lena.*

Aggie and Henry stood by.

Henry acknowledged him, his body stiff and wary. "Clinton."

"Sir." Clinton removed his hat and, holding it over his heart, faced Lena. "I've come to take you back, Lena. I'll say in front of everyone—I'm sorry for the trouble I caused. I miss you, and I miss the children. Forgive me. Give us another chance."

Lena felt her knees weaken. Every inch of her body betrayed her by longing for those words. She squeezed her leg muscles and tightened her grasp on the back of a nearby chair.

Henry cleared his throat.

Lena jolted to sanity. The look on her parents' faces. . . lessons from Aunt Caroline's. . . the times he'd pushed, hit, and forced himself on her. . . and thrown Ruth. She squared her shoulders and deflected his appeal with stoic pretense. "How. . . how have you been?"

"Been missin' you." He shifted. "Come back home, Lena. You belong with me."

Crossing her arms, she stood firm. "No, sir, I will not."

Clinton's face reddened. His lips pursed. His fists clenched, released, clenched, released.

Lena's body tensed and quickened, her instincts preparing her to bolt. She scanned the room, considering the quickest escape if Clinton were to sprint toward her.

"Where the hell have you been?" Clinton didn't pardon himself for his language, nor look at the men in the house. "Come home, or I'll take the children and you won't see them anymore."

At this, Lena's father stepped in front of Lena, toward

Clinton. George's fists clenched as he moved toward Clinton from the other side of Lena.

Clinton jumped back, out the front door, and ran away.

The men ran after him.

Henry's warning rang clear. "Stay off my property." He seethed as he came back inside, still panting. "He's a coward. Backed down from man. . . but takes his anger out on a woman. A coward, Lena, nothing more."

"I'm sorry, Daddy."

He wiped his brow and stood straight, his hands on his hips. His face softened. "Come here, darlin'." Henry pulled his daughter in for a good, strong hug.

A tear threatened to send her into shreds, but she gathered her wits and wiped the tear away. "Thanks, Daddy. But what am I gonna do?"

"We'll put our heads together." He put his hand on George's shoulder. "We might want to take matters into our own hands—he'd never hurt anyone again. But the rest of the family would suffer for it."

George drew in a deep breath. "Daddy's right. We should take time to think about it. Calm down a bit, talk about it, make a better plan."

"Calmer is better. How in the world you can go from being ready to fight to turning to tend to us, I don't understand." A half-smile, leaning her forehead against Daddy's, reinforced her admiration.

"Remember, I raised a few girls before you."

Lena crossed her arms. "Yes, sir. But I don't want to put this off any longer than necessary. I think we should bring his parents into this, at the very least."

Grannie made her way down the stairs, holding the railing.

"She's sleeping sound." "Everything's alright down here, now?"

"Far from it. Clinton threatened to take the children and keep them away from me unless I come back to him. George and Daddy drove him off the property."

"Hogwash." Grannie flipped her wrist. "Don't you worry. He can't raise those boys. His folks would tire of it, too. He'd be begging you to come take them off his hands in no time."

Lena hoped Grannie was right. She hoped to God.

* * *

Ruth awoke, cooing in the morning light. The now-chubby baby lifted her feet and grabbed her toes, rocking side to side. Lena traipsed to the cradle, exhausted, numb. Selecting a clean diaper, she began changing Ruth's diaper, emotionless, her face blank.

Ruth laughed at her—a darling and innocent giggle, her face shining with anticipation for a fun and loving interaction.

As darkness flees from the light of a candle, Lena's numbness gave way to joy. Looking into Ruth's shining eyes, she couldn't help but smile, and erupt into laughter in return.

Ruth wiggled her legs and toes as if to say, *Play Little Piggy with me.*

Lena gave her some tickles, and, with her lips on the bottom of Ruth's little feet, she blew blubbers. Ruth squealed with laughter. Taking her toes, one at a time, in between her fingers, Lena responded to her baby's wishes. "This little

313

piggy went to market, this little piggy stayed home. . ." At the end, Lena tickled Ruth from her pinky toe all the way up to behind her ear.

Ruth squealed with laughter again.

Lena joined her laughter, their eyes dancing together in love. Picking up her baby and pulling her in close, she kissed into the folds of her neck—to more rousing laughter.

As she turned to reach for her robe, Lena noticed Ruth's bottle on the bedside table. She picked up the bottle. *Warm. Mama must have snuck in and left it while I slept.* Another smile seized control of her lips. Lena nestled in her bed, adjusting covers and pillows to support her arms and Ruth's head as she offered the morning bottle. The sun peeked through the window, drawing Lena's gaze to the trees at the edge of the property.

She loved being a mother, despite the challenge of babies born close in age. When first wed, she considered herself an adult, ready for marriage, ready for anything. Her experience helping her older siblings with their babies led her to believe parenting would be easy. Her father had always been gentle with her mother, and with all the children. Lena never imagined a man would be rough with her. *Boys are not allowed to hit girls,* she recited from rules she learned growing up. *Why would a man think he's allowed to hit a woman?* Lena held Ruth close as she finished the bottle. "I'll never let him have you, baby," she whispered.

The smell of sizzling bacon wafted from the kitchen swelled Lena's appetite. "Time to go, little one." In the kitchen, she sat Ruth in the wooden highchair, snuck a piece of bacon to snack on, and warmed some porridge.

Daddy was in the kitchen having his morning coffee. A

page of his newspaper turned as Lena moved about the kitchen, and he spoke without looking up. "It's time we all had a talk." He looked up from his newspaper. "With his folks involved."

"You think that will help?" Lena spooned porridge into Ruth's open mouth.

"A man's accountable for his actions, and his family is the place to start."

"So, I had the right idea after all. But I'll need you with me if I'm to face them. Maybe more of us. The more the better."

Mama came in carrying fresh eggs from the hen house. "Good morning, angels. Can you lend a hand? I cooked bacon but I need help washing and cracking these eggs."

"Yes, Mama." Lena let Ruthie play with her spoon and joined her mother at the sink.

As the eggs popped in bacon grease, Mama agreed the time to go to the Smiths was nigh. "Grannie will tend to Ruth and the boys while we go." She served up the eggs and bacon. "No sense troubling about it. Let's do what needs to be done."

The buggy pulled onto the Smith's property. Mrs. Smith came out the front door, wiping her hands on her apron. She removed and placed her apron on the porch railing and propped her hands on her hips. "Well, I'll be." She muttered something to herself as her hand went out to greet them, along with a pursed smile.

"Good morning, ma'am." Henry extended one hand to greet her, removing his hat with the other.

"What can I do for you?" she asked, retrieving her lax hand from his. She waved her left arm to the side, directing them to the porch chairs.

"We need to have a conversation with you, your husband and Clinton, ma'am."

"Make yourselves comfortable." Mrs. Smith turned again to gesture to the seats. "I'll summon the men and bring tea. We'll set on the porch to talk."

In a few minutes the adults all had a seat on the front porch with a cool glass of mint tea. Mrs. Smith followed social protocol, in keeping with her typical insistence upon the organized and proper. Mr. Smith had shaken hands with Henry, while Clinton came from around back and tilted his hat, his mother running interference to awkward handshakes by handing him a glass of tea.

Mr. Smith started the conversation. "What can I do for you, Henry?"

Henry explained the situation as a gentleman, with restraint. "Well, sir, seems we have a problem between our children. They need help sorting out a solution." He twisted his wedding band, leaning forward in his seat. "I understand you are church-goers—willing to lend a hand wherever needed." He watched their faces, and having received the desired interest, he proceeded. "Their differences as they are, well, they won't be continuing their marriage. The matter of who is best to raise the children is at hand. Clinton thinks he should raise them, while Lena feels her motherly skills are what is most needed, at least for their early years."

Clinton couldn't keep silent at this. "What's between us is our business. This matter is not yours to decide. Lena has no right to take my boys from me. She needs to come back to me, not hide behind you. Do the right thing. The Bible says, 'What God hath joined together, let no man put asunder.'"

Mrs. Smith spoke up, her body stiff, her arms folded across her chest. "Sir, my son is correct in this matter. This is between them. And you, to try and put asunder what God hath joined? You speak as a reprobate."

Mr. Burriss cleared his throat, restraining himself. "Perhaps you and Mr. Smith are unaware of the nature of the problem. By my daughter's word, and marks I and my wife have witnessed upon her body, Clinton has not behaved in a Christian manner toward her. In fact, quite the opposite. Are you aware of his frequent drunkenness, infidelities, and violent behavior toward our Lena?"

Everyone looked at Clinton, who stared at the floor. His face reddened, his muscles tightened, and his breathing hastened.

"Son," Mr. Smith sighed, "Is this true?"

Clinton's hands clenched. He drew a deep breath and stood tall. "I admit I've had too much to drink at times. You and Mom both know. But nothin' else. Except if she needs correction. If she keeps at me and shows no respect or faith in me. And I've apologized for any wrong, more than—"

Mr. Smith raised his palm and his voice in somber admonition. "Alright, son, enough."

Looking to Mr. and Mrs. Burriss, Mr. Smith continued, "These matters call for reconciliation, with two sides to a problem, as in any marriage. Clinton admits his wrong. What about your side? Do you think Lena ought to have abandoned her husband, and refuse to see Clinton, even after he apologized?" His eyes narrowed. "When a person accuses another of infidelity, the use of a smokescreen ought to be considered, as a possibility, that the accuser is covering their own error. Perhaps Lena has a lover she ran off to see. We cannot rule out that possibility, can we? Maybe in her guilt, she egged on Clinton's anger, bringing him to the point of violence, giving her an excuse to leave him."

At this, everyone in the Burriss party shifted and tensed.

The hair on Lena's arms stood to attention. "How dare you suggest such a thing?" She leaned forward in her seat, her hands on the arms of the chair. "I can't believe you would think such a thing about me. Why, I never so much as look at another man. Clinton's been my everything since I was a child myself. You have no right."

Aggie placed a hand on Lena's arm. "Lena, calm."

Lena sat back in the chair. Her heart beat hard and fast in her chest, her face tingled, and her stomach tightened. She focused on slowing her breathing and pressing tears back.

Mrs. Smith cleared her throat and held her head high. "It appears our children have need of the Lord in this marriage. They should attend church regularly and meet with the pastor. No marriage succeeds without forgiveness."

Mr. Smith nodded in agreement. "In the meantime, the children should stay with us. Any mother who takes her children from their father cannot be trusted to do right by them. She will need to see how her own faults contributed to the troubles between them, before she'll be able to be a good wife to Clinton or a good mother to her children. Clinton has admitted his fault, which is a start for him, at least."

The Burrisses, gape-faced, exchanged glances with each other.

Henry stood. "With all due respect, Mr. Smith, we thought you and your wife would be objective. Your accusation against my daughter is serious, when she has done no such thing. She feared for her life—and that of the children's. Clinton's actions were criminal. He could be jailed for what he's done, and yet you insist the children are better here? Many a man in my position would have laid a heavy lesson on him."

"Are you threatening my son?" Mr. Smith fumed.

Harry turned his frame and intent gaze toward Clinton. "I will say this to you, Clinton." He shook his finger. "If you ever lay a hand on my daughter again, it will be the last time. Do you understand me?"

"Enough!" Mr. Smith stood up. "You are no longer welcome here. Get off my property."

Everyone stood, and the Burrisses shuffled off the porch.

Lena turned to face Clinton. "The children will stay with me." Holding her head high, she narrowed her eyes and spoke with firmness. "You know they should be with their mother." She turned to Mrs. Smith. "I'll go to counseling like you suggest, but the children stay with me."

The front door slammed, then reopened.

From the front porch, Mr. Smith lifted his shot gun in their direction. "The children will live with us."

33

Lena

Sandy Spring, Maryland. 1923

The Burrisses retreated to their buggy. Henry gave the reins a shake and they rode away. "They won't win," he said.

The stars sprinkled light across an indigo sky. Some sparkled strong and clear, occupying their place with surety. Some blurred—as if a hand wiped the first attempt and started over.

If Lena were Starlight, as Grannie and Mama dubbed her, tonight her glow dimmed in the Milky Way's blur—in the dust of splattered new beginnings. Pieces of herself dislodged and lived just beyond her grasp.

With all quiet on the Burriss farm, Lena drew her eyes from the sky back into her room, where she held a fully sleeping Ruth in her arms. The younger children quietly played in their beds across the hall, probably hoping the Sandman wouldn't sneak in to make them sleep. She laid Ruth in her cradle and headed down the stairs.

Daddy slept in his favorite chair. Mama sat by him, knitting a cap for one of her grandchildren. Drawn to the night sky, Lena went outside.

Grannie strolled toward the porch and sat on the swing. Her head tipped back, also watching stars.

Nestling into Grannie on the front porch swing, Lena laid her head on the strong woman's shoulder. She didn't want to discuss any further what had happened at the Smith's place. Enough had been said, all day. "Your stories always give me wings. Will you sprinkle some of your magic on me tonight?" She turned to admire her grandmother's face.

The folds at the sides of her eyes and lips drew up at the question—the crinkles of happy thoughts. "Oh, yes, Starlight. Rich memories are like magic, and dear to my heart."

"I loved meeting your sister. She and her family are a treasure."

"I'm glad, darling. I knew the trip would do you good."

"I'm not too old for stories. I want yours."

Grannie smiled. "What do you want to know first?"

Lena's mind raced. With so much she wanted to know, one question stepped forward and braved a chance. "How did you survive. . . hiding, afraid of being caught and sent away?" Lena slapped her hand over her mouth, shocked that she asked such a tough question of such a frail lady.

Eliza's brows lifted and she pulled her head back to glimpse Lena's face better. "You don't waste time, do you?" She chuckled and patted Lena's knee. Her eyes drifted up and to her left as she searched her memories for details. "When I think back, I think in the language I learned as a child, so I might need a while to find the words."

"I'll be patient."

Eliza spoke slowly, with frequent pauses as she pieced together a summary for Lena. "In my earliest memories, we hid. My mother. . . held me close. . . her hand over my mouth if she heard. . . or smelled. . . someone coming." She paused and shook her head. "The Bogeyman, coming to steal us away." Eliza chuckled. "Fear of the Bogeyman keeps children safe 'til they are old enough to understand."

"He's a useful old monster." Lena smiled.

Eliza's face grew somber. "Mother tucked us away, Caroline and me, hiding us deep in the rocks, bushes all in front of us. 'Hush, now,' she said, 'do not come out until all is quiet, or we come back for you.' I heard horses stomping and voices I didn't understand. We huddled there, holding each other. Then, quiet. We waited there, afraid to go. We fell asleep."

Lena noticed Grannie's lips quivering the slightest bit. Sorry she had asked, sorry to have brought up a painful memory to Grannie, at her age. She squeezed her hand.

Grannie smacked her lips a couple of times and drew a deep breath before going on. "Ezekiel, Mother's brother, came in with food and water, and stayed with us. He told us he would be our mother and father. I cried. I clung to Uncle Ezekiel."

Lena leaned forward and placed her hand on Grannie's arm. "Do you know what happened to them?"

"We never knew. They might have been killed, or forced west, as many others. Missing them broke our hearts as much as not knowing. We wanted to hate the whites for it. But Ezekiel said we must be brave, and imitate them, to be safe from them. To hide forever is to hide in plain sight, he said." Grannie reached for her tea and took a sip.

The words scattered light in Lena's mind, like stars across the Milky Way. *To hide forever is to hide in plain sight.* Childhood Bible stories connected with this lesson. *Baby Moses—*

"Turned out Uncle was right. Sacred Fire lights our lives, made of Good Medicine, not revenge or hate. Forgiving the thing the whites did is Good Medicine. Do not think all whites are the same—he knew good ones, he said. He taught us to speak English. He taught us everything—how to find food, water, even to weave and sew." Grannie's eyes crinkled again. "Though I do not think Uncle really knew how to weave and sew."

"What a fine man." Lena sat up straight and tucked her leg under herself, facing Grannie more directly. "What happened to him? I don't remember you speaking of him."

"He is gone, a long time." Eliza said. "But lives." She pointed to her forehead, then her heart.

Aggie shuffled from the doorway.

"My girl," Eliza smiled. "Come, sit with us a bit."

Aggie placed a shawl around her mother's shoulders and sat beside them in an old wooden rocker. The slats creaked as she pushed the chair forward and back, creating rhythm for the pensive mood.

"Grannie is telling me her memories, hiding in the mountains, losing her parents, and how she survived."

"I saw the glow through the front window," Aggie laughed. "Figured the wisdom of the ages must be flowing from my mama." She winked at them.

Eliza shooed her daughter's teasing with a wave of her hand. "You know, Lena, as time went by, I taught your mother many Cherokee ways. That blackberry tea she makes when your stomach is off, for example. Good Medicine."

Lena nodded.

"Foraging in the woods, gathering leaves and flowers to dry for special teas and dishes?" Grannie's pace grew with excitement. "Sassafras tea, yellow tea, rabbit tobacco and dogwood. . . so many things we use from the earth. You probably never thought much about it."

Aggie chimed in. "Yes, Mama told me, once I was old enough to keep the secrets. The good that comes natural to you, Lena, is Cherokee. Good Medicine isn't just for physical health—it's for our souls, our relationships. The way we are in this home—honoring, forgiving and respecting—is Good Medicine."

"Hmm." Lena's blurred stars began to come into focus. "It goes with the Bible, too. . . '*The leaves of the tree are for the healing of the nations,*' from the book of Revelations. . . and Jesus, he said all the Law and commandments sum into two: '*Love God and love your neighbor as yourself.*'"

Eliza and Aggie chuckled and exchanged a joyful gleam.

"Please, Grannie, more of your story?"

"Yes, yes." Eliza said, her tone reassuring. "Alright, where were we?"

"Hiding in plain sight and learning to forgive."

"Oh, yes. I don't know how he did it. He was a true hero. He gave more than ten years of his life to us, preparing us to safely hide in the white man's world. I suppose all that time he hoped we would find a way to live as Cherokee, to have our nation restored, but he never trusted the notion. He taught us to guard and keep our ways, in secret, for times ahead. I'll always remember what he said before we went our separate ways."

Using a deep voice, imitating her memory of Ezekiel, Eliza held up her index finger as she interpreted the words he had inscribed in her mind. "There will be a day when the world will be hungry, and our people shall bring our fruit to the world. The world will be ready then—ripe to harvest, each bringing her own gift, so that we all may go on. For now, we must be the seed. We must go into the dark soil and, in that hiding place, find strength to push out toward the light, and send roots deep into the soil to draw nutrients."

"Wow," Lena interjected. "That's a mouthful. I need to be writing this down."

"Uncle was a wise ole' injun," Eliza said with a wink. She had a way of saying a lot with a simple cliché, adding her own twist with her tone and twinkling eyes. "He knew how everything worked. He said that if we watch nature, she will teach us. Even the rocks can speak, he said. You must listen. All of nature has a voice, and something to teach us."

"The rocks?" Lena laughed.

Eliza took a breath and smiled again. "Caroline and I, we talked to the bugs, rocks, flowers, and the trees, and listened to see what they'd say." She chuckled. "We could hear them as children. We had plenty of these friends in the woods, mm-hmm. Learned all their names."

Lena and Aggie laughed at this.

"I can just picture the two of you, leaning down, ears to the rocks, eyes aglow." Aggie chuckled.

"Today you might call them fairies. We called them *Yunwi*

Tsunsdi, the Little People. They protected nature—taught us to take only what we needed, not more, not less. Uncle said many Cherokee believed the Little People had been killed by large birds, but we knew they existed. We saw them."

Lena caught herself leaning forward with eyes open as a child, delighted with Grannie's story of fairies coming alive in a forest of flowers.

Eliza grew more excited with her memories now. "They lived in tiny caves in the ground, covered with grasses and flowers. Only sometimes could we see them. As little girls, we took great delight trying to spot them—a fun game. Uncle warned us never to spurn them, for they also had power to bring us harm. 'Fussy Little People,' he said. They helped us, though. They pointed us to the right leaves and flowers in the woods to keep us strong and healthy."

The three stopped for a moment and watched the moon take command of the sky.

Eliza, gaining vigor, spoke again. "Oh, the beauty of the mountains in autumn. We see beauty here, but there? Gazing across a range of mountains blanketed in oranges, yellows, reds, and purples, sparkling in the sun or glowing in the violet evening light, that beauty brought unspeakable joy to my heart."

"I seem to have inherited your love of nature, Grannie."

"Could be." Eliza winked and nodded. "Uncle taught us that as the leaves on the trees change color and drop, we also must change. When conditions are harsh, and threaten survival, as frost does the forest, we learn from the trees. We may need to change the color and style of our clothing. We may need to change form. The wind may carry some of us to another place. But, when spring returns, we will grow again." Grannie's countenance softened. She paused. Her brows furrowed deep into the bridge of her nose.

"What's the matter, Mama?" Aggie questioned.

"The lesson of autumn leaves proved to be the one that saved us. . . perhaps more than all the others."

"Grannie," Lena said with tenderness, "I'm glad you survived those days. I'm sorry you lost your homeland. But I must admit I'm glad you're here and have been here all this time for Mama—for all of us. Is that wrong?"

Eliza perked at Lena's encouragement. "Why, no, Starlight, not wrong. I, too, am glad to be here. The Great Spirit and our ancestors see us here, for they see across the world. They bent trees in the woods, pointing the way, and we followed those trees to Maryland."

"The bent tree. Aunt Caroline showed me one."

Eliza nodded. "Mm-hmm. When I join our ancestors, we will see to it that you and your children find the way. The woman is the center of the family, and the leader. The white man said otherwise. You can lead, Lena."

"Me?"

"I have a new name for you. *Sasa*—protector. You will do all to protect and train your children toward good. No doubt about that. What seems a curse, turn to blessing, for generations to come."

"Protector. Thank you." Lena smiled and leaned into Grannie again. "I'll do my best to live up to it." Lena had not wanted to talk about her own troubles tonight, but Grannie's story weighed upon the present. *How could what's happened with Clinton prove to be a blessing?* Potential stirred like stars forming in distant galaxies inside Lena's mind. Grannie's words traveled from her mind to her heart and coursed through her body, reaching every part. *What seems a curse, turn to blessing, for generations to come.* A flash of energy sped through time and space. *Yes. Generations to come. Sasa.*

34

Becca

Rockville, Maryland. 1980

In the spring, sunshine and flowers and gentle breezes prevail. The heatwaves of summer shimmer off the road, creating a hazy mirage where all seems magical, moist and light. Then comes autumn. Long, cold nights steal the green, inflaming forests in lovely complexity, until the leaves release their grasp and fall to the ground to decay. The north wind blows, and once again, heads must go down to bear the icy blasts.

Winter came early that year.

Becca sat on the bed, head down, holding a small booklet. Letting it drop to the floor, she covered her face with her hands. Instinct rolled her body down onto the bed and pulled her knees into her chest. She wailed. "No, God, no."

A minute prior, the master bedroom toilet wouldn't flush. Having pulled the top off the tank to fix what was wrong, she'd seen a small booklet taped beneath the lid. She'd pulled the booklet loose. With a flip of the pages, a sudden frost crystallized her heart. *Mike?*

She'd walked mechanically to the end of the bed and turned to sit. Icy dark clouds chilled her soul, which broke into pieces and fell to the ground. *Why, God, why? Am I not enough for him?* Their intimate times flashed through her mind. Her new awareness of his mindset—lust—dirtied each memory. He had not been making love. She'd been a fool. *God, is there no such thing as a good man?* Falling back, she buried her face in the pillow and pounded her fist into the bed, screaming. "Why?"

Crying withered into spent numbness. She plodded to the bathroom and blew her nose. The red, swollen face in the mirror reminded her of old times. Hurt, again. Splashing cold water on her face until the numbness matched her heart, she retrieved the booklet from the floor and threw it in the trash. "Garbage."

No. He's going to know that I know. She retrieved the filth from the trash and tossed it on top of the toilet. Turning off the light, she shut the door behind her and went to fix dinner.

She took the ground beef out of the refrigerator and started breaking up the meat to brown in a fry pan. *This hurts so bad. I need to talk to someone.* She forced herself to continue meal preparation. "Onions, I need onions as a cover for crying." She peeled one and began chopping it. *What do I say to our small group? Our friends? I can't tell them his problems. Who can I talk to without ruining his reputation? I don't know what to do. Should I file for divorce, admit this was all a big mistake? Christine. What about her? I don't know what to do.*

Christine came in from playing at her friend's apartment downstairs. "I'm home, Mom. Going to my room to do homework."

"Okay." *Whew, she didn't look at me. I must act normal. She shouldn't have to suffer because of this.* Becca looked at the clock. *Mike'll be home soon. If he goes in the bathroom and sees it, we'll end up arguing in front of Christine.*

Summoning all her strength, she went back into the bathroom and re-hid the nasty booklet where she'd found it. She wanted to scream, rip the nasty paraphernalia into shreds, stomp on it, burn it, and walk out the door—for good.

Becca faked her way through dinner, clean-up and bedtime for Christine. As Mike brushed his teeth before bed, Becca lifted the top of the toilet and pulled out the booklet.

"I found this today." She plunked the pornographic garbage onto the counter and left the room.

Mike followed her into the bedroom, drying his face, which now bore a gray pallor. "This is not mine, Becca."

Becca's body language spoke for her. She sat on the end of the bed, her arms and legs crossed. Her face hardened as she bit her lip and averted her eyes. Inside, her heart pounded into her ears, threatening to burst her head open. One foot bounced violently up and down, releasing what begged to shout.

Mike sat near her on the bed. "I promise. Someone who worked here, building the place, must've left it. It's not mine."

Becca moved away from him but faced him. "Oh, really?"

She paced the floor. "How could you?" Her arms flailed. "What, I'm not good enough? You have to think of someone else?"

She stormed to the bathroom for the booklet. Opening it, she shoved a picture toward his face. "You think this is love? This is lust. Lust. Plain and simple." She ripped the book and let the pieces fly across the room. "If what you want is lust, then forget it. Forget about us. Forget about love. Because I'm not here for your stinking lust."

Mike broke down, sobbing. "It's not mine. Why don't you believe me?"

Becca stared off into nowhere. *How can I believe him? I can't.* A shiver up her spine threatened to turn her entire self into ice.

He gathered himself picked up his pillow. "Fine. I'll go sleep on the couch."

Becca tried to sleep. Shifting side to side, writhing in the covers, she argued with a Bible verse that seemed to torture rather than help her. 'Let not the sun go down upon your wrath.' *The sun's already down. Too late.*

Throughout the next day, Becca churned in the fallout. She managed daily commitments and chores with robotic duty. Switching on the radio to override her noisy brain, she tuned to the local Christian station.

A familiar voice, their pastor's call-in program, filled the room. A sex therapist, the day's co-host, discussed marital issues.

God, this must be from you. Should I call for help? She shoved her cry for help down with a hard swallow. *They'd know my voice.*

Someone else called into the program and described a dilemma similar to Becca's.

"This is not an unusual problem," the guest therapist said. "Many times, young men are not sure what to do to please their wives in bed. They begin to look for answers in magazines and such, and become aroused. Sometimes, this leads to worse problems, even habits. However, problems like these don't have to mean the end of a marriage. With God's help, the couple can receive prayer and counseling, and the marriage may be restored. Let's pray for you and your husband, and then you give our office a call to set up some counseling. Alright?"

She changed the station. *Maybe we can work this out.* Assembling the night's casserole, she pulled herself to-gether. *I did everything right with Mike. I can't fail now. Christine already lost one father. She shouldn't have to lose another.* The casserole slid into the oven as the clock dial turned to four.

After walking to the corner, she welcomed Christine at the bus. They stopped at the playground where Becca sat on the bench to watch.

What choice do I have?

Christine pushed herself up on the seesaw. Her feet swayed in delight, poised at the top. Her playmate pushed herself up in turn. Christine's side banged to the ground and bounced. She propelled herself up again, feet pressing against the packed dirt.

Maybe if I love him better.

* * *

Becca pushed away doubts, scolding herself for thinking them, and went on with married life. She applied portions of love verses from I Corinthians 13 as if they were love potions.

> *Love is patient, love is kind. . . does not dishonor others. . . is not self-seeking. . . not easily angered. . . keeps no record of wrongs. . . always protects, always trusts, always hopes, always perseveres. Love never fails.*

She would exemplify Christ's love, and blessing would follow. She committed herself to applying these words to her situation, and wrote in her journal.

> *I have God's love living in me, so I can love Mike. I will be patient and kind. I won't envy others who seem to have a perfect marriage. I won't dishonor Mike by telling others about this problem. I won't be angry. I won't keep a record of the wrongs. I'll protect him, trust him, hope for a healthy marriage and keep at it. If I love well enough, I won't fail.*

But the potion didn't help her make love. Her body betrayed her resolve, reacting as though he had cheated on her. She persevered through the winter of her marriage, wrapping her coat tightly around her core. Head down, pressing on through the icy hardship, she forced herself to pretend that loving Mike felt good.

But she wouldn't let him fool her again. Though on the surface everything was good again, the episode stuffed into the past like winter clothes in a box in the attic, Becca became hypervigilant. She checked all the possible hiding spots, compelled to know, hoping to find nothing.

Why did he come home late? Where did he go to lunch? How does he smell? Are his eyes sincere?

Finding no proof of further offense, the experience settled to the bottom of a dark, murky pool. . . where anything too hard to handle submerged, only to surface in unrecognizable form—at the edges—when something troubled the waters.

* * *

1981

Near Emmitsburg, Maryland.

Becca lit the candles she'd found in the kitchen drawer and placed them on the coffee table, next to the pink blossoms she'd gathered and placed in a glass of water. *Ah, yes, spring again.*

Standing back, she smiled at the impromptu setting she'd created for their first anniversary dinner. The fire blazing in the fireplace warmed the quaint cottage, found just an hour before. The long view from the living room window framed the valley below and mountains in the distance. "Perfect," she whispered.

Alongside the candles, she spread food from the only restaurant for miles around—Sesame Chicken for Becca and Cashew Chicken for Mike, along with wonton soup, egg rolls and fried rice. She poured a special treat—white wine—into plastic cups.

Becca longed to feel extra close to Mike tonight, after their earlier squabble. She had wanted their anniversary to be deliciously spontaneous, while Mike had wanted a concise plan and a schedule. Becca's loose plan—to drive to Catoctin Mountain Park, rent a cabin and hike the trails—ran amok. They arrived to find the area filled with tourists for a special weekend event. She and Mike argued over the issue, him spouting the virtues of proper and thorough planning, while she argued for the validity of her love of adventure. 'I want to feel totally free,' she'd said. His argument rolled around in her mind, uninvited to this moment. *'Now we're free, alright. Free to sleep in the car for our anniversary. Let's just go home.'*

They'd resolved the spat upon seeing a vacancy sign for this beautiful spot. The late afternoon whiled away, talking about their dreams, Becca's long-held dream of more children—three or four kids to make a 'real family'—and Mike's emerging dream to become a youth pastor. Mike had excused himself for a shower. As Becca prepared the place for dinner, the idea of spending their future in service to others warmed Becca's heart. His desire to live a godly life charged her desire to prepare the scene with a romantic touch. *Now I'm ready for things to heat up—in a good way.*

Mike's voice startled Becca. "Oh, this looks nice." He smiled, tightened the towel around his waist and headed toward the bedroom. "Let me put some pants on, I'll be right back."

"No need." Becca emitted her best 'come hither' glance.

"Oh, really?" Turning toward her, he blushed as he approached.

Why does Mike always looked sheepish when approaching intimacy? No worry, though. I'll take shy over lust any day.

Love. Love is what I want us to share. Pleasing one another. "Sit here." Becca placed a large pillow on the floor next to the coffee table. She had already positioned her pillow in the adjacent spot. Securing a bit of chicken with the chopsticks, she offered a bite to him. "Try this."

Mike reached for her arm and guided the food offering down to the table. "I think I'll try this instead." He pulled her in for a kiss.

The fire crackled and grew, as did their passion. They rolled onto the floor in front of the fire and entwined every part—arms, legs, bodies. Becca, enthralled by the romantic and unrehearsed nature of their interaction, slipped out of her clothes. Her deepest desire, to have him, the two as one, ached to be filled. Intensity heightened as they united on the floor in front of the roaring fire. Her body matched the fire's heat, pleasure coursing through her veins, heightening her sense of touch and commanding the pace of her breath. *I want this to last forever.*

In the afterglow, they lay entwined, breathing in sync.

Becca waited for her body to accept what did not happen. Keeping her disappointment in, she stroked his hair and kissed his cheek. "Happy Anniversary, honey." She smiled, her face still hot with desire.

Mike grinned. "And now for dinner." He stood and offered his hand to help her up. After cleaning up and donning robes, they returned to the coffee table and ate their tepid dinner.

Becca tried again later in the evening, but excitement evaded her. Sensing the struggle on both sides, she wanted to end the night on a good note. "If you just want to watch a movie, I'm fine with that."

"Are you sure? To be honest, a movie sounds good." He

switched on an old movie.

They spent their big night alone on their anniversary watching an old black and white. Mike drifted off to sleep by ten. Becca's foot freed itself from the covers and lashed side to side like a windshield wiper in a downpour.

Driving home the next day, Becca gazed out the window at the mountains and foothills. She'd always loved being in the mountains. They had honeymooned in the Appalachians. *I wonder if we'll live in the mountains.* She imagined their future family. Christine, already eight, would be a lot older than her little sisters or brothers. *Will we have two more? Three? Five, even, because I know we're going to be happy. We're going to be a good family. We'll have lots of fun together.*

A big farmhouse with fenced acres, a garden in the back, a view of rolling hills spotted with cattle or horses, and mountains in the distance, materialized in her mind's eye. Becca reached across the gearshift to take his hand. "I wonder why I haven't conceived yet. Without using contraceptives, I imagined I'd be pregnant soon after we married. Do you think we could start actively trying? Your job is good, and you like it, and Christine's already eight."

"Gosh, I don't know. We talked yesterday about me going to train to be a youth pastor. I don't think we need to try, but if you want to, we can."

"I do, but only if you're ready. We're still young. I had Christine young, and you're younger than me."

"By trying, you mean keeping track of your cycle, right? We don't have money for doctors and tests and all."

"Yeah, for now. Let's talk with Pastor Tom about ministry. You know what would be great? To have the position he used to have, leading a house for young mothers recovering from addiction. I wonder what training we'd need for that position."

"I don't know." Mike kept his eyes on the road. "But yeah, cool. We'll talk."

Pastor Tom, happy to hear of Mike and Becca's interest in ministry training, sponsored them in leadership and continuing education classes. Their new church's addictions ministry grew from small home groups to large weekly meetings, and spread to encompass recovering alcoholics, drug users and codependents. They'd meet as a large assembly for the lesson before separating into small groups for discussion and support. As a model couple, the two plunged into their new ministry roles, eager to fulfill the spiritual call to share God's love with others.

Mike and Becca became friends with Pastor Tom and his wife. Their children had become friends with Christine in Sunday school. The two families joined together for weekend fun and adventure. Becca had been taking Christine for walks in the country for many years. She welcomed the addition of friends to their weekend outings. While the kids loved scurrying around trails, finding treasures and identifying tracks, the adults would talk about ministry, mission work, and the joys and trials of raising a family. Tom's wife, Jody, always had a funny story to tell. Her outgoing, talkative, nature appealed to Becca.

"I wish I could be more like you," Becca confided in Jody after one of Jody's funny tales.

"Like me?" Jody laughed. "Gosh, I didn't think anybody would want to be like me! Why?"

"You're relaxed with yourself, not worrying about what other people might think. You can talk to total strangers like they're your close friends. I've never been good at talking to strangers. Do you think God will still be able to use me even though talking with people doesn't come easy for me?"

"Oh, yes, I'm sure he can use you as you are. Look for ways to share him and it'll happen. Why, I remember myself, new to ministry, and so shy—" Jody paused to see if Becca would react to her statement.

"You, shy?" Becca laughed.

Jody laughed with her. "Yes, me! Well, shy for me meant I didn't know how to speak to a crowd. I've always been comfortable speaking one-on-one. Anyway, Tom told me a trick he learned. He said, if you speak to a crowd, imagine them all with cabbage heads. I said, you're making me hungry." She laughed. "But, he said, if the cabbage heads don't work, focus on what they need. Think about what troubles they might have, and what might help them to hear from you."

"Oh, wow, good one. Why didn't I think of it?"

"Yeah, worth a try. Works one-on-one also."

"Thanks, I will."

Becca pondered the idea while Jody's chatting and storytelling continued. *Sometimes talkers don't notice when people have tuned them out. Then again, having a friend who keeps talking fills up the empty spaces.*

As she walked along with the group, watching the children run ahead and play, she wondered why she didn't recall good family experiences as a child. *In my childhood memories, the kids played in the yard, or close by in the neighborhood. I don't remember doing anything as a family, with my parents involved.*

35

Lena

Sandy Spring, Maryland. 1924

Lena approached the pastor for their Sunday afternoon appointment. This first appointment, to comply with her in-laws' demands, would be to explain the history of her entire situation with Clinton. Her heart beat faster as she approached the pastor's desk. *He only knows what Clinton's told him. He needs to know everything.* She slipped her hands into her white gloves and entered. *I hope this will bring everyone to their senses.*

"Lena," he said, after hearing her story, "I feel for you in this difficult situation." Drawing his shoulders back and setting his jaw, his eyes pierced hers. "This is what I can tell you on the authority of God's Holy Word." He turned his Bible around and pointed as he recited. "'What God hath joined, let no man separate.'" He turned to the next dog-eared page. "'Wives. . . be obedient to your husbands. . .

keepers at home.'" He sat back, closing his Bible.

"Your place is with your husband and children. God will honor your commitment to love and respect your husband. Go and submit to your husband, in faith, Lena. Remember, the Bible teaches us the husband is head of the wife. His laws, like an umbrella in the rain, shield you from the storm. If you step out from under the authority of scripture, you cannot expect God to protect you."

A knot twisted Lena's stomach, threatening to come to her throat. Words stretched apart in her mind. *What. . . hope. . . do I. . . have?* Under the table, she wiped her sweaty palms on her dress. *Reason. . . with him.* She wadded her skirt's cotton fabric in her fists. "But he nearly killed me. . . more than once. Do you really believe God wants me to stay?" Lena's watery eyes rounded, pleading her case to the pastor.

The man of the cloth sat back and crossed his arms and legs. The edges of his mouth turned down in grim resolve. He looked her square in the eye and pronounced his stance. "God will protect you if you trust in Him."

The sting of this harsh life-sentence pierced Lena's heart. Instinct drew her hand to heart. Her head, heavy as lead, tried to fall to the table. She forced her head high and her body to obey her will, excusing herself with appropriate politeness.

After supper, Grannie looked up from her knitting. "What's wrong, Starlight? You've been moping all day."

"Pastor says God's will is for me to return to Clinton. He said staying in the marriage provides protection from God. But I didn't experience protection from harm when I was with him before. The pastor's words condemn my soul and our children to a martyr's end. Is this what God wants?"

Grannie sighed and reached her hand out for Lena. "Will that bring goodness to the next generation?"

"I don't see how any good can come of it. I think I will stay away from church for a while."

"Church can take many forms. I say church is where out hearts agree with our Maker's, together, for love and goodness."

"Yes. Can we be church together, in our family, for a season, anyway?"

* * *

The Burriss family withdrew from traditional church for a season, in solidarity. The members of the church that met in the old white building on the hilltop at the end of the road continued to pray for the wayward souls in Lena's family, while the members of the church that met in the Burriss farmhouse encouraged one another toward goodness and love.

The family sat in their large circle in the living room, singing a favorite song, "The Green Grass Grew All Around." Lena played the mouth harp and the boys clapped their hands to the beat. Ruth swayed side to side.

Clinton came to the door. He tipped his hat as Lena opened the door.

"I need a word with you, Lena."

Polite manners dictated her automatic response. "All right." She waved him to the porch. Glancing at her father, who nodded and moved closer to the door, she slipped out.

Lena and Clinton found a seat on the front porch. The

rocking chair creaked, keeping time with the music inside.

"Would you care for some tea or lemonade?"

"No, no. I'm fine," Clinton said. He produced papers from his jacket pocket and unfolded them. "I have some papers the judge wants you to sign. It's all they need to grant us a divorce."

"A di. . . vorce?" He may as well have slapped her against the wall with his words. Her mind reeled. *He doesn't want me back. Not really. If he did, he would change, quit drinking, show me he means it.*

"Legal, so we can go on with our lives. You're not a wife to me anymore. Why should we stay married? I met someone else. Someone who wants to be there for me."

"What. . . what about the kids?" Lena demanded, leaning in.

"If you'll sign these papers, the judge will grant the divorce. We'll share the kids."

Lena reached for the papers and studied them. "I. . . I don't know what this is saying—"

"I know," Clinton spurt, "those lawyers have such fancy talk, but it boils down to agreeing we both want the divorce. I'm going to have a new bride soon. She doesn't want to have kids around all the time, anyway. I just want visits. You win. Sign it, Lena, you won't have to worry about the money. I'll pay for it. . . go on and sign it."

Trying again to read the papers, her seat poked her, her vision blurred, and her mind pressed her to hasten this disdainful but necessary task. *I've no money for a lawyer of my own.* "The children with me, you promise?"

"Don't worry, Lena. It says we agree to dissolve the marriage. If you sign these papers, I'll never hurt you again.

You won't be my responsibility or my problem anymore."
He pushed the pen toward her. "Sign it."

Her mind in a whirlwind, scrambling her emotions, she
wasn't sure what she felt—pain, or anger, or fear, or the
hope he'd never hurt her again. Love for Clinton might have
lingered beneath, pressing her to please him. Whatever
the reason, in a flustered state, she took the pen from his
outstretched hand and scratched her name across the line.

Clinton snatched the papers away and tucked them back
into his pocket. "I'm off."

A cawing black crow landed on the porch railing. Shim-
mying side to side, the glistening bird cast a beady eye at
Lena.

"Shoo," Lena said, with a flick of her wrist.

The lone bird flew off.

She sat on the porch long after he'd gone. *What did I do?*

The answer came three weeks later. An official letter, for
which Lena had to sign. She and her parents took the letter
to the town lawyer for interpretation of the legal jargon.

He looked up over his reading glasses. "Says here you
committed adultery, Mrs. Smith, and the judge granted
Mr. Smith a divorce on account of it. Mr. Smith is granted
custody of any children from the marriage."

Lena gasped. "The children, what? He told me the papers
said we would share the children. He told me he only wanted
visits."

"Adultery, ma'am, is a serious offense."

"Wait, this says. . . *I*. . . committed adultery?"

"That's right."

"He did, not me!"

"Is this your signature, ma'am?" He turned the paper toward Lena and pointed at her signature.

"Yes, sir."

"Well, you signed papers saying you committed adultery."

* * *

Clinton arrived with his parents. A woman she hadn't seen before sat with them. The barrel of a shotgun stuck out from the rear window of their automobile. He had papers in hand as he approached her. He held them out. "The children, now."

"How could you?" Blood left her head and rushed to her feet.

"You signed it." A half-smile quivered at the edge of his lip.

The boys ran around from behind the farmhouse, squealing with delight. "Daddy, Daddy!" They ran into his arms.

"See that?" Clinton narrowed his eyes at Lena. "They miss me." He turned to the boys, lifting Elliot and mussing Shaw's hair. "Come on boys, I have someone I want you to meet." They moved toward the automobile where the blonde woman sat with the Smiths. "Bring Ruth out. My new wife wants to hold her."

With no idea how to prove he was the one who cheated, or that she had not, or how he had beat her, and nearly killed Ruthie, or how he'd tricked her into signing those papers— Lena turned off. Behind a stone wall, where there is no feeling or reason or light or shadow, she packed Ruthie's clothes and bottles. She packed the boys' clothes and toys.

One word pierced the void as she kissed her children's cheeks and foreheads and released them to Clinton—*Stiyu.*

* * *

Lena pulled a shirt from the clothesline, folded it, and placed the plaid square in a basket. "Do they want to keep the boys as extra farmhands?" She reached for the next shirt.

Aggie nodded as she unclipped a dress and shook the wrinkles out. "Could be. No matter the reason, they will tire of having young ones to raise."

"You're a rock, Mama. You never seem to dream the worst." Grannie's words replayed in her mind. *Even the rocks can speak. You must listen.* "I suppose you're right." Taking the last shirt from the line, she placed the basket on the back porch. "Is that all the chores for now?"

"Yes, that's it. We'll press them tomorrow."

"I'm off for a walk then." Lena scrambled over the hill, and into the woods, to her old thinking spot. As a child, she'd come to this place often. Dappled with sunlight through the tree canopy, a creek ran by an outcropping of rocks. Nature's music played in this place—the brook keeping time, the birds singing melody and the leaves giving applause in gentle breezes. Lena climbed into her seat, a rounded hollow in the rock. *I still fit here.* Reaching her toes into the cool bubbling creek, she watched the water carry leaves downstream. "I will listen," she vowed.

Closing her eyes, she inhaled deeply. Woods, water, leaves, and wildflowers fused into a fragrant memory. The aroma, finer than any perfume, wooed her heart. She sought refuge here when she first fell in love with Clinton. Her feelings had overwhelmed her then, too. The conflict between her prior love for Clinton and her current feelings stirred a great tumult, forcing her eyes open.

She grumbled at herself, aloud. "I'm trying to hear rocks and trees." *I'm so confused. Dear God, please help my babies. Help Clinton be good to them. Help me.*

A tiny wren landed near her to take a sip of water and poke in the ground. Gentle, wise, and loving words rose in her heart.

> *Do not fear those who kill the body but cannot kill the soul. . . Are not two sparrows sold for a copper coin? And not one of them falls to the ground apart from your Father's will. –Matthew 10: 28 – 29*

It surprised Lena to have a verse, committed to memory years ago in Sunday school, surface to soothe her in this time of need. She smiled, but her lips pursed as she produced another worry. *How are they?*

A breeze lifted the leaves from the ground and carried them into the water. Lena had never seen the breeze come so far down the hill, not strong enough to blow leaves from the ground. The leaves floated downstream, each cradled in the water, eliciting memories of the Old Testament story of Moses.

Pharaoh ordered his Egyptian army to kill every boy born of the Hebrews so they wouldn't grow into a greater army than his own. Moses' mother hid him away for three months, then lined a basket with tar and pitch—creating a boat—

and set him adrift near the place where Pharaoh's daughter came to bathe. The princess took to the baby, and assigned Moses' mother to nurse him to the age she could keep him as her own.

Lena imagined Moses in a basket, floating down the river, as these leaves floated down the brook. Her chest pounded in her ears as she considered how Moses' mother must have felt.

She lost her son twice—once to the river, and later, to Pharaoh's house. What great strength and faith, releasing him into the hands of someone who would protect him.

"Please, God, protect my babies. Grannie says I'm the protector. Look at how I failed. Have mercy. Save us. Show me how to be their protector now."

The Bible story melded with Grannie's story. *They hid in plain sight.* Her words resounded in Lena's mind again. *A blessing, for generations to come.*

She looked up to pray. The beauty of tall, sturdy trees—reaching ever higher toward the light, their roots drawing water from this tiny creek—disrupted Lena's stream of consciousness. Within her, a whisper reiterated. *Do not fear those who kill the body but cannot kill the soul.*

At this, Lena stood tall, her feet in the water and her arms reaching up as branches of a tree. "God, you are bigger than this." She marched home.

On her way to bed, Lena relayed her experience in the woods to Grannie. "I was thinking," she concluded, "how Moses and his mother suffered a long time, but in the end, Moses led his people to freedom from Pharaoh's harsh rule—from four hundred years of slavery. The Israelites might have

never escaped Egypt if Moses' mother hadn't made a way
to save him." She leaned her head against Grannie's. "But I
didn't hear the rocks or trees."

Grannie raised her eyebrows. "Didn't you, dear?"

* * *

Lena went to town to search for work. In a small town, the
likelihood of finding a job is equally small. Lena determined
this in short order, with no shop in town having need for
employees. An older sister who'd moved to the city worked
as a government clerk. Lena hoped her chances for work
would be better there. When Abby visited, Lena rode home
with her.

Lena found a job on her first day in Washington. As a
food market cashier, she earned $11.00 per week, more than
enough to provide for herself and three children. Being
away from her children most days would be short-term.
She would learn to drive, buy a car, commute back and forth.
I'll hire a better lawyer. Get my children back.

36

Becca

Rockville, Maryland. 1984

"Come on in, Dad. What's up?" Becca opened the screen door and stepped off to the side, motioning for him to enter.

"Your mother is down near Charleston with her mother for the weekend, looking for a place for us to rent. I'll be heading out tomorrow morning."

"Have you had dinner?" Becca squelched her anxiety at being alone with him. *Be a good witness to him. Show him God's love.*

"No, not yet."

Becca stepped outside her comfort zone. "Stay for dinner with us. The roasted chicken is almost done. Mike's on night shift, so there's plenty for the three of us."

"Don't mind if I do." Her father smiled and winked as he entered.

They chatted through dinner with awkward conversation.

Christine filled the gaps with talk of her latest Nancy Drew mystery.

Becca considered what she might say to help her father turn to Jesus. She expected no real opportunity to talk with him about his faith once he and her mother moved to South Carolina. She chose to approach the subject carefully, because discussing religion, politics—or anything that could step on his toes—could backfire. "Dad, before you move, I've been wanting to talk to you about what God has done in my life. He's been helping me. He'll help you too, if you'll let Him."

Bristling, he pushed away his plate. "Well, thank you for the good dinner. I can't stay."

"You don't want to talk about this?"

"I have other plans." His eyes squinted.

She followed him to the door. Christine ran off to play. As they stood at the door, he looked back. Becca stood in the doorway, holding the door. "I love you, Dad."

He leaned in to kiss her goodbye. Instead of a quick kiss on the cheek, he turned in to her mouth at the last second, slipping in his tongue.

Becca drew back in disgust, fright, and disbelief.

He winked and puffed out his chest. "Bye." He turned and strutted down the stairs.

Becca shut the door and ran to the bathroom. Frantic, she washed her mouth, her face, and kept splashing water to rinse away tears—and the feeling. *What in the world? Oh my God, what do I do?* She did what came to mind. *Go for help.* After arranging for Christine to stay at her friend's house, Becca drove to the home of a recovery group leader.

Dinah led Becca to a private spot in the house. "You look

like something terrible's happened. What's wrong?"

Becca relayed the horrific story. In response to Dinah's probing, she relayed other memories of her father being 'inappropriate,' as Dinah called it.

"Don't speak to him or go near him again. Can you do that?" Dinah showed intense concern, her eyes making firm connection, and her hands on her knees as she sat across from Becca, leaning in. "Christine, either. You must make a clean cut from them at once. We'll get you into the office this week to start counseling. We need to know if he's assaulted Christine, or if anyone in your parents' house has, because she's still a minor."

"Yes, we can stay away. I don't want to be anywhere near him." Agreeing to let Dinah interview Christine, Becca headed to the door. "Thank you, Dinah. Again, I'm sorry to barge in on you like this."

"No, don't worry about that. I'm glad you turned to me. I'm sorry this happened to you. It never has to happen again, Becca. You'll have the help you need."

* * *

Relieved that Christine's interview suggested Dad had not assaulted her, Becca thanked Dinah.

Dinah gave her a book to read. "Make an appointment for you, this week."

"I will, thanks."

Becca devoured the story within a day—a personal account of a woman who had been hospitalized for mental illness, but really she had repressed being sexually abused as a child. After her repressed memories surfaced, she was able to heal and move on with a healthy life.

The book both moved Becca and troubled her. She searched the recesses of her mind, hoping the same wasn't true for her. Coming up empty, except for short clips of times her father showed his demented mind. She set the book aside and brushed her hands together. *Whew. At least I never suffered as that lady did.*

Her parents had moved eight hours away. Distance facilitated the process of letting the abhorrent memory go. *It's his problem, not mine. Why would I need counseling? I'm fine. God loves me. My husband and daughter love me. My situation wasn't as bad as hers. If only I didn't have to see my family, or drive near places we used to live. . . it could all just go away. I'm a new creation, not who I used to be. I need to take Christine away from them and move on with life.*

"Mike, let's get away from this city, the pollution, and smog. My family always wants our help but then refuses to change. Where your parents live is so beautiful. We've dreamt of Florida. Let's just move. Having healthy grandparents in Christine's life would be good for her, too."

Laying the newspaper on the table, Mike leaned forward. "Becca, I'd love that. I've been really frustrated with this job, as you know. Since the fellowship broke up, I've enjoyed the ministry at our big church, but I don't have any close ties there. So, yes, I'm in. I just need to find a job there and we're outta here."

"Of course we should pray first."

Mike smiled. "Of course. But we really have been for a long time, haven't we?"

"Yeah. I guess when you first suggested it, I wasn't ready to let go of what's always been home. Our church, our friends. . . but that's all falling apart lately, too. I think it's time for a change. A fresh start."

"I couldn't agree more." He reached for her hands across the table and closed his eyes. "Lord, you've heard our hearts and our words. If your will aligns with our desire to move to Florida, we ask you to show us. Lead us. Open doors as we seek. We give this to you and thank you for your love and guidance."

"Amen." Becca smiled, leaned over the table as she stood, and kissed Mike's cheek. "Want some more coffee?"

"No, thanks, I've got to get to work."

Southeast Florida. 1984

"Look, only one more exit and we're there." Becca pushed the edge of the map down from Christine's view and pointed to the road sign.

"Yay!" Christine cheered. "Only five minutes to go." At twelve, she had already mastered map-reading and enjoyed converting miles to estimated times of arrival. Christine folded the cumbersome map. "I was only three minutes off. Not bad for a twenty-hour trip."

"It'll be more like fifteen minutes, because I'm hungry." Mike eye-pointed at the restaurant billboard. "We'll pull in there, stretch our legs and grab a quick bite to eat before we find the house."

All agreed, since after twenty hours crammed together in the front seat of a rented moving truck, they felt no need to prolong the trip with a lengthy sit-down meal.

As they pulled off the highway and into the fast-food parking lot, Becca's daydreams carried her a few miles down the road near the beach. The salty summer air evoked images of a charming cottage near the beach, similar to ones they'd seen when they drove around on their visit to her in-laws' retirement villa.

She ordered a burger, fries and an orange soda and slid into the booth. Christine and Mike chatted excitedly, but Becca's attention seemed far away.

She imagined a place with a breezy Victorian-style front porch and a flower-laden picket fence. *I'll decorate with blue and white. Maybe fine one of those comfy, round-armed sofas, a white wicker rocking chair, and a braided oval rug. Christine's canopy bed will look perfect in her room, with a window on the backyard garden and oranges on the tree.* A dreamy master bedroom floated through her mind's eye, with large sunny windows, billowy white curtains blowing in the breeze and an antique chenille spread on the comfy queen bed. She pictured the family going for walks along the beach, enjoying the cooling relief of ocean breezes and inspirational views. Maybe they'd get a puppy. And a baby, *please, God?*

"Becca, where are you?" Mike snapped her out of her dream state. He gathered the empty food wrappers and piled them on the plastic tray. "Let's go. Don't you want to see how the new place looks before dark?"

"Oh, yes, sorry." She laughed at herself and helped carry the trash to the can. Having dreamt about the place many times, even before the trip, with no concrete form from which to imagine their new place, she'd imagined many scenarios.

Mike's father rented a place for them, sight unseen, not even a photo. Her father-in-law described the rental as a two-bedroom house a few blocks from the beach, with a small backyard and an established orange tree. Frightened by the idea of moving into a house she'd never seen before, Becca bravely agreed—to save time and money.

Following Christine's expert map-calling, they found the street and drove from one end to the other.

Becca pointed for Mike to turn right. "I don't see the house number anywhere. Go around the block and we'll look again."

"Are you sure you're looking for the number Dad sent us?" Mike reached for his father's letter with the lease on the seat between them.

"Yes, I'm sure. See for yourself." Becca, frowning at him for doubting her, handed him the letter.

Mike stopped the truck at the four-way stop. "Yeah, it's the right address. I'll turn around and we'll look closer this time." This was easier said than done, as great effort went into to turning the truck around—forward, back, forward, back. Becoming more frustrated with each partial turn, Mike told Becca to climb out and use hand signals to help him avoid hitting the bushes and mailboxes.

Becca blew a heavy breath of frustration. "It would have made more sense to drive around the block." She jumped down from the truck and headed behind it.

After heightened exchanges with a fury of waving arms to "Go" and flattening her palm to "Stop, stop, stop!", the truck finally faced the correct direction. Slowly cruising the street, the three of them scrutinized every possible house and mailbox number.

"I see it." Becca pointed. "See the two mailboxes right against each other?" The numbers barely showed through the sun-worn paint. "But where is the house?" She scanned the property. A small stucco flat—completely devoid of architectural interest—sat on a postage-stamp front yard with a scrubby shrub and weeds for a lawn. The front door displayed one of the two house numbers by the road—511.

Becca's heart sank at the sight. *No beachy cottage with a lovely front porch.* "Where is 513? Do you think we should ask the person in this house?" She looked at Mike. "I mean, I know you're male and all, so you don't like asking for directions, but what choice do we have?" The occasional playful jab she intended to lower their frustration level.

Mike didn't find the humor in her joke. Raising one eyebrow, he agreed.

Becca knocked on the front door.

An elderly woman in a flowery house dress opened the door. "Yes, 513 is behind this house. Go on back. You'll see. The front door is on the left side of the house, and the back door is on the right side, close to the driveway. A breezeway behind my place lets you walk from the driveway to your front door. Most folks use the back door when they rent that unit. I use the front yard, and you have the back yard to yourselves. Oh, and welcome, neighbor."

The new renters surveyed the property. The front door, not a front door at all, lay hidden past the back door, through a cluttered breezeway and down a narrow sidewalk. A huge Magnolia tree towered over the house near the front door. Becca compared this Magnolia with one she and Trista had in their country home. In this crowded space, such a lovely tree could not be appreciated. They squeezed by the tree to reach the back yard, crunching over the dropped brown leaves.

"This yard is about the size of the living room in our last house." An old Australian Pine overwhelmed half of the yard. Becca imagined both monster trees falling on the house in a hurricane.

Christine ran toward the small orange tree. "Look, oranges! Can I eat one now?"

Becca walked ten exaggerated steps to cross the lawn toward the oranges. *Enough space to toss a ball or play badminton.* She examined the oranges. "They look ready."

Christine pulled one off the tree and peeled it, dropping scraps of rind as they finished the trip around to the back door again, where the driveway ended.

Mike lagged a moment in the back yard. "The hedges surrounding the backyard are a nice touch. We'll have privacy."

"Except where we need it most—the commercial parking lot next door." Becca stood in the driveway and spread her arms out, presenting the wide expanse of asphalt between their driveway and the adjacent set of office buildings. "So homey, right?"

Mike shrugged. "Oh, well. Now for the inside." He jiggled the key and turned the doorknob. "Ta-da!" His arm, in grand welcoming gesture, led the way. "Ladies first."

Becca tentatively poked her head in. A musty smell caught her throat. *Ugh.* She stepped into the small kitchen and eating area. Terrazzo floors—a throwback to Maryland's linoleum—with mysterious gray concrete circles around the edges—disappointed. *If dingy were a color, this would be it.*

Christine stayed close to her mother as they entered the

living room. Old jalousie windows lined the back wall of the living room, their thin stacked panes disrupting the light and view of the back yard. Looped carpet in shades of brown gave the place a decidedly not-at-all-beachy air. *More dinge.*

They shuffled as a unit, saying nothing, into the square hallway from where they could see into the bathroom and both bedrooms. *The ceilings are so low, and the windows are so high. This is such an ugly house.*

Christine drew back, nearly shrieking.

Becca looked to see what was the matter. *Dead roaches in the bathroom. And mold.* She glared at Mike. *Your father picked this for us?*

Mike shrugged again. "At least they're dead."

After approving her room, Christine excused herself to go out back to pick some oranges, while Mike and Becca backtracked to the kitchen.

Checking the cabinets and drawers, live roaches ran. "I don't want to live here. I don't even want to be in this house, let alone sleep here tonight."

"The place is smaller than what we had in Maryland, but there's nothing really wrong with it." He checked the air conditioning and turned the thermostat setting down a few degrees.

"It's a third of what we had, Mike, and I hate it. This is not at all what I pictured. But worst of all, bugs. Live bugs. Huge ones. Ugh, no." Becca's face contorted as she crossed her arms and shuddered.

"But what else can we do?" Mike looked under the sink. "Dad looked for the best price in a good neighborhood. He made the down payment for us. We signed a lease, Becca." He stood and faced his wife. "We committed to a year."

"We'll only lose first and last if we break the lease."

Mike frowned at Becca. "Only? That's a lot of money. And start our life in Florida with a bad reputation? Our signature is our word."

"Does that mean we're slaves to reputation? All we'd lose is money." Becca knew she was being stubborn, but she took the risk. *Please, no more dashed dreams.*

"We can't afford it, Becca. I'll be making less than in Maryland."

Becca managed the bills and finances, and knew it, but this situation overrode her good sense. "Roaches, Mike. Roaches as big as rats." She exaggerated a shiver.

"Becca, you're bigger than them. You're overreacting. Besides, the truck is due in by six or we'll pay an additional day's charge." He put his arms around Becca to calm and persuade her. "Come on, it'll be alright. We'll unload the truck and return it, then go buy some bug bombs. We'll clean before we unpack anything."

As they lay in bed the first night in their Florida home, Mike fell asleep in record time.

Becca, keen to every sound, imagined little critters walking on the walls and ceilings and all over their things. Unable to keep her eyes closed, she pulled the sheets close to her chin. Alone on her side of the mattress, feeling a million miles from home, friends and all she knew, sleep evaded her. Consternation turned to prayer. *God, please help me. I really hate this place. I'm so disappointed. I wanted to build a good relationship with my in-laws, but now I can't face them. I can't pretend I'm happy with this. I hate it, Lord, I hate it. What am I going to do?*

* * *

Furnishing and decorating the flat to at least a tolerable degree of esthetic appeal, given her sparse budget, helped Becca focus on possibilities. She delayed job-hunting until school resumed, so she and Christine enjoyed daily walks to the beach. They explored boardwalk shops and packed picnic lunches. They'd laugh as they'd scurry under the nearest roof or bridge when deluged by the daily afternoon storm.

They'd shop with Mike's mother, who insisted they find something she could buy for them, and then savor their afternoon ice cream treats along the boardwalk. Summer passed in simple pleasures as Florida, with its warm ocean breezes and scrubby palmettos and sandy flipflops, became home.

The school year approached. Mike and Becca drove Christine to see the new school. Following Christine's careful directions from the city map, Becca pulled the car into a run-down section of town—the one Mike, now a police officer in town, had warned them was dangerous. Becca stopped the car at the corner. "Could this be it?"

At the intersection, in the worst section of town and surrounded by nine-foot-high fencing with barbed wire atop the entire perimeter, the middle school loomed. Christine pointed to the large sign that confirmed her mother's postulation. "Um, yeah."

Mike shook his head, his lips drawn in. He turned toward Christine and furrowed his brows. "Don't ever skip school.

I don't want you walking through this part of town."

Christine's eyebrows raised, then lowered. "Yeah. No problem there, Dad."

Becca called the school system to request a transfer so Christine could attend school in the neighboring town. She learned they did not sanction transfers. Her choice was clarified—move to the next town or find a private school.

"We can't afford either," Mike insisted.

They sent Christine off to the scariest-looking school Mike and Becca had ever seen.

Becca kept up daily with Christine as soon as the bus dropped her off each day. The first week went well. Her personality being friendly and sweet, Christine made friends the first week at school. By the second week, she realized the kids used drugs and engaged in sexual activity. Christine chose to withdraw from that group and sit alone in the cafeteria. All of this Christine volunteered to Becca as they plopped on the sofa with their daily afternoon snacks.

But it took time for Becca to figure out what happened next. Christine came home from school in a haze. Recognizing something off, Becca tried to convince Christine to talk.

Christine refused to speak at all. She sat, staring into the distance, locked in silence.

Mike came home and doubled the pressure on Christine to open up. "You've got to tell us. Whatever it is, we'll take care of it. What happened?"

She gushed out the story.

"Three boys. . ." Tears pooled and spilled onto her cheeks, though her face remained stoic. "They pulled me into a dark hallway behind the cafeteria. They pushed against me and tried to pull off my clothes."

Becca threw her arms around Christine.

She sobbed and regained her voice. "I cried out, but nobody heard me. I struggled against them, trying to get away, and shouting at them to stop. Then a cafeteria lady came around the corner. They ran off. And I ended up in the principal's office." She looked up at her parents, wiping her face on her sleeve, sucking in breath. "He called them in, but I got a reprimand for allowing them to do what they did."

Mike, who by now paced frantically across the floor with steam to blow, said nothing.

"Christine. You tried to get away."

"Yeah, but even the cafeteria lady, she said I flirted with them. . . that I asked for it." She sobbed again. "But I didn't, I swear."

"I believe you, honey." Becca held her daughter. Looking at Mike for agreement, she came up with a plan. "Your dad and I are going to speak with the principal. We'll set things right."

"I don't ever wanna go back there again." Christine's eyes pleaded with her mother.

"They'll need you there with us as we discuss it, but I won't make you go back to class there." Mike sat next to them and put his hand on Christine's shoulder. "Don't worry. We'll take care of it."

The next morning, they accompanied Christine to school to meet with the principal. After going over the incident, including what the cafeteria worker said, the principal chose not to suspend the boys.

"They've been reprimanded this time, as was Christine. If anything like this happens again, their parents will be called."

Christine, clearly traumatized, could not speak.

Becca spoke up for her. "She did absolutely nothing wrong and should not be blamed, but those boys did. They should be suspended. Their parents ought to know. At least tell us the parents names so we can tell them."

"I understand, but as this is a first offense. Our policy is to notify parents in cases where in-school discipline is ineffective. Besides," he turned his gaze to Christine, "how do we know you didn't go back there asking for it?"

"That's enough." Mike stood. "Come on, we're leaving this minute."

Becca sat in the back seat and held Christine all the way home. "It wasn't your fault, honey. We know you'd never ask to be treated like that." As she prayed for Christine and comforted her, Becca's heart ached. Under neath her calming manner, she also prayed for herself. *Once again, God, good dreams turned bad. Why? Why, why why?*

She blinked away the sheen that filled her eyes. *Once again, Lord, I failed to protect my baby, even though I tried with all my might. Please help us. I feel like I can't let her out of my sight. Creeps everywhere.*

* * *

They found an inexpensive private school in the next town and adjusted their budget accordingly. The school's associated home church welcomed the new family.

Christine blossomed, with new friends, a fun youth group

and babysitting jobs to round out her middle school lifestyle. Mike joined the worship team, playing his guitar, and Becca found her place volunteering in the Sunday School program. They transitioned easily into the church's support groups for addictions recovery, facilitating as they had in Maryland. The season went easy on them, for a while.

Until Mike suffered an injury in the line of duty. The surgeon did what he could, but the prognosis was not good. Mike would be transferred to clerical duty instead of active police work, an assignment he viewed as worse than torture. After months of hard work in physical therapy, Mike and Becca visited the pastor to discuss their new hardship.

They explained the situation and how their vision had always been for ministry, not police or clerical work.

"We felt called to serve," Becca explained, "but haven't quite figured out how to make that happen, or where."

"There's an excellent program in Central Florida." The pastor sat forward in his chair, both arms leaning on his desk, as he addressed the couple in his office. "They're starting a new training program for addictions ministry. They're especially interested in training couples right now, because we need more recovery programs for women—addictions, single mothers, that sort of thing."

Becca's eyes widened. Excitement welled. "Sounds perfect." She referenced Mike. *Will he think so?* "We feel especially drawn to help people who are really struggling."

Mike nodded. "I'm frustrated with police work. I risk my life to make the streets safer, and then the criminals walk out of jail on bond by the end of the day. And sitting behind a desk, pushing papers. . . I'm going crazy." He nodded at

Becca and smiled at the pastor. "Let's check the place out."

37

Lena

Washington, D.C. 1926

The city bustled. High rollers invested in a growing stock market, turning pennies into fortunes. New shops opened along the cobblestone streets of the nation's capital, fed by products arriving from far-off big cities. Women cut their hair—and their dresses—short. Gussied up Shebas and Sheiks jumped on streetcars to ritzy clubs and backroom Juice Joints to get corked and cut a rug. They shook the sequins and fringes of their glamorous high life in carefree celebration.

This glee swirled around, but not in, Lena. With one goal in mind—to win back her children—she worked, returned to her sister's apartment, did her chores, and closed her door, blocking the sound of frivolity. She saved all she could to find a lawyer—one that would make a difference. Going home on weekends became a rare splurge.

This weekend, she was glad she did. She had been at work but became distracted by an inexplicable yearning to be home. Her boss must have sensed her uneasiness, as he sent her home early, saying she deserved a break.

Sandy Spring, Maryland.

As she entered the house, she could feel something different. "Mama?" She wandered through the house. *No one in the main room or kitchen.*

"We're in here, come quick!"

Is something wrong with Grannie? She ran to her room. Grannie and Mama sat close by a small figure on the bed. "Ruth!" Lena rushed to Ruth's side, bent down, wrapped her arms around her body and laid her head against her baby's. "She's burning up with fever."

Mama laid her hand on Lena's back. "Clinton carried Ruth in. Said the doctor told him she has polio."

"Polio? Oh, no—"

"He couldn't put the others at risk, he said. I told him to bring her right in here. We know what to do." Mama handed Lena a cool cloth. "I've been laying cool wet rags behind her head and neck. Here, stroke her forehead with this."

Lena dabbed the cool cloth on Ruth's forehead. "Mama's here, baby." The cloth quickly heated up on the child's burning skin. Lena handed the cloth to her mother. "We'll need more cold water." *Polio.* The crippler and grim reaper of many a child's life. She bit her lip. "Will she be okay?"

Grannie nodded. "I believe so. I sent your sisters to gather healing herbs and plants. We said a prayer." Grannie ran her hand across the four small cowhide bags laid out on the bed—stores of dried plants, one for each of the cardinal directions—north, east, south, and west. "My supply of simples is low. They should be back soon. I gave them each a gathering basket with beads in them, and instructions. I told them that if they accidentally pull a plant by its roots, to bury a bead in place of the plant, and give thanks for the plant's sacrifice."

Lena kept her gaze on Ruth as she stroked her forehead. Her foot tapped with impatience. *I don't need the whole story, Grannie.* She called out loud enough for her mother, who had gone for water, to hear. "Mama, you comin'?"

"Fast as I can." Aggie carried the bowl of cold water into the room and sat it on the washstand.

Grannie watched Lena's foot tapping. She did not adjust her pace accordingly. "Take only a fourth of each plant, I told them, leaving plenty for nature to sustain itself. The dogwoods don't usually bloom this early. They flowered in time. Good thing, as their blooms will give life. I told them to take some flowers from the dogwood, and a couple of branches."

The kitchen's screen door slammed.

Oh, here they are now. Thank God.

Her sisters came in with their baskets.

Grannie stood and patted Lena's back. "You stay with Ruth, Starlight. Keep cooling her down. Your mama and I will brew teas for her fever and spasms."

Lena stroked Ruth's hair and repeatedly exchanged the hot cloths for cool.

After a while, Mama returned with tea for Ruth. She lifted her head and helped her take a few sips before laying her back down. "Let her rest now." Withdrawing a dogwood blossom from her apron pocket, she held the cross-shaped wonder in her open palm. Stroking each velvety bract, Aggie kept her voice low. "Remember how I told you, dogwoods are special? The four bracts represent Christ's head, arms, and at the bottom, where they nailed his feet together. See the red smear on each tip?"

Cordelia answered. "Yes. Christ's blood. And in the middle, the little circle of flowers is his crown of thorns."

Grannie entered, carrying a basket. "The leaves of the trees are for the healing of the nations," she said. "It may take some time, but she'll be alright. She pulled the newly picked Rabbit tobacco from her basket. Everlasting Life, they call this. Tea made from Rabbit tobacco will help her breathe. Laying soaked leaves from this plant on her muscles will ease aches or spasms. Come on, girls, I need you back in the kitchen. Lena can watch over Ruth while we prepare all she needs."

Soaking leaves and cloths in teas made from these natural herbs, they alternated cooling cloths on her neck and forehead with heated cloths over her body and legs. After warming her muscles, they massaged them several times each day.

Daddy and George brought in some large rocks. Using long strips of bedsheets, they tied one end to each of Ruthie's extremities, and to each rock on the floor at the corners of the bed, creating a traction system to preserve Ruth's spine and leg length. When Ruth had trouble breathing, Daddy and George created a way to rock the bed from head to foot, so that gravity could help her lungs work. They brought in a large log and laid it sideways under the center of the bed. The log lifted each end of the bed a few inches off the floor, creating a rocking cradle. Any of them could sit by the end of the bed and easily rock it.

The Burriss family took turns staying by Ruth, providing nourishment, herbal preparations, changing her position and rocking her. Constant prayer backed up their treatments, for several weeks, in round-the-clock vigil.

Lena let her job in the city go, staying home to care for Ruth.

At last, she spoke, her weak, crackly voice calling out, "Ma. . . ma?"

Lena's heart lept within her. "I'm here, baby. I'm here." She placed her hand on her girl's chest and patted.

Ruthie could say no more.

Ruth continued to sleep most of the time for the next two weeks, gradually staying awake longer periods of time. Pureed foods with added liquids helped strengthen her through this time. The family took her into the fresh air and continued helping her move her body so she could retain her muscle length and strength.

One evening, as the last ray of sunlight crept along the bedroom wall, Ruth spoke a sentence. "Mama, I sick."

"Yes, baby, but you're getting better."

Ruth cleared her throat. "Daddy and other Mommy go'ed out. Not come home. Shaw and Elliot and me got hungry.

We found somethin' to eat in the trash at the store."

At this news, Lena's blood ran hot, heating her face, her neck, and rendering her arms tingling. *My babies left on their own?* She patted Ruth's arm, mustering the strength to sound calm for her baby. "I wish I could have been there to get food for you."

"Why you not, Mama?"

"I didn't know they left you, but I'm glad I've got you now." Lena bit her lip, knowing she'd given a lame excuse that didn't answer her daughter's valid question.

"Okay, Mama."

* * *

It was two months before Clinton brought Shaw and Elliot to visit. Lena chose a time to ask them about Ruth's story.

"We're not supposed to tattle, Mama." The older boy squeezed the reminder into Elliot's hand.

"Ow!" Elliot frowned and pulled away. He studied Shaw's face. "Daddy said no, Mama."

Lena remained calm for her children's sake. but internally fumed throughout the day. When Clinton arrived to take the boys home, she fell silent. The anger flashing from her eyes must have reached his notice.

"Don't worry, I don't want the girl." Clinton spit on the ground and kicked dirt over the spittle. "But the boys belong to me."

Lena swallowed hard. "Why did you leave the children alone—and without food?"

Clinton half-cocked his face and squinted his eyes. "Them boys been feeding you stories?"

"No. You've got them trained—too scared to talk. Poor Ruthie told me, but she didn't mean any harm in it. She had just broken her fever."

"Must've been the fever. Don't pay her no mind." He whistled for the boys.

The boys carried a chicken around from the backyard, their faces aglow with delight. Hearing his whistle, they looked up. Their expressions dropped in unison. Shaw looked at Elliot, who let the chicken go. They climbed into Clinton's truck.

Lena stooped down and hugged them goodbye. "Take good care of each other, boys. I love you so much." Regaining her stance, she squared Clinton in his eyes and spoke with quiet firmness. "Don't leave these boys alone. If you have to go somewhere, I'm their mother." She placed her hand on her chest. "Bring them to me." She snapped around and marched toward the porch. With distance between them, she waved goodbye to Shaw and Elliot from the porch.

* * *

Grannie swirled the remaining drop of tea around her dainty cup, surveying the pattern as though she could see Lena's future therein. "You must go on."

Lena raised the teapot and offered to refill her grandmother's cup. "Ruth is here, that's good. But the boys—I worry about them. What kind of men will they become if he leaves them to stray like cats?" Returning the teapot to the center of the table after refilling their cups, she propped her elbow on the table and cradled her chin in her hand.

Grannie sipped her freshened cup of tea, then folded her

hands on the edge of the table. Her piercing brown eyes transfixed as she answered her question. "At creation, the Creator told the trees to stay awake for the first seven days. The pine, the cedar, the holly and the laurel stayed awake. The ones that didn't, well, now they lose their leaves in the cold. Stay awake, Lena, and watch. Be evergreen."

Awake. The image of an evergreen tree lit Lena's mind, brilliant emerald in a dark snowy forest, awake and stately through the night. "Stay awake for seven days?" She laughed.

"What is a day?"

Lena nodded. "I know, that's not the point." She pushed pieces of crust around on her plate. "I fell asleep—into a dream state—when I met Clinton. But I'm awake now. Your stories. . . well, amused me, when I was a child. Now they seem so mysterious. I need to hear them again. How do I know if I'm to change colors with the seasons, or, like you say, stay green?"

Eliza pointed to a spider spinning a tiny web on the daffodils in the centerpiece. "Be the Water Spider. Among all the animals, the Water Spider alone, though very small, was clever and brave. That clever spider wove a *tusti* bowl to carry a coal on its back, bringing fire across the water to earth."

Remembering the story Aunt Caroline told her, Lena scratched her head. *Carry a burning ember?* "I can't just go over there. But that's not what you mean, is it?"

"No, dear." Grannie folded her hands. "The Water Spider thought of a way."

Lena stood and picked up her plate and fork. Carrying them to the sink, she shook her head. "Honestly, Grannie, I wish you'd just tell me outright."

Azalea blossoms and daffodils traded their color into green as spring relented to the full, hazy days of summer. Grandpa Burriss carried Ruth outside to a little chair where she could watch the goings-on of the farm. Sometimes she'd scoot down onto the grass to look up at the clouds in the sky for shapes—one of her favorite games.

"Dat cloud bunny." Ruth looked up at her great-grandmother. "Tell me 'bout bunny and turtle."

A sky filled with white, fluffy clouds made stories flow from Grannie's imagination. She sat with Ruth most mornings, opening up more than she used to talk in the days of her secrecy. But as she told her story, her words jumbled. "And lettuth, no, carrots walked, no, yeth, phrryba. . .gonro. . . aye." Attempting to stand from her chair, she tumbled onto the grass.

"Grannie?" Ruth tugged on Grannie's dress, then cried out for help. "Mama!"

Lena, hanging laundry nearby, sprinted to them, calling out for others.

Within a minute the men arrived at her side. They carried Grannie into her room and laid her on the bed. One went for the doctor, while the others tended to her.

The doctor examined Eliza while the family waited outside the door. Before long, the doctor rejoined the family in the living room. He placed his worn leather bag on the table and dropped his stethoscope into it, clicking the bag closed. His deft fingertips pinched one button of his black suit coat into its buttonhole. His lips pressed tightly, turning down at each edge, and his eyes, as he looked up, bore a hint of sadness.

Addressing Henry and Aggie, he placed his hand over his heart. "I'm very sorry, but Eliza has suffered a stroke."

Aggie's knees faltered. Holding the back of a chair, she looked at the floor. "Will she—"

"She needs rest and hydration." Doc patted his brow with his handkerchief and tucked the moistened cloth back into his suit pocket. "Help her sit up to drink when she's awake. Moisten her mouth with a wet cloth if she cannot drink. Prop her right arm and leg above her heart, to keep the swelling down, and move them for her daily. Other than that, we wait and see. She could recover, or she could have another stroke and pass on. Too soon to tell." He reached for his hat from the coat rack.

Henry put his arm around his wife, holding her securely. "Thank you, Doc. We appreciate you coming by on short notice." After seeing the doctor out, Henry called the family together.

They gathered around Grannie, praying and caring for the one who had prayed and cared for them.

She awoke the next day, unable to speak nor swallow with any ease. The right side of her body remained completely flaccid. She could gesture with her left hand, and the left side of her face seemed to show her emotions. More often than not, she waved off offerings of food and water.

Lena entered Grannie's room early the next Saturday evening. She pulled the curtains closed, washed her grandmother with warm soapy water and a towel, and slipped a clean nightgown over her—all while protecting her privacy. Brushing Grannie's long silver hair, Lena hummed tunes she'd heard her grandmother hum. Fluffing pillows the way Grannie preferred—one under her neck and another under her knees—Lena relayed news from the day, speaking without pauses, so Grannie wouldn't feel the need to respond between each one.

As the room grew darker, Lena rolled a blanket to support Grannie's paralyzed right side. She placed her arm, hand and leg higher than her heart, as Dr. Bird had advised. A candle lit at bedside, Lena enjoyed the peace, the quiet, and the shadows dancing along the walls. With Grannie's hand in hers, Lena whispered, "I love being with you. You've always been the strong one. Wise, loving. For all of us."

Lena watched Grannie's face. A certain sadness clouded Grannie's weary eyes. Her face looked pale and drawn. *Does she want to go?* At times, Lena could almost hear Grannie's ancestors calling—*Eliza.*

"Grannie, you have many stories yet to tell. Please, fight back." Lena's eyes wandered around the dimly lit room, resting on a picture on the wall, a familiar old stereoview taken during the Civil War. "Like Granddaddy Lloyd. I need to know more about him. I know he made you proud, fighting that bloody war to his death." She smoothed a hair out of Grannie's face. "You told me he fought for unity, to set the oppressed free. . . and for me, though I didn't yet exist. But I want to hear how you met. How you fell in love. How you worked through problems."

She waited for Grannie to respond. *If I were in your situation, I wouldn't like it. Needing help to eat, drink. . . to do everything, and not be able to speak. I would probably want to go.*

The old cross on the wall, made of twigs held in place by woven clover strands, drew her attention. *Please, Holy and Great Spirit, heal Grannie. Or bring her home to You.*

Grannie's voice surprised Lena. "Sa. . . sa." Gazing straight into Lena's eyes, her crackling, dry voice strained a message. "Want. . . home."

"You want to go home? I guessed as much, but we still want you here, if you will, please." She longed for more, for an ounce of Grannie's wisdom and strength. Kissing her forehead and squeezing her hand, Lena snuggled in next to her in bed. After several long, slow breaths, she whispered. "But I understand if you want to go."

* * *

The morning sun kissed the paper-thin curtains, letting a gentle breeze drift across the room. Aggie combed her mother's hair and straightened her gown. Leaning over her to kiss her forehead, she whispered, "You were always here for me. May God grant me the strength to live up to your example." She dabbed a tear with her handkerchief and, hearing a sound behind her, glanced over her shoulder.

Lena stood in the doorway. "She's gone, Mama?"

"Yes, already, before I came in this morning."

"Oh, Mama. I'm so sorry."

The two held one another. They made their way to the porch. The sun, just rising, cast a gentle glow on the horizon. A robin's song greeted the day. Lena broke the long silence.

"How are you, Mama?"

"I miss her, Lena. Already. We've been together a long time. I've never been without her."

Lena fought the urge to weep, bringing all she had to support her mother. "Grannie's always been such a strong woman."

"She would do anything for us. I don't think she had any regrets."

"She gave me her Appalachian trip—the one she'd saved for. She never saw her sister again. Grannie knew better than I did. I needed the visit, and she didn't think twice about giving her trip money to me." Lena looked toward Grannie's room, where her body awaited burial preparation. "I will honor you always."

A whisper returned, not in her ear, but in her heart. *Never forget, Sasa. We are Aniyunwiya.*

"I will never forget what I learned from her."

"Nor I."

Ruth wobbled onto the porch from inside, her first independent steps since polio. "Mama and Grams." Ruth pointed to the sky. "Grannie fly!"

"Ruth, you're walking!" Lena reached out to welcome her girl to join them.

"Grannie woke me. I followed her here. Did you see her? She kissed you and flyed away."

38

Becca

"Folks, we have a new couple here in training—Mike and Becca. Give them a welcome."

Chairs screeched along the tile floor, and men in the program lined up to greet the new couple. "Welcome, brother. . . welcome, sister."

"Alright, everyone, let's get started."Attention turned to the large chalkboard, at the open end of the U-shaped teaching area, where the instructor, Bronson, cleared his throat. "Today we look at our family of origin. Most of us are adults and have our own family, but we all came from a family. The family you grew up with is your family of origin. We will look at that family, to see what we learned there. Draw me a picture of your family of origin."

He drew an example of a house-shaped box, with stick

figures inside. "Put them all in there if they were people who lived in the house you grew up in. Draw them in stick figures if you want. How well you draw doesn't matter. Represent what went on. Was Dad never home? Maybe he goes outside the house, off in the distance." He drew a large stick figure outside the box. "Was Mama in charge, or big brother? Draw the one in charge up at the top of the house." He drew a stick figure with a skirt in the pinnacle of the house-shaped box. "You can use a few words, but mostly try to draw it."

Bronson talked about family rules, functional versus dysfunctional relationships, and something called the Daily Moral Inventory or DMI. Everyone in class used the DMI form daily, for an honest self-examination of personal attitudes from the last twenty-four hours.

"Thinking about each of these attitudes, one at a time," Branson continued. "Ask yourself—Did I have an attitude of resentment yesterday? If so, put an X. If you had an attitude of gratitude all day, put a check. Then move on down the list. When you're finished, ask God about each attitude. Will you forgive me for holding resentment against so-and-so? Is there something I need to do reconcile with so-and-so after what happened yesterday?" He sat his chalk on the ledge of the chalkboard and roamed about as he spoke, making eye contact with the men in the room.

"This is not a time to tattle what someone did to you. This is a time to take responsibility for yourself. Own your choices—they're yours. No one forced you to have the attitude you had. Can someone make you think something? No. Thoughts are your choice. Attitudes are your choice. Ask for forgiveness, and ask God what to do about it. When you finish, record your insights in your journal. Bring the journal to group with you tomorrow, along with your family of origin assignment. We'll talk more about how these two—the DMI and your family of origin—relate to each other, tomorrow."

Morning class ended with a prayer circle, more hugs, and work assignments. Bronson called Mike and Becca to meet with him for orientation to ministry training. They walked up the path to a larger meeting room in the retreat center.

"No one in the program, whether in rehab or ministry training, spends all day in class, group, or reflection. Work is required." Bronson handed them each a map of the grounds and pointed out each work area as they walked the grounds together. "The construction crew meets here, while the cowhand teams, canning, baking, and landscaping crews head here after class." He turned his attention to Mike. "You'll be assigned to the print shop. We print a newsletter every month and our curriculum for the residents' binders, like the one you've got there."

Becca's binder, already reviewed, contained several workbooks. The rudimentary material—typewriter style print, and hand-drawn, stick-figure illustrations—suggested The Center's print shop hadn't yet met the computer generation.

"Becca, you'll oversee the cleaning crew."

Becca's eyebrows raised, then squished together as she processed the unexpected twist. *Overseeing a cleaning crew is ministry training?*

"Every job here is essential." He smiled as if he knew the assignment would be hard to swallow. "The orange groves bring in a substantial amount of the funding for the program. The cattle ranch brings in funds and food for men in the program. Beyond just funding, though, the work program provides a testing ground for the men. It's easy for them to think everything's fine when they're in class or groups. Their problems surface at work. Working together helps them recognize and get help with their real-life issues while they're here. Otherwise, they tend to get what we call, 'So heavenly-minded that they're no earthly good.' Religion can be an addiction, too. We aim to get to the root of that problem."

"That makes perfect sense." Becca breathed in the farm-fresh air—part cow manure, part orange blossom—and recalled how she'd dreamt of life on a farm. *The manure wasn't exactly part of the dream, but I'll take it.* "I don't mind cleaning crew supervision," she said. "I had my own cleaning business. If that experience can help the program and the men, I'm happy to."

After orientation, Becca searched for her cleaning crew. She reviewed Bronson's directions. *Down the dirt road, left at the dining hall, past the print shop, to the last cottage on the left before the pasture gates.* She found the cottage, its door propped open and the unmistakable aroma of pine cleaner wafting from a bucket on the porch. Becca smiled at the familiar scent. *Closest thing to the smell of Christmas in Florida.* She knocked on the doorjamb. "Anybody here?"

Stepping in, an affront to her senses made her stop. The pine scent shrouded a deeper, ingrained aura of wet wood, mildew, and old dust. She looked around from her stance by the door. Dust clung to paneled walls, ceilings, and windows—a half-inch accumulation on the cobwebs in the corners. A double bed with a deeply indented mattress, bedecked in a shabby gold-flowered bedspread, served as the focal point in the main room. A small table and two chairs completed the setting, their chrome legs crumbling from a flourish of rust.

Becca braved a few steps to peek into the kitchen, calling out again. "Hello?" The kitchen wall housed a refrigerator, sink, and hot plate. She gasped. *Roaches—the size of prehistoric giants.* She took a step toward the main room. *Guests have been sleeping in this cottage? I don't even want to be here in the middle of the day.*

The *woosh* of a toilet flushing in the other room confirmed the presence of life. Ned emerged, drying his weathered hands, and using the same paper towel to wipe the sweat from his deeply wrinkled brow. He looked surprised to see her. "Yes, ma'am, can I help ya?"

"Hi, I'm looking for the cleaning crew."

"Well, you found it, ma'am. Well, me and Jorge. He's cleanin' the cottage next door. What can we do for ya?"

Becca smiled. "Bronson sent me. He assigned me to oversee the cleaning crew."

Ned's jaw dropped and his eyes widened. He stood, gape-faced, for three long seconds. His jaw snapped shut to regain his composure. Terse, but buttered with manners, he stuttered, "Well. . . ma'am, please—wait right here a sec. I'll go fetch Jorge."

He scurried out the door before she could respond, sprite for a guy who'd been drinking for most of his sixty years.

"Jorge, what the hell ya doin'?" He shouted, approaching the adjacent cottage.

Becca overheard. She stepped onto the shared front porch. Looking down the road, she saw Ned hobbling along, trying to catch up to the one who must have been Jorge.

Jorge shouted without turning around. "I been puttin' up wit lots a tings since I got ta dis place, but not dis!" His arms flailed. "Ain't takin' orders from a mujer!"

Stunned, Becca paused. In the suburbs of Washington, D.C., females routinely ascended to supervisory levels. She had never met a man who believed a woman should not be in charge.

Ned abandoned his attempt to persuade Jorge to return. Turning back toward Becca, he disregarded Jorge's blow-up with the wave of his hand. "Don't worry, he'll be back. Or, he'll be hittin' the grade ."

The grade. The 17-mile dirt grade led to paved road, but town was another ten miles from there. "Hitting the grade" is what the men in the program could choose if they changed their mind about recovery. That is, if they didn't mind walking twenty miles among the twelve-foot long gators and throngs of mosquitoes, and without streetlights in darkness as impenetrable as a concrete wall.

"I am sorry, ma'am, we're not used to women around here, much less havin' one in charge." Ned stopped in front of Becca, looking truly apologetic for Jorge's behavior. "So, what do ya want us to do?"

The founder and Bronson both warned me this could happen, that being the first woman in the training program wouldn't be easy. Attempting to adjust to the deep south's more archaic ways with grace, she chose to give Jorge's reaction no extra attention.

Ned stood waiting, his expectant eyes fixed upon her.

Becca smiled and placed her hands on her hips. "Okay. First, tell me what you've been doing to clean these places."

He answered without hesitation. "Well, we vacuum, dust,

wipe counters, clean and stock the john, and make beds." With a sucking and clicking sound, he spat a dark wad from the side of his mouth to the ground and looked back at her without flinching. "Then we're off to the retreat center, where there's plenty more rooms to clean."

Becca resisted the urge to gag at the wad of wet, brown conglomeration of tobacco and sputum on the ground. She wished she hadn't seen the ungodly spectacle and made a mental note to walk the other way when leaving. A sand-filled flowerpot on the porch spilled over with cigarette butts—another stench. *A woman in charge means changes are in store for this cleaning crew. The families deserve better than this.* She turned to inspect the cottage rooms further as she composed her reply. "Okay, I'll have a look around, and we'll make a plan from there."

Beyond the musty smell, she noted more dusty cobwebs atop the curtains and doorways. All around. Cobwebs. Roach feces and eggs. She shuddered and forced herself further into the bathroom. Behind the mildewed shower curtain, charcoal gray grout lined the square pink tiles. More mildew and rust stains surrounded the drain. Daring to pull the sink's plug out an inch or two, she held her breath at the sight of black slimy threads hanging into the drain.

She'd seen enough. Patting the bedspread on her way out confirmed her suspicion. A cloud of dust chased her outside, where she sneezed uncontrollably. She found Ned in the cottage next door. "You've finished cleaning here today?"

"Yep, perdy much, ma'am."

"Okay, so here's what we'll do. We can't do everything today, but we're going to start deep cleaning, until you'd be proud to have your mom, your daughter or your grand-kids stay here.”

"But, what's wrong with it?" Ned shifted his stance, looking bewildered and annoyed.

"Well, let me show you." She pointed out one problem, then another. They headed to the bathroom. "And look at the grout and mildew."

"It won't come off. I tried." Ned's face was red and sweaty. He pulled some toilet paper off the roll and wiped his forehead.

Drawing from her experience with grout, she retorted, "Grab a toothbrush, I'll show you how."

He stared at her.

Is he angry? Confused? She decided to deal with the matter later. "And the bugs—"

"Can't help that, this is Florida." Ned's attempt at submissiveness met a swift end. "Besides, look at the space under the door, no way you can keep 'em outta here. And there's an exterminating crew." His face contorted into a troll-faced smirk.

He looks proud of himself for thinking of another crew to blame. She cleared her throat. "Let's go take a look at the other places, and then I'll work on a schedule for deep-cleaning."

The tour was informative, a firsthand witness of the conditions families endured on their weekend stays. Room after room, musty dust assaulted the nose and cobwebs lingered around the edges of the rooms and windows—all terribly short of clean. *It's been a long time since anyone in the cleaning crew had a scrupulous eye for a thorough, proper cleaning.* The longer Becca's list grew, the quieter Ned became. She hoped he wouldn't hit the grade with Jorge.

This would be a tough job for a dedicated crew.

* * *

She tossed her notebook on the table and stepped out back to see Shep. The family's Airedale terrier greeted Becca with excitement, the back half of her body wagging and her strong front paws and barrel chest bounding up onto Becca's torso. "Down, girl," Becca entreated, lowering Shep's legs to the ground and petting her head and ears. Throwing an old tennis ball, Becca raced Shep through the yard toward it.

Hearing distant thunder, Becca looked toward the sound. Across the field, beyond the neighbor's farm, a lone mass of storm clouds punctuated the otherwise clear view. Steel gray diagonal lines shot from the clouds' massive dark underpinnings toward the ground, blurring at the edges. Within the confines of the monstrous disturbance, lightning flashed, thunder crashing on its heels. Above it, a huge column of gleaming white mounds of cottony clouds burgeoned high in glorious splendor.

No wonder the ancients equated storms with angry gods. Becca pulled up a chair to watch. Knowing she would need to take cover soon, she savored the moment of cool breeze ahead of the storm.

The sliding glass door squeaked across its metal rail. Christine stepped out, home from school.

Shep ran to her, jumping and whining with joy.

Christine bent down, giving Shep a good belly rub, to which Shep gladly submitted, sprawling on her back with moans of appreciation.

Becca smiled and reached her arm out to Christine. "Grab

a chair and we'll watch the storm."

Christine dragged a folding chair from the storage room. She pushed her long brown waves behind her shoulder and kicked her shoes off by the edge of the patio.

"Mom, I never knew you watched storms without me. Awesome, isn't it?"

Becca nodded. "The breeze feels so good. The rain's almost to the Bradford's place—only a minute or two before we'll need to run for cover."

Christine placed her chair next to her mom's.

"How was your day?" Becca truly wanted to know, but the daily question had become a game—a predictable, amusing routine in which Christine evaded Becca's every attempt to pry into her school life.

"Fine." Christine pressed her lips together, the edges tipping up. Her brown eyes twinkled with impish delight.

"Mm hmm. And what did you learn today?" This next question, as usual, furthered the game.

"Nothing." Christine flashed her satisfied smile.

"Becca shook her head and laughed. "Let me guess. You're a whiz in science, so you aced the test, but you got bored in history, so you studied the Bradford's son instead." She eye-pointed toward the storm, which now swept across the Bradford farm.

"Not too far off." Christine crossed her arms. Her face waxed sullen as she watched the Bradford horses run toward cover in the barn.

"Well, since you didn't learn anything at school, tonight you'll learn how to cook fried chicken. How's that sound?"

Christine looked at Becca, her face lighting up. "You mean we don't have to go to the dining hall tonight? Good. I like being home, just us. But me, cook chicken?" She scrunched her face.

A loud clap of thunder paired with lightning broke the conversation, along with a blast of wind that blew the palm fronds to one side of the tree. Becca jumped up and grabbed her chair. "Let's go!"

Christine followed suit. They sprinted for the door, quarter-sized rain drops smacking their heads and arms. Shep followed, wanting inside, but Becca rerouted him to the storage room off the back porch instead.

Christine followed Shep into the storage room. "I'll sneak you in later." Propping the folded chairs against the storage room's open door, she scurried in behind Becca and shut the glass doors. "I'm goin' upstairs to watch the storm from my room."

"Okay, hon, I'll call you to help me cook in a few minutes." Becca called up the stairs after Christine. "Oh, and by the way, I miss Shep being inside with us, too. I wish we could change the rules. But don't sneak her in, we could be kicked out of the program for disobeying rules."

"Yeah, sure. Okay."

Becca could see Christine's eyes rolling in her mind's eye. She turned to straighten the house before starting dinner, then stood a few moments at the sliding glass door, which by now was pelleted with sideways rain.

Once the storm passed, Becca called Christine downstairs to help. Becca showed Christine how to prepare the egg and breading dips to fry the chicken. She took the chicken from the refrigerator and, pulling the plastic wrap open, offered the raw meat for Christine to prepare.

"Ew, Mom, I'm not touching chicken. Gross."

Becca laughed and, holding the defeathered, deheaded fowl by the spindly wings, shook it at her. "I am the ghost of chicken past."

Christine took off running.

Frightful raw chicken in hand, Becca chased Christine, both of them laughing as they scrambled around the dining room chairs.

As Becca turned the corner by the door, Mike came in. Nearly whacked by the chicken, he flinched. "What's going on here?" He placed his hat on the rack as the chicken chase continued. "I can see what you two do all day." Laughing, he headed upstairs.

Becca returned to the kitchen and picked up a knife. "Okay, if you're chicken to touch chicken, I'll cut and dip it, while you start the salad. But someday you'll be off on your own. What'll you do then?"

"I'll marry a chef." Christine flapped her hand, trumping her mother's one-up-manship. "That stuff gives me the creeps."

Becca shrugged. *At her age, I shopped and cooked and cleaned for eight. I didn't really have a choice. No one else would do it.* She turned the chicken in the egg mixture, careful to minimize drippage as she transferred each piece into the bread crumb mixture. *But I'm glad she doesn't have to live the way I did.* Patting the breadcrumbs across the top and pressing the meat into the mixture, she flipped the drumstick over and patted the other side. *Hopefully, though, she'll be able to cook chicken for her family.* Becca fit the last piece into the bubbling oil. Moving toward Christine, her fingers coated with the remains of raw chicken, eggs, and breadcrumbs, she cast a sly grin, lifting her curled fingers toward Christine.

"Ew!" Christine quickly picked up the salad tongs and fought her off. "Back off. . . you. . . chicken monster."

Pleased with herself for creating fun with her teen daughter, she nudged the faucet handle up with her forearm and washed her hands. She headed to the dining room to see if the table had been set correctly. *Everything's fine here.*

Christine entered with the salad bowl. Her face beamed with pride in her creation. Atop the lettuce bed she had arranged tomato wedges like petals of a flower, grouped olives in the center as the pistil, and tucked a few spinach leaves around the edges as leaves.

Becca's face lit up with delight. "Pretty Food!" Whenever one of them made an extra effort to make food pretty, the other imposed a cheek-kiss reward. She leaned into Christine's face and pecked a kiss on her cheek. "Mwah!"

Christine beamed, steering around her mother to place the salad on the table. "Okay, I've got a phone call to make. Call me when dinner's ready?"

"Sure, hon. I'll go make the fried chicken and mashed potatoes pretty."

Alone in the kitchen, Becca prayed silently. *Thank you that Christine's life is better than mine was. That's all I've really wanted, Lord, for Christine to have a good life.* Sticking a fork in the potatoes, she decided they were ready to drain and mash.

"Mm, smells delish" Mike descended the stairs, taking in a big whiff. "You know I love your fried chicken."

Becca's pride, purposefully tempered with humility, beamed. "I just fry the chicken and mash the potatoes."

"Better than anyone else's."

"Thanks." Becca still worked on just saying thanks when someone complimented her. Her old habit—either rebutting or returning a compliment—died hard. Years ago, someone recommended she simply say, 'Thank you.' She'd tried to ever since. "Dinner's ready. Will you call Christine?"

After supper and clean up, Becca took a long hot shower. Sneezing out what she could of the remaining dust from the day, she settled into bed. Her mind had been on the daunting task of deep-cleaning the old cottages and retreat center rooms, but the time had come to do her homework.

Draw my family of origin. Hmm. Drawing is easy, but how should I represent my family? Who was in charge? Dad was in charge when he was home, but he wasn't home often. What about mom? She did her share of yelling, and belt-swinging, but we usually found a way around doing what she said. The older kids, well, they were off doing their thing.

She drew an empty house, then the family of eight scattered around it, the parents yelling at each other in the distance and the baby of the house ruling Becca's mother. She drew herself out back, under the tree with the dogs.

As she scanned the stick figures representing her family of origin, memories played in her mind like a home movie—except not the moments caught on film. Daily arguments, Mom bringing up Dad's past mistakes, Dad yelling because dinner wasn't ready, or the girls hadn't done their chores, or because he worked all day while everyone else played. He'd storm out the door and stumble home hours later with frozen dinners for the family. Mom yelling about him spending all the money on beer. *And the house was always so messy. Roaches. Mold. Maybe that's why I can't—*

A shudder shook Becca out of the replay. With a heavy sigh, she laid her notebook down and looked around her room. Clean, tidy, cozy, and quiet. *Thank you, God. You helped me out of that mess. You're helping me build a family with love, patience, and kindness. Please, God, help my parents, brothers, and sisters to know You, too, and to find a better life.*

Prayer tucked her raw emotions neatly away, into the recesses of her mind, where she preferred them. "Good night, Mike." She kissed him on the cheek and rolled over. "Love you."

39

Lena

Sandy Spring, Maryland. 1927

Life went on after Grannie passed. It had to. She had said so.

Lena sat with Aggie on the porch, watching as the giddy Ruth chased lightning bugs across the yard, gathering them into a jar. Holes in the top of the jar and grass tucked into the bottom, she coaxed a few fireflies into the jar to serve as a nightlight. She let them free the next morning, to ensure the friendly little bugs would be happy.

"Soon you will go to school." Grandma Aggie looked up from her sewing. "Grandma's making you dresses, so you'll have something new to wear to school. You'll have a pail to carry your lunch in, too, and you'll learn reading and writing like a big girl." Fabric being expensive, Aggie crafted dresses from flour sacks. She stitched a smocking pattern onto the front of each dress, the colorful threads creating beauty from rags.

Ruth scurried to the porch to see the smocking Grandma held up. "Oooh, pretty. And look." She held forth her homemade nightlight with pride.

Aggie and Lena clapped for the little girl's creation. "We'll take them inside now and go wash up." Lena scooped up Ruth and tickled her all the way to the basin, while Aggie carried the jar of fireflies behind them.

After tucking Ruth in for the night, Lena met Aggie back on the porch, where she hand-smocked the bodice of Ruth's next dress. "Will you teach me to stitch like that? When I am a grandmother, I want to be just like you."

Aggie laughed and waved her hand. "Starlight, these are the simple things."

"Oh, Mama," Lena replied in earnest. "Now that I've worked in the city, with all the fancy cars, buildings, and such, the simple things are what impress me most." She watched and imitated her mother, stitch by stitch. The needle boring through burlap material, catching threads to pull the open weave together reminded Lena of her quest to draw her boys back into her care. *How can I draw them back? I'll never afford a better lawyer by staying home, sewing.*

"Starlight."

Lena startled, realizing she had left off sewing to staring off into the distance. "Yes, Mama?' Lena caught another stitch in the weave.

"I appreciate that you came home to help us." Aggie finished the knot in her line and trimmed the threads with her teeth. "But who can you meet here? Your life needs to go on. Daddy and I will be okay if you go back to the city to work. Lord knows we could use some extra money coming in."

Lena bit her lip. "I don't care about meeting anyone." Being with Ruth was her only relief now. "I want to stay here." She glanced at her mother. Seeing the sadness in her mother's face gave her pause. "Is money a problem?"

Aggie shifted in her seat and looked at the night sky. She drew in a deep breath and smoothed her dress across her lap. "The cities are booming. The farms—a different story. The bigger farms with their expensive machinery produced too much, so now there's less demand for what we do. We still owe money on the machines we bought when we were trying to keep up. Should've kept to horses, I guess. Honestly, though, between that and taxes, yes, money is a problem. If we don't pull out of this, we'll lose the farm."

Lena carried produce to sell in the farmer's market twice weekly, coming home to Ruth as often as possible. She longed to be with Ruth all the time, but with school and her parents keeping her little girl busy, pulling her weight to help with the farm was easier. Easier than when Ruth had been with her father.

Lena watched Ruth happily do chores for her grandma. Now that Ruth could walk again, the little girl helped in the garden, gathering fruit and vegetables, washing them and bringing them into the kitchen. Aggie—Grandma—let Ruth help bake the usual fifteen pies a week, and Henry— Grandpa—let her ride on the back of the plow as he guided the horses. Sometimes he let Ruth help him pick up rocks, which, Ruth told her mama, made her feel "real proud." She had grown strong and happy. This lightened Lena's burden.

Most weekends, family members from all around continued the tradition of traveling home to the farm to feast together. After the evening meal, they'd move chairs from all over the house into a big circle in the living room to tell stories and make music. Lena played the mouth harp, Aggie the washboard and spoons. Henry played a mean fiddle. Some brothers played guitar, banjo, and accordion. One brother, Edwin, couldn't play an instrument, so he clapped and stomped his feet.

Henry would start the line of social singing, "Old Bob Neal was a young cowboy; a young cowboy was he. . ." While the tune kept playing, and Edwin kept the beat, Henry would point at someone else in the circle, who would make up the next line. The resulting fun story, upon completing the circle, would end with a chorus of voices on a drawn-out end note.

These nights, like a glowing hearth in the center of their home, bolstered the family through sadness and painful memories. Gradually, their collective grief turned into a source of strength, bonding Lena's family and healing their hearts.

Fall, 1928

Lena pressed the ear piece of the phone harder into her ear. "What?"

"Clinton took Ruth. He said they need Ruth's help with her baby sister."

"I'm calling him now."

She forced her trembling fingers to dial his number. After three rings, his voice traversed the miles to her ear. Her seething voice returned through the wire. "How could you?"

"Me? How could you? You've run off, God knows what you're up to."

"Clinton, I have no choice but to work. I still want them with me."

Clinton laughed. "You have a fine way of showing it."

"And you? What's your excuse? Why did you and your latest model of a wife take Ruth to be your babysitter? She's only five."

His voice grew somber. "Times are hard here, too, Lena. We had to go into town to work for a while, that's all. We're home every night."

"Well, there's no reason she should have to be mama to your baby, Clinton. She needs to go to school. Let her stay with my parents and let your parents tend the baby."

"They're too old for that now."

"Then your wife should stay home. Ruth belongs in school."

"Alright. I'll talk to her."

Lena pulled her savings from the box on the top shelf of her closet. *Finally. This should do it.* Her hopes buoyed by this new era of women's rights, she believed her chances improved. Selecting a lawyer in the city, someone who didn't know the Smiths, she brought the divorce papers and shared her long story.

"Can you help me win custody of my children, Mr. Johnson? I've read the courts favor a mother raising the children, especially during the tender years."

Mr. Johnson listened to Lena's story, his brow furrowing and relaxing in turn as she relayed the details of her history with Clinton. He sat back in his seat and lit a cigar. A few pensive puffs later, as Lena sat in anxious silence, he leaned forward and looked directly into her eyes.

"I would sincerely like to help you, ma'am. The custom of the court has been to turn away cases of spousal battery and child neglect—especially after much time has passed, and without concrete evidence of such. Historically, a man answers for his family, and is therefore permitted to do what is necessary to discipline and control them as he deems best, providing, of course, life is preserved."

Lena shook her head, her lips slightly puckering.

Mr. Johnson drew a deep breath and sputtered. "Excuse me, ma'am." The large round man pulled his monogrammed handkerchief from a little pocket in the top left corner of his suit coat. He wiped his mouth, then folded and returned the soiled cloth to its pocket. After clearing his throat, he proceeded. "The law espouses the 'rule of one.' It is better not to hurt the children by forcing them to live in more than one home. In the last fifty years or so, the court has favored a competent mother as the more tender caregiver for young children. However, the court still leans toward a man having custody of his children, especially, Mrs. Smith, when the woman has limited means and/or a history of questionable character. When you add to the case your legal attestation of adultery, well, frankly, you should consider yourself fortunate to have occasional visits. The fact that he has permitted the girl-child to stay with you this last year is exceptional."

"My legal attestation?" Lena's voice quivered. Her hands

trembled. Her Scots-Irish and Cherokee blood fired up. "As I explained, the man tricked me into signing it. I had no such admission in mind. Nor should I have. My character has never been in question, nor my fitness as a parent. His, on the other hand—"

"Mrs. Smith, I would be lying to say your hard-earned money would be well-spent on a case such as this. But," he tilted his head to one side and squinted, "you're a pretty young thing. You'll be able to move on with your life. You'll have no problem attracting a second husband. Choose a better man and start over. Have more children."

Lena's mouth closed as her neck retracted her jaw. *The audacity. And to think I saved for years to pay for. . .* She crossed her arms.

Sitting back in his chair with his chest expanded, he looked down at her over his glasses, which perched on the edge of his nose. He explained the process if she were to proceed with legal action, and customary charges for his time, should she choose to retain his services.

Lena forced herself to politely thank Mr. Johnson. She found her way down the hall, the walls swirling around her. Pushing the massive, ornate door open with both hands, she stepped outside, leaned against the brick wall, and covered her face with her hands. *Start over? Have more children? How dare he so lightly dismiss me and my children?*

She ran to the alley and retched. Wiping her mouth, she looked around to see if anyone had seen. *No one.* A steady rain washed her tears, and with them, all remaining hope.

40

Becca

The Center, South Central Florida. 1985

"Hold on, let me grab my homework." Becca gathered her notes and drawings and crammed them into her binder. She joined Mike as he headed out the door toward class. "Do you have yours?"

Mike lifted his composition notebook toward her. "Yes. Come on, we'll be late."

They walked toward the dining hall at the end of the dirt road for their second day of class.

Becca sensed Mike's tension. "Relax. We have fifteen minutes, and in less than eight we can walk there."

"No sense cutting it too close."

Becca rolled her eyes. "I only made us late twice in five years of marriage." She gave him a playful jab with her elbow as she leaned toward him.

Mike threw her a raised eyebrow. "As you said, you made

405

us late, not me."

Telling her bristled back to settle, she took in the peaceful atmosphere on this dusty morning walk. "It's a beautiful morning." She pointed to the field. "Look at the white birds perched on the cows. Do you see how when the sun shines across the fields, the spider webs all across the meadow light up? They look like thousands of sparkling diamonds." With a deep breath, the balm of nature's beauty soothed her soul.

Mike looked at Becca and smiled. He took her hand as they strolled past the retreat center, the church building and picnic area. As they approached the concrete-block building that served as both dining hall and classroom, he let go of Becca's hand and picked up the pace.

Becca matched his pace. As they entered, she relished the charm of the early-rustic-on-a-budget decor inside this long, narrow room. Linoleum floor tiles in a random smattering of gray, red, white, and black, lent a playful air to the room. Above it, wagon wheels hung at intervals, each with eight candle-shaped bulbs in hurricane glass, providing a gentle glow. She strode into the dining area. Collapsible tables, in various stages of disrepair, surrounded by a mishmash of colorful stacking chairs, filled the room. At the far end, a rough-hewn buffet sported countless coats of polyurethane.

Her destination, the coffee bar, lay at the far end of the room. She headed toward the three large metal urns, stacks of plastic mugs, spoons, and condiments. Sliding a plastic mug under the spout of the 50-cup tank, she pulled the lever. Translucent brown liquid trickled into her cup, smelling slightly of coffee, but faintly of soap. She selected two sugar packets and tore the tops, spilling their contents into what she hoped would become a tolerable cup of coffee.

A full bottle of liquor with an unbroken seal caught her eye. She'd seen the bottle the first day, and Bronson had explained why such a thing would be in plain sight in an alcohol rehab program. *"Every man knows he has a choice every day. Might as well practice seeing it and choose to not drink while here."* Becca smiled with respect for the brave and unexpected reasoning.

Having blended creamer into her concoction, she headed to the U-shaped section of tables at the end of the room. Becca hadn't known ahead of time that the first six weeks of ministry training would be alongside the men in the program, as if she herself were newly sober. She sipped her lukewarm, soap-flavored coffee. *Well, here goes.*

Brother Will stood up to teach. "Good mornin' y'all, let's take a seat, and get started."

Mike and Becca chose seats near the far end of the U, where they could see everything and everyone, a habit learned when Mike was a police officer. The seats filled quickly with two dozen men in rehab, four group leaders, and three others in the ministry training program. Becca laid out her notebook and pen, ready to take notes.

Brother Will's appearance fit the scene. He dressed for his cattle rancher lifestyle a plaid yoked shirt with double pockets and snapped flaps, faded blue jeans, a cowboy-buckled leather belt, a frayed straw hat, and weathered western boots. A slightly plump fellow, his sun-worn face spread twice as wide when he broke into his trademark grin. Though his blue eyes sparkled when he flashed that smile, something in his look suggested he was about to lasso you with words, rope your hands and feet, and brand you as a yearling with his teaching.

His teaching style entertaining, casual and natural, he taught without notes. Becca could tell he knew the material inside-out, yet each story seemed crafted fresh for the day. His voice raised or lowered for emphasis as he spun anecdotal tales that delighted and captured the men's hearts.

This morning, Brother Will taught the Daily Moral Inventory, or DMI, a tool The Center developed to help participants examine themselves. He explained the negative attitudes on the DMI, giving realistic examples of how each may have reared its ugly head in their lives.

Using a whiny voice, he dramatized the role of a resident in the throes of denial and projection. "But, but, I couldn't help it, Brother Will, he made me mad!" He pointed at a man in the class, as part of his act. Then his left hand reached to grab his own right hand, the one with the pointing finger, and wrestled the finger to point in his own direction. The right hand struggled free and returned to point at others in the room. "It weren't MY fault that I lost my temper and stormed off! T'weren't MY fault that I drove the truck into the ditch! Why, if he hadn't a looked at me that way, I'd still be just fine, doin' my job."

Still in full acting mode, he turned his pointy finger toward Becca. "And, on top 'o that, if that wife o' mine hadn't a put me out, I wouldn't a drank that pint and wrecked the car." He postured, '*I don't know*,' with a woe-is-me expression. "Don't you see, Brother Will, don't ya see how people are always gangin' up on me and luck ain't never on my side?"

Everyone laughed—a laugh acknowledging their folly.

"Now," he went on, slowing his pace and lowering his voice. "I ask you." He stopped and peered directly into a client's face. "How old is that little boy?" He cast his shiny cowboy grin to men all around the classroom, pausing to let each man consider the question. "Seriously. How old is that little boy?"

Feet shuffled under the tables.

"Can you start to see how foolish it is to be pointin' the finger at everyone and everything else?"

A few heads nodded. Some crossed their arms.

Brother Will's voice stayed low and gentle. "The Apostle Paul said it somethin' like this. '*When I was a child, I thought like a child, I spoke like a child, I acted like a child. When I became a man, I put away childish things.*' You've probably all heard that Jesus said, '*Suffer the little children to come to me,*' and '*Come to me with the faith of a child.*' Do you think he meant childish or childlike? There's a difference. When we point our fingers to blame everything and everyone else, that's childish. We need to grow up. . . to take responsibility for our own stinking thinking. The way we've been thinking—denial and projection—is stinking thinking."

He wrote the words in large letters on the board.

STINKING THINKING

"Denial says I haven't done anything wrong. Projection blames everything on someone or something else. Gentlemen, thinking like that is what got us here. And it stinks. Stinks to high heaven—and God smells the whole mess. It's time we man up, fess up, and ask Hm to renew our minds."

Becca surveyed the men's faces. Every eye studied Brother Will. Every face shone with dumbfounded realization. *Brother Will has a gift. He pokes just enough fun, and includes himself in the blame, disarming their defenses.*

Brother Will sat on the stool in the center of the U. "Maybe your prayers have all been fox-hole prayers, begging for help after you get yourself in a fix. Maybe you blamed God for the fix you got in. When you come to Him admitting you're the one to blame, what will He do?"

Brother Will drew a long sip of his coffee. "Are you afraid He'll strike you down for what you've done?" His face spread into his signature grin. "Or do you believe He's a loving Father, willing to help you find your way?" Another long pause gave time to search hearts and minds.

"You're standing at the edge of a great chasm." He rose and drew on the chalkboard as he spoke. "On the other side is your heavenly Father's land, with everything you need for life and godliness. On this side, the bad guys are after you. There's an old wooden bridge, the only way to get across the chasm." He drew a cross as a bridge across the deep gap. "Saying you believe the bridge will hold you is easy. But unless you actually step out onto that bridge, the words mean nothing."

Becca connected with Brother Will's message, aware of the place in her heart that was afraid of God—as if His pointy finger in the sky sent lightning bolts of judgment to zap wrongdoers. She had prayed and studied her Bible for years, seeking to replace the frightful mental image with one of a loving Father. *Have I been blaming everyone and everything else? Do I really believe?*

"Some years ago, I went to a prayer retreat." Brother Will strolled into the U opening, using his arms to illustrate as he spoke. "I rushed in, wheels spinning fast from all the things on my mind. I carried my water bottle in one hand, my Bible and notebook in the other, and as I rounded the corner, I met another poor soul rushing around as fast as I was. Met him squarely, face to face." He clapped his hands together, demonstrating the collision. "Our papers and cups went flying and scattered all around us."

Chuckling gently, he paused to remove his glasses, wipe his brow, and replace his glasses. "Isn't this how we live our lives much of the time—carrying too many things, thinking so far into the future we barely notice our surroundings?"

Becca nodded. *Yes. Seems like I'm always busy. Lists of things to do. I never check them all off. . . I just move them to the next day's list.*

"Apologizing and making sure my poor victim was okay, I gathered my belongings and slipped into my class. As I entered, the retreat leader was saying something about prayer requiring us to slow down, filter out distractions." Another chuckle erupted, and Brother Will shook his head. " He said we'd learn to use our God-given faculties, including our imagination—our mind's eye—to talk and listen to God. Well, you can imagine how this fared with this country boy, who's used to workin' from before sun-up to after sundown. I didn't slow enough that day, so they made me stay a week."

Becca laughed along with several others.

"Believe it or not, this country boy learned to slow down, enter the quiet, and really pray—converse—two-way, with God. Now," he said with a resolute nod, "I'm going to teach you everything I know about prayer." Grinning again, he added, "In five minutes or less."

Everyone laughed again.

"Here we go. For a few moments, you're at a prayer retreat instead of a drug and alcohol rehab center, no extra charge."

Imagination, to pray? Wary of the concept, Becca breathed a prayer of her own. *Lord, be with me. Help me discern what's of you and what's not. Help me to trust You.*

"Everyone get comfortable in your seat, both feet on the floor." Brother Will moved to a plastic chair and modeled his instructions. "Pencils down. Close your eyes. Now, notice the sound of the fan, whirling around, swaying back and forth. Notice the birds singing outside. . . and your own breathing." He let silence fill the moment. "Notice and acknowledge how your body feels. Feel your heart beating deep inside your chest."

Becca welcomed calm. *Moving has been hectic, learning the lay of the land, all the new routines and people.*

"Picture yourself walking away from the busy places in your mind, going down the stairs. . . to your heart."

Becca followed Brother Will's lead until he mentioned going downstairs. The thought of this pounded her heart. *Downstairs?*

"Don't rush down. Go slowly, knowing you're going to spend some quiet time alone with your Creator in this special room. Your heart is where God sits on His throne, ready to meet with you."

Instead of imagining a cozy, warm place with her Creator, another picture jolted into view—stairs to the basement. She peeked to see if anyone noticed her discomfort. *No one noticed.* She closed her eyes again and tried to refocus.

"As you come to the bottom stair, you see him. God, the Father, seated on His throne. His eyes light up to see you. 'Come in, come in, have a seat,' he says. You walk to him and sit, knees to knees, and you look into his eyes."

Becca abandoned the idea of stairs and mentally caught up to Brother Will's lead. She pictured a figure in pure, white, glistening robes. His eyes sparkled with prisms of light, speaking volumes of love. At the envisioning of his arms open wide, she saw herself in his lap. He held her as a loving father would—gentle, firm, and secure. She felt safer than she'd felt in her life.

The sound of Will's voice reached her, muddled, as through a glass wall. "Now think back to the list of attitudes you checked off on your DMI this morning. Talk with him about it. Lord, I've been blaming everyone else, but it's me."

Becca mentally scanned her DMI from quiet time. Resentment had reared its ugly head. Shame loomed heavy on her heart. Not one to permit herself resentment, she pushed away anger whenever she noticed it.

Brother Will's voice came stronger. ""Ask him to forgive you and then wait, listen. What is he saying to you or showing you?" Again, he paused the gentle guidance.

Lord Jesus, I ask you to forgive me for this horrible attitude. Why do I keep snapping into resentment when you've blessed me so? When I am so loved and forgiven? Will you help me understand? Will you help me change?

Father God gently caressed Becca's face and lifted her chin—a sensation so real she opened her eyes, to see if someone was actually touching her. She closed her eyes again, returning to the Spirit's lead, in her mind's eye, in this room in her heart, where she sat snuggled in God's lap. Tears ran down her cheeks, the salty flavor real. God's eyes met hers, also brimming with tears, and glistening from His inner light. One trickled down his cheek, a rainbow of light bouncing from it.

My child, I'm so glad you're here with me. I forgave you from the beginning of time. I will help you understand. I will help you grow. Meet me here whenever you can, and we will walk through this new journey together. You are safe with me, my love. You are safe with me.

Brother Will's voice interrupted and faded the vision. "As you prepare to leave this special place, embrace God. Tell Him you'll be back soon. Be sure to thank Him for His love and forgiveness."

Becca embraced the Lord. *Thank you. I will return again soon. I'm so glad to be able to be with You this way.*

"Ascending the steps, slowly we come back up to the place where we live. You hear your own breathing—in, out. You're aware of the birds singing, the fan, the sound of the truck whizzing down the grade in the distance. You feel your feet on the floor. You take a deep breath and slowly open your eyes."

The room stirred with rumblings as men regained their typical positions, rubbed their eyes, and sipped coffee. One stood and went toward the restroom.

Brother Will continued. "This is the relationship with God each of us can have, every single day. You can talk with Him. He is as close as your own heart. You can receive from Him. With this type of prayer, called the Inner Journey, you can be partners with God in the work of renewing your minds and transforming your lives. Now, who wants to share? What did God say to you today?"

Becca read the room. The men looked joyous. Some beamed with excitement.

Brother Will called on a few to tell their experiences before closing class. "Do this every morning, record what you learned, and bring your journal to share in group tomorrow."

As class dismissed, Becca couldn't wait to return to her journal, to her next inner journey, to the safety of her Savior's arms. But it was time for Ministry Training class. Time to press on.

Becca immersed herself into The Center's program with her usual dedication, two hundred percent. Up at dawn with her Bible, DMI, and journal, she surveyed the last day's attitudes, thoughts and feelings, then scooted down the scary stairs to the throne room in her heart, where she bared her soul to God.

The Inner Journey prayer let her be herself with God as she'd never been before. An affectionate person, she loved envisioning herself curling up on her heavenly Father's lap. Sometimes she could physically feel Him holding her. She couldn't picture details in His face, but she could feel the comfort of His arms and sense His assurance.

For the first few weeks, Becca and Mike participated in the men's program, as if they were newly sober. They shared their daily DMIs and journals in small groups with the men in the program.

Becca, with no history of chemical addiction, had served the Lord faithfully for many years *I'm fine,* she told herself, *but I'll submit myself to the process, share my struggles and insights, and see what comes of it.*

Each member shared their DMIs and journals, then listened to the group's feedback. If someone thought another was hiding something, or gaming the system, they discussed the issue openly, encouraging one another into honest recovery. They supported good insights with congratulatory remarks and prayed for each other—prayers for renewed thinking and health for their minds, souls, bodies, and relationships.

* * *

Six weeks into the program, the second phase of ministry training began. Mike and Becca graduated into hands-on training as facilitators of the small addiction groups. Their own journals and insights would still be shared, but in the small ministry training group rather than with the men in rehab.

Within a few weeks, the ministry training group focused on Becca. One by one, they confided their impressions and concerns to her.

"You didn't look at me, or wave, when I pass you on the way to the dining hall," one said. "You seem aloof."

Another trainee nodded. "I felt that too. I thought maybe you don't like me."

Becca tipped her head to one side. *What? I didn't think—*

A third member of the group chimed in. "Yeah, seems you think you're better than us."

"You seem sad to me," one of the wives added. "With-drawn. You never join in the fun activities."

Becca's stomach twisted as she quelled her reaction. She squeezed the edges of the seat, listening, as group rules stipulate, but her mind spun. Her toes and fingers tingled. Longing to speak up, explain, or run and hide, Becca bit her lip. *I had no idea I came across that way.* Craig's accusation reared its ugly head from her long-buried past. *'You self-*

righteous—' She shook her head. *I've been kind, gentle, and open.*

Hidden portions of her journal came to mind—the ones she didn't bring to group. *Withdrawn? Maybe. But I can't share those things with this group.* She swallowed hard, the lump pressing hard against the back of her throat all the way down. *This hurts.*

Becca heard her own voice offer a humble apology. "I'll do better."

The group accepted her apology without pressing her. Much to Becca's relief, they prayed for her.

Becca wiped tears as she walked alongside Mike toward the dining hall for lunch. "I'm embarrassed. And perplexed. I didn't know they perceived me this way."

"You do come off that way." Mike tucked his binder close to his chest. Keeping his voice just above a whisper, he squinted his eyes. "You don't like to see yourself that way, but you worry about everything. You keep everything tight, in a tidy box. I know you've had a hard life, but to be honest, I'm getting really sick of always having to work so hard to please you."

The crunch of sandy dirt and stones kicking up beneath their steps, the oppressive heat of the midday sun beating down from above, and the air thick with molecules exploding into drops of salt water on her skin, all pressed against every inch of Becca's body. Surreal. As surreal as the words tumbling from her husband's mouth.

Mike squeezed her arm. "Hey, do you mind if I catch up with Branson? I have to tell him something about the print shop."

Becca shook her head. "No, go ahead."

She pressed on. *Mike and the group. Why didn't any of them come to me before to tell me how they felt? I've been trying to be friendly, but no one in the training program has opened to me, either. And Mike. Why did he wait for the one, two, punch?*

A group of four training students threw a football around in the picnic area. Becca made a point of waving to them as she passed.

Me, no fun? I thought I was pretty good at having fun. But they don't really know me. I've only been here a few weeks, and I'm dealing with a lot.

41

Lena

Washington, DC. 1929

As winter's gray cloak rolls in and lingers for months of cold, dreary darkness, so grief begged to settle in. She'd lost her children. She'd lost Grannie. She'd lost a year's savings on a fancy lawyer's heartless, condescending edict. The edict that snatched the strand of hope she'd held and nurtured for years.

But spring defies winter's frosty fingers. Sunshine streams across the city parks, flowers sport their brightest colors in every window box, and birds chirp and flit as they built their nests in gutters and eaves along the streets. All of these bastions of endurance worked together in concerted effort to defy Lena's gloom.

March's chilly evenings sped by, as did the cars alongside Lena. She walked toward her sister's apartment from an evening cleaning job. The people in the speeding cars looked warm and happy. Everyone seemed to be having the time of their lives, living as if prosperity would last forever. Lena didn't bother to dream of all that. Not right now.

But having a car would be nice. She had been secretly longing for an automobile ever since she'd seen one. What she deemed an unnecessary, frivolous thing at first, now seemed essential. With an automobile, she could travel to work and back daily rather than stay with her sister all week. If she could be with her children more, life would be better for them all.

She watched as prices on the Ford Model T dropped from an unthinkable $550 the year Ruth was born, down to under $300 in 1925. Then, every year, as she was about to buy one for herself, something else required her savings. This year, an early freeze damaged crops, wrinkling the tomatoes, crumpling the spinach and withering the lettuce faster than she could harvest them. The heartless blast of winter weather left her only a quarter of her typical yield at market. Lena took on extra cleaning and sewing jobs, but still suffered quite a setback.

People all around her in the city were buying goods on installment, even buying stocks, which they called "specu-lations," with only ten percent down.

"There's no reason not to, the market just keeps going up," Lena's friend from work had urged, as he talked up the stock market.

"I don't know," Lena had replied. "It doesn't make much sense, getting rich from someone else's money." But she had seen several co-workers and neighbors wearing expensive jewelry and driving the fanciest cars. Everyone seemed to be making money in the stock market.

As the next car sped by her, she decided to join the frenzy. Steeling herself against fear of the unknown, she hurried home, took her savings from the empty potato chip can kept tucked away in her room and called Barry to arrange the deal. Excitement quickened every cell in her body, spilling onto her shining eyes and rosy cheeks as she walked to meet Barry to purchase the latest booming stock.

On the way, she noticed an old tree leaning over the sidewalk. A breeze caught her cheek. Lena paused. *What was that?* She looked around. The tree bent further in the breeze. Instinct led her eyes to follow the direction it pointed. *Hmm. That's odd. Something tells me to go that way.* Lena shook herself from the brief, dream-like state. *No, that doesn't make sense. Barry's friend's office is this way.* She continued toward the meeting.

"I have everything." She placed the brown bag on his desk. "Two hundred and fifty dollars—count and see for yourself."

Stan's face lit up. "Oh, doll, that's great." He leaned forward over his desk and dropped his tone. "But, unfortunately, that's not enough to buy into this deal." His lower lip protruded, pouting in over-acted sympathy.

Lena's countenance dropped in response. Her shoulders slumped. She retrieved her bag and moved toward the door.

Barry hopped up, sped past his friend's desk and took her by the arm. With his lighthearted, confident manner, he offered advice and assurance. "Ish Kabibble, babe, it'll be fine. Stan here will advance you a loan. It'll pay off, no worries."

Barry and Stan stood, their faces excited as boys seeing a lighted Christmas tree lined with presents, awaiting her decision.

Lena conceded to their brilliance. "All right."

"Step right up, ma'am, you won't be sorry." Stan motioned with an open arm to his desk.

Before she could rein herself in, she purchased $2500 worth of stock with her $250.

"No worries, lil' lady, you'll have enough dough to buy the best jalopy there is in no time flat—and to secure your children's future and your parents' farm. Now, ain't that the cat's pajamas?" Stan puffed out his chest as he led her out . He locked the door behind them and turned to take her arm. "Take your pick, like this breezer I got here." Motioning to his car as they walked toward the curb, he opened the car door. "Jump in, I'll give ya a ride."

Lena bit her bottom lip as she slipped into the shiny convertible. Her hand slid over the smooth surface on the dashboard. *No.* She opened the door and scooted out as readily as she'd jumped in. "Thanks, Stan. I don't mean to be a killjoy, but I'll walk. Don't want to miss this beautiful evening."

"Whatever suits ya, doll." Stan and Barry sped off.

Walking back home to her sister's apartment, she slipped in quietly and went to bed early. She didn't know whether to celebrate or kick herself. *What have I done?* Desperate to make life better for her family, for herself, for the future, she'd traipsed between home and the city for years, bringing her pittance to help feed and clothe the family and paying a small rent to her sister and brother-in-law. She'd grown weary of well-doing. *These should have been times of pleasure and joy—years of happy marriage, raising children, meeting with friends and family for Sundays in the park.*

Looking toward the ceiling in the dark, the bed beneath provided no comfort. The space around closed in on her, taking her breath. Lines between herself and eternity blurred. She didn't understand. She slid out of bed, down to her knees. With her hands folded reverently, she cried aloud. "Please, God, let my investment multiply. Let us have what all these other folks do." Even as the prayer left her lips, her heart knew she'd missed the mark. "Forgive me, Lord, please forgive me, and help me to count my blessings."

* * *

She was in the city, tending her table at the farmer's market. Quite a commotion stirred in the streets and sidewalks. Lena craned her neck, looking for the source of the trouble. She spoke aloud, to any who might hear. "What's going on?"

An elderly woman perused goods on Lena's table, appearing to be in no rush. "Oh, the speculators, they're all in a tizzy now, dear. Nobody wanted to listen to reason. They wanted easy money. . . believed in it. Well, now the stock market's crashed. Everyone's rushing to sell their stock before they're completely broke."

Lena concealed her gasp, not wanting the lady to know she, too, had been a "speculator," foolish with her savings.

"Sell their stock?" Lena queried as calmly as she could. "How do you even do that?"

The elderly woman took a long look at Lena, up and down, over the rim of her glasses. "You too, dearie? I would have thought you'd have more sense in you than that. . . not the sort to be involved in such foolishness."

Blushing from embarrassment, Lena wasn't sure whether to be thankful the woman had such a fine impression of her or to be ashamed of herself for her lapse of judgment. She chose the latter. "Well, I did try it—a little—but I knew it was too good to be true." Lena took a deep breath and tried to encourage herself. She wouldn't be off work for several more hours, so to try to run and sell her stock now seemed pointless. "Maybe the market will bounce right back. After all, there's bound to be some ups and downs in that business."

Gathering her basket of produce closer into her body, the old woman sniffed. She pushed her glasses up and inspected the fine head of lettuce. "Well, I may be far from rich, but at least I know all my belongings are my belongings, and they will all be there when I arrive home. How much for this lettuce, dearie?"

"Ten cents, ma'am." Lena forced a smile. "Another nickel and you can have a tomato and cucumber, too. Will make a mighty fine salad for your supper tonight." She smiled, holding the tomato toward her customer.

"Very well then, here's fifteen cents. A salad sounds delightful. You're quite the saleslady."

"Here you go, ma'am. I wish you and yours a very nice dinner. See you tomorrow?" Lena grinned.

"On the 'morrow, young lady. Good day to you."

"Good day, ma'am."

Lena ducked beneath her table, pretending to restock her vegetables from the bins underneath. She held onto her face with both hands and took a few deep breaths. *Oh, dear Lord, dear Lord, please don't let it all be gone. What will I do?*

Rockville, Maryland. 1932

Without running water, maintenance or garbage collection, the city became an unhealthy place to live. Lena intended to return to live at her parents' place on the farm, but nothing there would help pay her enormous debt from the market crash. Her older brother and his wife, Robert and Theresa, offered her room and board in exchange for cooking and cleaning. She left the city and moved in with them.

It didn't take Stan long to find her. He called to collect the monthly payment toward the stock loan. His voice, deeper than in the days of carefree living, relayed the serious nature of her debt. "You're five months in arrears. I got people after me. How can I pay them if you don't pay me?"

"Stan, I need to find a job. There's nothing in the city, but I'm looking here. I walk as far as I can every day, going into every store. If I don't find a job, I've got nothing to pay you."

His throat cleared loudly into the phone. "The lenders mean business, doll. You have to come through for me."

"How about if you put me to work? I can clean, or cook, or mend for you. I'll be glad to do any chores."

"That won't help."

She heard him take a deep breath and blow it out.

"Can you sew? I know of a shop that needs a seamstress. I could get you in to talk with the owner. But you'd owe me one, Lena. Good jobs don't come easy, so you'll have to do right by her."

"Of course!" Lena stood, her heart lightened as if the job were a sure thing. "Oh, thank you so much, Stan. Tell me, where do I go, and when? I can be ready in half an hour."

"Whoa, whoa there, young lady. I'll speak with my aunt and then call you back."

She hung up the phone and went right to her wardrobe. *Now what could I wear?* She took out two dresses and inspected them for flaws. *Can't go in there scraggly and expect her to believe I'm a seamstress.*

Mama's sewing lessons paid off, landing Lena the seamstress job. Or, rather, as she apprenticed and became approved, a dressmaker. Society's elite members visited The Dress Shoppe for customized dresses. The wives of politicians, ambassadors and successful investors frequented the shop, needing a new dress for every event. For them, the Great Depression was like a tornado, devastating the other side of the road while leaving their houses intact. Lena held on through the tempest, sewing night and day to meet their exacting requirements, their deadlines, and her obligations.

Sandy Spring, Maryland. New Year's Day, 1933

Lena had been home since Christmas, but this was the first day Clinton allowed the kids a visit. They'd enjoyed a big breakfast in the kitchen before everyone scurried off to tend their chores. Shaw and Elliot had gone to the barn with Grandpa Burriss. Mama had creaked up the stairs to make beds. Ruth had stayed in the kitchen with Lena, prattling on through clean up time.

She plunked herself in a chair. Her tone changed into

angry muttering.

Lena dried her hands and pulled a chair beside Ruth at the kitchen table. "What did you just say?"

"Daddy told me there won't ever be presents for me. He wasn't kidding. My little sisters got dolls and new clothes. I got nothing." Ruth crossed her arms and huffed.

"Oh, honey." Lena sat beside her and wrapped her arms around her gangly pre-teen.

Ruth leaned her head against Lena's arm. "Mama, I don't like living there. I don't get to go to school. Mostly I babysit. When the first one came along, okay, but now there's three of them. I don't wanna do this anymore."

Lena squeezed her girl. She ran her hand down her smooth brown hair, tracing to the end of her long braid, which she spun around her finger while she pondered her response. "Doesn't their Mama stay home with them?"

Ruth shrugged and wiggled her shoulders, gaining her freedom from the long hug. She sat up straight. "Some-times, but other times they're both gone—for days or even weeks. They said they had to go where they could find work, but they come home walking all funny—like a couple of newborn calves who can't stand on their legs."

Lena's nostrils flared with a gust of air. Her voice quivered as she checked her response. "It shouldn't be that way. I'll speak to your father again." She reached toward the center of the table where winter roses lilted over the edges of a milk-glass vase. As she stroked a silken red petal, several other petals fell to the table. "Times are tough, Ruth. Work is very hard to come by now. Some of us must leave home to work so our families will have what they need. Like me."

"But I don't care about clothes, or even food." Ruth

pressed into her mother. "I want to be with you. I want to go to school, and I want to play. This is not fair."

"You're right about that. It's certainly not fair." She swept the fallen petals into her hand.

Ruth's eyebrows furrowed. She slammed her fist down on the table. "Why aren't you here for me, Mom?"

Lena stood and pushed in her chair. "I told you. I must work." She pointed her finger at Ruth, and with a firm but gentle voice, added, "And don't you slam your fist in this house, young lady."

Ruth huffed, folded her arms and stiffened her back, feet apart on the floor. "Okay. But there's more to it. I just know it. You always tell me I'm smart. So, tell me."

Lena sighed as she lined the petals along the windowsill to dry in the morning sun.

"Tell me the truth."

She leaned a hip against the cabinet and faced her daughter. "I'll tell you this." She picked up a dish towel and dried a large ceramic bowl. "Your father and I were not a good match. I wanted to keep you, but the law gave your father custody." She placed the bowl on the shelf. "I've been working all these years, hoping to win you and your brothers back. But we've had huge setbacks. Things we couldn't help. My heart is broken, Morning Star." Her eyes beamed sorrow and regret to her daughter's. "I wish I could do more."

"It still doesn't add up. . . why they'd give us to Daddy instead of letting us be with you. There must be more you're not telling me."

Lena dried another bowl. "Never mind that. You're my Morning Star. You're good-natured. . . kind and gentle. You make life fun, honey." She nestled the smaller bowl inside the larger one on on its shelf. "And so good to your little sisters. You sing with them and take them outside to play. You told me you help them find animal figures in the clouds—like you and Grannie used to do. You taught them how to pick flowers from the hillside and how to gather eggs for breakfast."

Ruth relaxed as her face gave way to a slight smile, followed by a forlorn look. "I try to be like you, Mama. Shaw and Elliot. . . they're hardly here anymore. They have to work on Grandfather and Grandmother Smith's farm. I end up being the mother, alone with the babies. I must do something to make them happy or they just whine and cry all the time."

Lena sighed. "You have no idea how much my heart breaks for you, and for them. I do what I can do. I pray hard. . . and try to trust God with what I can't do. Remember Grannie's story about the water spider bringing fire?"

"Yeah." Ruthie tapped her foot.

"We keep doing the best we can. . . being creative and looking after others too. Look, your brothers are growing up to be respectful, hard-working men. Having plenty to do helps."

"I guess." Ruth uncrossed her arms. "Except Shaw. He works hard, yeah, but he can be awful, too." She rolled her eyes and scrunched up her nose as she stood and pushed in her chair. "Unless we're dancing. You know me. I like to dance. Shaw does, too."

"Then let's dance." Lena turned the radio dial to a perky song and danced across the kitchen.

Ruth's face beamed with delight. She jumped around the kitchen with her mother. Together they shimmied and stomped their blues away.

42

Becca

"Consider this a fast, but from the indulgence of speaking your mind." The visiting speaker explained *Poustinia*, the Russian word for desert, as he prepared the ministry training students for a week of prayer retreat. "For the next week, we'll live like monks, in a vow of silence. We'll seek God, tune our senses to Him, and to turn down our internal jabbering as well. We're tuning into quiet, solitude—the posture of listening."

He handed information packets to the nearest person to pass around. Moving back to the podium, he gave detailed instructions and dismissed the class. "You will be sorely tempted to speak, but if you do, you'll miss out on the lesson silence offers. Keeping your mouth shut will bring much to light."

Becca determined how to manage the assignment while

walking back home. *Most of the participants are away from home, staying in the retreat center. Mike and I live here, so it'll be harder. I can do it, though. I'll just communicate with pen and paper.*

She scribbled a note to Christine, telling her why she and Mike would be silent and what to expect for the week.

"Does it really matter, Mom? They won't know if you talk or not."

Becca smiled and shrugged. She wrote her reply. "I'll know, silly. I'm not in ministry training to pretend to be something I'm not."

Christine's eyebrows shot up. "Oh." She laughed. "Could'a fooled me. Well, then, this should be an. . . interesting week."

Becca placed the communication pad on the dining room table and wrote on the top page. "We'll leave this notepad here all week for messages, but try to help us by doing your best this week, okay?" She pointed to what she wrote for Christine to read.

Christine read the note aloud. "Sure, Mom."

Becca wrote in response. "Okay, off I go. I'm going to walk the orange groves."

As Becca strolled through the orange groves, she focused on listening. She tried to let her internal verbiage dissipate. The exercise proved futile. Mike's words from last week, '*really sick of always having to work so hard to please you,*' jabbed repeatedly, as if in replaying them, she would understand what she'd been doing wrong. How they ended up here, in ministry training, but so distant from one another and so devoid of passion. They could talk about work. They could talk about raising Christine. They could talk about anything but what was really the matter. Frustrated, she slipped back into the house to prepare dinner.

Surprised to hear Mike's voice breaking the silence, she looked out from the kitchen, down the hall. He came out from Christine's room, looking surprised to see her. Becca's heart skipped a beat, and tension pulled at her stomach. The unwelcome alarm bells of suspicion intruded, pealing louder than ever during this period of silence.

Is Mike molesting Christine?

She held her tongue, eyeing Mike for facial or body language that might answer her question. *No. I am overreacting. Why would I think that? All he did was talk to her and walk out of her room.* Turning back to the kitchen, she placed the chicken in the oven.

Her thoughts disobeyed the inner parent that chided her for unfounded suspicions. *I need to check it out.* At Christine's doorway, she saw Christine on the floor by her bed, doing homework.

Christine glanced up. "Hi Mom."

She looks okay. Becca smiled and waved in response. Still, though, Mike didn't usually go into Christine's room. Wanting to ask Christine why Mike had been in her room, she also didn't want to convey mistrust. She observed for a moment, believing—hoping—that if anything were wrong, she would sense it.

Christine changed positions, tapped her pencil, and frowned at her mother.

The frown fueled Becca's concern. A sense of urgency swelled, rendering her vow of silence all but impossible. She remembered the retreat leader's admonition. '*You will*

be sorely tempted to speak, but if you do, you will miss. . .'
She didn't want to spoil half a day's silence with an over-reaction. Still, she desperately wanted to know. *Why did Mike talk during Poustinia? Had Christine done something wrong?* If so, Becca needed to know. She knelt by Christine's homework and and wrote on her scratch paper. "What's going on?"

Christine shrugged. "Nothing."

Teens—such detailed answers. She went to the dining room table for the notepad, then approached Mike, writing, "Is everything all right?"

He peered over his newspaper and shook his head to the affirmative. He wrote back. "She didn't do her chores, but I settled it. Nothing to worry about."

Becca tapped the notepad with her pencil. *Hmm, I wonder why chores became important enough to break silence.* She went back to the kitchen.

God, is he?

The harder she listened, the more elusive God's voice seemed.

By the end of the week, Becca, more exasperated than ever at her fearful suspicions, wrote in her journal to close out the lessons of Poustinia.

This time of quiet brought me face to face with how much I want to control everything. I watch Mike like a hawk. I'm always on alert to catch him doing what I'm afraid he'll do. I'm inundated with worry that Christine might be abused—right under my nose. I'm afraid to trust God because I'm afraid I'd use that as an excuse to blind myself into idealistic oblivion. I don't want to be blind to anything that could hurt my daughter.

I don't want to be caught unaware or fall short of being a good mother. Would I blind myself? Then again, would I really want to know? Everything we've built will come crumbling down. Or everything I thought we'd built.

More aware of her discomfort and distrust of Mike, she questioned if—or how—she should discuss the problem with him. After denying her suspicions for many years—since the first year of their marriage, when she'd found pornography, and when Mike came home smelling of woman, she had decided against it. Never sure if Mike was cheating or not, she had given him the benefit of doubt—the doubt of her own intuition.

I don't want him to know my mistrust. If he's been faithful, this will hurt him. I don't want my problem to hurt him. Besides, if I told him now, he'd just think I was turning the tables on him because of what he told me he's feeling.

The week of silence also illuminated how she had been forcing herself to pretend to enjoy sex, and why. *If I don't satisfy Mike, he might have reason to turn elsewhere.* She had been forcing herself to participate even though arousal made her vulnerable to intrusive memories or fears. *This is not how marriage is supposed to be.*

She checked her DMI. Fear? X. She pushed back the pages, quickly reviewing the last several months of her DMI's. Fear. X, X, X, X. Every day. The connection struck her. Her aversion to sexual pleasure was aversion to trust, fear at her core. She avoided trust like a dangerous drug—a potion that would expose her to—ensure her of—victimization. *How can I trust when trust has only ever made a fool of me?*

Her problem with trust, sex and control had distanced her from Mike, driving a wedge between them. She had avoided facing her part by blaming him for their problems. All these years, she'd been blaming him for not reading her mind, for not noticing her distance, and for not coming after her when she distanced herself. Her resentments against him had festered into an oozing ball of puss in her gut.

It's me. My problem with trust. My lack of trust is ruining our marriage. Her spine stiffened. *I am our worst enemy.* Setting her DMI aside, she closed her eyes against the onslaught of mixed emotions. All fingers pointed at her. This was her problem. She would be responsible for a failed marriage, for a broken home, for hurting her daughter.

Why am I like this? I need to know why I'm so deeply afraid. I must face this, no matter what the root is. Clenched fists tucked under each arm, she closed her eyes and entered her inner throne room, the child inside longing to climb into God's lap and let Him hold and comfort her.

God, please help me. She fell at his feet, her tears spilling upon them.

He reached down and placed his hand upon her head, no hint of anger or judgment emanating from His being. "Come to me, my precious daughter, come and rest a while with me."

Becca cried. "You've laid down your life for me, yet I can't seem to trust you, or anyone. You said the righteous will live by faith. But me, I'm broken, Lord. My faith is puny compared to my fear. Fear is driving me crazy, Lord. I'm even afraid of being afraid. I don't want to be this way. I don't want to ruin everything. Please, if something really is happening, help me to face it. Help me to do whatever I need to do to protect Christine, and to deal with reality in my life instead of this fairy tale I've been trying to create."

He took her chin in his fingertips and drew her face to meet His loving eyes. She looked up, trembling, fearing what he might reveal, but ready to face it. His intensity pierced her soul. She reached for His hands and climbed into His lap, where she could bury her face in His chest, in His robes, and not have to see His face. The size of a child in His larger-than-life body, she curled up against Him and wept.

"I'm still afraid, Lord, I'm sorry. Lord, I know my dad did me wrong, but not to the point I should feel this. Please show me, Lord. Please reign in me. Whatever it takes, Lord, I give myself to you. I love you, Lord. I want to love you with my life."

He held her, his strong arms providing gentle firmness around her curled up body. "I will heal all of you. You are ready. Come with me, have a look."

Despite her pounding heart and furrowed brow, despite the warring thoughts and trembling hands, Becca slightly relaxed to draw in a stilted breath. Finding just enough trust in His holiness to allow Him to lead, she consented. "Okay, Lord. You have control."

They traveled in time to a scene from her childhood. The edges dark and hazy, she saw what he revealed as they stood to watch from a distance. She sensed His white flowing robe next to her and held on to watch.

The family room appeared exactly as she'd remembered from twenty years back—wide, knotty pine paneling on the walls, a windowed wall overlooking the backyard, and a television at the far end of the room, facing the couch and recliner. Her mother was out Christmas shopping, the two oldest kids with her. Becca heard faint sounds of Carlton and Missy playing in their rooms. She saw herself, as a child, watching television with her Daddy.

On the television screen, a couple kissed passionately. The exuberant young Becca jumped up and stood on the couch. Placing her hands on her hips, she quipped, "Daddy, I know how grown-ups kiss."

"How?" He smiled at her.

"They kiss on the lips." She laughed at her own silliness.

Daddy's eyes lit up. One side of his mouth turned up in impish glee. He moved over to where she jumped on the couch. "Show me."

"Oh, they put their lips together and turn their heads back and forth and mess each other's hair up." She giggled as she pretended to kiss an invisible person.

"No, show *me*."

"Huh?" Becca didn't understand.

"Do it to me." Becca's father moved closer, his index finger to his lips.

Becca's body tensed as she watched the scene from afar. She squeezed her Savior's arm tighter.

Her Savior reached across her and the scene switched. She saw the same room, from another angle, after her mother returned. The child Becca sat on the floor near her mother's chair, unable to stop crying, well after the other children had gone to sleep.

"Stop crying and go to bed," her father grumbled from his recliner.

The young Becca cried harder. She couldn't catch her breath. She couldn't stop.

Her mother yelled at her father, "What in the world happened? I can't even go out for a few hours without something happening."

"There's nothing wrong with her. I was watching a show and she started crying."

Becca's mother tried to calm her and urged her to say what happened. She gave her a bowl of ice cream—the expensive brand she saved for herself. Torn between her intense pain and a rare treat, Becca finally settled enough to eat a bit.

"What happened, Becca?" Mommy plied.

"I. . . don't. . . know. . ." Becca burst into sobs again, pushing the ice cream away.

The scene faded. Becca curled up in her Lord's lap, in the throne room of her heart. She sobbed, heaving and shuddering from the depths of her soul. As if no time had elapsed since she was a child, the feelings rushed over her. "Oh, God, oh, God." She clung to him. "I didn't know the words to say."

The Holy Creator of the universe held and rocked her, His white robes enveloping her in pure love. When God said, "I love you, my child," His meaning rang pure, holy, and unselfish.

Becca's store of excruciating pain released in sobs too deep for words. After several minutes, her sobs calmed.

He stroked her hair and spoke. "It wasn't your fault, my dear one."

Becca sobbed again. "But I never should have—"

"It wasn't your fault. It was not your fault."

Three times. When God wanted to drive a point home, he made three repetitions. Becca swallowed hard and repeated the important message aloud. "It wasn't my fault." The words, more difficult to utter than she imagined, resonated true, yet they hovered, ethereal, like a wisp of morning mist above deep waters.

"My child, healing will be a journey. I will be with your every breath. You will know how loved you are. You will see yourself as I see you. You will see reality. I do not condemn you for feeling fear. I do not condemn you for trying to prevent injury. I do not condemn you for trying to protect yourself and your daughter. Fear, distrust, and protectiveness are normal reactions to being abused. You will learn to let my Spirit replace those feelings with a balanced sense of control. You can do your part in protecting yourself and your family and do so with me rather than hiding in shame."

Becca had been trapped in a small crate in this part of her soul, concealed, even from herself. As she emerged from the cage, she noticed her stiff, pained and stunted state. She stretched. *Being free of this turmoil will be good.* She sang a worship song. "Lord, you are. . . precious, kind and true."

He joined in and sang back: "Child, you are. . . precious. . ."

Pain gave way to wonder, peace, and joy. *The Creator of the universe, the Almighty God, the King of kings and Lord of lords, El Roi—God saw me. He rocked and comforted and sang—to me.* She smiled at Him, humbled, uplifted, thankful.

He wiped her tears with His gentle hands. Take this song with you, and come and see me again soon, my child." Embracing her, He set her back on her feet.

She hated to go, but sensed the time. Returning His embrace and climbing the stairs from her heart to her mind, Becca opened her eyes. Her room was the same as a few minutes prior, but Becca was not. She wiped more tears away, blew her nose, and opened her journal.

> *It wasn't my fault. I didn't know I had blamed myself.*
> *I didn't even remember. But it happened. As soon as I*
> *saw the family room, the experience all rushed back,*
> *intensely real, as if it had just happened. My father*
> *molested me. I was seven.*

Becca released the pen onto her bed and stared at the words it had formed. Another tear wriggled down her cheek. Her fingers followed their instinct, to brush away the tear as something to be ashamed of—something wrong. She grasped the pen again and let the ink flow out with words for the interior clamor.

> *What he did messed up love for me. I loved my Daddy,*
> *wanted his love, wanted him to pay attention to me,*
> *joke around and play with me, but I didn't want him*
> *to hurt me. That was not love. Not at all. How could*
> *he do such a thing?*

Shock set in, transporting her from reality into the surreal place where time slows and all is like a dream. Her emotions faded into the background, as if screened by a thick glass wall. She set her pen down and scuffed into the bathroom, each step an accomplishment. Who she saw in the mirror didn't even look like Becca, but rather some sad waif lost in a dream. Holding a washcloth under the faucet's stream of cold water seemed to be the action of a robot, not her own.

Wringing the cloth nearly dry, she pressed it against her swollen eyes.

I've got to get to Ministry Training class. But how? How can I go like this?

She washed her face and plodded back to her room. Pulling on her jeans and a baggy shirt, she noticed her journal still on the nightstand. *Christine can't see this.* Becca slipped her journal between the mattress and bedspring, straightened the bed sheets, and headed to class.

As she walked, questions surfaced like words in an inverted Magic 8 Ball. *Why didn't God stop it?* She shook the thought away. Another popped up. *What else happened?* Then another. *Did I imagine it?* Again, she shook the vague thoughts away, only to meet another. *Did he abuse any other kids? . . . my sisters? . . . Christine?* The last question more than she could handle, she forced the subject out of her mind. *No! No more of this today.* With decisive force, Becca heaved open the classroom door and stepped in.

From across the room, she saw Mike. He hadn't noticed her enter as he talked with his friends. She didn't want him to notice. *He'll see my puffy eyes and red nose. He'll ask what's wrong. Could I lie? I never lie.* Letting her long hair fall across her face, she looked down toward the books she carried, as if trying to find something, while she passed the other classmates toward her seat. Arriving at the table next to Mike, she pretended to be absorbed in preparations for class.

The teacher introduced the day's lesson.

Becca sighed with relief. *Mike didn't notice.* Becca continued looking at her notebook, and tried to listen to the teacher, but concentration eluded her. *How will I break this to Mike? He already knows my dad had come on to me, told me he wanted to make love to me—at fourteen. I don't think I blocked any memories at that age.*

"We're going to have some guests visit our training class next week." The teacher's voice interrupted Becca's train of thought. "The authors of our textbook. Be sure to have finished at least chapters. . . "

Becca managed to write down the assignment, until rumination overtook the teacher's words again. *Disgusting. I just froze. Why didn't I fight him off?*

Teacher's voice came to the forefront again. "The Lord isn't only interested in improving our behavior. He prefers to clean up and heal what's on the inside, where the big difference is. The real miracle Jesus brings—relationship with our Abba Daddy—renews us to rest in and enjoy him forever."

Becca usually listened with rapt attention to Pastor Richard. Thankful to be in this setting, at this time, where healing is a part of ministry training, she savored every word as a treasure. Today, though, her mind wandered as never before.

I hated what my father did, but I loved him. He was my daddy—the one who put a roof over our heads and food on the table. He comforted me when Mom rejected me, when she wanted me out of the house. I wanted him to come to know the Lord.

Saying anything to my family about what Dad did would undo all my efforts sharing Christ's love with them. I wanted to forgive him, to understand him and for him to seek help, but I hadn't realized his sickness was so bad—and went so far back. How did I forget what he did?

Her notes from class turned into mindless scribbles in

the margins of her lined note pad. Her attention rested on her drawing—a series of squiggly lines entangled upon themselves like the center of a golf ball. Tiny black bands wadded together inside a hard, white sphere—the one golfers smacked with clubs in celebrated effort to sink in a hole.

Pastor Richard drew the layers of an onion on the blackboard. "Going through healing is like peeling off one layer of an onion at a time. The outer layers are the hardest to peel, but inside, the stink is so bad it makes you cry!" He laughed, and the class chuckled with him.

Becca pushed back a tear.

"Recently, in a large assembly of clergy, a show of hands suggested approximately eighty percent had a family member with a substance abuse problem. That's astounding. The very people who are trying to help addicts are hurting from the effects of addiction, probably too much to pass on true health themselves." He paused and sat his chalk on the ledge under the board. "Unhealthy clergy, who may not even realize they're unhealthy, tend to pass on dysfunctional messages. Messages filled with all you *should* do. You should forgive. You should smile. You should give beyond your comfort level. You should behave this way, perform that way. A life of should's is a life of performance—of facades, not a life of faith in the Good News."

He leaned against the back of a chair with both hands, his voice lowering and his eyes scanning the room. "This group of ministry training students has an opportunity unlike what's offered in seminary—the opportunity to be real, to drop your masks, your facades, and all you've learned you *should* do, and let people know your true selves. You don't have to be perfect to help another. You just need to be in process—the process of receiving the good news of the Gospel, that you truly are loved, accepted, and forgiven, the process of being in relationship with Abba Daddy, letting him heal your wounds and renew your minds, and being willing to share your journey with others."

He pointed to the layers of the onion he'd drawn on the board. "As I said, peeling an onion makes some people cry." He looked at Becca. "And that's okay."

Becca felt tears wash her cheeks. She nodded and looked back down at her notes. She drifted further into memories. *Soon after we moved to Florida, everyone wanted us to go to Mom and Dad's house for Easter. After the experience with Dad, we decided not to go. I told them something had happened, and I would send letters to explain it. But everyone went into an uproar over my decision. Emily accused me of being a terrible excuse for a Christian. Complete turmoil. Seven years hoping to be a good witness to my family, all shot by rocking their nice little boat—all because I wouldn't join them for Easter.*

She wrote on her notes, next to what she'd written from Pastor Richard's lecture about dropping the mask, being real, and peeling the onion.

The boat I rocked has a name. EVERYTHING'S FINE HERE.

Becca's mind drifted into lessons she'd learned in the last year about dysfunctional family systems. Connections between their lessons and what happened in her family lit up her brain like fireworks. An elephant could be in the middle of the room, but if the alcoholic said, "No, there's no elephant here," then everybody else in the family better agree, and shut up about it, and tiptoe around that elephant.

She had learned that people tend to stay rooted in patterns

they learn in childhood. If the boat isn't rocked, nothing changes. But even when the boat is rocked, no guarantee of improvement follows. Picturing the dysfunctional family system as a mobile shaken out of balance—teetering and tottering, but returning to balance. Becca's family had been shaken when she refused to join them for Easter, but they regrouped and went on without her.

She looked at her notes. "EVERYTHING'S FINE HERE."

I've played the game, too. I persuaded Mike to be civil to my family when he wanted to take them to task.

Becca faced a huge decision. Let the secret out, regardless of the fallout, or find a way to shove her feelings and memories back down, to wear a mask. *Here I am, pretending I haven't been crying, like everything's fine. Everything isn't fine. I need to change, or the pattern will continue.*

Pastor Richard's voice rose above Becca's mental stream. "Every dysfunctional family lives under three unspoken rules."

Becca felt his eyes on her, as if he'd noticed she wasn't paying attention today and increased his emphasis to gain her attention. She looked at him and indeed, he was addressing her directly. Becca lifted her pen to the paper and looked at the board, ready to write down the three unspoken rules.

"The first is, don't talk."

Becca wrote—1. Don't talk.

"Now, this doesn't mean you can't talk at all, of course. In an alcoholic home, you can talk about pretty near anything, except for the alcoholic's drinking. What happened in your home of origin when someone talked about the alcoholic's drinking?"

Hands raised and, when called upon, a few students shared

what their father or mother did when someone brought up drinking as a problem. The alcoholic parent made the person who spoke up look worse than him or herself, or the whole house ended up in a huge fight and the alcoholic had a reason to leave and head to the bar. Becca had lived those stories.

"Rule number two is don't trust."

Becca wrote—2. Don't trust.

Pastor Richard continued. "It could have been as simple as the alcoholic promising not to drink again. Every day, or week, or month, the same promise. Every day, or week, or month, the same violation. We learned NOT to trust. We learned the lesson over and over, all throughout childhood. Maybe Dad promised he would come to your ball game but ended up drunk instead. Maybe Mom promised she would take you and move somewhere else, but never did. Dysfunctional families don't follow through on promises. They find a way to return to their former homeostasis. Children learn not to trust their parents."

This struck home. She couldn't trust her father. He had abused her. And her mother? She didn't do anything to protect Becca from him. *Mom followed Dad's don't talk rule.*

"The third rule in dysfunctional families is the most insidious. Don't feel."

Becca wrote—3. Don't feel.

Don't feel? But I grew up being called a crybaby. Some said she'd cried her life away. *My feelings are too intense—they've led me into trouble, too many times.*

Pastor Richard clarified the don't feel rule. "You may think you're feeling, but a dysfunctional family offers no healthy means to process them. Emotions aren't acknowledged. Children don't learn how to manage their emotions. If some feelings are tolerated, others are disallowed. Some members are allowed certain feelings, others not. Maybe Dad is angry all the time, but if anyone else is angry, they're in trouble—big trouble! Maybe little Suzy has a good reason to cry, but instead of someone finding out what's wrong and comforting her, she's ridiculed for being a crybaby."

Becca gulped. Had Pastor Richard been in her family of origin? Her eyes widened and she sat her pen down, listening.

"So, if we're going to be ministering to hurting people, we first need to examine ourselves. We need to pay attention to how well we're breaking the big three dysfunctional rules— so we can learn better, healthier ways to manage life. Then we'll be able to pass on a healthy example for those we hope to minister to." He placed his hands on his hips as he surveyed the room's responses. "Yes, you heard me right. These rules are meant to be broken. In our groups, and in your quiet times with the Lord and in your relationship with your spouse, it's time to talk. Take a chance on trust again. Let yourself feel and bring all of your thoughts and emotions to the Lord for renewal. He will teach you how to process your emotions in a healthy manner."

Becca examined faces around the room. Everyone responded to this lecture—some gape-faced and stunned, some shifting in their seats, some with tears streaming down their faces. She looked at her notes again. She drew a large circle around the three rules and slashed a line through them. Beneath it, she wrote in large capital letters—

BREAK THE RULES!

43

Lena

Rockville, Maryland. 1933

Lena carried a large quilt made from scraps of old clothes—a gift for her brother and sister-in-law. Stitching in secret during weekends at home and quiet moments at work, she hurried to present the quilt to them as a token of gratitude for their generosity through tough times. She headed toward Robert and Theresa's house, after a delivery truck driver, who often let her ride along on his route from Sandy Spring to Rockville, dropped her at the corner.

As she walked, another man drove by in his work truck, and, upon seeing Lena, he abruptly stopped the truck. The gears gave a loud *krunk, clonk, crunch* as he shifted the old pickup into reverse and backed up, stopping next to Lena. He pushed the gearshift into neutral and pulled the screeching hand brake.

"Ma'am." He tipped his hat as he leaned toward the open

window on her side. "I see you're carrying a large load. Can I give you a ride?"

"Well, that's kind of you, sir, but I'm nearly there." Lena noticed his rugged good looks through layers of dust, presumably from manual labor. "I'm going right there to my brother's place." She pointed with her eyes, her hands being fully engaged in carrying her package.

The truck door swung open and out he launched, with a boy's energy. Smiling with eyes so kindly Lena wanted to melt, he quickly pulled his suspenders up over his shoulders where they belonged. Wiping his hands on his pants, he scurried toward her, reaching toward the quilt. "Well, let me carry that for you, ma'am. A pretty little thing like you ought not to be carrying such a large package."

Pretty little thing. Those words again. Lena hated that term, ever since that first lawyer used the term with disdain. *But he meant to compliment you.* She looked away briefly to avoid signaling her discomfort with the term. "Thank you, sir." Politely releasing the quilt to his open arms, she straightened her gloves.

Together they walked two houses down the street, to Robert and Theresa's. Dorsey set the quilt on the front porch swing. "Forgive me for not introducing myself. I'm Dorsey." He held his hand out in proper fashion. "Dorsey Reeves. I live behind this house of your brother's." The handsome stranger careened his neck around the post to see through from one back yard to the next. "I'm surprised I haven't met you before. And you are?"

"Lena Smith. Nice to meet you, Dorsey. Thank you for your help." She responded with her hand toward his, palm down, as customary and added a slight curtsy as her sisters taught her. Doing so felt silly, which warmed her cheeks.

Dorsey lifted her hand toward his face and kissed it. His eyes tilted up toward hers as he did, watching her response. The tip of the right side of his mouth curled up, as if delighted to see her cheeks flush and a light flash in her eyes. His smile dropped as he caught a glimpse of his dusty clothes. He stood up straight and increased the formality of his tone. "Well, I must be going, ma'am. I hope to meet you again."

Lena sensed her heightened pulse. She placed her hand on the wall to keep herself from swaying. Her feelings rapidly fluxed, from her initial slight annoyance at his "pretty little thing" remark, to intense attraction, to shy embarrassment, and now, slight confusion at his sudden change in tone. "Of course, unless. . . Would you like to say hello to my brother while you're here?"

Appearing relieved at the invitation, Dorsey thanked her but kindly requested another time, so he could make himself presentable. They agreed to him returning after dinner for tea and dessert.

Lena pressed her skirt down around her and checked her hair in the mirror by the door. She opened the door for Dorsey, with Robert and Theresa right behind her.

"Good evening, Miss Lena." He smiled and tipped his hat.

Lena caught her breath. She'd noticed his handsomeness even in his dusty work-clothes earlier, but now, cleaned up and dressed for dinner, she forced herself to look away so as not to gape. "Good evening. Do come in." Arm motioning the way, she stepped aside and turned her glance to her brother and sister-in-law.

"Yes, come in, Dorsey, good to see you." Robert reached for Dorsey's hand.

The men shook hands. They had been neighbors for years and exchanged neighborly man-talk over the back fence at times. Only after meeting Lena did they first gather inside the home.

"May I take your hat, sir?" Theresa's pleasant manner respected social propriety in friendly, casual style.

The four gathered at the kitchen table for tea and pie. Conversation flowed, and the hour passed quickly. They discussed Dorsey's carpentry work, as well as family, weather, and farming. Lena spoke of her family, their farm in Sandy Spring, of work, and her love of animals, sewing and gardening.

Each time their eyes met, his seemed to glimmer, as though they'd been eagerly anticipating hers. To engage in direct eye contact may be too forward, so she attempted to limit herself from the game. Yet her eyes found their way back to his countless times, her face warming each time. *But why? His sense of humor, or his big, strong chest and arms. . . and hands?* Although laughing at herself for thinking this way, her best efforts to resist fell sway to his charm.

The next night, and the one after that, and nearly every night for the next three weeks, Dorsey courted Lena with flowers, strolls around the neighborhood, and long talks on the porch swing.

They talked about everything. Lena learned Dorsey had never been married, but he'd come close a couple of times. Something made him wait. If he were ever to marry, he'd said, he'd marry someone he could trust, someone with a good sense of humor, who would be comfortable being themselves. No interest in pretense or fancies, he wanted someone who shared his faith, his love for a simple life, and honesty. Lena found herself hoping that someone would be her.

Their evening stroll ended as they approached Robert and Theresa's door. An old porch swing, wearing faded white paint, chipped at the edges, stood ready to receive visitors. "Dorsey, there's something we need to talk about. Can we sit a spell?"

"Of course." He held the swing steady for her as she sat, then he sat beside her. His feet pressing against the porch floor, he propelled the swing.

"Well, you've heard me talk about my children." Nervousness shook the edge of her voice.

Dorsey laughed. "Yes, a time or two."

His laughter soothed her nervousness. "I guess I have talked about them—quite a lot. You've never asked me why they don't live with me, or anything about my first husband. I. . . just want you to know. . . you can, if you want to, ask."

Dorsey's eyebrows raised. His lower lip puffed out. He slipped his arm around her shoulder and gave her a squeeze.

"Well, thank you. I appreciate you offering the explanation. I haven't asked, because I didn't want to pry, or be rude. If you feel ready to talk about it, I would like to know. Let me say, first, you couldn't tell me anything that would make me stop caring for you."

Lena's nervousness dissipated, leaving her smiling. She leaned her head toward his and replied. "Well, I appreciate your patience. I do feel I can trust you with this." Watching the sunset, she relayed her story.

"We married at sixteen. Naive, of course. In the first year, everything went well. Well as could be expected, younguns like us learning to be parents while still adapting to being married, and to managing a household on our own. But soon after the first one came along, Clinton started coming home late, and drunk. Always full of excuses, but none good. Then, when Elliot came along, Clinton took to staying out all night. He told me he couldn't get enough sleep with the babies crying. Said he couldn't concentrate at work. I managed them both on my own."

Dorsey squeezed her shoulder and patted her arm. "That must have been very hard for you, and so young."

"Yes, hard, but matters turned worse still. He'd come home drunk and force himself on me. At first, I told myself to do my duty, so I gave in and let him. But then I refused because he smelled of liquor and cigars. . . and perfume." She bit her lip. She hadn't spoken of the painful experience for years and now the intensity of emotion that accompanied that revisiting caught her by surprise.

"He did see other women. I knew when he told me he had a right to, since I didn't do my part. Then—" Lena paused to consider if she should tell him everything. *If I don't tell all now, then when? I want to get this out. . . to know how he'll react to the whole truth.* She cleared her throat. "If he didn't like what I said, he'd smack me. Hard. To get me in line, he insisted. He pushed himself on me, no matter if I cried or pushed him off, or what. Even when pregnant with twins, he kept pushing himself on me, strangling me near to death more than once." Her composure crumbled.

Dorsey reached both arms around to comfort her. "Honey. No man ever has any business treating a lady like that." He let go with one hand long enough to retrieve and present her with a handkerchief from his pocket.

Accepting his thoughtful gift, she pulled herself together and wiped her tears and nose. "There's more." She apologized for her ridiculously long, sad tale, to which he shook his head and begged her go on. "The twins came early. The boy didn't make it." She drew a deep breath, her eyes on the flower garden, her body still except for the crumpling of the soiled hanky in her lap.

"Clinton blamed me. Then he blamed Ruth. His anger spilled out on me, and then on Ruth, too. He shook her—a five-month-old." Lena blinked away blurring vision, which let moisture streak her cheeks again. "That's when I left. I took Ruth, loaded the children in the baby carriage and left. Later, he convinced me to sign divorce papers. I didn't understand all the legal mumbo-jumble, so I shouldn't have signed. Turned out the papers said I admit to adultery, but I didn't do any such thing." She turned to Dorsey. "I was faithful to him through everything. I wanted him to sober up. . . for us to be happy together. I lost the kids because I fell for his trick."

Dorsey did not hesitate. "I believe you. Don't need another second to consider it." He reached toward the table, pulled a violet from the vase and handed the tender flower to Lena. After leaning his head to hers for a moment, he turned his gaze toward the road. His jaw stiffened. "If I ever see the man, I'll be sorely tempted to repay him—with my fist in his face."

"No, no, not that." She studied him, reading the lines of his face, the quiver in his jaw, the far-off look in his eyes. On his lap, the briefly tightened fist relaxed. Sorrow, rather than retribution, prevailed.

"But Lena, don't worry about this keeping me from you. If anything, I care more for you." He turned to her. Stroking her hair, his eyes on hers, he quieted. "I wish I could have been there to protect you."

"Thank you." Lena pressed a kiss onto his cheek. She sat forward on the swing, smoothed her dress, and turned to face him. "It feels good to get the truth out. If this proves too much, I understand. I don't want retaliation, but I am working with some lawyers to get my children back."

"It hasn't been too much for you, so it's not too much for me. I'll do what I can to help." His eyes roamed from hers, to her hands, which lay folded in her lap, and back to her eyes. "You're a strong woman." Replacing his arm around Lena's shoulder, he pulled her close.

They watched the sun go down in silence.

Sandy Spring, Maryland.

Aggie placed her dish towel on her shoulder, propped her hands on her hips, and tilted her head at her happy daughter. "Starlight, I do believe you've a special glow. You've been dancing around the kitchen, singing songs." She pointed a finger and leaned in. "You have something to tell your Mama."

Lena giggled. "Is being happy so unusual? Can't a girl just love life. . . love being home with her family?" Her feet slid across the floor while she carried a stack of dishes to the table.

"Well sure, but you've been home with family often. Aunt Caroline's family were all here with us just three weeks back, and you didn't act this happy. No. Something is different." Aggie grabbed the dish towel from her shoulder and scooted after Lena, catching Lena's bottom a playful snap with the towel. "Tell your Mama!"

Lena sat the plates on the table and turned to her mother. Her face beamed with joy and excitement, hands clutched together at her chest. "Mama, I'm in love."

"I knew it! You've got that glow." Aggie threw her hands up with excitement and wrapped them around her daughter. "I'm so happy for you." She pulled out a chair. "Now sit right here and tell me all about him."

Lena guided her mother into the chair instead. "No, you sit, Mama. I'll just dance and talk."

Lena cut a rug around her mother, amusing them both. She pulled another chair in front of her mother and sat facing her to spill the news.

"His name's Dorsey. He lives right behind Robert and Theresa. A gentleman, Mama—kind, and sensible, and thoughtful, and understanding. Oh, and handsome, too! But not so handsome that he thinks all the Sheba's should be after him. He's been courting me for several weeks now, and I can't find a thing wrong with him."

"He sounds wonderful. What does he do for a living?"

"Construction—a superintendent. A sharp mind—and hard work doesn't deter him."

"And has he stated his intentions?" Aggie lifted her eyebrows and gave her head a short twist.

"Not full out, yet, but he's hinted, and I believe he feels the same." Lena's composure returned. She read her mother's eyes as she spoke. "I never thought I'd feel this way again. Sometimes the feeling scares me, so I want to take my time—see what he's really like, including how he behaves when he's mad." Lena smiled. "But for now, I feel exquisite. I'm a schoolgirl again, blushing and feeling my heart go aflutter."

Aggie's lips tightened and spread wider as her head nodded. "Good. There's no need to rush. When do we get to meet him?"

"Soon. Let's talk with Daddy and the rest of the family at supper tonight, and, if everyone agrees, we'll plan it. Robert and Theresa like him, so one hurdle's cleared."

The screen door slammed, and Ruth's voice rang out. "Mama, Grandma, you in here?"

"Your girl." Aggie said to Lena. "I'll go hang the wash to give you two some time alone."

44

Becca

The Center, South Central Florida. 1986

After preparing for an early night, Becca sat on the edge of the bed near Mike. *I hate to burden him with this. It'll upset him. God, I need your help.* She turned half-way toward Mike and cleared her throat. "The Lord showed me something this morning."

Mike, already under the covers and reading, didn't look up. "Hmm."

"Mike, I really need to talk."

"What?" He shot a look at her, brow furrowing. "I have a lot of reading to do." He returned his attention to his book.

Her voice cracked. "Oh." She averted her eyes, which welled with tears at his terse response. *Mike thinks I cry for attention, or to get my way. I won't have him see me cry because that's not it.* She tried keeping her emotions at bay.

Mike huffed, put his book down and pushed himself to a

sitting position. "What? What's the matter now?"

Her heart raced and pounded, boiling red heat to her face. Entreating Mike to talk with her was hard enough, but when he placated her as if she were a bothersome child, an imposition on his busy life—*Hmph! No way I'll tell you now. Not when you act as if your very presence is God's gift—*

She stopped her thoughts. To lash out, pointing out his error, would be to her shame. No doubt, she'd end up apologizing. Waiting for his return apology would catapult her back to fuming. *I won't lash out. I'll just not need him.*

Usually, her stoic side repudiated her needy side. But not this time. Whether due to the intensity of this morning's experience or the cumulative effect of over-stuffing—or both—she couldn't convince herself not to need him.

"Mike, my dad—" Sobs burst, cracking a huge gap in the dam that held pools of tears at bay. Becca turned her back to Mike. She wrapped her arms around herself as her chest heaved. Fighting to push down, hold back, repair the breech, she buried her face in the pillow and folded into a ball.

Mike's tone changed, from annoyance to genuine concern. "Did something happen to your dad?"

"I remember now." Becca's words rode the stream between uncontrollable sobs and stunted breath. "I remember. . . he. . . molested me." The final words rang foreign, yet eerily true. She grabbed a wad of tissues from the box on the nightstand.

Mike put his hand on her back. He lay next to her, with his arm around her.

After a while, Becca's explosion settled. "I'm sorry."

"No, no. Don't apologize for that. You didn't do anything wrong." He sat up, his legs over his side of the bed. His body tensed and his voice lowered. "I want to pay that man a visit. I wish I still had my service weapon."

Becca turned and saw him clenching and opening his fists. She heard him breathing out the way one does before taking a long breath to swim underwater. "No—not that. You'll end up in jail. And then what?"

"I know. I won't. I'm just saying, it's what he deserves."

Becca's uncoiling ball of emotions was enough for one night. *I can't handle his, too.* Drawing a deep breath, she laid a hand on his thigh. "God's going to help me with this. I just wanted you to know. Like Pastor Richard said today, I'm going to talk, trust and feel."

Mike laid face to face with Becca. "Okay. You probably need someone else to talk with about this, too."

"You mean a counselor? I don't know. I'm exhausted, though. That's all I can do tonight. I need sleep." She turned to her other side, away from Mike, now conscious that her face must be an ugly sight. Pulling an extra pillow into her chest, she hugged it. "Just hold me."

As she drifted into sleep, she entered a magical garden, with pansy beds thick enough to rest in, dogwood trees blooming all about, and daffodils waving in a gentle breeze. Fruit trees and vegetable vines thrived, and lilting birdsong filled the air. A gardener knelt in the pathway, facing away from her, engrossed in his work.

Becca approached. She watched as the gardener skillfully pulled a huge weed from the soggy ground, taking great care to get every bit of root. She marveled at the long and intricate roots.

The gardener held the withering foe up. His face, from

the side, shone gentle, calm, unperturbed, and perhaps even joyful, as he admired his accomplishment. "This one planned to take over."

Becca chuckled at his confidence, and as she did, the gardener turned. An immediate connection with his smiling face gave her a sense she'd known him all along.

He spoke to her. "If I'd tried to pull this one from dry, hard soil, the sneaky invader would have broken off at the top. These roots in the ground would have produced more weeds—all through the garden." He waved his hand over the teeming garden.

Becca's eyebrows pressed together and she tipped her head to one side. *Who is he?* Dressed in blue overalls, kneeling by the side of an impressive flower garden, he seemed relaxed and confident—not at all perturbed by the stubborn weed. *This is his garden.* She looked around. Seeing no clouds in the sky, no evidence of recent rain and no bucket or hose nearby, she asked, "How is the soil so moist?"

The gardener pulled his hand out of his glove and reached up to touch her cheek. A tear from the outer corner of her eye trickled onto his finger.

"Your tears did it. Let them flow."

* * *

Many families at The Center practiced relationship building by hosting father-daughter dates. Tonight, the plan included dinner and a movie. Mike and Christine waved goodbye and drove off in the family car. They'd meet up with the other fathers and daughters after having dinner in town and then sit together as a larger group for the movie.

As the car disappeared in a cloud of dust down the road, a cloud of dust stirred in Becca's heart. Worry and fear struck her, hard. Though she planned to use the evening alone to refresh herself with a bubble bath and a good book, she couldn't shake off worries that Mike would abuse Christine while they were out.

After nervously cleaning the house, then doing her aerobics to the videotaped instructor, she turned on the hot water to run a bath. While the tub filled, she picked up her journal. *Maybe if I write about it. Get the words out of my head and onto the paper.*

She wrote a prayer. "I'm so scared Mike will abuse Christine. Why, Lord? Did I stuff away a memory of that, too?" She closed her eyes to descend the imaginary stairs to the throne room in her heart. Jerking away, she added to her journal. "And the stairs—why do they look like stairs to the basement in Maryland? Why do I freeze when I picture them?"

A gentle response rose in her heart, which she also wrote. "Shall I show you more of why you mistrust men, and why the stairs bring you such dread?"

Tensed, and wondering if he would take her to another scene of forgotten abuse, she steeled herself to cooperate. "Yes, Lord. Whatever it takes." Releasing the pen and closing her eyes, Becca pictured herself on God's lap. She held on for dear life. *Go ahead, Lord.*

A scene unfolded, viewed from a corner of the ceiling. Becca's oldest brother carried the nine-year-old Becca down the stairs to his basement room—a cold room in a large cinderblock basement. Hanging sheets surrounding a mattress on the floor defined his room.

Immediately, the memory surged. He told her he loved her, and that this made him feel good. Becca remembered confusion. On one hand, she felt sort of good, that he loved her, like she was something special. That gave her pause. But no, she didn't like the weird feeling. Wrong, her gut told her. She didn't know what he would do. She made a move to get away. He was on top of her, telling her shush. . . hold still.

The child Becca turned her head away, squeezing her eyes shut, and forced herself somewhere else in her mind, as if willing reality away would make him stop kissing and touching and pressing himself on and in her, hurting her, making her do wrong. When he finished, she lay there, frozen stiff, eyes squeezed shut, tears streaked down the sides of her face and pooling in her ears.

His whispered warning replayed in her mind.

"If you tell Mom, she's going to know what you did—that you're not a good girl. Keep our secret. I love you, Becca, you're my favorite girl."

The scene faded.

Her gut a ball of tangled turmoil and horror, Becca felt as if the abuse had just happened, but this time, with an adult's comprehension. Shudders from those cruel years caused her body to tremble and heave. So many times, both her father and her brother. Nowhere to go to escape. *Why didn't I scream? Why didn't I stop them?* She recalled a time she'd wrestled out of it and run up the steps to tell.

Hearing the water running in the tub, she reached out and turned the faucet off. She slipped into the tub and closed her eyes.

Telling didn't stop it.

A prisoner in her own home, childhood meant hiding, guarding, fearing sleep. Becca sobbed, rocking to and fro, holding herself. *I escaped by turning off my mind, like life was a TV channel I could just switch.* She trembled, freezing, and opened her eyes. The bathwater had turned cold. She stood, dried, and wrapped herself in a terry robe. Taking her journal with her, she curled up in a chair and sought the Lord again.

"Now do you understand?" His tone, his being, exuded sadness mingled with patience and love.

I grew up not just abused but confused. Love meant sex. Scanning her boyfriend history—from the first, to Luis, Noel, Craig, and all the others. *All liars. They pretended to love me, but they just wanted sex.*

"It's no wonder you're afraid. You experienced the worst. This is not what I created man to be. This is an abomination, not what I created families to be. I don't want you to condemn yourself for your fear or lack of trust. Let yourself feel what you feel and bring everything to me. I will comfort you. I will restore what they took from you. I will heal your wounds. You are not bad, my precious daughter. You needed love, but you did not ask for, nor want, abuse."

Becca wept with God. After a long, deep cry of release, she looked up and braved a question. "Is anything happening now? I want to be brave enough to face it. Please don't let my denial and repression leave Christine compromised."

His look reassured her. "Not all men are like that."

My worries spring from what I learned about men in my past. Those worries make sense in light of my experience. "Lord, thank you. Yes, please do heal me. I need your love and comfort." She wrote in her journal. "Not all men are liars. Not all men are abusers. I grew up in an extremely sick family. They taught me wrong. Now I will learn what is right and true."

She paused to reflect on her written words. *My family. Extremely sick.* Guilt welled in her throat, stifling the anger that clenched her neck and jaw. *I shouldn't judge them like that. I'm sorry, Lord.*

"Becca, you do love your family—at your own expense." His voice pruned the deformed branches in her mind. "Have you taken the blame to shield them? You did not cause the abuse. Let me deal with them."

I have taken the blame. I have been trying to shield them, as if the abuse was my fault, and as if anything you might do about it would destroy us all. I've been forcing forgiveness across the whole lot of us like a blanket of protection. My flimsy excuse for a blanket has just let the offenses go on—undercover.

Becca stood and paced the room, her thoughts reeling.

I skipped over my natural and rightful anger. I've been condemning myself for not loving them enough, applying the Gospel like a Band-Aid over a gaping, festering wound. . . all because I'm afraid that you'll reject me if I don't forgive.

She searched herself to make sense of the whole picture. *Now that I can see myself as a child, I realize I have been brutal to myself. I would never treat a child the way I've treated myself. From now on, I will treat my inner child as I would treat my own child—with kindness, gentleness, support, and encouragement.*

"Yes, my child." The edges of his lips turned up and his tone sweetened. "How can you love your neighbor if you do not love yourself? Join me in loving Becca." His eyes sparkling and his voice gentle, he continued. "Let's not focus on fear for now. Let's focus on love, on what holy love is, and does—and on meeting your need for real love. Loving yourself is not selfish. It's essential." He squeezed her in a gentle embrace, drawing her into his heart.

"Wow." She sunk in, enjoying the security of His arms. After eight years enjoying news of His unconditional love in the Bible, unfathomable depths of His love lay ahead, yet to discover. Delighted by the idea of love expansive in height, depth, and breadth, she, in contrast, was small, barely sprouted, not healthy or mature enough to serve the Lord in full-time ministry. *But God knew that. He called me anyway. I am what I am, Lord. I can't pretend to be more.*

She rested, her mind wandering back over the last several months, of the many times she'd seen fear as her worst enemy. "You know what just occurred to me, Lord? I've been focused on eradicating fear from my life because I'm afraid of being afraid."

They chuckled. The Lord lifted her and smiled at her, his sparkling eyes speaking volumes of love. "Fear is not a sin. Fear is an emotion that signals danger. When you experience fear, the feeling alerts you and energizes you to act against the threat. Fear is not the opposite of faith. The opposite of faith is not believing—not believing me, what I've done for you, what I say about you, and who I am for you. If you want to focus on eradicating something, let's go after the lies you swallowed. Let's replace them with believing what I say about you."

Another vision formed in her mind's eye—a picture of an infected wound, but in a brain. The infection of repressed, neglected memories surrounded invasive, thorny lies, clogging neural pathways in her brain. She invited God to clean out the pus, to expose and pluck out the lies, and to cleanse and dress the wound for healing with the balm of truth.

She slipped her pajamas on, poured a cup of hot apple cider and settled at the dining room table with her journal, to record the evening's revelations.

> . . . I've believed all these lies somewhere in my brain: It's all my fault. I'm no good. I'm bad. All men are liars and secret predators. God will punish me if I don't forgive them even though they haven't repented. I can take the blame for them and save them.
>
> But here are the Truths: It's not my fault. God made us good, male, and female. God will not punish me—on the contrary, he will guide me into all truth. I am willing to forgive, not excuse, because of what Jesus did on the cross. Jesus is the Savior, the Sacrifice, not me. God's job is to administer justice and to offer redemption, and each person has free will to choose to accept or reject his offer.

After recording the exchange in her journal, Becca curled up on the sofa by the Christmas tree. Mike and Christine still out, Becca relaxed into the present moment. She basked in the comforting aroma of the cinnamon stick she swirled in the cider. Her gaze skimmed along the tree, from the twinkling lights to the manger scene beneath. The sight of the newborn baby wrapped in burial cloths and laid in the cow's feeding trough struck her. Jesus, Emmanuel—God with us—one with the Father in Heaven from before time, hadn't been too proud to start over again as a babe. *Neither will I. And this time I'll have the best Father ever.*

Truth sprouted in the tilled depths of her heart and soul. *I am accepted. I am precious and holy in His sight. I am loved. I matter. I have a purpose. I am equipped and capable to fulfill God's purpose in my life.*

* * *

1987

Bronson moved an old milking stool to the center of class and sat on it. "You see how easily I can sit on this stool? I'm not going to fall off, am I?" He wiggled around on the firm seat.

Someone in class replied. "No, sir."

He stood and went to the chalkboard. He drew a simple three-legged stool. "That's because the stool has three legs. If I cut one of these legs off, would I be able to sit on it without falling off? Not without a lot of work, right?" He turned and watched the men nod. Facing the board, he wrote as he spoke. "The stool's legs have names. This one is God, this one is self, and this one is others." He wrote the names along each leg. "To have stability, we need healthy relationships with all three—God, self and others. If we saw a leg off, the stool won't be balanced. Have we cut off our relationship with others?" He erased the leg named others.

Bronson pressed his fingers together at his chest as he walked around the class, speaking in solemn, matter-of-fact surety. "The disease of addiction needs blaming and gaming to survive. Admitting how we've hurt other people is hard. Knowing how to make amends is hard, too. If possible. There's no guarantee others will forgive us. Our task is to see what we've done, to become willing to make amends, and to try to make amends. Take out your pencil and notebook and jot down what you've done to cut others off. Don't worry if you don't think of everything. Just write what comes to mind in the next five minutes. Later this week, we'll write letters of apology."

Becca had long ago apologized to everyone she could recall hurting. As a ministry training student, she regularly examined herself for anything she hadn't thought of before. During the five minutes, she recalled no unattended offenses. Instead, she considered what the Lord had reassured her about the abuse not being her fault.

Deciding to ask Pastor Richard about her ongoing relationship problem with her family of origin, she headed to his office after class. She'd been keeping him apprised of her personal recovery situation in a pastoral counseling relationship. "Have I cut them off my three-legged stool? I'm confused. I've done what I could to apologize for ways I might have hurt them when I was an angry teen. But the distance we created is to protect Christine. Am I taking too much or too little from what Bronson taught today?"

"Becca, I think you've already taken more than your share of responsibility in your relationship with your parents." Pastor Richard leaned forward over his desk. His rounded features conveyed the certainty of grace. "Instead of a letter of apology to your family, how about a letter extending honest and loving confrontation?"

Becca's eyebrows launched upward as her eyes opened. "Confrontation?"

"Yes. Pray about it. I'll be glad to look your letter over before you send it."

That night, Becca settled into a quiet spot with her Bible, notebook, and a pen. She closed her eyes to pray. The Lord stood as a mighty warrior, composed, yet infuriated at the evils imposed on the child Becca. She saw herself standing between her father and the Lord, her arms spread out as if to guard her earthly father from her heavenly one. As a mediator, she looked at the Lord.

His face spoke to Becca's heart, and she knew.

She gasped at herself. "I'm still trying to protect my abuser—from you."

He waved his arm, gesturing for her to step aside.

"I can't, Lord. I don't want you to give him what he deserves. Please, there must be a reason he became what he did. Please, forgive him."

Father God stood, arms open, his face solemnly asking her to trust him.

This is God, the creator—the one who sent his only Son to save us. If I cannot trust Him with my father, then who? I need to stop protecting my dad. "You have more love for my father than I do." Stepping aside, Becca took her place at God's side. Opening her eyes, she knew what to do next.

Dad,

My memories came back. I must have some-how pushed them out but now I remember. You did sick, wrong, and inappropriate things to me, including molesting me when I was only seven.

You hurt me. I still struggle to trust anyone. I am receiving help for problems stemming from what you did, and God is healing me.

You need to stop abusing people. I don't know why or how you got so messed up, but you have no right to impose yourself on, to hurt others. You can change if you want to, if you seek help. Turn to God and professional help.

I am telling the family what you did because they deserve to have a chance to protect their children from you. Your behavior is unacceptable, and I won't expose myself or my family to sexual abuse any longer.

Love, Becca

Not a perfect letter, but a start. She also wrote to her brothers, her sisters and mother, telling them what had happened. Her letter to Doug was confrontational, like the one to her father. After sharing the letters with Pastor Richard for approval, she put them in the mail.

As she walked toward home from the row of mailboxes, a distant storm thundered. The peal reverberated in her soul and called her eyes to scan the skies for the source. *Nothing.* Nothing but a cloudless sky. Becca whispered a prayer.

"Lord, you know I don't like war. Mailing those letters, I feel like I've launched the first cannonballs, starting war. But the war began long ago. This is my first counteroffensive move. Let the truth hit the target, Lord. Destroy the altars used for their vile sacrifices. . . and put an end to abuse."

45

Lena

Bethesda, Maryland. 1934

"Daahhling, do be a dear and take the hemline up for me. I need this dress tomorrow."

"Of course, ma'am." Lena opened the dressing room door. "Please, slip on your lovely dress and then step right up here." She waved her hand toward the platform next to the dressing room.

The congressman's wife, a regular in The Dress Shoppe, stepped into the dressing room and drew the curtain.

"Did you bring the shoes you'll wear with it?"

"Indeed." The sophisticated patron stepped out from the dressing room. She turned for assistance with fasteners on the back, slipped her feet into her beaded heels and stepped up onto the platform.

Lena stooped at the foot of her statuesque client and began pinning. "Here, Mrs. Lewis?" She looked in the mirror for a response.

"Yes. But please, call me Flo. That's short for Florida, not Florence."

"Oh, are you from Florida?" Lena pinned the hemline, circling around the platform as she worked.

"Oh, goodness, no. Florida is my real name. It means beauty and thriving." She held her chin high and peered at her image in the mirror, appearing pleased with herself.

"Both qualities you possess, ma'am." Lena flashed her eyes toward Mrs. Lewis, sending a warm glance. "I mean, Flo." She turned her eyes back to her job.

Flo smiled. "Speaking of thriving, I'm going to a very important dinner hosted by the Women's Club. Many of us are exercising our influence with our husbands, who will attend with us, since we haven't yet outnumbered them in matters of governance for the country."

Lena removed a pin from between her lips, her eyes widening. "How exciting. Which matters, ma'am?" She returned to pinning.

Her client continued her eloquent elaboration. "I'm sure you've heard of the work of the former Roosevelt, Teddy, toward establishing a better understanding of child health and development." She glanced at Lena, and back to the mirror. "Since the depression hit, his findings and initiatives, as wonderful as they were, fell by the wayside. The government had no choice but to focus on bringing this country out of financial ruin and rampant unemployment, as I'm sure you know, dear."

"Yes, ma'am. Many of our fine customers discuss such things—"

"Now, though, we see an opportunity. My husband has

put forth a bill which primarily addresses the needs of our labor force and elderly, but we will be advancing the idea of incorporating children's welfare into the bill's final form."

"Oh, that sounds wonderful." Lena's mind drifted toward her children.

"Yes. Including government funds for homeless, neglected children, foster care and the like. And those born less fortunate, say for example, with a physical or mental deficiency."

"I know some very neglected children myself." She sat back on her heels, still propped at Mrs. Lewis's feet. Taking the last pin from her mouth, she focused on her client's eyes. "Is there anything I can do to help?"

"Oh, you mean you personally know some children in trouble?" Her face grew troubled, her furrowed brows settling over her questioning eyes. She gathered her dress and stepped off the pedestal. "Sit with me, here. Tell me. . ."

* * *

Lena clutched a small notepad in her white-gloved hand as she approached the grand steps to the Congressional Country Club. She tracked close to Flo and her group of influential women from the club.

"You'll do just fine, don't you worry." Flo patted Lena's arm. "And you look stunning in that dress. How wonderful of Frances to loan her dress to you, sight unseen. Did I tell you she's on the president's cabinet?"

"No, ma'am, but I sure do appreciate you inviting me to speak. I never imagined—"

She had never imagined. Nor had she wanted to do such a thing. Her soul shivered at the very idea of revealing her personal troubles to anyone—much less an audience of some of the country's finest leaders. Her deepest fears rose to taunt her. Clinton would become enraged, would kill them all. Or worse. But Lena had determined to do this, for the sake of all children in need.

"Yes, yes. First female Secretary of Labor, she is, and a great advocate for child labor laws. Everyone here tonight simply must hear your story. We need all the votes we can get, Democrats and Republicans alike."

"So kind of you," Lena whispered. "I just hope I don't forget anything. . . or get choked up in the telling."

They entered the grand meeting room. Ornate columns flanked with golden light sconces adorned one side, while massive arched windows, framing pristine courses of rolling hills, lined the other. All around, chest-high marble pedestals supported elaborate arrangements of white lilies, orchids and roses, each at least a wingspan in breadth and height. A formal-clad seating of violinists played *Beethoven's String Quartet Number 14, Opus 131*, recognizable to Lena from the cyclical playing of classical recordings as background music on The Dress Shoppe's phonograph.

Lena had never seen such elegant grandeur. *Just yesterday morning, I was pinning a hem. Now, here I am, among the elite, dressed like one of them. Still, . . . it's just me.* She drew a deep breath and composed herself. Following her group, she found her name card at the seat among those of pristine manners, education and status.

As the meeting commenced, the speaker introduced Mrs. Roosevelt. The first lady provided a sincere and pleasant welcome to all. Handing out hearty endorsements for the gentlemen who joined their wives for this special evening, Eleanor wielded humorous anecdotes with the skill of a master-at-arms. She conveyed a strong sense of duty in this great democracy—duty to serve and support those less fortunate. Defining the groundwork for the evening's agenda—primarily social insurance, mother's pensions and children's health—she introduced the next speaker.

Various speakers took their turns at the podium, while tuxedo-clad waiters inconspicuously served and removed plates and drinks. Some speakers elaborated on the myriad of possible solutions being proposed to institute social insurance, with their pro's and con's, and hailed Congressman Lewis and Senator Wagner's proposal as the best for the nation. Some speakers emphasized the need to consider homeless and neglected children along with the elderly.

Mrs. Lewis elbowed Lena. "Finish up that cake, dear. We're next."

"And now, with sincere pleasure, I introduce to you, Mrs. David Lewis and her special guest, Mrs. Lena Smith." The speaker held her arm toward Flo, who stood.

Flo offered her hand to Lena, and they strode together toward the podium.

Lena took the seat next to the podium. Her thumbs rubbed the blue ink on the notepad held in her lap as if to absorb and imprint them indelibly in her mind.

Florida spoke with great charisma, applauding the efforts of her many friends in the room on behalf of laborers, elders, and children. "Now I want to introduce you to a very fine woman. She has a true story of great importance to us all, to our nation, to our posterity. Hers is a story that you, fine ladies and gentlemen, hold the power to change. Please, give a warm welcome to Mrs. Lena Smith."

The crowd applauded.

She stood, placed her notes in front of her on the podium and nodded. "Good evening, and thank you for the kind welcome. I am honored to stand before you fine men and women who are dedicated to increase freedom and justice for all Americans. As Mrs. Lewis requested, I will share my story with you tonight. Though my story is sad, I want you to take heart, because we're not finished yet! You have the power to enact legislation that will help not only my story, my children, but ensure all children in our nation a better future."

Lena paused, flipping a page of her speaking notes. Her dry throat seized. Looking at the side of the podium, she saw Flo handing her a fresh glass of water. *Bless you, Flo.* She took a sip, cleared her throat and drew a deep breath.

Familiar faces in the crowd—women she'd read about and recently met in The Dress Shoppe—buoyed Lena's resolve. Gertrude Simmons Bonnin smiled at her, giving Lena goosebumps. An amazing woman, known as Red Bird, she wrote and labored for equal rights for women and Native Americans. Lena had followed her writings for years. Next to her, Marie Bottineau Baldwin beamed at Lena. Marie had also been in the shop for alterations to her modern native women's clothing. She'd recently retired from the Office of Indian Affairs after a lifetime of advocacy. Dolly Curtis Gann was there, too, Vice President Curtis' half-sister who served as second lady. Dolly gave Lena a thumbs up along with her contagious grin.

I'm in good company, chin up.

"I grew up in a happy rural town about 20 miles north. Mama and Daddy lovingly raised fifteen children, and countless cows, chickens, goats and pigs."

A murmured chuckle passed through the room.

"My family and my town instilled the highest ideals. We had a good school and a free library, both of which we put to regular use. Upon entering mature life, I found, as you likely have, many surprises. Unexpected hazards, you might say. My marriage began well. When my husband served in the Great War, for which we all are proud, he returned home in anguish. He grew distant, angry. We all tried to reach him. Despite prohibition, he found solace in strong drink. His drinking temporarily alleviated his personal pain, but took, in exchange, his self-control. Unfortunately, my children and I bore the brunt of his poor choices. . ."

Lena told it, the whole story, with poise and grace she hadn't known herself capable. She told of his beatings, and how they worsened with time. She told of their anguish at the loss of a child, and how he turned against their daughter, threatening her life. She told of his deceit with divorce papers, of losing custody, and the lawyer's rejection. She told how he returned her daughter with polio, and how she and her family, with her Cherokee grandmother's knowledge of natural remedies, nursed her back to health. She told of her struggle to find work as a woman, of Clinton removing their daughter from school to babysit his new wife's children. She told of her folly in the stock market, and how the crash left her with impossible debt.

Lena carried her story to the present, emphasizing Clinton's ongoing neglect and misuse of her daughter.

"This country outlawed slavery over sixty years ago, yet

children still live like slaves—without laws to protect them. I'm sure you've heard of the recent case in New York, in which an animal protection law was applied to rescue an abused child. Animals have greater laws protecting them than our children do. I may be of simple beginnings, but I know enough to see that this ought not be."

Taking a sip of water, Lena cleared her throat, straightened her arms and braced her hands against the podium. Her voice erupted—strong and emphatic.

"Children grow up quickly. Growing up without their needs met places them at great risk of delinquency, of a life of ill-will. Deprivation can fuel depravity. I ask you to consider the urgency of this bill for the sake of the children. Act swiftly. Ensure this bill prompt funding and administration, that not just my children, but the children of our great nation and of the future, may be saved."

Applause erupted. Chair legs scraped the floor as each attendee stood. Many dabbed their eyes with handkerchiefs or napkins, nodding at Lena and clapping.

Carrying her notebook, she returned thankful gestures and made her way back to her seat.

Flo reached her arm around Lena's shoulder and pulled her in. "Lena, you must join our women's club. We simply must have you."

"How could I? I'm no one."

"Please! Your dues have been paid." She tipped open an envelope containing a check with many zeros—more than Lena had ever seen. "An anonymous benefactor has come to your rescue."

The room's ambrosial bouquet of floral and sweet delicacies suddenly turned pungent. Her stomach quivered and leapt. Her fingers and toes set afire, tingling and filling with fluid. Her head threatened to float from her body's hold upon it. "Please—excuse me, I'm feeling quite faint." She stood and flitted to the nearest powder room, where she splashed cold water on her clammy face and neck.

A semblance of calm returned as she patted her skin dry. Reaching into her clutch, she powdered her nose and made her way back toward the hall. Her high heels clacking on the marble tiles echoed in the long expanse.

The muffled sound of leather soles joined, matched, and then doubled her pace. She glanced behind.

A man. One she did not know. Dressed as a server. He gained on her, his fevered pace matching his look of urgent consternation.

Is he after me? For what—for telling my story? What world of politics is this? I don't belong here. He would overtake her if she did not hurry to the entrance of the banquet hall. Her racing heart hastened her steps.

Just as she was about to turn into the banquet hall, he caught her arm.

46

Becca

The Center, South Central Florida. 1987

Becca's oldest brother, Doug, responded to Becca's letter with a phone call.

"I'm so sorry, Becca. What I did has been tormenting me all these years. I hated to bring up the subject because I didn't know if you remembered it, or if you hated me forever."

Stunned, the room spinning, she reached for the chair and sat. "Oh."

"I wouldn't blame you if you did. I hate myself for it."

"I don't hate you. I hate what happened, but you, no. But you need help."

"What, you mean like counseling? I can't do that, Becca. You've gotta understand, if I told anyone what I did, they'd put me in jail. I can't be in jail."

"What about your daughter? Have you—?"

"No." Doug's voice became worried, terse. "Never. Barb won't let me see her anymore, anyway, since I'm like two years behind on child support. You don't have to worry about that."

Becca tossed the ideas in her mind. Does what he's saying make a difference? She didn't know. She expelled a frustrated breath through her nostrils. "I don't think you'd go to jail for what you did as a teen. So go to counseling. You'll need professional help to work through all the mess inside after the family we grew up in. I need help. We all need it."

"I can't take that chance. How would I ever get to see my daughter again, if they knew?"

"I'm telling Barb either way. I'm finished with covering things up out of fear. No. This secrecy and covering has to stop. Barb needs to know so she can protect that little girl of yours from this sick family."

Doug's silence extended longer than Becca could wait for a response.

"Like I said in the letter, I forgive you. Partly because of what Jesus did on the cross to forgive us all, and partly because you've admitted it. You stopped well before you were eighteen. Trust is another thing. How do I know you've stopped completely? Without major changes inside and out, we're doomed to repeat our mistakes in one way or another. That's why we get help from God, and from counselors."

"Okay. I understand. I'll read more about it, and pray, but privately." His voice grew shaky, tentative. "I just don't think I can trust the system to not punish me for something I'm not even doing anymore. You know what they do to child molesters in jail. I'd never survive it."

I don't know what else I can do. "Our relationship will have to stay distant," Becca said. "I won't take a chance of anyone touching Christine." Becca hung up the phone and let her head fall into her hands. *Help him make the right choice, God.*

The phone rang again, on the heels of the first.

"Becca?"

"Carlton. I just got off the phone with Doug, like five minutes ago."

"Yeah, he told me. We both got your letters and we've been talking." His voice quivered. "What happened was horrible. I should have done something to stop it, but I was just. . . I don't know. . . something inside of me just shut down." The sound of full-on crying came through the line, but muffled—as if he had cupped his hand over the phone to conceal the loss of control.

A lump caught in Becca's throat as tears wet her lashes. "You've always had a tender heart. I didn't want to have to tell you what happened. But I've learned that stuffing painful memories is leaving weeds in the garden. They take over. But the Lord is my gardener now and he's pulling out the roots. I thought you should know, because the Lord can heal your memories, too."

"Maybe this is why I stayed high all through my teens. To block it out. You're the reason that I even know the Lord. You're the one who encouraged me to attend fellowship meetings with you. You used that word, en-courage, and the meaning came alive in my heart—courage, on the inside. I'd been afraid of God, of giving my life to Him, but I found the courage—because of you."

Tears gushed. "Thank you. I'm glad. But this. How are you going to deal with what happened? Did what happened then cause you problems at home? We live so far apart now, I don't know your struggles."

"No. I dedicated my life, all of it, body, soul and spirit, to God."

A question loomed over the dark waters of her yet un‑charted journey. *Is what he's doing enough?* She didn't know.

"I'm so glad for that. I think I have to say, though, the same thing I said to Doug. Dad was so sick, and the things he did to me got buried deeper than my conscious level. They've ruined my trust for anyone. But God wants to do a deeper work. He wants to dig those weeds out of my mind and plant truth, deeper than I ever knew before. I want you to dig with us. Dig into God deeper, ask Him, and reach out for a counselor to help. We need extra help to not to inadvertently pass our flaws to our kids, and to protect our kids better. How are your kids, by the way?"

"They're good. We're okay, really. Living on the west coast, I never have the money to go see Mom and Dad anyway. But I will. I will pray, and see if there's a godly counselor anywhere nearby who I can talk with."

They settled the call, and Becca waited. *Two down. One to go. Talking about this shakes me to my core. Confrontation is so hard. But there's no going back. The battle is yours, God. I am your reluctant but willing soldier girl.*

* * *

Two weeks passed, and her father did not write or call. Becca picked up the phone.

"Mom?"

"Becca? That's a surprise."

"You got my letters?"

"Yes." Mother's voice cracked. "Caused quite a commotion around here."

"I want to speak with Dad."

She heard the phone clunk onto the counter and her mother's steps fade in the distance. A few seconds turned into a minute. Becca wished for some elevator music in the phone to make the time go by faster.

The phone clunked again. Mom's voice returned. "He won't speak on the phone to you. Says he'll only talk to you in person. I wouldn't come, though, if I were you. God knows what he's capable of. Why do you feel the need to bring this up again, anyway? After so long?"

Both her father's ploy and her mother's pain and anger stung. Becca drew a deep breath. *Lord, what do I say?*

"Just let bygones be bygones. Leave the past in the past."

"I can't, Mom. The past is still alive. What about your grandkids? What if he's still doing those things? We can't just bury our heads in the sand, as if nothing's happening. I won't. Not anymore."

"He's too old for that anymore. All he does is work, burn trash out back, eat, drink, and sleep. No point in rousing a sleeping lion."

"You need help, too, Mom. This family's a mess. Wouldn't you like a better life—one with love, and peace, and closeness?"

"Hmph. Of course I'd like those things. But not everyone's as lucky as you are. You got out, but you have no idea how stuck I am."

"You're not stuck. You just think you are. If you really

want out, there's a way. I'll help you any way I can."

"Just don't come here."

Becca took her mother's command to her knees, to her sovereign commander. After praying and discussing the matter with Pastor Richard, Becca decided to defy her mother's order. She would go.

"Mike, please stay with Christine, at home. Christine will be safe here. There are too many children at risk there. No one is listening to my plea to protect them from my dad."

"I don't know," Mike said. "Are you sure you'll be safe?"

"This is something I have to do. He's not going to hurt me."

"I'd feel better being there to protect you."

"But then who would protect Christine? And what if you lost your temper and lashed out at him? You could end up in jail, and Christine and I would be without you, too. No. Stay here, please. I have to face him, to stand up to him against his lies."

"You've already written. Isn't that enough?" Mike shuffled his feet under the table. "You gave him a chance."

"I did. I tried. He said he wants to talk to me in person, so I will go so far as to meet him on his ground. I'll show him I meant the letter for his good. If he turns down my solid offer of hope through spiritual and professional help, then at least I'll know I've done all I can to reach his heart. If need be, I'll call the police. I promise."

Outside of Charleston, South Carolina. 1987

At the end of an eight-hour drive, her car turned into the driveway of her parents' mobile home, situated on a large parcel of rural land. Her mother's rose garden bloomed at the far northern end of the property, a tiny square of beauty in a large expanse of neglected acreage. Freshly whacked weeds posed as a front lawn. Empty frozen-dinner packages, tissues and half-crushed cans stuck to dead flowers by the front steps, a warning sign to passersby—Garbage Welcome Here. Something about this dump, a step down from the run-down homes her parents previously rented, sent her skin crawling.

The gear shifted into park. Leaving her purse in the car, far from the roaches that roamed freely in her parents' house, she locked the car door and shoved the key into her pocket. Her clenched hand instinctively pressed on the knot her stomach. Becca willed herself, one foot at a time, up the four metal steps. The storm door creaked open, she knocked.

47

Lena

Bethesda, Maryland. 1934

Lena spun to face him, to get a good look at him, while bracing her stance to provide a swift kick with the pointed toe of her patent leather shoe.

"Lena, is it really you? I can't believe it!"

Her brows knit as she studied his slightly familiar face. "Let go of my arm, at once. Do I know you?"

He let go. "Oh, I'm so sorry. Did I frighten you? I was just so excited to see you. I wanted to catch you before you went back in to the banquet." The dark-haired man smiled—a pleasant, youthful smile that set Lena's heart at ease.

"Is there something I can help you with?" She brushed her gown to straighten it. "I must get back to the meeting."

"I'm Adohi, Aunt Lena. Remember?"

Her eyes must have glazed over, as his face lost its sharp

angles and morphed into that of a twelve-year-old boy. The gold brocade wallpaper and lofty mahogany ceiling beams behind him dissolved into log paneling. The scent of blackberry tea and pine tickled her nose. "Adohi?" She felt the corners of her lips turn up as light returned to her eyes.

"Yes! It's me!"

Her hand clasped her mouth, concealing her glee from the crowd in the next room. She threw her arms around his shoulders and leaned her head into his chest. Drawing back, she held him by the upper arms to admire him. "My, how you've grown. What are you doing here? I had no idea you'd left the mountains."

He motioned toward a settee against the wall in the long hallway. "Please, come sit with me. I can only stay a moment. If they catch me talking with one of the members like this, I'll be fired."

"I'm no member, my sweet boy."

They sat, their knees angled toward one another, Adohi placing his body at an angle to keep watch for anyone coming into the hall.

"I work here part time, but I'm apprenticing for my uncle. My step-uncle, really. Your Aunt Caroline's step-son. I don't know if you remember her talking about him. He had left the farm before you arrived. He's a lawyer here now, and I've just finished law school."

Her eyebrows raised, Lena took his hands in hers. "That's wonderful news. I'm so glad to see you."

"I heard your speech and knew it must be you. When my grandmother passed, we could not find her letters, so we didn't know how to find you again. She was our only connection."

Expelling a heavy breath, Lena's sorrow pressed tears to the edges of her eyes. "I didn't know. When did she pass?"

"Two years now."

"I'm so sorry. She was such a special woman. And your family was so good to me."

"We're your family, too. And here I am, finally." He smiled and puffed out his chest. "I remember racing the wagon away as you left. You said to come see you again."

"Yes, Adohi, I'm so glad you're here. Is Enna here as well?"

"He is, and our parents. Grandfather, you remember, Gatlin, sold most of the farm to fund our schooling. Enna attends Georgetown University.

Lena clasped her hands together at her heart. "This is wonderful news." She reached into her clutch and produced her notepad and a pen. "Give me your phone number and address. We will get together soon." She handed the notepad and pen to him.

He scribbled his number. "When I heard your story, I knew we could help. I've wanted to help since I first met you. Why, you're one of the reasons I studied law. Please, call me soon. Tomorrow."

* * *

They arranged a formal meeting with Aunt Caroline's stepson. Lena entered his law office, a Victorian house in pristine condition.

Adohi and Enna greeted her at the door and showed her in. The front room welcomed clients in formal manner, with jabot window dressings and mahogany furnishings. A long conference table and chairs filled the room to the right side. Mr. Bradley sat at the far end, perusing an old leather-bound book with yellowed pages. His ample grey mustache nearly concealed his smile, but the wrinkles at the corners of his eyes revealed his pleasure upon seeing her.

He stood and approached, extending his hand. "Welcome, come in, have a seat."

Once seated, he cleared his throat. "Adohi tells me you're one of Aunt Eliza's Maryland tribe." His eyes rested on Lena. "I see the resemblance."

"One of fifteen, yes." Lena placed her hand on the table and leaned toward him. "I'm sorry to hear about your step-mother. Aunt Caroline was a wonderful woman. And you— Adohi told me so much about you."

Adohi winked at his great-uncle. "All good, I assure you."

Lena laughed. "Yes, all good."

"She was a wonderful woman, indeed." Mr. Bradley took a deep, whistling breath. "Don, will you make some hot tea, please?"

"Yes, sir, right away." Adohi stood.

Lena looked at Adohi. "Don?"

"My nickname. Uncle says Don will go over better in business than Adohi. At least until we Cherokee secure our rights."

As the young man disappeared into the kitchen, Mr. Bradley squared his eyes with Lena's. "He's a good lad. Will be a fine lawyer, soon. As will young Enna, here."

"Yes, both very good." Lena smiled at Enna.

"Don tells me of your troubles." He paused to take a deeper breath. "I think we can help. For nearly fifty years, wife-beating has been a crime in most states, but I am yet to see our judicial system use its power of enforcement in such matters. I want to change that. I moved to this city to have a greater influence on our laws as a nation."

Lena fought the urge to look down. Many years had passed since Clinton had levied his unjust punishments and self-centered coercion upon her, but still, her feelings tended to wade in the muck of shame when she thought of it. She stepped out of the muck by keeping her eyes on his. "Thank you for working to improve the system, Mr. Bradley. I'd like to see the matter changed, too."

"Call me Harris. We're practically family, after all."

"Yes sir, Harris."

"Your Grandaunt Caroline, as you know, was my step-mother. When my father first brought her home, he told me she would be my mother. I protested at first. She was not my mother, you understand. Caroline was good to me in every way and loved me as well as she did her own son. I soon took her to heart as my mother and loved her dearly."

Adohi returned, with tea. After pouring a cup for each of them, he sat beside Lena.

Harris held the teacup near his mouth and inhaled the steam through his nose. "Thank you, son." He cleared his throat. "When I was a lad, the people I grew up around—in town, school, and sometimes even in church—said things I didn't like. They thought they were better than the people whose skin was darker. I'd come home, and put my white arms around my Mama's waist, and lean into her chest. There's nobody better than you, I'd say. Nobody better."

Lena listened with rapt attention. She'd grown up learning about differences between the North and South. Living at their junction, Lena had embraced the views of the people in her town, Sandy Spring—the Maryland town that emancipated slaves well ahead of the Civil War. *Yet here is a man born and raised deep in the South who's more a defender of the needy than Clinton, who also grew up in Sandy Spring.*

"Now one thing I learned, in all my years defending the oppressed. A person ought to be judged by their actions—their character. We ought not judge by their state in life, their physical attributes, nor their education—or lack thereof."

Adohi stood and clapped his hands. "Bravo, Uncle, bravo."

Harris waved the lad down. "Sit down, Donnie. I don't need that nonsense."

Lena leaned in toward Harris. "Many years passed since my husband mistreated me. My proof—bruises and such— are long gone. I only have verbal testimonies of people I told, of my family. Nothing else. But he hasn't changed. I don't think he has. He's been horrible to our daughter. He uses her like a slave. What evidence would we need to take legal action against him for that?"

Harris' lower lip protruded as his head rocked in small arcs, up and down. He detailed instructions of case files for Adohi to gather. He interviewed Lena with meticulous detail, asking Enna to take notes.

"I wonder, though, how much might this cost?" Lena considered the generous gift from that anonymous donor. Thus far, she hadn't wanted to cash it. She didn't know how to manage such a thing and a whirlwind of busy appointments had swept the week away.

"It will be my pleasure to serve you, Lena." He waved a hand dismissively. "There may be some minor fees associated, but I am at your service. The way I see it, Adohi here needs the practice, and I can put him to most of the tasks involved. We can make a good case and lay down precedents that will move us closer to our goal overall—for freedom and justice for all."

"Oh, my." Lena laid her hand over her heart. "You're so kind. Now, after all these years, will my prayers be answered? Sir, you are a God-send."

Harris chuckled. "I've been called many things. God-send is a new one."

"I have this check, from a benefactor who wants to help. I've been holding on to it, not sure how to proceed. . . "

Harris looked at the check and cleared his throat. "An es-crow account will keep these funds protected and minimize any taxes due the government. I'll work on all of the legal arrangements if you'd like."

"Very much, yes. If I could, too, is there a way I could use some of the funds to pay a debt as well?"

48

Becca

Outside of Charleston, South Carolina. 1987

"Hey, sis. Come in." Missy stood aside and opened her arm for Becca's entry. Leaning in for a half-hug, she seemed at ease, her usual happy self.

"Good to see you." *She's so nonchalant. Does she know why I'm here?* Becca entered and scanned the room. The plaid sofa and chair they'd had for several moves, from Maryland to South Carolina, made the place look much as she expected. Beyond the main room, she saw her mother in the kitchen, pouring a glass of milk. "Hi, Mom."

"You made it. How was the trip?" Cecelia moved toward the living room and sat on the sofa, watching television, as usual. The square box blared repeats of her mother's favorite sitcom from the 1950s, which seemed more interesting to her mother than Becca's presence.

Becca moved toward the breakfast bar between the two

rooms. She sat on the edge of a stool, not wanting to settle in. *They're acting like everything's fine. I have to break the niceties.* "Where's Dad?"

"He's out back, burning trash."

"I need to talk to him."

"You're gonna go through with it?" Cecelia looked away from the television long enough to shoot Becca a look of disdain. "It's no use, you know."

"You said he'd only talk to me face to face. I have to try." Becca let her eyes do the pleading. She longed for Mom to join her mission. Hope, knit with longing, neediness, and sorrow, tugged her heart. *I've wanted a happy family all of my life. But if we're ever going to be happy, we've got to face problems.*

Cecelia shook her head. "I told you—your father is disgusting. I wanted to leave him years ago, you know that." She looked back at the TV. "I don't see what good dredging up old business now will do. He'll never change."

"Your grandkids are reason enough. We need to protect them."

"I keep a close eye on him." Her mother cleared her throat. "The grandkids aren't here often. A little girl lives next door," she said, her eyes averting as she considered the idea. "He talks to her a lot. . . but he's an old codger now. I don't think he'd do anything at this point."

Mom. Why do you close your eyes to this?

Becca glanced at Missy, who busied herself washing dishes. The kitchen counter and cupboards provided some distance—some protection—from this conversation. *Missy. You look so uncomfortable.*

Becca decided to talk with Missy later, to see if she could

reach her, to see if she realized the danger of leaving her children with Mom and Dad. She looked back to her mother. "Mom, if you think he might be doing something with that girl, you need to call the police. Not reporting him is completely unfair to the kids."

It struck her. *She's afraid. That's why Mom has never. . .* Becca cleared her throat and swallowed. *Now that I'm here, I can sense their feelings. I want them to be here for me, but they need me to be here for them.* She sat next to her mom and softened her tone. "What are you afraid of, Mom?"

Becca's mother looked out the front window, her arms and legs crossing as her brows furrowed. Her voice began as a whisper. "You have no idea what he's capable of." She sat forward as her voice took on strength, burgeoning into anger, then frightful fury. "The other day, I was out back taking care of the dogs. He was up on the roof, working. A huge piece of sheet metal came flying off the roof and almost cut my head off." She used her arms to demonstrate how she ducked from the metal. "I screamed and looked up, and he was just standing there, laughing like an evil man." Her eyes filled with terror as she spoke. "I think he's trying to kill me."

Missy stepped back into the room. "Seriously, Mom?" She shook her head with disdain, as if she were the parent speaking to a wayward child. "It was windy, and the metal slipped out of his hands. He laughed when he realized you were okay. You're overreacting. Dad wouldn't try to kill anybody."

Becca didn't know what to think or say. Tempted to be dismissive of her mother as overly dramatic, she allowed that perhaps Mom had some good reason to fear. *The terror in her eyes. . . so real.* But with Missy bent on protecting her father, she decided to shelve this discussion for later. *No big family disputes. And no chickening out.* "I'm gonna go talk to him."

Becca opened the back door to the expansive yard. Her father stood by the burning trash, about 50 yards back, poking at the fire with a long stick. He had aged considerably, pure white hair replacing what had been peppery gray. With some added weight and a rounded white beard, she wasn't sure she'd have recognized him if she'd seen him elsewhere. Yet his usual quart bottle of beer was a dead giveaway.

He glanced her way, then back at the fire.

Becca steeled herself, breathed a prayer, and headed toward him. "Hi Dad."

"Hi, girl." He stifled a grin that said he'd won the hand—she was on his turf. "You look good."

The compliment flirty, not fatherly, Becca chose to ignore its echoing chill. "You look. . . different."

He laughed. "Yeah, they call me Papa Smurf or Santa Claus."

Both figures kids love. He and kids should not be together. She steeled herself at the thought. "You said you wanted to talk in person."

He guzzled a few swallows of beer and stirred the fire. Squaring his eyes on hers, they narrowed, the way they did when he meant business. "What you said in your letter, you're right, I did those things. I did a lot more than that. You don't remember." A wry smile crinkled one side of his face, his eyes intent on staring her down.

This is what he wanted to say to me? Becca dug in. "I remembered more since I wrote the letter. You molested me more than once." Her gut wanted to heave her forward into a ball on the ground. Tears threatened to gush out, robbing her strength, showing her neediness. *Not the time to lose composure.* Becca fortified herself and fended the strong tide of emotion by pressing into her purpose. "Dad, you have a huge problem. Being sexual with a child, and incestuous. . . the books you left out in the bathroom when Mom was out of town—with bestiality and incest. You left them open as if you wanted us to read them—"

"Just my reading preference." His voice grew angry. "You can't slight a person for their reading preference. Besides, you don't remember most of it." A gleaming eye showed his pride at being one-up on her.

Just your reading preference? Her stomach soured. *Unbelievable. How can he dismiss this disgusting, warped way of thinking as a reading preference?* Becca's knees wobbled. Locking them, she half-turned from him. *I won't be dissuaded. I came all this way. Help me, Lord.* She faced him again. "No. Healthy people don't prefer perverted sexuality. Do ducks mate with chickens, or pigs with sheep? If a male dog goes after a relative in heat, the puppies turn out sickly and weak. Inbreeding is not right, Dad. You need professional help. . . and help from God Himself."

The man she had known as Daddy, once, directed the poker further into the fire, pushing trash into the embers. Not looking at her for this part, he spoke as if an authority on the matter. "I told you before, this is my preference. You shouldn't judge or call a preference right or wrong. Humans are no different than animals in heat—we do what we feel the urge to do. The survival of the fittest. If you feel it, do it. You should enjoy sex whenever you can, with whoever you want. Don't try to moralize it." He gave a side-glance and clicked some spittle into the fire.

Becca could hardly believe her ears. *He's hardened against how he hurt me. . . and surely, others.* The stench of burning garbage matched his mindset in repulsiveness. *The burnt offerings in Israel. . . at least they smelled good. He's burning an offering to evil.* Choosing to stand near him and his abominable blaze a few more seconds, Becca asked God for help with a response, then spoke.

"Dad, I'm sad to hear you excuse yourself by calling it a preference. We are not just animals. We can resist primal urges. You cross the line when you don't respect or care for others. You hurt me more than I'd even want you to know. Maybe you were hurt as a child. I don't know why you're like this, but what you've done is wrong." She watched his face for any indication her words touched him. "Being hurt is no excuse to hurt others. God can heal you and forgive you. You can stop hurting others. . . and yourself."

Becca counted to ten in her mind, searching for what else, if anything, to say.

Her father brought the brown quart-bottle to his mouth and ingested more of the chemical that sustained his dysfunctional downward spiral. A piece of cardboard took flight from the fire, escaping with the wind. He bent to retrieve the fleeing bit and forced it deeper into the embers.

Repentance is further than I imagined. She sighed and noticed a leaf, also carried by the wind, had landed at her foot. *Time to go.* Looking into the fire, Becca relayed her boundaries in no uncertain terms. "I hope you'll reconsider because, believe it or not, I do love you. I want the best for you. What you've been doing is definitely not the best. So,

Dad, I can't be around you, or trust you, and I won't bring Christine around you. The rest of the family has to know about this, so they know the risk." Seeing no response again, she spoke the rest of her mind. "I'm going now. Don't do this again. Don't hurt anyone else. Please, turn to God with this, and get professional help for your alcoholism and for your pedophilia."

"That won't be happening, so I guess I won't be seeing you again." He brought the beer back to his lips.

Her choice perceptibly right, but stinging to the core, she walked away. The weight of leaving her unrepentant father fully upon her, she bid a solemn goodbye to her mother and sister. She closed the car door and backed out of the driveway.

Dad chose alcohol and perversion over me. It was not my fault—not at all.

On the drive to a nearby hotel, the conversation intruded upon her thoughts, but she willed The Center's mantra and her heart's cry to overpower it. *I cannot change another person by direct action. I can only change myself. Others have a tendency to change in reaction to my change. God, I can't change him. But I still want him to change. Please let my words sink into his heart. Please help me keep changing toward you, toward healthy choices, toward standing up for the children in danger. Be my Daddy now, more than ever.*

That night, Missy joined her for dinner. As they finished eating, Missy offered her thoughts, speaking low enough to not be overheard by surrounding diners.

"Dad never did anything wrong to me. I want to believe what you say, but. . ." She sat her fork down and folded her hands. "I work with him. He's so nice to everyone. People see him as good-natured. They like him."

Becca weighed her choices before speaking. *I'm not sure I believe Dad never molested her. If he did, she's blocked it out like I had, even more so.* "Well, I'm telling the truth. I don't rock the boat unless it's important. You know I hate conflict."

"Yeah, I guess. You used to love to shock everyone, but that's not you anymore."

"No, not at all. Here's the main thing. Don't trust him around your kids."

Before leaving the next morning, she called the local police station, gave them a synopsis along with his name, address and number.

"I have to get back home, but you should know. There's a little girl next door, and my sister's kids go visit all the time."

"We'll send someone out," the phone clerk said.

In the twelve-hour drive home, Becca longed for an inner journey form of prayer. The pain, an empty hole churning in her gut, she shared with her Father, God. *He refused help. Refused change. Refused me.* She sensed that God also ached, for all His creation who turned away from His love.

She turned onto the highway. *He chose alcohol and perver sion over me. That hurts—so bad.* His horrible decision lay behind her on the road, disappearing from her tear-blurred glances in the rear view mirror.

The road ahead came into perspective more clearly with every mile forward. *There is no reason to let my time be consumed over other people's poor decisions. God will see to*

Dad, and all of my family, because He loves them even more than I do. My part is done, at least for now. What lies ahead? God will put to use what I've been through to help others who are wounded. Others who want to heal and grow .

She turned on the radio. Becca hadn't kept up with current events since she and Mike moved to The Center. Television wasn't permitted in the dorms. It would distract the men in the program from the work at hand, they believed. Mike and Becca had agreed to the same rule at home, and she never had time to read the paper. In the car, on the long drive, catching up on the news of the day seemed a welcome distraction.

President Reagan's speech in Berlin was the news of the day. "Mr. Gorbachev, tear down this wall."

It had been a long time since the first handshake in space. At the time, Becca thought the act signified a new unity between the nations, but war had continued—under the sea in nuclear submarines and on land via spies and listening devices. The Cold War was better than the mushroom cloud of nuclear war—the one she'd imagined most days when walking to high school, when everyone knew duck and cover would really mean ducking your head between your knees and kissing your ass goodbye.

Tearing down the wall in Berlin resonated in Becca's life. She was tearing down walls too.

The Center, South Central Florida.

Back at home, Becca found new confidence in every rela-tionship. Facing fear—facing her father—though heart-breaking in one way, proved to release her true self more than she'd ever experienced. Where repressing her true self had been like grinding gears and spinning wheels, feeling and sharing her true self with others shifted her into drive. The process also deepened her intimacy level with Mike—in every aspect.

The rest of the year of ministry training sped by. Becca engaged in several areas of ministry—facilitating a support group for adult children of alcoholics, co-leading a marriage support group, and designing and facilitating a recovery group for women overcoming sexual abuse. Embracing the long journey ahead toward full health and maturity, Becca practiced the art of comforting others where she had received comfort.

In the spring, she and Mike graduated from the program and began searching for where the Lord would lead them in full time ministry.

"Riverside called." Mike's face lit up with excitement. "They offered me a position as a recovery pastor. They want me to facilitate small groups and do recovery counseling."

Riverside, their home church before moving to Florida, seemed a backward step. "Back to Maryland? I'm glad for you, but no. Let's wait and see if any of the Florida ministries are interested in hiring us."

"Becca, this is a great opportunity. If I turn down jobs, worker's comp will stop paying, since I graduated."

Becca took a breath and considered his point. *Don't react. Respond.* "Tell me more about the job. Do they want me, too?"

Mike's demeanor changed from excited to serious. "Well, no, they only have one in the budget. But you can volunteer." His face perked up, his eyes begging her to join his excitement.

Becca pushed back at her natural tendency to give in to his desire. "I was a volunteer. For years. Mike, I'm sorry, but this disappoints me. I went through every minute of training that you did. I worked really hard. I know God has a calling on my life. If you work at Riverside, and I volunteer, I'll end up cleaning houses or bookkeeping again. Is that what you think I should be doing after all this? I think we should wait for an offer to work together. We're a team."

Mike paced the room. "Becca, if you volunteer, they'll see how good you are, and if all goes well, maybe they can provide for you in the budget for next year."

No, I don't want to go back. Becca tried to slow her frantic heart. Tempted to slip back into her habit of de-selfing in the name of love, she felt herself wavering. *But maybe Mike is right. How many positions in addictions ministry exist for couples, anyway? I hoped The Center would hire us, but they're not. We have to do something, but we don't have to give in so easily.* "Let's pray first—take a little time before deciding. Another offer may come in."

"Sure." His face took on the sheepish look he adopted when revealing something she wouldn't like. "But I already accepted."

49

Lena

Rockville, Maryland. 1934

All of the Burriss family approved of Dorsey.

"I do," she'd said, laying aside her reservations. *He's not at all like Clinton, and I'm not who I was before.* She'd held her bouquet with minimal quivering, her family around her, and her dedicated man's gentle, loving, soothing looks calming her nerves.

After a simple ceremony with the justice of the peace, Dorsey carried Lena over the threshold of his home, behind Robert and Theresa's.

It was a lovely little cottage, surrounded by hedges, with a metal gate at the front sidewalk. The white clapboard home beckoned her to sit awhile on the ample front porch, with blue-painted wood floors and ceilings—the sort of porch that called for a large pitcher of lemonade as a constant. Inside, a plain wood rocker and side table rested on an old, tattered rug. In the corner was a radio so large it stood on its own as furniture.

Having been a man's home, needing a woman's touch, its simplicity welcomed Lena. "Hmm, I think we need a little more furniture in here," she said with a wink. "The rocker will fit better on the front porch anyway. Let's find a sofa and some big, comfy chairs for this room."

Dorsey smiled. "I should'a expected this. . ."

She couldn't get over the kitchen. She hadn't imagined a carpenter would have such modern kitchen appliances—a gas stove, a working refrigerator, and running water in the deep porcelain sink.

"Now this is a dream, dear." Lena sparkled as she tied her new apron around her waist and kissed her big smiling man.

Complete with electric lights and free-standing electric fans to cool them in the hot Maryland summers, Lena's new home seemed luxurious compared to the little house she'd bid goodbye to on the farm, her room in the city, and her room in Robert and Theresa's house. She shoved away pangs of false guilt for having such a nice place when so many people lived in squalor in these days of the Great Depression.

"Now, where is the flour?" Lena searched the cupboards, pulling out the essentials needed for fresh biscuits and gravy.

"This part's a dream for me." Dorsey grinned.

Dorsey and Robert installed a gate between their properties so the two couples could easily visit. They shared gardening, flower and vegetable seeds, and many evening meals together in their back yards. They settled into a happy life here. Lena loved gardening. She nurtured each seedling as a treasure.

Soon their little property included chickens and a fine pair of pigs. Dorsey built the chicken coop, and Lena enjoyed gathering fresh eggs each day. Their little yard sustained them well, for Lena knew how to farm and cook.

Though she loved her chickens, she knew their place. "Thank you for your service," she'd say, holding a chicken by the neck and snapping a quick jerk around. She'd pluck, clean and butcher the bird, knowing just where to cut through each joint to separate the breasts from the back and the thighs from the drumsticks.

After soaking the fresh meat in salt water all day, she'd dredge each piece in finely seasoned breadcrumbs and flour alternately with buttermilk and eggs, and gently settle the breaded meat into sizzling bacon fat in a cast iron skillet. Paired with fresh lima beans, potatoes and homemade cornbread, Lena's fried chicken dinners were feasts to remember, surpassed only by her fresh berry pies.

Lena's happiness, though, felt like a cake baked without sugar. She missed her children terribly. She didn't talk about her sadness much, but she struggled even through the best days. Sometimes, as she lay her head on her pillow at night, tears would flow.

"I'm doing all I can do," she cried. "I'm so grateful for Mr. Bradley and Adohi taking my case, but the whole thing is taking so long. I want to gather them up like a hen takes her chicks under her wings, but I can't."

Dorsey recognized Lena's frustration. He tried to ease Lena's pain. He picked flowers and set them on her pillow at night. He did silly things to make her laugh. He came home with pets for her—first came the Mynah bird. "He'll even talk to you when I'm not here!" A pet monkey soon joined the family too. The couple had many fun evenings and weekends with their families and pets.

Friday nights were the couple's favorite. Tired from the long week working, they set aside Friday nights to be alone together. After a simple meal and drinks on the porch watching the sun go down, Lena and Dorsey would retreat to the living room to listen to the radio. Dorsey usually sat in the chair, while Lena curled her legs up beside herself to be comfortable on the sofa. She worked on her stitching, making clothes for Ruth. They'd reflect on the week or just sit quietly. These were special times, when they forged their mutual bond of support.

"Life is what you make it, darling," Dorsey said in his light, philosophical voice. He smiled and motioned for her to come sit in his lap.

Lena, enjoying Dorsey's masculine way of approaching life, responded in kind. Moving over to him, she slipped her arm around his neck and lightly placed herself on his lap.

"If you say so, handsome. Let's say I make it with you," she flirted.

"Now you're makin' sense!" Dorsey pulled her in tight and kissed her, then scooped her up and carried her to the bed.

* * *

Dorsey hung the cupped earpiece onto the handle of the candlestick telephone and called to Lena. "Just got a call, Shaw's been in trouble at school again."

"Oh, that boy! What happened this time?" Lena laid aside

her sewing and joined Dorsey at the kitchen table.

Dorsey sighed and shared the sad news. "Apparently, Shaw hasn't learned his lesson about how to treat a young lady. He cornered a girl in the back of the school yard and kissed her while she screamed for help. They've kicked him out of school. The Smiths want us to come get him."

Lena sighed, a heavy sigh, as if in so doing she could breathe out the anger, sadness, guilt and compassion that rushed to pool in her chest. "Let's go get him."

The couple drove to get the lad in silence. Calling on Lena and Dorsey in times of trouble had become common-place. Whenever one of the kids was sick or unmanageable, the Smiths—either Clinton and whatever woman he was married to at the time, or Clinton's parents, if the kids had been left on their farm while Clinton and his woman gallivanted—called on Lena to get them back in order. They wouldn't permit the children to stay long enough for Lena and Dorsey to make a lasting difference, but Lena embraced any opportunity to have what positive effect she could.

Looking out the window as they rode past the broken down buildings and trash-littered streets that had come to be normal by the mid-1930s, Lena's heart ached. Times were so hard. Everyone was struggling, everywhere. Lena's struggle had been going on her entire adult life now, and she regretted ever leaving her boys—nearly every day. She ached for her boy. His life had been a series of troubles, most of which she probably didn't even know. *He's always been industrious,* she thought, urging herself to think the best. *He pitched in to help on the Smiths' farm from a young age, learning to work with farm tools and on vehicles way before I would have let him.* She thought about how often Clinton had left Shaw in charge. *He pretended to be the man of the family, no emotion. He did things he saw men doing; things that weren't so good for him.*

She turned and looked at Dorsey as he drove. *I wish he could have been around Dorsey more. Way before I met Dorsey, though, Shaw needed him. Smoking by age seven, by golly. I blame Clinton for this behavior, really. Shaw saw his father with the ladies and started imitating him. He was too young to know the rules of engagement, so he ran right through the bases with young girls. His grandfather put a whippin' on him, but nothing seemed to faze him—he shrugged off correction. Just like his father.*

The truck slowed, then turned into the long dirt driveway of the Smith farm. Shaw stood, with his bag, waiting on the front porch.

"Get in, young man." Lena got out to let him slide into the middle of the front seat. She wanted to hug him, but she also wanted to yell at him. Silence seemed the best choice.

He climbed into the car, and they headed toward home. Passing by the Sandy Spring Store, then farmland on either side of the way before Rockville, the only sound for miles was the whir of the engine and thump of tires over the bumpy road.

Finally, Lena broke the silence. "Son, I'm disappointed."

Shaw shifted his eyes from the floorboard to the front window. "It wasn't like they said. Those teachers, they just hate me. They make up stories to get me in trouble all the time. That girl wanted me to kiss her."

Dorsey piped up. "No matter, you had no right to take advantage of a young lady like that."

"Hmph." Shaw crossed his arms. "If you don't want to

hear the real story, then I got nothin' to say." He returned his gaze to the floorboard.

Dorsey spoke sharply. "Fine with me if you've got nothing to say. You ought to be shutting your mouth and opening your ears."

"Yes, sir, would be your best choice of words, son." Lena's nostrils flared.

"Yes, sir." Shaw frowned.

A week with Dorsey and Lena seemed to turn Shaw back into his younger self. Shaw's fowl attitude yielded to their firm but kind ways. He smiled again. He seemed to love his mother's cooking, her joviality and her attention. He even seemed to love her stories, how she'd hide lessons in silly tales and leave Shaw to figure out the meaning.

Lena wasn't sure what Dorsey had said to him when they had their talks, but since Dorsey had always treated Lena properly, she trusted he was the best person to teach Shaw how to behave with the ladies. Discussing such things was a man's job, not a mother's.

"We have to take him back now," Dorsey announced after another phone call. "They said there's work to be done on the farm. Even though school is over for him, he needs to go home and work for his living."

Lena sighed and turned to look out the window where Shaw was throwing the ball for the dog. "I wish he could stay. He's sixteen, but look at him out there—he seems more like ten or twelve."

Dorsey tucked his arm around Lena's waist and snuggled into her ear from behind, looking out at Shaw with her. "I know, baby. You're such a good mama, and he didn't get enough of you. Maybe that's his problem, but it's not your doing. Clinton runs in his blood. Elliot didn't get enough of you, either, but he's not like that." He kissed her on the side of the cheek and patted her.

"I guess so." Lena wiped a tear that welled at the corner of her eye. *He's right. Elliot's not like Shaw.*

Just a year younger than Shaw, Elliot tagged along with most things Shaw did, but he had a certain caution about him that Shaw seemed lacking. Maybe seeing Shaw get in trouble so much taught Elliot extra caution. Maybe he had more of his mother's nature than his father's. Whatever the reason, Elliot always watched out for his older brother and his younger sister.

He wasn't as good at concealing his emotions as Shaw, either. Once, when he'd spent a weekend with Lena, she had slipped in to see him sleeping, and found him crying. She'd learned he worried about his mama, his sisters, Shaw, his grandparents and even his father and step-mother.

For the most part, though, Lena thought, *the kids usually find ways to have a good time.* Lena recalled things they'd told her about living with their father. So many times, they'd turned chores into games and made the best of tough situations.

They stood in the kitchen a few moments, watching Shaw play with their dog.

Dorsey slid his arm out from around her waist and opened the back door. "Shaw," he called, "get your things together. You've been called back to work on the farm."

Shaw dropped the ball and plodded into the kitchen.

A flowered tablecloth covered the old wood kitchen table, set with lacy white china and finished with fresh cuttings from the flower garden. Lena's scrumptious scratch rolls, fresh eggs from the chicken coop, and crispy bacon served as a pleasant distraction from the pending sad trip returning Shaw to his grandparents.

* * *

Sandy Spring, Maryland.

As they pulled into the Smith farm, Elliot and Ruth ran to greet them. Throwing her arms around them both at once, Lena missed the opportunity to say goodbye to Shaw. He grabbed his bag and scooted into the house as quickly and quietly as he could.

Lena and Dorsey never went inside the Smith home—not since Mr. Smith had sent her and her parents scurrying away at gunpoint, so long ago.

"I wanna come stay with you." Ruth whined. "Please."

Lena whispered into her ear as she squeezed her tighter. "I want you to come, too, my beautiful girl."

Elliot pulled back from his mother's hold and shook Dorsey's hand. "Thanks for bringing Shaw back." His attempt at a manly voice betrayed him, cracking.

Dorsey acknowledged Elliot's attempt at maturity. "You're welcome, sir. I trust you'll be keeping your big brother in line, now, won't you?"

"Yes, sir, as easy as herding mice."

Mrs. Smith emerged from the house, wiping her hands on her apron. She called out from afar. "Come back inside, children. There's plenty of work to do, I won't have ya loafin' around out here all day."

"Aw, do we have to?" Ruth gazed into her mama's eyes, begging her to take her from this house of hard work and misery.

Lena smoothed Ruth's tousled hair and caressed her cheek in her hand. "Well," she teased, "there's work at my house, too, darling."

Ruth rolled her eyes. "Oh, Mama! Any work at your house is better than play here."

"Hmm." *Is she teasing me, or is she really that miserable here?* "I wish I could take you, Morning Star, but we have to live with what is, not on our wishes."

"Come on, Ruth." Elliot tugged his little sister's arm.

"Okay, now, you two keep up your schoolwork, and keep after each other. We'll be able to get you to come stay with us for a month as soon as harvest is done."

"Yay! Really, Mama?"

"Really." Lena gleamed. "Now give me some sugar. . . and tell Shaw I said to be good."

50

Becca

Delray Beach, Florida. 1987

Becca parked near the beach and grabbed the loosely woven bag she kept in her car for times like these. She crammed her wallet and journal into the beach bag, alongside a beach towel. Slinging the pack over her shoulder, she shuffled over the passageway between dunes, toward the sound of lapping waves.

Curling her toes into the cool sand with each step, Becca reached the clearing. She stopped for a moment to breathe in the view, feel the breeze and smell the salty air.

This view—so vast. You are here, and so far beyond what I can see. Seeing fewer people to the left, she found a spot to spread her towel. Opening her journal and flipping to the next blank page, she wrote her prayer.

On my wedding day, I promised Mike that where

he goes, I will go. But Lord, I really don't want to leave here. I love Florida. I love what we're doing here. Moving to Maryland feels like going backwards.

She let herself feel the ache in her heart. The idea of leaving Florida, of leaving the soothing waves and balmy breezes of the beach, or the vastness of the horizon and blue skies above, but most of all, of leaving his family, which had become her own, only better, and her new family of friends at The Center—her safe place—all merged to one pulsating, hungry, frightening sense of impending loss.

A small, childlike part of her cried out. *Don't you care about me in this? Mike didn't seem to. He refused to go back on their offer. He's so afraid of going a day without a job that he just threw me under the—*

But I will trust you. You know what you're doing, and you have good in mind for me. By the power of your Holy Spirit in me, your strength in my weakness, I will go where you lead.

She listened for his still, small voice in her heart. An hour passed as she listened, running her fingers through the sand, gazing out upon the horizon, soaking the warm sun into every pore. The waves laid a rhythmic beat upon the shore, splashing spray and foam upon the borders of their unending journey. Too brief, their glorious moment of arrival, their splendor all too quickly succumbing to the depths in which they started, beneath the sea.

"I can speak to you wherever you are, my dear. I will lead

you beside still waters as I have led you here."

She recorded this day's experience, so rich to her senses, in her journal. As she made her way back to the car, still pensive and listening, pondering all of these things, she noticed a gnarled Seagrape tree. Round leaves fluttering in the wind applauded the glories of the sea. While many Seagrapes hugged the dunes, this one stood alone. The weather-worn and aged trunk stretched up and over the sidewalk.

Doubtless, this tree survived and grew through many storms—storms that pressed shoreward. Many branches crouched to the ground, where they rooted and sprouted new sections. These offshoots flourished in their new setting, lush with green leaves that also clapped in the wind. Becca aligned her body in parallel with ancient winds that had sculpted this masterpiece.

North.

* * *

Rockville, Maryland. 1988

The family sat down to eat around the table and said the blessing. Becca had just enough time to make dinner after her four a.m. shift calling substitute teachers, followed by cleaning two townhouses and picking up Christine after school. She dished a scoop of Christine's favorite casserole, a bubbly mix of cheeses, ground beef, enchilada sauce, cream of onion soup and chopped up tortillas, and handed the plate to her daughter.

"Mmm, you made Yummy." Christine received the plateful from her mom and dug her fork in. She blew on it, preparing to savor the cheesy pleasures.

"How was work today?" Becca handed Mike his plate.

"Rough." He received the plate. "The new pastor said we have to attend every service since I'm on staff. That's four times a week, plus our support groups." He sipped his soda.

"Plus working full time?"

"Yes. And he says we need to sign a commitment to church membership. I think the pastor they brought in is worse than the last one. He wants to control everything we do."

Becca rolled her eyes. The last pastor had been ousted after an adultery scandal, which had become almost commonplace. Nearly every month, another famous preacher's reputation bit the dust. She'd seen so many of them sobbing their crocodile tears on TV that she'd come to expect it from church. "The whole system's more dysfunctional than we realized. I miss our church at The Center, where no one had to pretend to have it all together."

A knock at the door interrupted dinner. Christine ran to answer it, and returned to the table, followed by Becca's father and younger brother.

Becca hadn't seen or heard from her father since the day they'd talked in the backyard in South Carolina. *Did he have a change of heart?* Taken by surprise, she started to greet him, but her body stiffened like Joan of Arc in battle armor. Her mind was on Christine. She did not want them in the same room.

Mike stood and, ignoring his father-in-law's offered

hand, spoke harshly. "What are you doing here? I know what you did."

Becca's father dropped his outstretched hand. His body language bristled. "What are you talking about? I didn't do anything."

"I know my wife. She wouldn't make those things up. I've seen how much you hurt her."

"Are you calling me a liar?" He cast villainous eyes at Mike while he straightened himself, puffing out his chest. "Because I've killed men for less."

"That's it. You need to leave here, now." Mike pointed to the door.

"I'm not going anywhere unless my daughter wants me to go." He looked at Becca.

She stood, her napkin sliding from her lap to the floor. "Go, Dad. I'm not having this, threatening my husband, acting like nothing happened."

He glared at Becca. His lip quivered, hinting at the existence of a tiny bit of heart inside. The lip's weakness corrected under a swift bite from his

front teeth. A strong exhale flared his nostrils. "You want me to go? I'll go. But I'm telling you this." His attention shifted to Mike. He jabbed his finger in the air, toward him. "I've put curses on people before. . . just by thinking. You don't know who you're messing with."

Mike pointed toward the door. "Go now, or I'm calling the police."

He turned and shuffled out.

The couple followed Becca's father outside. Stopping by the car, Becca made another appeal, expressing her love for him. "Dad, I want the best for you. I want you to get help. I can't trust you until you do."

The loud *caw, caw* of a crow startled Becca, drawing her eyes toward the bird's rapid descent from above them. The black bird plunged toward a nest of fledglings in the tree outside their door. *Where's Jake?* Becca followed her instincts back into the house. As she opened the door, a sick feeling caught her gut. *Something is wrong.* She heard a zipper.

Becca stopped at the entrance to the living room. Jake and Christine sat several feet away from one another on the couch, their faces stunned at her entry. The air felt dank, as if some evil spirit lurked around the edges. Christine uncrossed her arms and legs and looked at her mother, her eyes beckoning for help, on the brink of tears.

Becca locked her gaze on her younger brother. His eyes, she could tell—even though his long blonde curls spilled over them—averted hers. "What's going on here?" Not waiting for answer, she lowered her voice to convey authority. She pointed him to the door. "Leave, now. Dad's waiting for you outside."

As Jake hurried out the door, Becca turned to Christine. The pool in her daughter's eyes spilled over the edges. She rushed to her and put her arms around her.

Christine leaned in and sobbed.

Becca held and rocked her.

Christine's sobs waned after a few minutes. "I need to tell you."

"What happened?"

"He exposed himself and wanted me to touch him." She sobbed again, her face in her hands on her lap.

Becca's head spun as her heart wrenched. *We were only*

gone a second.

Christine, with unmistakable sincerity and anguish in her posture, her face, her tears, her tone, her trembling hands. . . let loose the truth she'd held back too long. "He's been bothering me like that since I was five, but I could never tell you. I thought you would blame me or hate me, or think I wanted to do it. I just froze."

Becca thrust her emotional reaction aside to be present for Christine. She held her, rocked her and apologized that such a thing happened. "Jake was wrong. It wasn't your fault. Telling can be so hard, I know. I'm so proud you spoke up. I won't let this happen again."

After sobbing a while, Christine sat up. An ashen sheen veiled her face. "Do we have to call the police? I'm not ready to talk with police or a judge about it. I never want to see him again." Tears returned.

Mike, who'd since come in, had been listening from the outskirts. "There isn't much the police can do about what happened before without evidence. Jake was a minor then. Not this time. We should call. Maybe the investigation alone will scare him off. But we don't have to call tonight."

Becca knew the battle— loyalty to family versus legal action, taking a stand. She knew how the fear of retribution haunted a person. Christine was but a young teen, and Becca, an adult, hadn't yet taken legal action against her abuser. "I won't call them yet if you're not ready, but I will confront him myself. I have to. He needs to be stopped."

Christine calmed at this.

The torrent of emotions swirling inside threatened to render Becca helpless. She drew on her honed skill of steeling her emotions, erecting a levee against the flood.

"I wanted more than anything to protect you from this." A trickle leaked through the tiniest of holes, threatening to deluge her baby with Mama emotions. She fought to constrain what came out. "I wish I had been able to face what was going on in my family sooner. I should have never let them babysit you. I'm so sorry, honey. I'm so sorry."

"Mom, he even got to me when we were visiting your mom's mom, with all of you in the living room. Jake and I were in her room. He started rubbing against me. Your uncle came into the room. He walked in on it. I was so embarrassed and ashamed, I couldn't do anything." Christine cried as she spoke, her voice and body quivering. "But he didn't say anything. Jake stopped, and I just stood there as if nothing happened, playing with the brush and hand mirror. Frozen. Then your uncle just left the room. He didn't say anything either. I've been wanting to tell you all these years."

"Uncle Jiles?" *My mother's brother, also covering up knowledge of abuse? How much further does this thing spread?* Becca let the question hang. "You know some of what happened to me, and how I've been healing. We can help your heart heal from this. We will. I promise. Freezing is not at all unusual for abuse victims. The central nervous system—that's supposed to choose fight or flight when threatened—goes awry for some of us, and we just freeze."

Christine sat forward, her face revealing connections being made in her head. "So that's why I froze when those boys attacked me in middle school. I'd already been conditioned to freeze. . ."

After Christine went to sleep, Becca cornered Mike and led him into their room. She shut the door and sat in the window seat with him. "Mike, I need to talk more. I'm about to explode but I didn't want to in front of Christine. Promise me first you won't go kill anyone. I can't lose you."

"I get it. I promise, but you know I want to already."

The levee broke. "I can't believe it. Mike, what are we going to do? I can't believe it. Oh, God. She's been hurting for years. Because of *my* little brother. Damn it! How could he do such a thing?" Tears streamed down her face. Her body shaking, she wrapped her trembling hands around it. Her body rocked forward and back as she sat on the edge of the seat, pulsing as if the tide would explode through every pore.

She stood and paced the room. "I feel responsible. I should have known. How could I be so stupid as to think I could live in their house and protect her from the very things I couldn't protect myself from? God. I hate that I repressed everything and went into denial. I hate that I was so afraid of my dad."

She pulled her hair at each side of her face, as if the pressure would ease the eruption inside. "I want to kill him—and Dad. Strangle them, kick them, shake them, jump up and down on them! I can't stand it. Not my baby. My poor baby." Becca collapsed onto the floor. Her knees drew into her chest, and her body rolled back and forth. "God, how could You let this happen? How? God, no!"

Mike knelt beside her and put his hand on her back.

Becca could barely feel him. She covered her head with her arms and cried with sobs too deep for words. Overcome, trembling and rocking, she sobbed until the room came back into her awareness again.

Mike stayed by her, stroking her hair and holding her. He

kissed the top of her head.

Mucous blocked her airways. Barely able to breathe, she whispered, "Tissues?"

"Yea, of course." He brought tissues and waited while she blew her nose and wiped her face.

"I'm sorry." Becca's voice but a whisper, she pushed into a tailor-sit position.

"No, no, don't be sorry, Becca." Mike shook his head. "You've stuffed your anger too long. You should be mad as hell about what they've done."

"I guess you are, too. I'm sorry for my family. I'm sorry I brought you into all this."

"You don't have to apologize for that. You are good. So good. I'm amazed that someone as good as you came from them."

"You know any credit goes to the Lord. You know, the one I was just yelling at?" The pressure of her swollen face resisted her attempt to smirk at herself. "But I don't really blame God. I'm just so mad."

"Be mad. It seems right to be mad."

After a long pause, Becca's heart settled down a bit. She looked into Mike's eyes. "I forgive you now."

He scrunched his brow. "Huh?"

"For what happened the first year we were married. I've held it beneath the volcano all this time. Watching you. Worrying. I thought all men were liars, but time has shown me you're a good guy."

Mike's face pinked up. His puzzled look melded into calm. "Thank you. But it really wasn't mine."

The sun rose again. Pressing her swollen face into a cold wet washcloth, Becca checked on Christine.

"Let me sleep." She pulled the covers over her head.

"Okay, honey. It's Saturday anyway. I just wanted to see if you were okay."

Christine grunted.

Becca poured her coffee and picked up the phone. "Emily, how are you?"

"Terrible."

"What's wrong?"

"I always said I remembered everything from my childhood. But now I remember more."

Becca listened and prayed and encouraged Emily as her memories poured through the phone, along with her tears. Dad and Jake had struck there, too.

When their conversation ended, and having learned from Emily that Jake and Dad were staying at Doug's, Becca dialed his number.

"Hello?" Douglas answered.

"Put Jake on."

A long pause ensued, and then her younger brother answered the call.

"I know what you did. What you've been doing—"

Jake cut her off. "You don't understand. Just. . . let me come over and I'll explain it to you."

"I don't understand? No, I guess I don't understand. I don't understand how there could be any explanation that could possibly justify it." She forcibly restrained her emotion-laden words. "There's nothing you could say that would be an excuse for what you did. Nothing."

His voice cracked through the line. "Please—"

A myriad of conflicting thoughts rushed through her mind. Her little brother. The one she'd rocked and played with, read stories to at bedtime and—the one that hurt Christine. "Look. You know I have a relationship with the Lord. I'll go so far as to say the Lord can forgive you." Becca swallowed hard and pursed a curt whiff of air. "But I'm drawing a line. You're not welcome here. If you think you can explain things to me, fine. I'll meet you at a restaurant, just you and me, to see what you have to say. But here's what I already know. Both Dad and you need help. You need counseling and a relationship with God to help you change from the inside out. Our family is sick, Jake, and the disease keeps spreading from generation to generation. It stops here. I won't let this happen again."

"Okay, I'll meet you."

* * *

He didn't show. Instead, he called to say he'd left town. "I've always wanted to see the states. A friend was going to Arizona, so I hitched a ride. When I got here, we went to a church." He paused, as if expecting an excited response. "I went forward when they asked if anyone wanted to be saved, and I prayed with the pastor. I was born again."

Caution overrode what would have been joy. *This could just be a ploy to smooth over the damage done.* She cleared her throat. "Okay. . . that's a good start. Now keep at it. You have a long way to go." She wanted to lean into his tender side, but she knew she must hold the line. *He's no baby anymore. He abused my baby.* "Learn all you can. Seek the help you need to change your life. Let me know when you want to meet me, but otherwise, the ball is in your court. What are you going to do with it?"

She hung up the phone. *Dang it. Now he's across state lines. What would the police even do?*

51

Lena

Rockville, Maryland. 1934

"Ruthie!" Lena ran to greet her daughter. "You're here. I hoped you could come this weekend. Let me see you." She held Ruth by the shoulders and beamed. "Honey, you're getting' so tall! But thin as a rail." Ruth's face showed signs of weariness, but Lena chose to abandon the negative. *Ruth should feel welcomed, not scrutinized.* "But, oh, you're a beautiful sight for my sore eyes."

Ruth smiled and tucked her head onto her mother's shoulder, snugging her arms around her mother's waist. "I miss you so much, Mama."

Lena returned the hug, their heads nearly the same height now. "I miss you too." She held on until Ruth relaxed her hold. "Come sit on the sofa and tell me everything."

Ruth complied, plopping on the sofa as lanky teens do. "I hate living with Daddy. He's horrible." Spying clove candy in the bowl on the coffee table, she leaned forward and popped one in her mouth.

Lena's skin crawled every time Ruth said she hated living with Clinton. She still fought the urge to take Ruth and run away somewhere her father would never find them. *Focus on what's best for now. Just listen to Ruth. Be here for her.*

Ruth didn't wait for her mother's response. "Awful." She pushed the hard candy into the side of her mouth, talking over it, recounting her dramatic stories about being her father's slave, babysitting her step-mother's children night and day, and not being able to attend school. "He hates me. I don't know why, but he does."

Lena listened and validated Ruth's feelings. Typically, Ruth needed to blow off steam before she could enjoy her weekend with the Burriss family. When Ruth stopped ranting, Lena tested the water to see if her daughter was ready to cheer up. "With all that off your chest, would you like to see the new dress I made you?"

"A new dress?" Ruth sat up straight. "You betcha."

They clattered up the stairs, where Lena presented Ruth with a hand-sewn jumper dress. Midi-length and bright yellow, the dress portion sported red top-stitching, and the puffy-sleeved blouse repeated the colors in plaid on a white background.

Ruth shrieked and clapped her hands. "I love it!" She flung off her old dress to try on the new.

As Lena helped pull the new dress over her daughter's head, she gasped. "Ruth. You have bruises. What happened?" She placed her hand over the multiple sites of purple and green blotches covering Ruth's back, lightly caressing each of them as if her touch could heal.

Ruth winced. "Oh. Those. I fell."

Lena took her daughter's shoulders and gently led her face to face. "You fell on what?" A suspicious eye investigated Ruth's response.

Ruth stammered.

"These look like hand-prints. . . and these, like fist marks."

"I told you, he hates me—but don't tell him. It'll get worse—"

Lena put her arms around her girl and cried. "I'll never let him near you again, even if I have to go to jail to keep you away from him. I'm so sorry, baby. I should have kept us in the mountains, far away from that monster."

"The mountains? What are you talking about, Mama?"

She wiped her tears and composed herself. "Never mind. That was long ago. But now, no, we're not running away, and I'm not sending you back. We're gonna fight this thing. Don't you worry, honey, he'll not get his hands on you again." Lena went to the telephone, picked up the earpiece and spoke into the horn-shaped mouthpiece on the wall. "Operator?"

A female voice answered. "Number, please."

Lena spoke with resolve. "I need the Bradley Law Firm in Washington, D. C."

"One moment, please."

The earpiece clicked, and Harris answered. "Bradley Law. May I help you?"

She told him.

"I'll send a photographer there to document this evidence. Better yet, I'll send someone to get you both. As horrible as this is, the new evidence will help—and hasten—your case."

* * *

Rockville, Maryland. 1935

The massive brick building, a bastion of righteous power, dominated Lena's field of vision as she craned her neck to take in the expansive sight. Atop the wide stairway, six huge, ionic columns supported a Roman-styled pediment and frieze with the inscription, "Montgomery County Court House." Grasping Dorsey's arm with her left and Ruthie's with her right, Lena and her little group began their ascent into the halls of justice.

Shaw, Elliot, Harris, Adohi, Enna, and several aides preceded them.

Harris stopped every other step to take in the spectacle, each pause punctuated by several raspy breaths. "An impressive new build." Step. Step. "Did you bring all the folders, Don?" Step. Step.

At the massive wooden doors, Ruth gasped. "Do giants live here?" She raised one eyebrow at her mother.

Harris nodded. "Designed to emphasize our comparative size to the law, no doubt."

Ruth frowned. "What does he mean, Mama?"

"Maybe that the law is bigger than us."

The group progressed, through voluminous, paneled halls, to the courtroom, where lofty, coffered ceilings maintained the inhabitants' sense of smallness. They slid along the hard wooden benches to await the judge. Ruth clung to Lena. Dorsey slid in after them, creating a barrier between them and Clinton's side of the room. Shaw and Elliot took the bench behind their mother.

Across the center aisle, the lone lawyer checked his watch, the door, and his watch again.

"All rise," the plaintiff said.

The judge entered and called the case.

Clinton's lawyer spoke first. "Your honor, if I may approach the bench, sir."

The judge consented, motioning for both lawyers to approach.

Lena tried to read their lips while tilting her ear toward the lawyers as they conferred with the judge.

After some deliberation, the lawyers returned to their seats.

The judge, his face stoic and serious, filtered through papers. Having reviewed them, he jutted out his lower jaw and picked up his gavel. "As Mr. Clinton M. Smith has not appeared before this court today as ordered, he stands in contempt of court. In light of recent evidence on file, this court grants sole custody of the children of said Mr. Smith and Mrs. Lena Durriss Smith to their natural mother, now known as Mrs. Dorsey Reeves. Visitation rights for Mr. Smith to be withheld and reconsidered upon completion of arraignment of the accused and subsequent findings of that inquiry." He lowered his gavel. The decisive pound echoed in the vast open space.

Lena squeezed Ruth's hand.

"What did he say, Mama?"

She looked to Harris, and, upon receiving his nod of approval, she turned to Ruth. "It means we won, Morning Star. We won!"

Dorsey threw his arms around his wife and step-daughter.

Shaw's fixed jaw gave way to the smile in his eyes. He reached forward and squeezed his mother's shoulder.

Elliot let out a triumphant hoot. "You did it, Mama." He turned and thanked Mr. Bradley, Adohi and Enna as they made their way out of the courthouse.

Lena's heart pounded as excitement rushed through her. Outside of the courthouse, years of longing to gather her chicks under her wings met an abrupt culmination. As she stretched out her arms to receive them, their arms went around her waist, lifting her from the ground in a flurry of joyful relief. The grouping circled around, squeezing and laughing and wetting their cheeks with tears of joy.

Lena motioned toward a bench in the shade. She sat, holding Dorsey's hand, absorbing the surreal shock, while the rest of the group chatted. Ruthie raced after the morning doves as they strutted through the grass by the fountain.

It had been a thirteen-year battle. *Shaw will be eighteen soon, Elliot's sixteen. And Ruthie—oh, what she's been through. She's a big part of the reason we finally won—telling all. And Dorsey, what a man.* She leaned in against him. *And Adohi, Enna and Harris. . . if not for them, I might not have won.* In a few seconds' time, her mind raced back to the day everything changed—the day she'd told her story to Mrs. Lewis in The Dress Shoppe, the day she'd been invited to speak at the banquet. *And President Roosevelt—the stroke of his pen changed everything. I could just kiss him!* Tears filled her eyes and erupted into streams. She let them flow down her cheeks.

"Dorsey, I'm going to pray right here, right now." She took his hands in hers and their foreheads met. "Thank You, God. You know I've railed at You. You know I've begged and struggled and fought and. . . failed so many times. But You helped me choose to love, and to keep trying, no matter what. So, I thank You. Thank You for bringing my children back to me." Peace settled over Lena's body, from her head to her toes she basked in sweet relief.

"Okay, let's get the house ready!" She sprang to her feet and pulled on Dorsey's arm.

He stood. "I'll drop you and Ruth off at home and take the boys to get their things. Sound good?"

"I'll have paperwork to go over with you, but go on, enjoy your family." Harris reached for Lena's hand and planted a kiss on her cheek.

"Thank you, Harris. And you, Adohi and Enna. You've all been such a wonderful help."

The complete family joined together in the living room — Dorsey, Shaw, Elliot and Ruth, their eyes fixed on Lena, and Lena, her eyes scanning them.

"You're home. You're finally home. It feels so good. I've no words—"

"Mama," Elliot said. "No words needed. We've always been home when we're with you. Now we get to stay." He leaned forward, his arm on his leg, tilted his head and raised his brows with the most impish grin . "Now, where in the world will you fit us all?"

They laughed.

"Ruth will have the guest room, as we've always done."

Dorsey headed toward the kitchen. "Come have a look back here." He led them to the back porch he had enclosed.

"Plenty of room here." Shaw plunked on the daybed. "But where will you sleep, Elliot?" He tossed his hat at his brother.

"Hey!" Elliot caught the hat and tossed it back at his brother. "We'll take turns. Cushions on the floor one night, the bed the next."

Dorsey moved between the boys. "No need. A new bed should be here this afternoon."

Both boys looked stunned. "But. . ." Shaw started, "how could you have known?"

Dorsey grinned. "Just a hunch."

Ruth looked up from where she sat on her bed that evening. "But Mama, what about my sisters?"

Lena pressed her lips together. She sat next to Ruthie. "They're going to stay in a home with some very nice people who want to help them, while your father and their mother sort things out."

"But I want them here, with us." She pulled a pillow onto her lap and fidgeted with its fringes.

Lena sighed. "I'm afraid that's not possible."

"Why not? I've always taken care of them. They're more like my children than theirs."

"I know, and you've been wonderful to them." she leaned her shoulder in against Ruth's. "But your step-mother and father have the legal rights to their children until the court determines otherwise, and for now, at least we know they're safe. Foster families are special people. People who welcome children they don't even know into their home."

"I want to be one of those."

Lena took Ruth's chin and turned her face to smile eye to eye. "One day, perhaps. You'll make an excellent foster parent someday. But for now, let's get you back in school."

Ruth nodded. "Yes, Mama. I would like that. Are you sure they'll be okay?"

"As sure as I can be. We'll check on them tomorrow. And we'll stay in touch."

"Promise?"

"Promise." Lena kissed Ruth's forehead. "Now into bed with you. Tomorrow's a new day, and it'll be here before you know it."

Shaw swung open the screen door from the back yard, followed by Elliot, and traipsed across the rug.

"Hey, I'm reading here." Ruth fussed at her brothers, shooing them away.

"Stop right there, young men." Lena pointed them toward the door. Using her firmest tone, which wielded authority despite the endearing cheerfulness her eyes emitted, she issued her entry edict. "Shoes off! Don't track mud through my clean house."

Pushing his shoes off by the mat by the door, Shaw held up a letter. "I got a letter, Mama." He sat beside her at the table and tore open the envelope. Unfolding the letter, he read aloud. "This is to inform you that your request for room and board has been accepted." He looked up, eyes lit with excitement. "Woo-hoo! I'm moving to Atlanta."

"What?" Lena reached for the letter.

He released the unfolded paper to her. "My boss said they needed carpenters there. It'll be great, Mama. Room and board for a song, and plenty of work. I'll earn enough to send you money every week."

Lena shook her head in disbelief. "No, son, no. I just finally got you back."

Shaw stood and kissed her forehead. "I'll be back to visit. But Atlanta, Mama. I'll get to see the world. This is just the beginning." He bounced his way through the kitchen and into his room, shouting behind him. "Time to make tracks."

Lena's shoulders slumped. She rested her chin on her hand, which propped on the table. "Not you, too, Elliot?" Her sad look entreated him.

Aligning their four shoes near the back door, Elliot stood tall. He brushed the dust off his overalls and smoothed his hair. "No way, Mama. You're gonna have to give me the boot before I go." He smiled and sat beside her, smirking and beaming at her. "The food's too good here."

"Thank heaven." Lena partly stood and kissed his forehead. "No rushing off. I waited too long for you all." She slid back into her seat.

The phone rang.

"I'll get it." Elliot sprinted to it.

Lena heard the earpiece hit the wall and footsteps across the kitchen.

"Mama." Elliot stood in the doorway, short of breath. "Something's wrong with Grandpa and Grandma Burriss."

Lena dropped her sewing and rushed to the phone. Ruth sprang from the floor and followed. Lena pressed the phone to her ear. "What's wrong?"

52

Becca

Rockville, Maryland. 1988

Mike at work and Christine at school, Becca had the morning alone. Troubled and skittish from conflict and from trying to keep things together for Christine all weekend, she had no time for pleasant scenery or comfortable sofas with her coffee, Bible and journal. She plopped into bed in her clothes and got right to business, journal and pen by the bed.

She prayed aloud. "Lord, as you know, I know about Christine's abuse. I'm angry and fed up. I'm done with sugar coating. I'm tired of bleeding out the gills for the abusers in my family, hoping they'll be saved. I just want to get to the truth, the whole truth, and nothing but the truth. Memory after memory, I've faced so much, for years, but I want every root out. There's something beneath I haven't seen yet—I know it. Please show me and let's be done with it. Pull the whole root out, God, please. I'm totally Yours."

She closed her eyes and pictured herself walking down the stairs from her head into her heart, and entering the throne room, where God—Father, Son and Holy Spirit—resides. Today she found herself at his feet, wiping His feet with her tears and her hair.

God bent to the girl kneeling at his feet. He lifted her onto his lap and tilted her face to meet his. Wiping her tears and tucking the hair out of her face, he spoke without words. "There is one more, the root of all others. You are ready. Come now, with me, and I will hold you while we face it, together."

She opened her eyes and beheld his glory. The heavenly Father, unlike her earthly one, was the Father she'd needed but hadn't known. He never used or abused her—but always built her up and treated her like a precious gift. He delighted in her. With the heavenly Father was the Son, Jesus, the human embodiment of the Father's heart. Jesus stood in for her where she fell short. He understood her human frailty. Jesus confronted bigotry and rescued the persecuted, fed the hungry and listened to children. Becca had come as far as she had because of what He did. Invisible, the Holy Spirit connected them all. From the inside out, the Spirit renewed Becca's mind and empowered her to overcome evil with good. Becca could rely on the Spirit to guide her into all truth.

"Okay, let's do this."

They appeared in the house she had seen in her first inner journey. This time, though, she and the Lord walked toward her bedroom. The Lord stopped at the bottom of the attic entry. He reached up and pulled the folding stairs down, then opened his arm, guiding Becca up the stairs. She crept up and saw the built-in beds along each slanted wall, and the window at the end of the room. The room was empty. Becca looked at her Lord. *What?*

He reached toward the doorknob leading into the small room in the other half of the attic. An abrupt breath caught in her lungs and she her stance froze. She had forgotten about that room.

"My child, I am with you."

She moved closer to the Lord and peered in. There she was, as a child, lying on a table in the center of the room. Though Becca knew she was not on the table at present, her body shook with cold, fear and terror. She clung to the Lord in her mind's eye, and His presence calmed her.

She saw her father standing at one side of the table and Doug on the other. Her father recited strange ritualistic words, which she didn't understand. A "rite of passage," she heard him say, making her brother "a man." In the shadowy edges of this room, she saw Carlton curled up in a ball in the corner. *A ritual. Dad forced Doug to abuse me, and Carlton to watch.*

Becca didn't need to see more. She turned her face into God's chest, held on and wept. Together, they traveled back into the throne room in her heart, into the safe place she'd come to treasure, where she continued to weep and shiver.

The need for a tissue to blow her nose forced her to open her eyes. Her body continued to tremble uncontrollably, heaving from deep in her gut, shuddering with heartbroken sorrow. Becca fully remembered it.

She had told her mother she hurt "down there" while trying to ride her bike the next day. Her mother had insisted the bicycle seat hurt her, even though Becca had said, "No,

Daddy and Douglas hurt me."

Her mother had laughed. "You can't blame them, silly. They're not even here."

More memories of her brother terrorizing her flooded back, with their accompanying horror. All attempts to tell had backfired. She'd survived by avoiding and denying reality. She wept for herself, and Jesus wept with her.

"How I wanted to intervene, to swoop you up and set you in a safe place, my child."

Becca, eyes closed again, curled up in her Lord's lap, stiffened. "Then why didn't You, God? Why?"

God knew all. He could do anything. Why didn't he stop it? From some unknown store deep within, a fissure cracked. Red magma spewed from her gut, bursting the fissure into full-blown eruption. She blamed him for not intervening, for not doing something to stop her childhood abuse and save her. Rising to her knees, facing him, the small child beat his massive chest with her fists, screaming and crying at once.

"You could have helped me. You could have helped all the people—throughout time—who needed rescuing, who suffered unthinkable abuses, diseases, and disasters. Why didn't You?"

As the volcano spewed, Becca recalled letting her anger go at her father. She was thirteen. Her father beat her in return, his fist buried in her stomach, again and again, until she escaped. Her wrenched gut and frozen soul had locked away anger—in any real form—knowing reprisal would come, swift and harsh.

God could banish her forever for this. But she would not hold it back. No more. She would be her true self with him, no matter the consequence.

The Holy One didn't flinch or retaliate. He let her pound his chest until, at last, in exhaustion, Becca's arms lost their fury, her rage released.

Tears streaming down her face, she leaned into His arms, sobbing with loss, heartache and need. "But I know you to be love. I don't understand."

He comforted her without words. His radiant love, no scolding or correction, whooshed through her body. His Spirit cradled every cell.

After a time, his hand gently on Becca's back, Father God spoke. "Becca, you want to know why I've allowed such horrors. I am willing to share my heart with you, as you have yours with me." He sighed, and with his exhalation, sorrow permeated the air.

Curious at the weighted air, Becca wiped her tears and looked up at him. Furrows of deep affliction framed the far-off look in his eyes.

"I must suffer unimaginable atrocities to be—for now. If I were to use my power to control people, forcing them to honor me against their will, people would only know fear, or, worse yet, be no more than robots."

Becca listened, uncertain how to fathom the information.

"Without free will to choose or refuse me, there is no freedom to truly love." He leaned his forehead to hers. "I am wholly committed to your freedom, my dear one. I am completely delighted you have chosen to come to me, chosen to love me and to let me guide your life. We suffer many things for freedom. Eternity is free from the sin that drives people into horrific acts—I promise you that. In the mean time, people, governments, and laws must do their part to protect the innocent and restrain wrongdoing."

Becca let his words soothe her questions. He experienced the pain of being a parent who—for whatever reason—couldn't prevent his child's suffering. Becca knew that pain. His explanation may not have been enough for some people, but it satisfied her aching heart. After relating to God and knowing his tremendous character and reliability for over ten years, she let trust rush into the void where rage had lived.

As Becca returned to peacefulness, her body no longer trembling, her heart expunged of terror and pain, she gathered herself and hugged her Lord goodbye. "I'll be back soon." She opened her eyes and looked around her room. Everything looked the same, except the clock. Four hours had passed.

It is done. That was the taproot. Now I know the worst. I was not a bad girl. I was a victim. They had no right to use me that way. They were wrong. Dad aligned himself with evil. I was trapped between loving and needing my family and wanting to escape. God was with me, longing to intervene, comfort me and set me free. And He has—I am free now. He can bring good, even from this. I can be someone who brings His essence into the toughest situations.

Becca opened her journal, two hours before Christine would come home from school, and wrote everything she remembered, then posed a question—

"God, why do the memories only seem real when
I am praying in an inner journey with you?"

"Because you closed the memories off to survive. They were too much unless you feel safe with me. Now you have faced them. You are a pioneer for your family, braving this new frontier and blazing a trail they can follow. I will protect you and guide you and your family and bring good fruit from this labor of love. Your trust in me will bring forth blessing for many generations. You can rest now, my child. I am pleased."

"Thank you, Lord. Even though sometimes I'm tempted to think I've imagined all these memories, I look at the outcome. Dad admitted—he even told me there was more than I remembered when I first confronted him. Strong emotions attached to every memory. I couldn't have made them up. But above all, I know the work you've been doing through your Holy Spirit to renew my mind. You've pulled out those nasty, matted roots and the thorny bramble-bush of tangled emotions and helped me to feel them, one at a time, soothing and comforting each one. You've spoken the truth of your love for me and assured me that you're delighted with me—all deep in my heart and soul. I feel normal, now, Lord. No, even better—I feel whole and healthy. Thank you."

The second hand on her bedside clock continued its *tick, tick, tick* around the dial. Becca went on with her day. As she did her chores, her mind kept returning to what she had learned from the last inner journey. Her thoughts tumbled around, scraping against one another as stones are smoothed and polished, making sense of the pieces.

The ritual. A cycle of familial abuse. Dad came to Maryland because—

The realization set off alarm bells—alarms she may have heard earlier, if not for her warring emotions repressing her common sense. *My father. . . lives in a van, not far away. He came here on purpose. Jake wasted no time going after Christine. All I did was turn my back for a second. Is he preying on other kids? My nieces? Will Dad try to silence me? Would he kill us? Set fire to the house while we're sleeping? Would he steal Christine?*

Awareness called for action. She phoned local family who might have contact with him and warned them. Then she got in her car.

As she drove, she watched for his van. *Now that I know fear is appropriate, and not just some fault on my part, I won't guilt myself out of it. This is a valid fear. He's a pedophile. A ritualistic one. A danger.*

Parked in the parking lot of the local police station, Becca crunched through the icy slush, checking behind and all around. *Did he follow me here?* Her hands trembled as she entered the station. God's words urged her forward. *You have governments with laws to protect the innocent and restrain wrongdoing.*

She hoped they wouldn't recognize her as Mike's wife—he used to work from this station. Back then, she'd come here to meet him for lunch. This time she came to tell them her father and brother are dangerous criminals. A pallor of guilt by association swept over her. She drew a deep breath, straightened her back and shoulders and stepped up to the counter.

"I have something to report."

An officer led her down the hall to a desk, where she took a seat.

Through her trembling voice, she told the detective what she knew. "I want you to know about a potentially dangerous situation. My dad. . . he's a pedophile." Her fingers quivered. She bit her lip to hold back her tears. "I've tried to convince him to seek help, but he won't. I'm afraid he might lure a child into his van and abuse them."

"I'm sorry to hear that, ma'am," the officer said. "Tell me more about that."

She relayed her story, in brief—that he was a vagrant, living in his van to work in Bethesda. Holding back her stomach's inclination to retch, she described where she heard he parked at night, a parking garage near Doug's. She gave them Doug's address in Bethesda. All she knew about Jake's location was his word, that he was somewhere in Arizona. Fidgeting with her tissue, which by now was torn to shreds, she reassured them their work would not be in vain. " I'll press charges if you'll arrest him. I won't back down. I can't stand the thought of him still molesting children. Please, take this seriously."

The officer finished his notes and laid down the pen. He interlaced his fingers and rested his arms on the desk, then steadied his eyes on Becca's. "I appreciate the courage you've shown by coming in with this problem. I'll notify the Bethesda office, and we'll keep an eye on him." He drew in a deep breath. His eyes took on a forlorn cast. "Unfortunately, the statute of limitations to prosecute sexual abuse is seven years. Since your father's abuse happened over ten years ago, I'm sorry ma'am, but there's nothing more we can do unless he repeats the offense. And, since your younger brother has left the state, he's out of our jurisdiction. Let us know if he returns, though."

Frost on the windshield blocked Becca's view to leave of her spot from the police station parking lot. After sitting a few moments to let her heart stop pounding, she donned her gloves and opened the car door. Opening the trunk, she found the scraper and cleared the windows.

This was one of the few times Becca didn't notice the beauty of the quiet snowfall around her, gradually changing all that was gray and grimy to sparkling white.

Back in her seat, her gloved hands gripped the steering wheel. She let her spinning head slump onto her hands. *Nothing more we can do?* The lump in her throat pressed hard. *Seven years? I needed longer than that to remember it.*

Agony sunk a heavy anchor to lodge in her gut. *Nothing more we can do?* She shifted the car into drive and snapped the turn signal wand down. Methodically, stoically, numb, she drove as if the car knew the way home. The wipers' *thum-squee, thump, thumsqee, thump* kept time with the detective's taunting words—*Nothing, more, we can do. Nothing, more, we can do.*

Idling at a traffic light, a sparkle caught the corner of her eye. A cluster of early hyacinths bloomed beneath a rusty old cattle fence. The light of her turn signal lit up the dusting of snow, sparkling on the lavender flowers and the snow-covered barbed wire. With that image, his words in her head stopped.

Whitewashing a barbed-wire fence doesn't make the barbs less painful. The statute of limitations needs to be extended for cases of sexual abuse, especially on children. Becca's brows pressed down upon her eyelids. What would it take to change the law?

The light turned green, and she continued driving home. She thought about all she'd been doing, raising her daughter, building a marriage, ministry training, inner healing. *What can I change? What can I not change?*

Becca turned the car onto her street and into her driveway. *There is something I can do.* She shifted the gear into park and pulled her purse onto her lap.

She opened the car door and watched her feet swing out, land and adjust to the fresh layer of ice and snow beneath them. Standing, she closed the car door. *God, help us. We need it.*

As she walked toward the front door, she noticed how the streetlights cast a warm glow upon the lightly drifting snow. The yard, the sidewalk, the front railing, all glistened snow white.

"Lord, this is why you brought me back to Maryland. I had to find out what happened to Christine, and I had to know what Dad and Jake were up to. You're showing me the bigger picture."

53

Lena

Sandy Spring, Maryland. 1934

Lena lifted her black veil enough to press a handkerchief to her swollen eyes. The funeral procession stopped, and an attendant opened the limousine door for her. Dorsey must have quickly darted around the back of the vehicle because his hand appeared almost from nowhere, extended to assist her. She let one foot slip out onto the street, then the other. Pressing against the sides of the car door to stand, she took his arm, and stepped toward the open gravesite. Each second ticked, slow and precise.

Folding chairs lined the grassy walkway, pointing the way to the flower-laden caskets resting beside the graves. Four. At once. Lena's knees gave way.

Dorsey leaned in, slipping his arm around her waist, supporting her against his side. He kept her from falling as he led her to her seat. Her siblings, the children, along with many family members, friends and neighbors, filed in, each finding a seat without a sound.

The pastor stepped to the front and opened his Bible onto the portable podium. He opened with the usual request to bow heads together, entreating God's comfort for the loss and expressing gratitude for the better place to which they'd gone. He began his homily. "It is great sorrow to lose a loved one, no matter the time or reason. But when a tragedy strikes suddenly. . ."

His voice trailed off into the background, along with sounds of cars whizzing by, leaves rattling in the breeze, and the clanging of metal grommets against a flagpole.

In place of the pastor's voice, mental images of the explosion and fire replayed in Lena's mind. Horrific scenes haunted her every thought. *Mama. Daddy. Cordelia. John. All gone. Sitting around the kitchen table, and then. . . gone.* Her mind constructed various possibilities of what it had been like for them, all terrifying. *I hope they went quickly.*

Her eyes opened and scanned the row of children to her right. They varied in height, from full-grown to only ten. *Cordelia's children, all looking so brave. Orphans. God, how could you let this happen?* Lena had helped her sister raise some of those children, before her own had come. And Cordelia had nursed Ruthie back to life. Cordelia was Lena's favorite sister and confidant. *How will I live without her?*

Daddy. Mama. They had always been. They were the core of this loving family. *What will we do now?* She asked herself these questions countless times, yet they cycled around in her mind again and again, a broken record. *What will we do now?*

John and Cordelia's home exploded and burned. Something went awry with the gas stove while the four of them worked in the kitchen.

The family met at the Burriss farm after the funeral. The neighbors brought casseroles and pies and huge jugs of iced tea. *Pies. Mama always made pies.* Lena wafted through the crowd, a surreal experience with people around her laughing and crying, perusing photograph albums and eating and drinking. Children chased one another as if—

An afternoon comforting one another and retelling fond recollections, dissipated with the crowd into the evening's task—deciding what to do with loose ends. Who would take which of the orphaned children? Would they let the farm go? Having been unprofitable through much of the decade, selling the farm made sense. They could divide any profit among them, with the largest portion going to raise John and Cordelia's children.

No consensus on the matter meant more discussion and details. Lena slipped away from the discussion and meandered into her parents' room.

Visiting the top of her mother's dresser, as if Mama might be there, Lena ran her fingertips along the soft bristles of her mother's silver-back hairbrush. She selected a hair comb and tucked the jeweled trinket neatly into her curls, then spritzed some of Mama's cologne on her wrist. As she reached up to touch a dot of the heavenly scent to her temples, her hand traced the edges of her face. Peering at her image in the faded mirror, she whispered. *Mama. In me. I miss you so much, already. What will we do without you?*

Turning about, she noticed her father's valet stand, which stood, at the ready, near the clothes closet. His Sunday suit no longer draped around the valet's wooden shoulder pads. *Because they buried him in it. But I always think of him in his overalls.* She sat on the valet stool and picked up one of his work boots left lying by the bed. Running her hand along its tattered leather edges, she savored the aroma of soil he had faithfully plowed, grain he had reaped, and a hint of mud from the creek's edge. Pulling the boot into her embrace, she curled herself around the leather symbol of Daddy and wept.

What will we do now, Daddy? This farm, our home. . . they're talking about selling it. How can we think of such a thing when you were here last week? This is the best place in the entire world. I can't let your farm go. You are here. We are all here, still singing around the circle, still chasing fireflies in the pasture. I'm still here. The girl I was. Me as a teen. My kids as babes. Oh, God, we can't lose everything. No.

Grief sent her sliding off the short stool and onto the floor, where she lay on her side in a ball, her knees to her chin and her arms around her legs. Deep waves of grief rolled over and through her. All lost, never to be found again. She felt as if a bomb passed through her gut, tearing a gaping hole through her core. She emptied her store of tears, crying until heaving gave way to the occasional deep breath, until her arms and legs relaxed, and her eyes drifted open. She lay on the floor by the bed, absorbing the quiet. Gradually, the clatter of family downstairs and people outside returned to her awareness. She blinked away tears, and a box underneath the bed came into focus.

What's this? I don't think I've ever seen it before. She reached for the box and slid it out from under the bed, pushing up to side-sit on the floor. Examining the large wooden box, she brushed away a layer of dust, then traced the hand-carved engravings with her fingers. Not recognizing any of the symbols along the edges, she studied the large insignia decorating the top of the box. *Surely this means something. Are these initials? Is this Cherokee, Celtic, Gaelic?* She pushed a small dowel out of a brass loop and opened the box. A mild scent of cedar filled the room.

Letters. Inside the fabric-lined box she found neat stacks of letters, bundled in separate stacks, and tied with string. Leafing through the edges of each stack, she recognized Aunt Caroline's and Grannie's handwriting. *Should I read them?* She returned the stacks neatly, and was about to close the box, when a small parchment fell from a pocket inside the box's lid and landed by her hand. Tenderly, for the paper was home-pressed and fragile, she opened it.

> *My Dear Children,*
>
> *When I am gone, yes, read these letters. Before Aunt Caroline passed, she returned the letters we sent to her. I have combined them with her letters, preserving them for you. Life is too busy, or ends too abruptly, or does not afford correct timing, to tell all that needs saying. Write your important matters of heart. Add to this collection and pass them on. Continue this legacy of love.*
>
> *With all my love,*
> *Mama*

Lena held the precious letter to her heart and wept again. She gathered herself and carried the box to the kitchen table, where her siblings continued their engagement. She placed the box in the center of the table and sat in her chair.

Her siblings quieted, all eyes on the box, and then on Lena.

"What's this?" Two or three of them asked in unison.

"This?" Lena cleared her throat and reached one hand onto the box. "This is what really matters." She stood and opened the box, then read their mother's note aloud. "Who wants to read them with me?"

One by one, each raised a hand. "Aye."

They spent the evening opening and reading. They started with the oldest—letters between Grannie and Aunt Caroline.

The first letters between the Cherokee sisters were illegible. Lena recognized Tsalagi, their native language, but could not read it. Gradually, their letters incorporated English. Eliza noted her memories fading, including her native tongue. She confessed her growing love for the man their uncle arranged for her. His noble character had won her heart. Caroline had grown to love her spouse as well.

Eliza wrote with immense pride for her husband's dedication and bravery as he embraced the Union cause. This matter slowed the sisters' letter writing for a time. Cherokee infighting produced horrific outcomes, and Caroline exercised prudence, withholding letters for several years.

After the war, Eliza wrote of her husband's death. He died in battle, along with most of the troop he led, and Eliza grew angry at never finding his grave. Fearful to file a claim for a veteran widow's pension, thinking to do so may bring her Cherokee to light and endanger Aggie, she ended up destitute. Eventually, she took on manual work alongside freed slaves, and lived with them in sparsely furnished cabins. She taught her daughter at night, by candlelight, until the landowner noticed and helped send

Aggie to school. Finding a friend among the former slaves, she found safe companionship for over a decade. He was older, but kind, and good to her. Eliza tended him to his death. By then, Aggie had married Henry, and the young couple took her in. Her later letters displayed how Grannie's life grew in gratitude and contentment in her role as matriarch, grandmother, and great-grandmother.

Letters from Aggie to Aunt Caroline proved more difficult to read, for the content fell as salt on raw wounds. The siblings chose to persevere, deciding the time was right, and believing the balm of their mother's words could help soothe their grief in the end.

"My Dearest Aunt Caroline," one letter read, "How painful 'tis to stand by as my daughter suffers the loss of her children. I want to take her in my arms and soothe her. I want to magically bring the babe she lost back to life. I'm tempted to ask God to remove their father from this earth so Lena may have her children."

"Are you sure you want me to continue with this one?" Lena's oldest brother sent a tender, understanding eye with his question.

"Yes. Go on." Lena reached to hold her younger sister's hand.

He continued to read. "My own memories resurface, how Henry and I grieved when we, too, lost babes, more than once. Yet we had each other, and our other children. Being a parent to adult children and a grandparent holds untold blessings, yet at times the weight proves unbearable. Why do our lessons lie in waste, while the next generation freely make their own mistakes, not gleaning from lessons we've learned? Can we not spare them suffering? But we cannot force knowledge upon them, no more than we can assume their responsibilities as our own. It would not be right. So, I relegate myself to stand by. . . to help when asked. . . and to pray."

"Mama." Lena let her thoughts spill aloud in the presence of her siblings. "I wish I'd told you how important you are to me. The advice, but moreover, your example, and Daddy's, guided me through every step. You helped recover my footing from every misstep. Did you not know your value?"

A brother leaned in to comfort her, holding her until she raised her head. They continued to read, letter after letter, into the wee hours of the night. As a rooster announced the arrival of dawn, the last letter opened.

My Dearest Aunt Caroline,

I write today even though you are gone. I want to write a good thing, after years of making you endure my grievous letters. You should know, I see now.

Hardships and suffering are the only way we humans truly learn. Book knowledge and gleaning wisdom from elders are all well and good, but personal experience is the best teacher. Looking back, I could not spare any of my children their rich learning experiences. Each has come full circle. Soon they begin letting go of their children, to let them make their own mistakes.

Thanks be to God for his indescribable gift of mercy, to patiently endure as we mature into His image— into love. . . patient, kind, full of mercy, and slow to anger. Thanks to you and my mother, and my dear husband, I am more accepting now of what is beyond my control. I see how my children love me. I have been important to them and to my grandchildren.

Lena finally has custody of her children, and Cordelia and John have asked us to their place. They are ready to take on the mantel of hosting our family each weekend, so Henry and I can rest. The farm has been difficult going this last decade, and we hope when we are gone the children do not feel they must maintain that which is but a relic of the past. The torch passes generation to generation, and it is well with my soul.

By His Grace,

Aggie

The golden letter lay in the center of the rough-hewn farm table, glowing in the last candle's flickering light. Lena scanned her siblings' faces. Each held sorrow, yet with it, a glimmer of light.

Mama had told the whole story in one last letter. She'd served an ample slice of rich family legacy, a blend of smooth and chewy textures, complementary sweet and sour flavors, and better than any pie she'd ever baked.. Mama's letter told Lena and her siblings where to go from here.

"Mama, you knew. God bless you."

54

Lena

Bethesda, Maryland. 1934

Lena leaned over Harris' desk and signed the last of the documents.

"That will do it, my dear." Harris gathered the stack of papers and stood them on end on the desk, tapping them into alignment.

"Now, there's the question of money." Lena sat back in her chair and reached for Dorsey's hand.

"Yes. I've looked into the matter as you requested, and you may use what you need to pay off any existing loans you may have. Doing so is in the best interest of your success, which seemed to be the donor's intent. Our expenses may also come from the fund. However, there is quite a large sum remaining, even after those expenses. Have you given thought as to how to best invest those funds to secure a better future for your family?"

"We have." She squeezed Dorsey's hand. They exchanged encouraging looks. "My benefactor was too generous, yet being anonymous, we have no way to return the extra funds. So, we've been thinking. The dreams I had as a girl—they were grand, indeed. I was planning to travel to all the lands I'd read about in books. I wanted to visit all the museums. Wear the finest dresses. Dance in the greatest halls."

"You certainly have enough to make those dreams come true now." Mr. Bradley said.

"But those dreams faded. I've since realized that what I really wanted was to have the very thing I left when I was just a girl. The family I was raised in—my father, my mother, sisters and brothers. The farm. A good education. I had a wonderful childhood." She sipped her tea and placed the glass on a coaster.

Adohi pulled up a chair. "I enjoyed such a childhood as well. Enna and I often wish we could go back."

"But it's too late to recreate that for my children. Their farm experiences were not so idyllic, and farms everywhere are suffering. Daddy and Mama, John and Cordelia are gone. We must face what is. At least the children are with us now. We make enough to care for them. They don't need wealth as much as they need love. There are many children who still don't have enough. Children who are pulled out of school to work, with not enough food to eat, clothes to wear, or love to guide them." She stood and paced the room, rolling her handkerchief between her fingers.

Dorsey stood and placed his arm around her shoulder. "It's alright, love. I am with you."

Lena squared herself toward Harris, letting her arms fall to her side. She took a deep breath. "We want to create a fund for children who've been abused and neglected, for women escaping violence in the home, and for the hungry. And for your mission here, too, Harris, for Indian rights. Is there enough to create a fund like this, one that will be philanthropic and continue to grow by strong and wise investments?" She pursed her lips and held still. Her breath steady, she kept her eyes on Harris.

The air grew thin and quiet. At the window, a cardinal landed on the wooden trim and peeped into the room.

Harris cleared his throat. "There is."

"Can you help us with that?"

"We would be honored."

"Good. Make it anonymous, like the gift was to me. No one should know it started with me. Use the name Grannie gave me. Sasa."

Harris turned to Adohi and Enna. "How about this cousin of yours? She is *Aniyunwiya*, no?"

55

Becca

Rockville, Maryland. 1988

"I want you both to be the first to know." Becca pulled the chairs together in the living room as they prepared for weekly game night. "So, before we start our game, we need a quick family meeting."

"Oh, no, not another family meeting." Christine rolled her eyes. "Mom, come on, you said this would be a fun night after such a rough week."

Mike patted Christine on her arm. "It has, but your mom wouldn't stop fun for just any news, right Becca?" He grinned and winked at her.

"Very funny." Becca tossed a pillow at him. "I know, I know. I am all too serious. This has been a rough week. I want to have our game night, but this news just happened. I want you to know. Just a few minutes, then we can pray and play."

Christine placed the game board on the coffee table and plopped onto the sofa. "Okay, what is it?"

Becca sat, curling her feet under her in the chair. "Okay, here goes. How about a news sandwich? First good news, then bad, then good." She watched their faces for approval. "Good news first. I finally overcame a long-held fear and I feel pretty darn valiant for it."

"What did you do, Mom?" Christine's face lit up with interest.

"I went to the police station. . ."

Christine's mouth gaped.

". . . and reported my dad and Jake." Becca widened her eyes, taking in their responses.

Mike's eyebrows raised as his chin tucked. "You did?" His face recovered from the shock to show genuine interest and approval. "Good for you. What did they say?"

"Well, that's the bad part." Becca's lower lip protruded, caught by her teeth on one side. "They said they'll keep an eye on my father, but that the statute of limitations passed."

"The what of what?" Christine sat up and leaned in.

"Statute of limitations—the number of years after a crime that charges can be pressed. I'm no lawyer, but in cases like this, limiting the years seems ridiculous."

"Neither am I," Mike added. "But when I was an officer, there was no statute of limitations on murder or felonies. Seems like there wouldn't be for child molestation, either."

"Exactly, right?" Becca waved her hands with exasperation. "I couldn't believe it. I told him that I hadn't even remembered the abuse until the last couple of years. He said the statute of limitations on child abuse is seven years after the child reaches the age of majority. I would have had to report him by the time I was twenty-eight."

"Mom." Christine sat, dumbfounded. "You just missed it."

Becca sat back in her chair. "I know. And the laws vary by state. We weren't even back in Maryland until this year. Jake's on the run. We'd have to track him down to prosecute. He's left the state where he exposed himself to you, and before that episode, he was a minor. It looks like we won't be able to do much to stop him, either. Except—"

"Leave the state." Mike spoke firmly. "I'm the one that led us back here. I'm the one charged with protecting you both, my family. If the law's not going to afford us protection, then we're going to go somewhere safer. I'll start the job search Monday."

Becca, stunned, raised her eyebrows. "Seriously?" She breathed a sigh of relief. "That's not what I was going to say, but I'm all for it."

"Wow." Christine got up and paced the room. "Move, again? I didn't want to move back here anyway, but isn't there anything else we can do to stop them?"

Becca's lips pressed together in firm resoluteness as she prepared her answer. "That's the second good news. We're not completely powerless here. I don't believe God intends for us to just roll over and take this. We can overcome it. First, we need to find you a safer place so you can heal, Christine. I've already told everyone in the family, so they'll know to keep Dad and Jake away from their kids. But we can't stop there. We're gonna find people who will help us change the law. I'm not going to bury my head in the sand or kiss our butts goodbye. This means war."

"Wow, Mom. Way to be fearless." Christine beamed at

Becca and sat next to her. "You know what? I'm proud of you. I still never want to see Jake again, even in court, but someday I'll be ready."

"I'm sure you will."

Mike shook his head. "I guess I should have studied law after all, like my parents advised. Who knew I'd need a law degree for this, though?" He moved closer to Christine and put his arm around her shoulder. "I don't want you to have to suffer for what he did. If you can't stand the thought of seeing him, then we won't pursue that—yet. I do want you to have counseling, though. That way you win, no matter what."

Christine leaned into his hug and then pushed away in proper teenage form, opening the game box and spreading out the board. "Deal. But we can't solve everything in one night. For tonight, can't I just be a teenager? Let's play Monopoly. I'll be banker."

"Dibs on the boot." Becca grabbed and held up the boot token. "I'm in the mood for some some butt-kicking." She laughed.

"Oooh, watch out, Becca's got her Irish up." Mike winked in jest as he reached for the sports car. "And I'll get us outta here!"

The next day, Becca made several calls to local associations, trying to find anyone she might align with to fight the statute of limitations law on child molestation. The best she could find was a telephone clerk who told her how much money she'd need as a retainer to start a case.

"I don't have that kind of money." She hung up the phone, her heart fluttering from embarrassment at telling her issue, combined with frustration at the sparsity of resources and the enormity of the task.

I know nothing about changing laws. What should I do? I'll need years studying and saving up for a lawyer before I can change anything—years of Dad and Jake. . . possibly hurting more kids.

She shook the image from her mind. Shelving the yellow pages, her finger pressed the numbers she knew by heart. *Christine's my priority.*

"I'm so glad you called." Pastor Richard's tone reflected sincerity and relief. "I was just about to call you."

"Oh?"

"Yes. We've decided to open a women's recovery program, and to re-write the curriculum. We interviewed various couples, but we couldn't stop comparing them to you and Mike. I know you just recently left, but will you come back?"

* * *

Their new plans firmed within the week. Mike, Becca and Christine prepared to move back to Florida, this time to work at The Center. Christine looked forward to starting counseling with The Center's church youth pastor, who would facilitate inner healing. Mike and Becca would work together on new curriculum, begin a women's recovery program and develop outpatient support groups.

Before Becca could leave Maryland, one last visit beckoned. Since her negative childhood memories had surfaced and resolved, positive memories more freely floated to the surface. The best were the ones with her grandmother.

Becca's earliest memories with this magnificent woman lifted her soul. She was the one bright spot in Becca's childhood.

Tucking her journal and Bible into her bag, she drove to the cemetery where Grandma was buried. As she drove, Becca remembered one special night at Grandma's. Though very young then, she recalled Grandma's hand holding hers, squeezing tight, easing her fear. As her family's car turned the corner out of sight, so did Becca's fear, lilting down the street like a dandelion fairy tumbling in the wind.

"Well, come on inside, Grandma's got a surprise for you."

"For me?" Becca could never recall a time in her life when she'd felt so special, so noticed, so *there*. "What is it, Grandma?"

Grandma playfully initiated the hunt. "First you have to find it."

They walked hand in hand past the hedges along the sidewalk and pushed open the iron gate that led to Grandma's yard. Between the gate and the front porch, a rectangular area welcomed them, a green carpet of soft, cushiony grass. Lovely flowers in varied heights and colors lined the borders. "Hmm. Nothing here."

Becca bounded up the three wide wooden steps to the front porch. Nothing under the rocking chairs. Nothing under the cozy round rug of colorful knotted scraps or the table. Nothing behind the lamp or cheery potted geranium. She picked up the chenille pillows as she climbed on the porch glider. "Not here."

"Let's look inside." Grandma opened the squeaky screen door. Her blue-gray eyes twinkled, and her cheeks, when smiling this way, were as round and rosy as Santa's.

"Okay, here I come." Becca slid off the glider and peered in the house. At once she saw—perched on the sofa, with a big red bow—"A doggy!" She ran to her delightful surprise. "I love it! I always wanted a doggy all my own."

"Yes, sweet pea, he'll be your very own special friend. You can take him for walks, see?" Grandma showed her how to pull the toy dog along, making its feet clack and the springy tail wag. "He likes going for walks, see? His tail wags."

It was a lovely toy, made of wood and painted like a beagle, but shaped more like a 'hot-dog doggy.' She could almost hear the big, pouty eyes say, 'Walk me.' Becca gladly complied. "Can I take him for a walk?"

"Sure, you can. You can walk him up and down the sidewalk while I start supper." Don't go far, though. Grandma needs to see you from the window."

Becca sped out the door, talking all the way to her new doggy, whom she named Snoopy. She walked him up and down the sidewalk for what seemed like hours.

Grandma made me feel so loved. Becca pulled into the cemetery and slowly headed to the section she recalled visiting as a child. She drove the curvy roads, looking mostly to her right, hoping a landmark would ring familiar. *Hmm, finding her grave won't be as easy as I thought. Everything looks different after all these years.*

Then she saw it. An old oak, now bigger than Becca remembered—yet much the same. *That tree.* Her eyes followed its crooked trunk, then the lower branches as they skimmed the ground. The lowest branch touched the ground and turned back toward the sky. *There.*

Parking the car nearby, she sidestepped the monuments

so as not to step on anyone's resting place. At the top of the hill, she circled to take in the scene. A beautifully landscaped cemetery with rolling hills and age-old shade trees made a lovely place to spend the afternoon, even if among the departed. A gentle breeze blew a strand of hair into her face. Brushing the strand aside, she noticed beds of purple, yellow and white flowers swaying in the breeze. Compelled to see them closer, she drew nearer.

"Pansies." Becca stooped to feel their velvety smooth petals. "Happy flowers." Cradling one smiling pansy in her hand, she tugged ever so slightly and tucked its smiling face into her journal. A favorite Dickinson poem echoed in her mind.

> 'Apparently with no surprise
>   To any happy flower
>   The Frost beheads it at its play—
>   In accidental power—
>   The blonde assassin passes on—
>   The Sun proceeds unmoved
>   To measure off another Day
>   For an Approving God.'

The poem resonated in her soul when she was a teen, so she'd committed the poem to memory. She had been only six when her grandmother died, too young for such eloquence, but at the time she imagined that God didn't care if she suffered. Death robbed her of the one person who had given her light, love, and kindness, all of which she so desperately needed.

Settling in to sit next to grandmother's gravestone, she

ran her fingers along the rocky edges. She opened her journal. With pen and ink, Becca shared her painful loss, her grief, and her long-held misgivings with God. After spilling her anguish, she yielded her soul to the One who had become her inner light, love, and kindness.

If it had to be, Lord, that Grandma had to leave, and You approved, which I still don't understand, I'm glad that I've had her memory with me all these years, and I'm glad that she's with You.

At once, she sensed His response rising in her heart. She let the ink flow with His words.

She is with me, and we are with you. We have always watched over you. You are precious in my sight. You are my child—my delight! I will hold you in times of sorrow and dance with you in times of joy. I grieved with you, but I knew the end all along. I knew I would be with you, and you would receive my comfort. You share all things with me, my beautiful daughter. Together we will sow and reap, tear down and build up. I love being with you, and I love sharing this world with you. I know I can trust you to do well with all I give you, my dear.

After a moment of shared silence, she looked again at the pansy. Stroking the velvety petals, she remembered her grandmother's words. *"Whenever you're sad, come pick a flower—especially a happy flower like this one. Listen closely. It'll cheer you up."*

Becca had sensed her grandmother watching over her from heaven, especially when she noticed pansies. She brought the pansy near her ear. "I'm listening, though I feel quite silly, Grandma, my happy flower." Closing her eyes, she listened.

A gentle breeze waved the velvet petals against her cheek as a soft touch from her loving grandmother. A deep sense of calm grounded her. The grass beneath cradled her. The wind carried wisps of clouds like angels across the sky. She breathed in deeply and imagined tracing the air circulating through her body, bringing energy and life to every cell—her brain, her heart, her torso, her limbs. Expelling the old, she breathed in the new.

Becca opened her eyes and scanned the rolling cemetery hills. A pair of cardinals poked at the ground nearby, flitting between the lawn and their nest in the branches above. Flowers danced in the breeze under every tree as far as her eye could see—beds of pansies, all smiling, all happy to be.

She grasped her pen again. *Grandma*, she wrote, as if she were alive to read it, *I want to be like you when I am a grandmother. I want to treat my grandchildren as precious treasures. I'll pass on what you taught me, to tend our gardens and see God in the smile of a flower.*

She sketched the likeness of a pansy beneath this entry and closed the book. Standing, she gathered her things to go. Just before leaving, she gingerly kissed her fingers and delivered the kiss to her grandmother's name on the tombstone:

Lena Burriss Smith Reeves

"I will keep praying for your son. You couldn't have known what Shaw did. Your heart would been broken, as has mine. I'll do my best to stop him from ab

using anyone else. And Jake. . . and anyone who does what they did. I don't know what could possibly make anyone do such heinous things. *What happened to him, Grandma?* But I do know it wasn't your fault, as it wasn't mine. I'm going to war against abuse, first by helping victims, but someday, we'll change the world. I feel it, Grandma."

Becca breathed in the sweet, warm air and remembered her grandmother stooping to take her into her arms. "Somehow, I think I got that from you."

56

Becca

Becca kissed Mike goodbye as she walked out of the dining hall, heading down the dirt road to teach her class. "I'm so glad to be back here. Thank you, honey."

Mike smiled and squeezed her waist. "Me, too. Christine's been doing well in her counseling. Moving back here was the right choice."

Setting her books down in the new classroom, a large open area in an old church building, Becca drew a 3-D thinking template on the chalkboard.

"Welcome, everyone." She smiled as the women entered and took their seats. "Let's get started."

The women, ranging in ages, sizes and backgrounds, shuffled to their seats and opened their notebooks.

"As we learned yesterday, our recovery will involve three-dimensional thinking, which is a way of considering the past, present and future at once. We learn from the past and make best use of the present to press toward a better future."

She sat on the stool at the end of the U-shaped table grouping and took a sip of her coffee. "I'm sure you each have a goal for your future. You've told me you want to see your families restored, have a good career, help others. These are all excellent goals for the future."

One of the women raised her hand. "But I've tried to fix things, so many times, and I just keep making the same mistakes. That's why I'm here."

"Yes, thank you. How many of us feel that way?"

A show of hands spread across the room.

"The past has a way of creeping up on us, destroying the present and future. Unless we learn from it. Running from the past doesn't help. Have you tried repressing the pain of the past, pretending things didn't happen?"

Several women nodded.

"Maybe even repressing the present?"

Nods turned to puzzled faces.

Becca smiled. "Some of you might believe that all men are liars."

Several chuckles ensued, and one person spoke under her breath, "Ain't that the truth?"

Becca chuckled along. "All men might be liars, but not all liars are men." She paused, her eyes lighting up playfully. "Oh, you don't think you lie?" She smiled. "How about this?" She stood and shifted her weight to her left leg. Using a deep voice, she started the mock scenario. "What's wrong, honey?"

Becca shifted her weight to her right leg as if she were the female in a couple. "I'm okay." She bit her lip.

Back to the man's side and deep voice. "No, really. What's wrong? You can tell me."

She switched to the woman's voice and side. "I'm okay." Her foot tapped furiously.

Shifting again to the left leg, she crossed her arms and used a sarcastic tone. "Yes, you're OKAY, alright:

Obstinate,

Kerfuffled,

Angry, and. . . and. . . and. . .

Yellow."

A few ladies chuckled.

Becca lowered her brows, crossed her arms and used a female tone. "Oh, you think you know everything. Well, you misused the word, kerfuffled. Kerfuffle is a noun. So there."

By now, everyone in the room was giggling or laughing.

"Dishonesty hasn't worked for us, whether we're talking about the past or present. In recovery, we come out with whatever is wrong. If we're not okay, we're not okay. Be real."

Becca sat back down on the stool. Her voice soothing, she continued. "I don't spend much time looking back anymore, but for a long time, I had to, because I had a lot to face. I grew up in the Vietnam era and in a family that fought all the time. I didn't want to fight. I didn't realize the battle going on inside. It wore me out."

A sip of her coffee and a deep breath, she had their rapt attention. "I took the time to face my past, and receive comfort, and lo and behold, I'm not torn or controlled by painful memories anymore. God helped make something beautiful out of my painful past, and now I'm better equipped to help you with yours."

Returning to the board, she drew entwined, thorny branches. "This bramble-bush of thorny vines represents our damaged emotions. Pull one, and they all come along, scraping and hurting along the way. It can be overwhelming."

Next to it, she drew another bush, with separated branches, each reaching for the light. She turned to face the class. "In recovery, we'll separate the tangles, one by one, so they can be pruned and restored to a healthy, functioning tree of life." She pointed at one branch. "Eventually, you'll be able to feel one emotion at a time, without them all rushing in. Sad, for instance. . ." She pointed at another branch. "Or glad. Whatever you feel, you're allowed to feel. We'll explore their accompanying beliefs, and, you'll be healthier. Steadier. Ready to find your place in the world without the need to numb yourself."

Placing the chalk on its tray, she observed her students. Their faces and positions spoke of their varied responses. Some sat forward, eyes on the teacher. Others leaned back in their chairs, legs crossed, and doodled in their notebooks. One turned, gazing out the window, her face wet with tears and streaked mascara.

Becca placed a hand on the crying client's shoulder and softened her tone. "We're with you. For you, not against. Your personal journey of recovery will help you to help others, from the inside-out, where the Spirit is working. But the work isn't easy. It takes—" Becca followed the sullen student's gaze out the window, to the crooked old tree reaching toward the sun. She stretched her arm toward the tree for the class to see. "Like this tree, healing takes as long as the arduous, beautiful journey. . . takes."

> *I am not now what once I was*
> *Nor am I yet what I will be*
> *One thing I do, and in 3-D*
> *The past, with comfort, I release,*
> *The future, reaching forth in peace,*
> *In present, focused, I press on—*
> *with Love's high call*
> *for you and me.*
> *-Philippians 3: 13-14*

> *Paraphrased for The Bent Tree Path*
> *by Joan T. Warren*

End of Book One

Continue the journey—see **excerpts** of **The Bent Tree Path, Book Two**, as well as discussion questions, words from the author, resources, shout-outs and trigger information, all in the pages that follow.

Find and follow www.joantwarren.com
and author Joan T. Warren on Facebook, Instagram, Amazon, Goodreads and IngramSparks.

Excerpts from Book Two of The Bent Tree Path

Becca, 2022

"Our sister, may you increase to thousands upon thousands; may your offspring possess the cities of their enemies." – Genesis 24:60

Becca placed the envelope into the mailbox and raised the red flag. *Done.* Sliding the phone from her pocket, she called Christine. "Hey, hon, gotta minute?"

"Sure, Mom. I'm working, but I can take a couple of minutes. What's up?"

"I did it!"

A slight chuckle through the receiver tickled Becca's ear. "Did what?"

"I mailed my retirement papers." Becca bit her lip. "In four months, I'll officially be over the hill."

"That's great—except for the over the hill part."

Becca's playful tone softened. "I wouldn't mind an easier road on the other side of retirement. I'll still be raising Clara, but I'll have more free time. Maybe time to do more just for

"

pleasure."

"You deserve that, Mom. You've been working hard since you were fourteen. I'm sure you made the right choice."

"Thanks, hon." Becca paused to enjoy sense of fulfillment their relationship held. Christine had been her sidekick since they were both kids—first as single mother and daughter, and later, as adult friends. "I really appreciate that."

"So, you'll get to visit more?" A wistful air permeated her voice. "There's a hammock waiting up here for you with a great view of the lake and mountains."

"I hope so, but I still need to be here most of the time—with Clara in school."

"Yeah, but a girl can always wish."

"I'll have more time for projects. I'm thinking of making an extensive photo album for Joy. . . one that relays our family history."

"Joy would really like that. I'll dig through some of our pics and make some copies to include, if you want."

"Absolutely—thanks. Well, I should let you get back to work. . . "

"Yeah. I'm glad you called, though. I'm excited for you."

"Thanks, Christine. Have a good day. Love you."

"I love you too. . . and congratulations!"

As Becca entered her home office, framed diplomas on the wall caught her eye. No degree had come easily. She'd put college off until Christine grew up. Any career aspirations Becca might have fancied when she was young—being a professional dancer, an interior designer, or a psychologist—paled in comparison to being there for Christine. She'd spent her time as a young mother learning to be an adult herself, a good parent, and then in ministry, helping people recover from all sorts of painful pasts. When she finally attended college in her late thirties, she'd become an occupational therapist.

With over forty combined years serving people of all ages and with all sorts of illnesses, disorders and challenges, Becca had pretty much seen it all. She'd worked in rehab programs, hospitals, outpatient clinics, skilled nursing facilities, assistive living facilities, schools, and—her favorite—clients' homes. In home practice, Becca specialized in pediatric occupational therapy, helping children and families with special needs.

She'd seen children far exceed their specialists' predictions. Children with autism learned to connect with their parents, to talk and to be educated on level with their peers. She'd helped babies born with flaccid paralysis of one arm to swing by both hands from the monkey bars by the age of three. Sometimes babies didn't progress, even after tying all approved treatment strategies. In those cases, Becca trained families to understand their child's needs, and to embrace a new normal.

Yes, it would be hard to leave her professional career. Becca turned from the diplomas on the wall and picked her journal and pen up from her desk. She headed to the kitchen, poured a cup of coffee and snuggled into her favorite spot in the garden.

The words flowed from her pen, the answer flowing freely as soon as she breathed another prayer for reassurance about her new direction.

"Your efforts have not been in vain, my dear child.
You forged new territory, a pioneer. You leveled a

trail through wilderness, leading to beautiful pasture. I will continue to work through you as you set your mind to fulfill your new journey. Follow the ideas that delight you, for these are the ones where we'll meet to work together on this new creation."

Becca closed her journal, inspired—but a bit sheepish, for the Lord's words to her heart both humbled and encouraged her. She loved journaling when God's words went straight to her pen—which happened again regularly now, after years of not hearing Him, years she spent lost again, a dark night of her soul that lasted over ten years, after Mike—

* * *

Joy, 2006

"The gloom of the world is but a shadow. Behind it, yet within our reach, is joy."
      - Fra Giovanni Giacondo (c. 1435-1515)

"Thanks, Nana." Joy hugged Becca's neck. Placing the necklace around her neck, she turned to Christine. "Mom, will you help me with this clasp?"

Christine fastened the necklace—a little silver cross with a tiny diamond in the center—and turned Joy around to behold her ten-year-old daughter. "Perfect. Just your size, and beautiful, like you." She turned to the group in their living room. "Okay, everyone, let's go."

The extensive family squeezed into three cars and headed to the church for Joy's baptism.

A bounce in Joy's step kept her visible to the rest of the family as she led her large group to the front pews. "We sit in the front row today. That's what Pastor Nick and I planned. Here." She waved her hand, directing them to the first row to the right.

Joy had written and practiced her speech., ready to go through the "outward expression of an inner experience," as the pastor called it.

Pastor Nick motioned for her.

She stepped down into the tub, holding her notes above the water. *Ooh—chilly.* An urge to swim stirred her. Swimming always made cold water feel warmer. But no. This is baptismal water. *Be calm, keep your speech dry.*

The pastor put his arm around Joy and turned her toward the congregation. "I present to you Joy Mäkelä. Joy is a vibrant addition to our Sunday School. Her family joined us just a year ago, and we are blessed to have them. Joy is a delight. She's quick to think of great ways to organize things and keeps us all entertained with her great sense of humor. She enjoys gymnastics, playing with her dog, and of course her family and friends. Joy tells me she's prepared a speech to share with you today as she affirms her faith in our Lord and Savior Jesus Christ through baptism. Go ahead, Joy."

Joy looked out at the congregation. She beamed at her family—all eighteen of them, including the ones from New York. In the third row, she saw a hand wave. It was her best friend. *Lizzie made it too—good. They're all here. Here goes.* She opened her folded notes and took a quick look at them.

Her forthright manner and confidence made every word an adventure. "Hi, folks, I'm Joy. You should all know this 'cuz you're my brothers and sisters—and Pastor Nick just told you my name."

Chuckles rippled along the pews.

"I've known about Jesus for as long as I can remember. But, one day last year, I was feeling guilty about—well, something. Doesn't matter now. Mom told me that when a person asks God for forgiveness, He throws their sins to the bottom of the ocean, never to be found again."

Someone in the back said, "Amen."

"Mom said all I had to do was accept Jesus into my heart and I'd be forgiven. So, I did. And bada-boom—He forgave me! And bada-bing—I was saved!"

The congregation chuckled.

This response, which Joy had hoped for, buoyed her confidence. Her tone grew more serious. "I am ready to tell the world that I am a Christian through baptism." She turned her notes over to continue, reading from them. "I thank Him for his bittersweet death, and today I celebrate his resurrection."

She cleared her throat as she began the last section of her speech, telling herself to try and look at their eyes—or noses. "This is for you. God is walking through the church today, putting His hands on our shoulders, telling us He loves us. Jesus gives us joy and life. Celebrate new life with me and my best friend, Jesus Christ."

The congregation broke into applause, cheers, and amens.

Joy placed her arms over her chest. "Okay, Boss!" She slipped one hand up to hold her nose.

The pastor lowered her into, and raised her from, the

waters of baptism.

As she stood again from the water, Joy pumped her right fist like an athlete after winning a tough match. "Woo, hoo!" She laughed and stepped out of the tank.

Her father held a large towel for her. As she leaned into it, he wrapped the towel around her shoulders and hugged her. "I'm so proud of you," Pete said. That was awesome."

A warm sensation rose from deep in Joy's heart, filling her with warmth and peace. She cherished the feeling for what may have been only a nanosecond, then bounced back to her bubbly, lighthearted state. "Thanks, Dad. Gotta go change outta these wet clothes."

In the dressing room behind the baptismal, Joy recalled the scene that led her to need forgiveness. On her way to school, bullies had threatened her, day after day. She'd done what Mom said, what the teachers said, what everyone said to do about bullies, but it never stopped. Finally, she'd decided to take matters into her own hands. Her brother's pocketknife clicked open when the bullies got in her way—and they scattered like scared rabbits at the sight. Joy ended up in trouble—suspended from elementary school, even after her parents told the principal that the school should have done more to protect her and to punish the bullies.

Weird, how I ended up both the good guy and the bad guy at the same time. I got suspended, but they got to keep going to school. But at least they won't come near me again. Who cares what anybody else thinks? I get to start again. That's what the Bible says, and it makes sense to me, so that's the plan.

After the ceremony, the family gathered in Joy's house.

Some chatted on the brown leather sofas in the living room, and others mingled in the kitchen, helping Christine get the food and drinks on the counter for a buffet-style lunch.

In the family room at the back of the house, a light flashed through the plantation shutters. The room was empty. Joy crossed through the filtered sunbeams on the floor as she approached the windows on the other end of the room to peek out the window. She tipped the shutter up to see and cringed. *An ambulance. At Lizzy's house.*

A touch on her shoulder told her someone had joined her at the window. *Mom.* "What's wrong, Mom?"

"Don't go. Let me call." Christine headed for the phone.

But Mom, Joy tried to say. Her voice caught in her throat under a burst of confusion and fear. *Lizzy and her mom were in church today. They just got home a few minutes ago.* She started for the door.

"No, Joy, don't—"

The door slammed behind her faster than the sound of her mother's voice could travel. Running across the back yard and toward the ambulance, Joy's heart pounded. *Did something happen to Lizzy? We were just riding bikes last night. She was just in church with me. She has to be alright.*

The paramedics came out the side door toward the ambulance. They wheeled a stretcher toward the vehicle.

Joy strained to see—who? Her breath caught in her throat.

A sheet covered the person's face.

Lizzy? No!

* * *

Continue the journey in **The Bent Tree Path, Book Two**.

Find and follow www.joantwarren.com
and author Joan T. Warren on Facebook, Instagram,
Amazon, Goodreads and IngramSparks.

Discussion Questions

The following questions are for personal, book club or support groups. Readers are welcome to provide constructive feedback via blog comments on www.joantwarren.com. Your positive reviews on Amazon, Goodreads, Facebook, et al., help the cause. Please take a moment to spread the word. Many thanks.

1. Compare and contrast the times this story covers. How did legal systems and/or cultural and societal norms either help or hinder the main characters in their quest?
2. Which of today's societal norms made this story difficult for you, and how?
3. Did you feel the need to press through any personal bias to finish the story? Share this struggle and what insights you can take from it—did you learn from your own reactions? Are you glad you stuck with it, and why or why not?
4. Describe the influence each generation's struggles and victories had upon others. . . Eliza's and Caroline's Cherokee history, Aggie's life, Lena's story, Shaw's, Becca's and Christine's?
5. How do Lena's and Becca's upbringing and early lives differ?
6. How do they harmonize?

7. Which character do you most relate to, and why?

8. What most frustrated or infuriated you during the story's unfolding?

9. What most surprised you?

10. What most touched your heart?

11. How would you interpret Becca's sense that she'd reached the tap root of her painful past? Was there a particular emotion that she'd had the most trouble admitting, permitting, or processing?

12. What theme(s) do you note from The Bent Tree Path?

13. What do you most want to know as you begin book two in the series?

Words From the Author

We've come a long way since Lena's early 20th century experience, but even now, a hundred years later, domestic violence is far from being a thing of the past. In 2023, the Center for Disease Control and Prevention (CDC) reported that approximately 41% of women and 26% of men in the United States have experienced domestic violence[1], also known as intimate partner violence (IPV).

That's four of ten women you know, and one of four men.

Of the 260 million adults who live in the United States currently, over 114 million report having experienced psychological aggression by an intimate partner in their lifetime.[1] That's almost half of us, my dear readers.

Perhaps it hasn't hit home for you. You don't even know anyone who's been through it. Please, read on, because those who have been abused need those who haven't been abused to be informed and supportive as a lifeline in a healthier community.

For many people, the damage begins early in life. About a quarter of those who reported experiencing IPV in their lifetime said that they first experienced it *before age 18*.[1]

The damage goes on, leading to chronic health problems,

mental health problems, and in some cases, death. U.S. crime reports suggest that—

- One in five homicide victims are killed by an intimate partner, and
- Over half of female homicide victims are killed by a current or former male intimate partner.[1]

Don't skim over that. If a homicide victim is female, the culprit is an intimate partner—
MORE. THAN. HALF. of the TIME.

Even surviving has its cost. According to the CDC, the lifetime economic cost associated with medical services for IPV-related injuries, lost productivity, criminal justice and other costs, is $3.6 trillion.[1] As of this writing, that's *over 10% of the US gross national debt.*

To prevent IPV, we need to understand factors that create risk. We need to provide protection and promote healthy, respectful and nonviolent relationships. We need to find lasting, internal change and set appropriate boundaries in intimate relationships.[2] This kind of change—the earlier, the better—passes health forward to future generations.

Marginalized people from racial and ethnic minority groups face higher risk of the worst consequences.[2] Of all racial and ethnic minority groups, it is the Cherokee who have experienced the worst when it comes to domestic violence and abuse.[3] Stay with me as I share a bit more about this phenomenon.

In this story, Lena's grandmother, Eliza, is Cherokee.

Since the fictional portrayal of Eliza began, well over a decade ago, the "Cherokee Grandmother Syndrome" has blossomed into what many now consider an offensive stereotype.[4] I considered removing Eliza's portion of Lena's story, not wanting to risk offending the very people I desire to elevate. I chose to keep Eliza because her story is not only dear to my heart but is timely. America's understanding of what it means to be Cherokee needs to grow.

The most recent US Census (2020) contains a significant upswing in people claiming Indigenous ancestry—from under a million in 2000, to 5.2 million in 2010, and to 9.6 million in 2020, the largest growing group being Cherokee. Since birthrates among members of the Cherokee Nation could not account for this upswing, the difference is in how census questions changed. And change, they did. In 2020, the US Census permitted citizens to record *more than one* ethnicity.[5]

Since Cherokee intermarried with Europeans for centuries, and the number of potential ancestors doubles every generation, exponential growth could conceivably skyrocket from thousands to millions within three centuries. If, indeed, millions of Americans have Cherokee or other Indigenous ancestry, it behooves us to better understand their cultures, including their suffering.

The cultural assault upon indigenous peoples that occurred during our nation's expansion era inflicted generational wounds, whether on the Trail of Tears, in lives of secrecy after escaping, or in boarding schools, adoptions and foster homes across the continent.[6] The fallout of those wounds still reverberates in their frightening victimization statistics, especially against their women: the latest report by the National Coalition Against Domestic Violence states that 84% of Native women experience violence in their lifetime.[7] Post-traumatic stress disorder is also higher among traumatized Indigenous peoples, with rates similar to that of combat veterans.[7]

Eliza's story introduces awareness and respect for those who endured mass genocide, cultural oppression, loss of homelands and heritage. Eliza's story (including a prequel to come in the series), beckons us to improve understanding and respect for Indigenous people's generational wounds, and to learn and honor their lifeworld and spiritual practices for healing trauma—a construct known as epistemological hybridism. These factors have been cited as vital to recovery for this significantly impacted minority.[8] Positive affirmation and respect can promote health and healing for all. This story alone cannot impart such vast knowledge, but hopefully it lengthens a compassionate bridge.

Becca's story highlights an example of potential outcomes of child abuse. Her effort to end the cycle of abuse advances the cause but is far from complete. The U.S. Children's Bureau reported over 500,000 substantiated cases of child abuse in 2022.[9] The CDC suggests that one in seven children in the US experienced abuse or neglect in the past year, but *only a fraction of what really happens ever gets reported.* Children in families with low socioeconomic status are reportedly five times more likely to experience abuse and neglect than children from families with a higher socioeconomic status.[10]

Outward signs of child abuse include unexplained bruises, overly aggressive behavior, lack of necessities, and drastic changes in behavioral and eating habits. Abuse may also underlie character traits such as low self-esteem, taking on too much responsibility, being overly loyal, overly fearful, or extremely achievement oriented.[10]

Abused and/or neglected children are at increased risk of experiencing future violence—victimization and perpetration—and sexually transmitted infections. Another major long-term problem associated with child abuse and neglect is delayed brain development—with toxic stress increasing post-traumatic stress disorder, learning, attention and memory difficulties. These children are more likely to face lower educational attainment, substance abuse, and limited employment opportunities.[11]

Prevention, as with domestic violence, involves understanding and intervening. Children need more help than adults, as they depend upon adults to intervene. Many victims live with fear in their own homes, dependent upon abusive parents to survive. They need adults to rise to the challenge, to notice, to break the stigma and act, to lower risk factors in the community, and to increase nurturing relationships and environments. Early intervention is crucial—the earlier the better, because sensitive periods in childhood's rapid brain growth lay the foundation for a lifetime of function—or dysfunction.[10]

There is hope. With personal effort, brain health and function can improve. Scientists have demonstrated that our brains have neuroplasticity, which means neural connections can be remodeled, or rewired.[12] Purposefully replacing negative thoughts, beliefs and actions with helpful ones, securing places and interactions that nurture self-compassion, adding faith, prayer and meditation to regular routines, choosing appropriate nutrition, physical activity and community involvement—all have been shown to be effective methods to remodel brains.[13, 14]

As with Becca's story, these changes take time. Her choice to shift from blaming herself and others into discovering and owning personal responsibility for her recovery led her to untangle the knots in her thoughts, emotions and beliefs. This heroic work cleared a path to stop abuse and promote health in her family and those in her circle of influence. The complex tangle of love, personal needs, loyalty, and abusive or neglectful relationships deserve deep work if change is to be wrought.

Trauma of any sort can impact future generations. Scientific research in epigenetics reveals how prior generations' trauma and coping strategies are passed on not just by demonstration or behavior, but genetically.[15] This means our great-great-grandparents' trauma can still trigger us toward action. My hope is that The Bent Tree Path will elicit awareness, respect, compassion, kindness and healing for all people—and especially bless the world's oppressed and abused.

Please—pass it forward, *healthier.*

A great deal more is needed to end domestic violence, child abuse and neglect.[16] Book Two in the series carries readers further in the process of making such a difference and explores the potential inter-generational effects of positive change.

Citations informing Words From the Author:

1. U.S. Centers for Disease Control and Prevention. 2024. *Intimate partner violence prevention: About Intimate Partner Violence.* Available from https://www.cdc.gov/intimate-partner-violence/about/?

2. U.S. Centers for Disease Control and Prevention. 2024. *Intimate partner violence prevention: Risk and Protective Factors.* Available from https://www.cdc.gov/intimate-partner-violence/risk-factors/index.html

3. National Coalition Against Domestic Violence. 2016. *Domestic violence against American Indian and Alaskan native women.* Retrieved from www.ncadv.org

4. Sneed, Anthony. 2024. *Director Statement, The Great Cherokee Grandmother.* Film Freeway. Available from https://filmfreeway.com/TheGreatCherokeeGrandmother.

5. Van Dam, Andrew. "The Native American Population Exploded, the Census Shows. Here's Why." *The Washington Post*, October 27, 2023. https://www.washingtonpost.com/business/2023/10/27/native-americans-2020-census/.

6. Pember, Mary Annette. 2017. Intergenerational Trauma: Understanding Natives' Inherited Pain. *Indian Country Today Media Network.* https://amber-ic.org/wp-content/uploads/2017/01/ICMN-All-About-Generations-Trauma.pdf

7. National Coalition Against Domestic Violence. 2016. Domestic Violence Against American Indian and Alaska Native women. Retrieved from www.ncadv.org

8. Bassett, Deborah, Ursula Tsosie, and Sweetwater Nannauck. 2012. "Our Culture is Medicine": Perspectives of Native Healers on Posttrauma Recovery Among

American Indian and Alaska Native Patients." *The Permanente Journal 16 (1): 19-27.* https://www.theper manentejournal.org/doi/10.7812/TPP/11-123

9. U.S. Department of Health & Human Services, Administration for Children and Families, Administration on Children, Youth and Families, Children's Bureau. (2024). Child Maltreatment 2022. Available from https://www.acf.hhs.gov/cb/data-research/child-ma ltreatment.

10. U.S. Centers for Disease Control and Prevention. (2024). *Child abuse and neglect prevention.* Available from https://www.cdc.gov/child-abuse-neglect/about/ind ex.html

11. Patoine, Brenda, for The Dana Foundation News & Insights. (2018). The abused brain. Published online October 9, 2018 and retrieved 2024 from https://dana. org/article/the-abused-brain/

12. Amen, Daniel, Dr. "Change Your Brain, Change Your Life." YouTube, June 8, 2011. https://youtu.be/MLKj1 puoWCg?si=g1wkjE4Ii9PNFIUL.

13. Best, Steven R., Natalie Haustrup, and Dan G. Pavel. "Brain Spect as an Imaging Biomarker for Evaluating Effects of Novel Treatments in Psychiatry—a Case Series." *Frontiers in Psychiatry* 12 (January 13, 2022). https://doi.org/10.3389%2Ffpsyt.2021.713141

14. Amen, Daniel G., Kristen Willeumier, and Robert Johnson. 2012. "The Clinical Utility of Brain SPECT Imaging in Process Addictions." *Journal of Psychoactive Drugs* 44 (1): 18–26. doi:10.1080/02791072.2012.660101.

15. Howie, Hunter, Chuda M. Rijal, and Kerry J. Ressler. 2019. "A Review of Epigenetic Contributions to Post-

Traumatic Stress." *Dialogues in Clinical Neuroscience* 21 (4): 417–28. doi:10.31887/DCNS.2019.21.4/kressler.

16. Vieth, Victor, Theodore P. Cross, Robert Peters, Rachel Johnson, Tyler Counsil, Rita Farrell, Betsy Goulet, and Karla Steckler Tye. 2024. "'Unto the Third Generation' Revisited: The Impact of a National Plan to End Child Abuse in the United States within Three Generations." *Journal of Child Sexual Abuse* 33 (3): 265–89. doi:10.1080/10538712.2024.2354266.

Resources, Books, and Links for Your Recovery Journey

You are invited to follow author Joan T. Warren's blog at http://www.joantwarren.com for her latest updates, publications, and contact information.

Her compatible guide, My Road to Recovery: A 12-week Guide for Inner Healing, is designed to assist anyone with a wounded heart who seeks healing. This manual includes simple lessons and journal prompts, is faith-based, and therapist-approved. The author took great care to ensure the guide is non-toxic, but some who have wounds closely associated with religion desire a secular version, which is in the works at the time of this writing.

The following **books** by other authors may also help:

Boundaries and Relationships: Knowing, Protecting and Enjoying the Self by Charles Whitfield

Codependent No More by Melody Beattie

Faith that Hurts, Faith that Heals: Understanding the Fine

Line Between Healthy Faith and Spiritual Abuse by Dr. Stephen Arterburn and Jack Felton

Healing the Wounded Heart: The Heartache of Sexual Abuse and the Hope of Transformation by Dr. Dan B. Allender

Healing the Soul Wound: Trauma Informed Counseling for Indigenous Communities by Eduardo Duran

It Didn't Start with You by Mark Wolynn

The Domestic Violence Sourcebook by Dawn Bradley Berry

The Transformation of the Inner Man by John and Paula Sandford

The Wounded Heart: Hope for Adult Victims of Childhood Sexual Abuse by Dr. Dan B. Allender

Websites with Resources Dedicated to Ending to Abuse:
www.zeroabuseproject.org
www.thehotline.org
www.nomore.org

Shout-Outs from the Author

This book is a complex piece—over a decade in the writing, and more than a half-century compiling the experience necessary to skillfully handle the sensitive subject matter. Listing every name the author wishes to thank is a task quite insurmountable. Some people, though, stand out as my most hearty supporters—in life, writing, editing and publishing. These I've listed, in no special order except that I've listed my family first. You all have my eternal gratitude and deserve more than words can express.

- **Randy**, my husband—for countless hours enduring the light of my laptop computer next to you in bed, well into the wee hours of the morning, for patiently waiting for and helping with late meals while I "just finish this section," for listening to me go on and on with ideas that may or may not have been interesting or compelling to your science-fiction oriented mind, and for constant encouragement and affirmation during my moments of self-doubt and exasperation. *Thank you, my sweet man!*
- **Denesia** and **Megan**, for letting me probe your inner-most thoughts and emotions to enliven the mindsets of certain (good) characters in the story, and for reading long sections of first drafts. ***Now you get free copies!*** *(No,*

not every person named Denesia or Megan—just the ones in my family. Sorry.)

- My **children**, **step-children** and **grandchildren**, who gave up time I could have spent with them or for them while I researched and wrote instead. I hope you barely noticed it! Thank you for your undying love and inspiration and for all the joy you bring. *Yes,* ***Angelina,*** *this includes you!*

- **Grace Anglican Church of Fleming Island**, especially members of small groups who have personally supported, encouraged and prayed for me and with me, and demonstrate love in action as you reach out to help others in need in non-preachy, meaningful ways. *You've made a place for me after I'd lost trust in churches, and oh, what a good place it is.*

- Members of two critique groups: **Word Weavers Fleming Island** and **Word Weavers Page 52 Historical Fiction.** You provided countless hours of feedback which helped improve many chapters and excerpts of this book, always sandwiching constructive feedback with positive specifics at the beginning and end of each turn. *Pure awesomeness in the nightmarish land of edits.*

- **Word Weavers International**, for your publications, conferences and critique groups for writers. *What a find!*

- **Florida Writers Association**, for your publications, conferences and podcasts supporting writers. *So good!*

- **Zena Dell Lowe** of The Storytellers Mission, for your consultations, workshops, podcasts and YouTube lessons for writers and your new class, Hollywood Story Structure Made Easy, which helped me restructure and rewrite this novel and will help those in the future. *You* *da bomb, girl.*

- **Sherri Stewart** of Stewart Writing, and **Jan Powell** of Writing with You, for awesome feedback, encouragement, and editing suggestions. *(Look for Sherri's books online)*

- **Reedsy.com**, for your amazing FREE website that provides a place to write, edit, learn and typeset in multiple formats for printing. Oh, and the free classes. *Blimey!*

- YouTubers who regularly post informative and helpful content for writers, including but not limited to: First Line Frenzy with **Rebecca Faith Heyman** *(I tried!)*, **K.M. Weiland** with Helping Writers Become Authors *(wow— amazing)*, **Jericho Writers, The History Quill, Jerry B. Jenkins, Sarah Nicolas, Design With Canva, Simon Sinek, Alpha Ministries Okeechobee, Alyssa Matesic, iWriterly, Author Learning Center, Eva Marie Everson, Ancestral Spotlight, Abbie Emmons,** and **Visit Cherokee Nation**. *There are tons more, but the book must go on.*

- **Dunklin Memorial Camp** in Okeechobee, Florida, for consent to use depictions, descriptions and modified lesson material in a fictionalized manner, and for helping many with inner healing and ministry training—*just knowing you're still doing so after all these years makes my heart happy.*

- **University of Florida Department of Occupational Therapy**, for academic excellence equipping and training therapists to employ the art and science of occupational therapy—to lovingly and skillfully help people with functional challenges to adapt and achieve their best in life. *Go Gators! Go change the world!*

- **The American Occupational Therapy Association**, for ongoing commitment to improving therapists who facilitate maximal functioning for people with mental and/or physical challenges through the use of meaningful activities. *Living life to its fullest!*
- **Alcoholics Anonymous**, for creating a pattern of recovery and support groups worldwide that help people with alcoholism as well as co-dependency, family members and people with other addictions, and keeping things simple from there. *Kiss!*
- **Tim Tebow**, for advancing awareness of human trafficking and doing something about it. The Tim Tebow Foundation and Her Song. *Donate to help!*
- **Zero Abuse Project**, for collaborating resources and facilitating mutual support for victims of abuse and being committed to ending sexual abuse. *You're a big behind-the-scenes player in Book 2!*
- **Jerry Wolfe**, the first Beloved Man of the Eastern Band of Cherokee Indians in over 200 years, for your service in World War II and your years of dedication to serve the Cherokee community with lessons about culture, language and stories. You were amazing to meet, and your personal warmth and knowledge are an inspiration beyond your time here on earth. *Stiyu.*
- **The Cherokee Nation**, for supporting the creation of media and places that facilitate reclaiming the many lessons and virtues that were nearly lost by merciless treatment during the quest for 'Manifest Destiny' in America. *May this work honor all of America's first peoples.*
- **Matthew Hawk Eldridge**, award-winning author (and

"mostly" Indigenous person), for your generous contribution of time and feedback as a sensitivity reader for Cherokee portions of the book. You went above and beyond, and I deeply appreciate you. *Read his books, folks!*

- **All recovering abuse victims**, for your dedication to not only recover, but to pass on keys to recovery for those in need, to go on loving, and to eradicate abuse from the planet. *Press on to the good ahead, and keep bending those trees for the next generation of travelers.*
- **All writers, counselors, therapists and people who dedicate themselves to help abuse victims, and to better the laws and the world.** *Angels, every one.*

Thank you. Thank you.Thank you. Thank you all, and thank you, Lord.
—Joan T. Warren

Sensitivity or Trigger Alerts

Below is a list of possible triggers in The Bent Tree Path. The purpose of sensitive material is to facilitate awareness of issues and healing pathways for victims, not for entertainment or explicit use.

- Violence, death: Mildly graphic depictions of domestic violence.
- War: Discussions related to war and its impact, but not graphic.
- Abuse and RAMCOA: Mild to moderate depictions/discussions of sexual abuse, child sexual and physical abuse, and neglect.
- Alcohol and pornography addiction: Discussions, not graphic.
- Consensual sexual activity: Discreetly handled, not graphic.
- Discrimination: Sexism, racism, discussion handled tastefully and appropriate to timeline.
- Stereotypes and politically 'correct' term use: The reader might interpret stereotypical depictions or politically incorrect use of terms related to gender, race, national origin, ethnicity, age, religion, or other status characteristics, but the author made thorough and sincere attempts to maintain consistency with timeline

norms while treating each with respect and sensitivity.
- Christian faith: While there are no passages intended to be preachy or evangelistic, some religious beliefs and practices are depicted, including some that may be considered toxic, but are consistent with timeline norms and drawn from real-life experiences. The overall theme is consistent with building healthy, balanced, affirming relationships with God, self and others.

Please enjoy this book for what it is worth.
Provide constructive feedback and register for updates by
emailing:
joantwarrenemail@yahoo.com

www.ingramcontent.com/pod-product-compliance
Lightning Source LLC
Chambersburg PA
CBHW060557300726
48975CB00005B/1361